SYRUP
TRAP
CITY

by Penny Grubb

SYRUP TRAP CITY

by
Penny Grubb

First Published 2017 by Fantastic Books Publishing
Cover design by Gabi
ISBN (eBook): 978-1-912053-58-2
ISBN (paperback): 978-1-912053-59-9

Chapter 1

Maximilian Corder would have walked past the restaurant without a thought had a waft of fresh coffee not tickled his nostrils. *Hull's premier cup of coffee,* a sign proclaimed. He didn't want a hot drink, but he slowed. The long strides that had brought him this far had boosted his circulation, suffused him with the certainty that it was good to be alive. If he carried on at this speed he would be early and have to wait. He didn't do waiting. It made sense to stop for a drink. And anyway, he enjoyed watching people squirm.

He stepped inside.

'Table for one, sir?'

He hadn't noticed anyone at the hostess-stand. The girl was slight, dwarfed by the tall desk, her face unfamiliar. He looked her up and down, teetering on the brink of a curled-lip snarl but his good mood still bolstered him so he allowed her a gracious smile and said, 'Fetch me Meriç.'

She jumped with gratifying speed to obey his command, her expression scared as she scurried away. She'd realised who he was. He liked that. He tracked her zigzag path between the tables to the end of the bar where she whispered urgently in the ear of a second woman, this one older, slender but solid. Another new face. The place must be doing well.

Then Meriç was hurrying forward, rubbing his hands together, a bead of sweat forming at his temple. 'Max, how good to see you. It's been too long … far too long. A drink? A pastry? Something more substantial?'

The remnants of the condescending smile he'd turned on the hostess still played at Corder's lips. He let his gaze wander above Meriç's head as he looked all around. 'Just passing. Looking in on my investment.'

As he spoke, the slight girl eased herself behind them and back to her station. 'New staff since I was here last. I trust that means business is good, not that you're squandering my money.'

Meriç's attempt at a light laugh strangled itself into an unconvincing throat clearing. 'Yes, yes. Assistant manager. I'm training her up. Plans to expand.'

Eyeing the rookie at the hostess-stand, his inescapable conclusion was that Meriç had lost his head for a bit of skirt. That did not augur well for the smooth running of the business. But then Corder smiled, equilibrium restored. It was the other woman Meriç was looking at, the solid blonde.

'Yes, get me a drink,' he said with a dismissive wave of his hand. His glance ran across the tables, resting on a six-top with a reserved ticket bordered in tinsel. He pushed aside the cutlery at one of the place-settings and sat down.

Meriç scurried away. The young hostess looked self-conscious, her attention bouncing from the menu board in front of her to the doorway, never once straying Corder's way. A middle-aged waitress, a familiar face, emerged from the staff-only door carrying a tray of steaming coffees and elaborate pastries. The blonde, the new assistant manager, followed carrying the plates that wouldn't fit on the tray. She looked efficient enough, though if Meriç intended leaving her in charge for significant lengths of time she might bear closer scrutiny. He didn't much care. As long as the place ran smoothly, his investment was safe.

Meriç returned with a fancy glass on a tray. Mineral water, crushed ice and a sliver of lime. The perfect accompaniment to his present mood. Inwardly, Corder applauded.

'Did you ... uh ... was there any business you came to discuss?'

The tension crackled behind the implausible casualness of Meriç's question.

One word and he could pull the rug from under this man's whole life, but what Meriç could never grasp was that if he pulled the plug, there was no more fun to be had in these encounters. 'No, just a drink on my way somewhere else.'

Meriç backed off with deferential murmurs and went to busy himself behind the bar. The hostess let in another group, taking them to be seated at the far end. They were six. Corder wondered if they'd been destined to sit at the table he was occupying. Another group arrived and another close on their heels. Like a relentless conveyor belt, he thought, bringing customers and disgorging them at the door. The hostess and the blonde juggled roles to keep things moving while the waitress marched back and forth from kitchen to tables with practiced ease. Not enough feet on the floor, but maybe they had extra staff arriving for the lunch trade.

The hostess was still dealing with the previous arrivals, and the waitress making drinks behind the bar, when the conveyor belt spat out a young couple who laughed as they entered, eyes only for each other. Corder set his gaze on the blonde. In a single movement she plucked menus from the shelf and turned towards the newcomers.

Then the fluidity of the machine jarred and crashed. Instead of coming forward with a smile of welcome, she spun round, grabbed the arm of the waitress and spoke in her ear whilst thrusting menus into her hand. Then she was gone through the staff-only door behind the bar.

The waitress looked alarmed as well she might. The lunch trade was building. This was no time to lose a pair of hands.

Corder leant back in his chair and watched. Meriç was out on the floor now bustling between tables, picking up used crockery. Corder watched the waitress welcome the couple that the blonde had run from. Their attention remained exclusively on each other; besotted, completely off guard. He tensed as he realised he knew the

3

man, recognised him from a different context. He was a detective sergeant from … no, he couldn't quite remember where … not hereabouts … the memory would surface. Gossip concerning a forthcoming marriage … he made it his business to know about people. That must be the new wife. He wondered what they were doing in Hull.

It was unlikely that he would be recognised but it was time to go. As he slid from his seat, detective sergeant whatever-his-name-was turned looking for a waitress. Corder let his movement swing him round so his face was out of the man's line of sight. He strolled further into the restaurant, up to the bar where everything lay reflected in the mirrored wall that ran behind the optics, close to the door that led through to the clatter and steam of the kitchen, close enough to overhear a rapid-fire exchange, to learn some names.

The young couple were wrapped up in each other again so he veered round, making straight for the door and the fresh air. They didn't even glance his way. He'd learnt that the would-be assistant manager, the one who'd run away from that policeman, was called Annie. Nothing to ruffle the smooth calm of the morning, but a useful snippet to squirrel away. He wondered what it was about, and if Meriç knew.

A frown creased Meriç's brow as he slammed shut the safe on tomorrow's float. The place was quiet, lights dimmed, doors locked on the last of the revellers. Just the two of them. She'd been ducking and diving out of his way since lunchtime and it had been too busy to corner her, but she had nowhere to hide now. He'd planned to be gone an hour ago, to leave her to lock up. What, after all, was the point of paying an assistant manager's wages if he couldn't carve out a little more time for himself?

There she was, pulling on that beige jacket of hers all ready to leave. Oh no, you don't, my girl, he said to himself as he called sharply, 'Annie!'

She wore the disarming smile that he'd come to distrust, and trotted out some pleasantry about tomorrow.

'What was this morning about, Annie? You can't hide away like that, not when we're busy.'

She screwed up her face into an apologetic smile. 'The guy who came in; he's a detective. He'd have blown my cover. He works in York, or he did when I knew him. God knows what he's doing over here.'

'How do you know him?' Meriç experienced a moment's worry. Corder's unexpected visit … it wouldn't do for detail of Annie's role to leak to certain quarters. But that wasn't going to happen. These were diversionary tactics because she knew she'd been caught out. He folded his arms and looked at her. He would like to see a bit more deference from Annie Raymond who hadn't as yet accorded him the respect that was due to a boss. He sensed the chance to take her down a peg.

'We … uh … ran into him on a case we were involved in. He's called Ahmed. He's a detective constable based in York. I don't know who the woman was.'

So much for her grapevine. He allowed himself the tiniest of smiles as he asked, 'We? *We* ran into him?'

'Uh … me and … Mrs Peters.'

'Ah … your boss at the agency.'

'She's not–'

He watched her swallow the words as resentment flickered across her face. 'Sorry,' he said. 'I mean of course, your business partner.'

The hidden agendas crackled across the silence that hung between them, but he wouldn't push her just to satisfy his own idle curiosity. He had stopped to chat at the young couple's table. He knew the woman. Her parents had been regulars for years. Annie herself had served them more than once in the brief time she'd been here. He'd heard more than he wanted to know about their daughter's forthcoming marriage to the policeman. He allowed his expression to harden.

'His name's Ayaan Ahmed,' he told her. 'He's not a detective constable, he's a detective sergeant. He has leave over the festive season. He and his wife are staying over here with her parents.'

'They're not booked in for tomorrow?' She blurted out the words, a level of panic underlying them.

Meriç blew out a breath and snatched at the diary. Annie Raymond peered over his shoulder as he ran his finger down the bookings. Satisfaction welled up inside him to see the length of the list. Business was booming. Or rather … he shivered as a shaft of ice played down his back … on paper business was booming. The reality didn't match.

Their eyes met. It was as though she read his mind. 'I'll get to the bottom of it,' she murmured, and in an instant they'd swapped places. He was the one reliant on her skills.

'No,' he snapped. 'They're not booked in under his name or hers.'

'What if they call in?'

'We don't get walk-ins on Christmas Day and what if they do? If they don't bring the extended family, I'm sure you'll fit them in.'

'But …'

'But nothing, Annie. You're the manager here in my absence. So what if he recognises you? Your cover story's solid.'

She went as though to speak but stopped. She'd worked in Hull years ago, and had devised a tale in case she ran into any old acquaintances. He knew she didn't want to use it. He assumed some false pride thing to do with the loss of face it would entail, but maybe there was another angle, maybe her cover story was closer to the truth than she wanted to admit.

Chapter 2

It was late Christmas afternoon. Annie ran her finger down the list of bookings just as Meriç had done the day before. The neatest service of the year. Every reservation accounted for and served.

The last two family parties lounged over coffee and crackers, but there would be no more business now. They had had one walk-in, a group of four, already halfway to drunk, attracted by the lights and laughter at the height of Christmas Dinner service. Annie had told them, no room. She could have fitted them in, and head waiter, Yağız, had waved the rag a bit at her decision. She'd taken it as an instinctive gesture to stir things and had given him a hard look. The piercing blue of his eyes had matched her stare for a moment, then he'd looked away.

Money for old rope, Meriç had told her. She wouldn't go that far. Her feet ached and tiredness swelled out from her bones. The end of the shift was in the air now as the waiters moved about their jobs, being subtle about clearing and cleaning around the stragglers but wanting them gone. An occasional clang and muffled expletive from the kitchen reassured Annie that the behind-the-scenes clean-up was well underway. Once the back of house was scrubbed to clinical cleanliness the staff there would be gone via the back exit into the alleyway. They were supposed to await her say-so but the head chef resented her intrusion into his world and took every opportunity to assert his autonomy.

A movement from one of the remaining customers caught her attention. The elderly matriarch of the group by the window was rising to her feet. Good. They would all follow her lead, then once the smaller group in the corner was exposed as all alone, the air of family bonhomie would evaporate, they would sense the presence of the remaining staff, feel the subtle pressure to be gone and let their servers savour a bit of the festive day for themselves.

Annie fingered the phone in her pocket, twisting her head to glance down, to see if any new emails or texts had come in. In her role as manager, she would roast any staff member caught checking their mobile, but she'd been bombarding Pieternel with texts, calls and emails since that almost encounter with Ayaan Ahmed. Pieternel was solidly on voicemail and auto-responses.

Annie had shocked herself with her reaction to seeing Ahmed again. He'd been entangled in the traumatic case that snowballed into the near-collapse of the agency; a case that brought out all the latent paranoia in her senior partner. If none of it had happened she wouldn't be here doing this job for Meriç. Or would she? Pieternel would tell her, *it's a job and a good payer, be glad of it.* She didn't want to meet Ahmed again; didn't want to have to convince him of her cover story, that she'd swapped professions.

... lost my nerve after all that stuff in York ... contacts in the area ... catering was my first choice profession anyway ...

That last bit was a lie but Pieternel had sown the online trail and tinkered with the databases so that it would look credible to anyone who checked. Only she didn't want him believing her story; if they had to meet she wanted him to guess she was undercover and then leave her alone. But he had too much of the nosey copper in him for that. And as Pieternel would no doubt say, thank heavens for it or you wouldn't be here at all. But she hated that he was a sergeant now and she, who had been at the peak of her career had not only stood still in her profession, but appeared to have bailed out and gone backwards.

She stood up straight and moved forward to usher the larger group out of the door with smiles and thanks. Her work here was done anyway, not just the Christmas shift but the puzzle she'd been brought in to solve. She had already left a brief message for Meriç to tell him so. And tucked at the back of her staff locker lay a pen drive with a detailed report on it that she would use to back up her assertions. If he wanted it for perusal later, she would copy it on to the office computer. The miniature drive was a good piece of kit, high-capacity, expensive. He could buy his own if he wanted one. The thought annoyed her. She should be beyond the need to worry over the cost of a pen drive.

Once the penultimate group had disappeared into the encroaching dusk, she issued a low command to the waitress at the bar. 'Carol, keep an eye on things for a mo.' Carol was an experienced server who'd been with Meriç for years. Annie could rely on her to recognise incipient trouble, not that she expected any from this last sedate party.

She slipped through to find a moment's privacy in Meriç's office. She would leave a message for Pieternel to expect her back in London before the tinsel had disappeared from the capital's streets.

When she returned it was to see the door close behind their final guests as cloths were whipped out to give the last few corners their pristine polish before everyone could go. Annie glanced at the time. Ten minutes before the official end of shift. They'd done well today. She hesitated long enough to make sure that all that was needed was a final sweep up of the floor around the last two tables before clapping her hands and announcing, 'Good job, everyone. Get yourselves off home. I'll finish up.'

Yağız stiffened as though about to argue, but subtle vibes from his colleagues kept him quiet. They all wanted to go. She even had a smile and a 'Happy Christmas' from a couple of them.

The task she had left for herself was essentially housework, something she had always gone to enormous lengths to avoid, but the key value of cleanliness to this business had caught her interest. It mirrored the importance of being thorough in her own profession. She found satisfaction in the gleaming face that Meriç's restaurant showed to the world. She wiped down the chairs and pushed them aside before wielding the broom to draw together the myriad particles that had floated down.

It was as she bent to pull the tiny heap of dirt into the dustpan that she heard the click of the front door. Thoughts flashed through her mind as she spun round. It was late … deserted … she should have slid home the bolt as soon as they'd left … Yağız had deliberately failed to click the lock.

It was Meriç.

'I didn't expect you today.' Her tone was sharp in response to the shock he'd given her. She softened it to add, 'It's been busy, all bookings honoured.'

'That door should have been bolted. I expected to have to go round the back when I saw we were closed.'

But I bet you were pleased you didn't have to, thought Annie, keeping her expression neutral. 'I sent everyone home a moment ago. I was just finishing here and about to lock up.'

'Even so …'

She let him grumble on as he went to flick through the day book and she wondered if he was here because of her message. It was the perfect opportunity in any case. The only time she and Meriç had chatted privately for any length of time had been in his riverside apartment at the start of the job. Subsequent communications had been snatched moments at the restaurant. This was her chance to reassure him he wasn't the victim of any criminal activity.

Her problem was not in convincing him – her surveillance had been thorough – it was Pieternel's silence and Meriç's contract. Pieternel's fault for tying them in to a six-weeker. It was clearly never going to be that. And Pieternel would have to pay the price. Annie had nothing to give him.

'I'm glad you've called in,' Annie told him. 'I need to have a word with you.'

'And I with you,' Meriç responded. 'I know you think you've got to the bottom of things.' He tipped his head towards the dustpan and brush in her hand. 'Finish up and we'll talk.'

As Meriç disappeared through the door to the kitchen, Annie felt the buzz of her phone. She snatched it out of her pocket. Pieternel! At last. It was a text.

Don't wrap it up yet, will be in touch.

Annie punched in Pieternel's number, keeping a wary eye on the door behind the bar.

You have reached the voicemail of …

Christmas meant nothing to Pieternel other than an opportunity to corner people in their homes, and that would be what she was doing, pulling in favours from years of networking, from players who'd forgotten they'd ever known her, doing some serious damage limitation to keep the agency at the top of the league. Their other operatives including Annie, the prize milch cow, were all out doing overpriced work to keep the coffers topped up. She understood the need for it, but that didn't make it less annoying and clearly Pieternel hadn't got the point this time.

Nor for that matter had Meriç. She hadn't got to the bottom of anything. The problem was in Meriç's mind, not in his business. Sure the numbers she'd managed to squeeze out of him showed a downturn, but she'd found no hint of fraud or wrongdoing, and she couldn't sort out his business affairs. He needed accountants or consultants, not a private investigator. The best she could do would be to advise him to tighten his business practices, be more aware of the expanding competition they faced in this area, shake up his staff, get them back on top of their game. She wondered if she could drop in a particular hint about Yağız.

Meriç would not leave here tonight until she'd convinced him, and Pieternel would get the point just as soon as Annie could pin her down long enough to explain. Pieternel would be pleased. She must be desperate for another pair of experienced hands back at HQ.

She had stowed the cleaning materials in their cupboard when Meriç returned. He held out a paper that Annie recognised as the agency contract.

'The job's not over, Annie. If you leave, I want my money back.'

'Yes, but just hear me out–'

'All my money back, Annie. Right now.'

She felt her smile become fixed. 'Well, that's not quite …' She lifted the contract from his hand and ran her finger down to the relevant clause. The words *full refund* and *immediately* leapt out at her. How had Pieternel let that through? It must have been a concession to persuade Meriç to sign up to the overpriced six weeks. She handed it back.

'The job's done, Meriç. No one's trying to cheat you. You've hit a mini recession. Christmas was good. It'll pick up.' She watched for any sign that he was taking this in; didn't see any. She thought of the pen drive in her locker. As well as her report, it held all her surveillance records. He had no idea what she'd been doing. Not quite time yet to bring that into play. It was never a good idea to let the client know how deeply you could penetrate their operation. She would hit him with the evidence if she had to. 'Look, I'll talk to Pieternel. Since I've wrapped this up so quickly and you paid up front, I'm sure she'll agree to refund something. But the job is done.'

He turned over the printed contract. Annie registered that it was longer than usual.

'Not unless you intend to pay me from your own pocket,' he said, his finger tapping on one of the clauses.

She leant in to read it. Pieternel had tied in both sides with a straitjacket. No matter how quickly the job was done, five minutes, five days or five weeks, and as long as it was done to his satisfaction, no refund would be made … but if she dropped the job before he was satisfied that it was done, then he was due a full refund. She had to hold herself in an iron grip not to react as her mouth went dry. Not just a full refund but payment before she left.

What the fuck's she playing at? She was close to saying it aloud, but pursed her lips and drew in a breath. She and Pieternel had been through a lot together. This wouldn't be the first time they'd clashed. Somewhere underneath it all there would be logic, but once again Pieternel had kept Annie in the dark. They'd never worked in the same way but fundamentally they always landed on the same page. She had to hang on to that.

'OK, I'll stay on until I've had the chance to discuss this with Mrs Peters, but we need to talk. I want to take you in detail through the observations I've made.'

'First, let me show you something, Annie. Come with me.'

She followed him through the door to the kitchen. Ambient light gave an eerie glow to the newly polished surfaces; reflected moonlight pierced the slanted windows, melding with the solitary streetlight that shone from the alley, catching the stainless steel of the line, creating orange and silver starbursts, breaking the clinical contours. They pushed past the cold-store and through the makeshift door that separated an awkward corner behind the walk-in. This cramped spot served as the office; the configuration of chair, desk, computer and filing cabinet leaving room for one person to ease themselves in. Meriç could sit in here happily for hours. Annie found it claustrophobic.

He fired up the PC. 'I want you to see this.'

She watched the finance spreadsheet scroll up the screen. She'd seen it before. He'd already shown her the areas he considered to be losses, and she could counter these figures with her own calculations showing that they were an accurate reflection not of fraud but of declining business.

He slotted a pen drive of his own into the PC.

Another spreadsheet. More detailed inventory on this one. 'I haven't shown you this before.'

'I asked to see everything, remember?'

He spread his hands in a gesture of admission. 'You didn't need to see it then. Now you do.'

His initial reluctance to show her this set of figures focused her attention. The reason people like Meriç came to private investigators was to keep a lid on their own secrets, which was not usually a problem. Client confidentiality was paramount though all their contracts had an exception clause for 'serious criminal activity'.

Meriç moved the mouse, reducing the size of the windows to show both sets of figures side by side. Annie was ahead of him, doing the calculations in her head, feeling a frown crease her brow.

'But that's not ...'

He nodded. 'Not wastage, not business declining.'

She stood upright, let her gaze lose focus. 'Why didn't you show me this before?'

The question was automatic, a sign of her annoyance. His answer wasn't important. She already knew he had secrets, didn't want anyone crawling over his books, but those figures contained information she needed to know.

Shock prickled her skin. Two of the dates he'd highlighted were shifts where she'd been present making her own meticulous observations. But if the figures were right – and why should she doubt them – someone was systematically defrauding the restaurant and she'd failed to spot it.

Chapter 3

Despite the tiredness from a demanding shift, Annie stayed up into the small hours, papers spread about her. Her rented room was at the top of a decrepit terrace, reasonably central but little better than the place she'd camped out in when she'd first worked in Hull; in a past lifetime it seemed. As she added the figures, cross-checking with the stock lists, trying to work out how the scam operated, bursts of music and laughter from nearby cut across her thoughts.

She had come to Hull all those years ago on a wing, a prayer and a temporary post with the Thompson sisters. From that unpromising start she'd built an empire. Now somehow she felt she'd come full circle. No money then; no money now. How had it come to this? At least back then she'd had her ambitions and she'd built a network of friends.

The sounds of late Christmas revellers still celebrating the day shone a spotlight on her isolation. There had been no more from Pieternel since that text.

Who did she know in Hull after all these years? The Thompson sisters were still around but they mustn't know she was in the area effectively taking work from them. That left Ayaan Ahmed, and he was only here over Christmas. In the old days she'd have called on anyone on the slightest pretext if she'd wanted company, but Sergeant Ahmed, especially given the context in which she'd come to know him, was one of the few upon whose doorstep she could not plant herself. What would she say?

Remember me? I'll bet I remind you of people and things you'd rather forget, but I need someone to have a drink with, can I come in?

The thought of the dismay that would blanket his face made her smile. She wasn't that desperate for company yet, hopefully never would be.

With a sigh she turned back to the lists of dates and figures. Meriç had a genuine problem and a far more subtle one than she'd imagined. Her mind had been rerunning the key shifts to work out what she'd missed. And yes, she could home in on occasional memories; bursts of annoyance that someone wasn't quite on song, someone else not where she'd thought they were. She'd taken it as part of the wall of hostility she'd been up against since she started, but looking back, she was no longer sure. Why hadn't she checked more deeply? How had she dropped the ball to this extent?

Was the simple shameful truth that she, Annie the high-flyer, partner in a successful London firm, couldn't bear the thought that someone from her past would see her working in a restaurant?

It was as though she'd assumed from the off that there was nothing to find. But she'd never worked like that even on the most unpromising of cases. She thought about how easily she'd dismissed Meriç's fears, thought him paranoid. And now it occurred to her that the distrust hadn't started with Meriç. From the day this job had first been mooted, she hadn't quite believed Pieternel either.

Did she stay or go? And if she walked out on Meriç without compensation and without finishing the job how much trouble could he cause? Their business had taken a huge knock. This wasn't the time to open up new battlefronts. She pulled out her phone and once again clicked in Pieternel's number.

We're not fighting for our lives this time, she thought as she listened to the ring tone, we're fighting for our place in the pecking order, repairing the damage of having the security services' spotlight on us.

'Listen Pieternel,' she said to her colleague's voicemail. 'I don't know why you've pushed me out.' She paused. 'OK, if I'm honest,

I don't even know *if* you've pushed me out, but it feels like it and it wouldn't be the first time. I should be helping you, not stuck out in the sticks. We might not always see eye to eye but we'll get this sorted more quickly together than apart. And at least you know you can trust me.'

A flare of some sort lit the high window and the slurred rendition of a Christmas carol floated into the room. Annie thought with envy of the carefree revellers making their unsteady way through the night while she was trapped.

'It's clearly a staff scam,' she went on. 'It's clever, it's something more subtle than the usual snatch and grab but it'll not be hard to track down now I'm on to it. The thing is I'm the last person who should be in the field right now. I can't concentrate. Any half-baked PI could do a better job of it than me right now. I'm going to call on the Thompson sisters and hand it on. With the head start I can give them, they won't muck it up. You've had plenty of money off Meriç for us to pay them and still come out on the winning side. But I might need you to sell the idea to him. I'll get to the Thompsons tomorrow evening and let you know what's what.'

Annie sat back with a smile of satisfaction. A good practical way out. Why hadn't she thought of it sooner? The Thompsons would be pleased to have such an easy earner plonked in their laps.

She and Pieternel had been at the top of their game before they inadvertently drew interest from unwelcome quarters and found themselves on the radars of the sorts of people everyone wanted to avoid. It would take some nifty footwork to get through the maze without losing every prestigious client on their books, but they could do it. Hell, they'd faced worse over the years. Pieternel had reverted to type, forgotten that Annie was no greenhorn these days. It was time for her to come out of the shadows and get back into the thick of it.

Meriç let his expression harden as he turned his back to his paying clients. He pushed through to the kitchen where Yağız was reaching for a carefully crafted salad.

'Wait!' Meriç stopped him, whipping a linen serviette from the side and wiping an invisible blemish from the pristine rim of the plate.

Boxing Day was always hectic, especially over lunch time as the sales shoppers pushed in to grab a bite to eat.

'Where's Annie?'

Yağız gave a half smile as he tipped his thumb towards the office. 'Been in there all morning.'

Meriç strode the short distance past the cold-store. 'I don't pay you to skulk about when we're this busy. It's chaos out in front.'

Her gaze snapped up to meet his, one of her fingers rested on a row of figures on a page in front of her. 'It was fine a minute ago.' She sounded surprised. 'I was just checking something.'

'Well, don't do it now.'

'I thought you had a meeting somewhere. You said you wouldn't be in today.'

He leant in close to be sure his words wouldn't float out to anyone in the kitchen. 'I should have been looking at the new premises,' he hissed from close range, fixing her with a glare. Only she and Yağız knew what he was planning and it had to stay that way. He would tell the rest of the staff when he was ready. They'd be delighted to hear about expansion, room for promotion for the lucky ones, but there were certain ears that mustn't be reached. Maximilian Corder or anyone who knew him. The new venture was Meriç's stepping stone out from under Corder's yoke. Not that Annie knew anything about Corder.

'You came to me highly recommended.' He kept his voice low, stared hard into her eyes.

'I'm not psychic,' she shot back. 'You kept vital information from me. But I'm on it now, it won't take long.'

He toyed with a challenge about not having had the benefit of her specialist skills despite the premium price, but there was some truth in what she'd said so he left it. And for all that, she'd done a competent job running the place. He believed her assertion that she'd only been back here for a minute over Yağız's accusation that she'd deserted her post all morning. He knew Yağız didn't like her, didn't approve a stranger brought in over his head, but that was good. He didn't want a manager who made friends of his staff. In other circumstances he might consider keeping her on while he wrestled with the new place.

'I need to get back out there,' she said. 'We're busy, and I know we'll have a stack of regulars calling in.'

Yes, she had an instinct for it, knew how to cosset the old clients and welcome in the new. They walked through together. He couldn't fault the demeanour she turned to the public face of his operation, the instinctive way she greeted his regular customers with just the right mix of deference and welcome. She had a gift for reading people. He supposed it was a useful skill in her chosen profession, but how much more productive in his? Annie Raymond had taken the wrong path, but anyway, now that he'd given her the right push he would get the benefit of her talents in both roles for as long as she stayed.

This scam had to be unearthed and snuffed out before Max Corder got a whiff of it. Corder might enjoy playing the touchy investor and watching them all jump, but he would shut them down in the blink of an eye if he caught an inkling that the restaurant was victim to a scam. It made the set up too vulnerable. Max Corder was the reason he'd gone to this expensive London firm in the first place. He daren't use anyone from Hull for fear Corder would get wind of it.

The boss of the London agency had assured him that Annie would stay. He'd spoken to her this morning. 'Be firm about sticking to the letter of the contract,' Mrs Peters had said. 'She won't rock the boat.'

He wasn't so sure. He'd been alarmed to hear from Mrs Peters that Annie had suggested handing over to someone local. She'd said, 'It won't come to that. Just sit tight and do what I tell you.'

As he stood watching Annie move forward to greet some new arrivals, it occurred to him that Mrs Peters' motive might be more about keeping their conversation a secret from Annie. What if he told her, what if it caused a rift between her and her boss? Could he use that to his advantage? She was good in this job if she'd only stop turning up her nose at it.

Look at her now, hurrying forward, her smile mirroring the one with which the couple at the door greeted her. He heard the words, 'Annie, come and meet my daughter and her husband … Cari, this is our new friend, Annie. She'll look after us.'

No!

His feet wouldn't move, and if they had he was too late. The young couple laughed at each other, not looking at Annie, but they turned as the introduction reached their ears. From the way her back stiffened, he knew that realisation had hit Annie. Then he watched the laughter drain from the on-leave policeman's face as his and Annie's stares locked.

Chapter 4

Things wound down towards the early evening lull. Meriç sat in the cramped office listening to the bustle of the kitchen behind him, the clang of metal on metal. He thought back to that jarring encounter between Annie and the off-duty policeman, the uncomfortable pause, the man's mouth gold-fishing as he fought to contain his surprise. Annie had been the one to recover her poise first, to smooth things over, to fuss around the older couple as a way to glide past the awkward encounter. Then as soon as she could extricate herself she had hurried away and pushed through the staff door.

Meriç had watched the policeman's stare follow her; had seen a sudden spark of suspicion flare in the eyes of his wife as her parents exchanged a glance and pretended to be engrossed in a menu they must know by heart.

An intangible hum of satisfaction had rippled through the back of house. They were pleased to see Annie knocked off balance. Everyone noticed something wrong even if it wasn't immediately apparent what it was. The grapevine would have sorted that out as the day wore on, and if they hadn't known to start with that the new son-in-law of these regulars was a policeman, they would by now. The obvious assumption was that the unpopular new manager had things to hide. Meriç could only hope they didn't find out how much.

He'd pulled her into the tiny office, shutting them both in. But before he'd got out a word, she'd been at him.

'I can't risk running into him again, having him ask questions. I have to drop out of sight. I've worked out how.' Then she'd given him the bones of the scheme Mrs Peters had warned him about; the scheme to hand over to a local firm.

'I know the Thompsons,' he'd said. 'And if I'd wanted them involved, I would have gone to them in the first place.' It was what Mrs Peters had told him to say. He'd never heard of these Thompsons, whoever they were. He hadn't been convinced it would work, but Mrs Peters clearly knew her colleague. Annie had given the ghost of a shrug and had tried another tack.

He was to let it be known he'd sacked her, but she would keep a set of keys and put the restaurant under covert surveillance for the 'few days' she had insisted was all she needed.

'And what am I to do for a manager in the meantime?' he'd shot at her.

Cutting things short, he'd set her to expediting, which she wasn't very good at, and had pushed Yağız out on to the floor for the final shift. It annoyed him all the more that she was prepared to let it be thought he'd sacked her in order that everyone would assume her gone. How could anyone have that level of contempt for a position that others would kill for? But his initial determination to force her to stay on in her visible role wavered as he considered the angles. In talking with the family group earlier, he had gleaned that the young couple would stay at least another week. That meant his assistant manager useless in the restaurant, jumping round every time the door opened, so unless a juicy murder cropped up to curtail the policeman's leave, he would have to rethink.

He'd ended the discussion with a terse, 'I'll speak to you after we've closed tonight.'

It was past midnight by the time everyone was gone. The restaurant lay in darkness but for the dim 24-hour lights and the office lamp that he'd yet to turn off. In the hours since he'd spoken to Annie, Meriç had had time to put some meat on the bones of his ideas.

'We're closed tomorrow,' he said as she came through to the office. 'That gives you a day to set up. If you can prove to me you can do this job arm's length, then I'll allow you to take a couple of days leave. I'll say it was short notice, some family problems, something like that. Tomorrow to set up, and you can have two days after that. But if the job's not wrapped up, you're back on the floor. I'm falling behind on my schedule for the new place.'

'I need a week. This scam's sporadic. Two days isn't enough.'

'Then you're back working openly from within the restaurant.' He was too used to people wanting to stretch things; time off, overtime, leave, to be swayed by anything she had to say. A week might have been better because then he could tell her with confidence that the policeman had returned to his lair at the other side of the county, but he was pretty certain there would be no more family excursions after the look Ahmed's wife had given her.

She nodded, apparently conceding the tight deadline. He found himself wondering if she could do it given the time to focus and room to manoeuvre. If she didn't push him, he might allow her the week she wanted.

'I need uncensored access to the books and the back end of the systems,' she said. 'A real manager would have it.'

'You're not a real manager. You won't even be a pretend one if I let you run with this plan. And I'm not letting you run with it until I see the set up. Tell me what information you want and I'll see that you have what you need.'

'You're making it difficult when you don't give me the full picture.' He heard irritation in her words, but she drew in a breath and swerved away from picking a fight about it. 'Ayaan Ahmed, the policeman, he's going to be a regular in here, isn't he?'

'While he's over here, maybe. His in-laws have been good customers for years. But police officers don't get much leave, do they? He'll be gone in a week or so.'

'He'll tell people. He'll ask around.'

'What people? Why would he bother? What will he tell anyone anyway, that you've fallen on hard times?'

He saw her flinch. 'I didn't mean that. He must know I'm undercover.'

'Wasn't he convinced by your cover story?'

She gave a tut of annoyance. 'I didn't stop to talk. How contrived would that have looked? If he's curious he might come back and ask, but more likely he'll go off making his own enquiries and he'll end up blabbing to the wrong people.'

'And who might the wrong people be?'

The annoyances stacked up; her lofty assumption that her role as a private eye was so superior to a job in good restaurant; her presumption that she could call the shots; her failure to unearth whatever was going on that was slowly crippling his business. By the 'wrong people' she meant anyone who'd known her in her high-flying days who might think she'd sunk to the dregs by working here. There was only one 'wrong person' who might persuade him but she knew nothing about Corder.

She paused before she answered his question as though making sure she had his full attention. And suddenly his full attention was exactly what she had. Something in her expression ran a shiver down his back.

'I know I shouldn't have ducked out of sight when Ahmed first came in,' she said. 'It just made it all the worse when we came face to face. He took me by surprise. But I wasn't the only one who ran away from him.'

She paused as though to let him ask the question. He didn't. His mouth had dried.

'Corder,' she went on. 'Maximilian Corder. Soon as he was sure Ahmed wasn't looking, he was off like a cork from a bottle.'

Meriç stared at her. She shouldn't even know Corder's name.

Chapter 5

Annie could have bitten her tongue. She'd had no idea that Meriç would react this way. That one time Corder had come in during her tenure, she'd seen the way he deferred to the man. Sure, she'd been distracted by the unexpected appearance of Ahmed but it hadn't blindfolded her, and distracted or no, she was an investigator first and foremost. Of course she'd made enquiries. After all, Corder might have been central to the scam she was chasing, not that she'd believed in the scam at that juncture.

Meriç visibly struggled to hide his anger and surprise and she had to find a way to let him off the hook or she had no chance of talking him round.

'Tomatoes,' she said, making herself look alarmed.

Meriç shot her a blank stare.

'I forgot. There's a box of tomatoes been left out. I need to put them away.'

As she turned to escape the cramped space, he eased out of her way. She was being a manager; looking after his best interests, he could let her go.

Once in the clinical emptiness of the space-age kitchen, she reached for the switch. Meriç was no fool but he hated to be surprised. If she'd known it was such a big deal, she'd have drip fed bits about Corder until she'd accustomed him to the idea that she already knew whatever was to be known. The overhead strips clicked on; brilliant white sought out every corner, bouncing back at her from the polished surfaces. She heard a scurry from the alley outside. Light had burst through the high skylights to scare off some living being that thought it had found a secure corner for the night.

Ah! A cardboard box sat under one of the counters. She pushed it towards the cold-store. Freeze-dried apple, not tomatoes but its scraping across the tiled floor gave weight to the subterfuge with which she'd dived out of the conversation with Meriç.

This should give him time to glide past her ill-advised mention of Corder and pretend it hadn't happened. She needed him on board with her plan for arm's length surveillance, not only to avoid Ahmed, but because she had an added sophistication to sell him.

Covert surveillance cameras were not hard to install, and not illegal as long as she had Meriç's agreement. But even though the equipment wasn't expensive these days, it was beyond her current budget. Her plan was to persuade Meriç that she should put together the set up and leave it for his use after the job was done. That way he could pay for it.

Not that she would mention it tonight. All she needed was his agreement to the overall scheme, then she would source it on Pieternel's credit, show Meriç what could be done and he was sure to want it, especially as he planned to open a second restaurant and he couldn't be in two places at once.

'Is that everything?'

She hadn't heard footsteps and jumped as he appeared behind her.

'Yes, all done.'

'I heard sounds from the tenfoot … uh … alleyway.'

'It's fine,' she snapped, annoyed at his assumption that Hull slang was beyond her comprehension. 'It's all been checked.'

'It could be rats. Are the bins secured?'

'Yes, of course. It's …'

'Check again before you leave. I don't want trouble from the council.'

She pursed her lips as he turned away. It was the chef's responsibility to see that the bins were checked. She sighed. It was her job to check on the chef.

Two days? It wasn't enough, but there was no point in arguing now. She would put everything in place tomorrow while they were closed and then talk him round.

'No one's job is safe,' he grumbled at her. 'Even if we have a long friendship. In business hours, everyone must pull their weight. Even you.'

Ah, she'd thought he was grumbling aimlessly but this was for her benefit. He didn't like it that she was outside his jurisdiction, but maybe she'd unearthed the reason for the huge fee Pieternel had prised from him. Was she supposed to be his genuine fulltime manager as well as an undercover investigator?

'I have sacked good managers before,' he went on, and unexpectedly she felt a stab of pride that he'd called her a good manager. 'Mrs Peters assured me you didn't drink strong spirits. I wouldn't have taken you on otherwise. You won't know about the previous manager I had in here. I found him one morning sound asleep … drunk … couldn't wake him for hours. But when I did, I sacked him on the spot.'

Annie murmured sympathetically and let Meriç chunter on. She was happy to go along with the pretence that he was her boss as long as he never tried to act on it. She knew about the manager he'd sacked. She'd done the intel before she'd started the job.

She walked with him to the front entrance, locked and bolted the door behind him before returning through the gloom of the empty dining room, round the bar and into the kitchen. The overhead strips lit every corner like it was a bright midsummer day and gave her an idea.

Her original plan had been to go out with her torch, lock the door behind her and give the narrow alley a cursory check as she made her way the few metres to the main street; it had more or less become her routine anyway. But both she and Meriç had heard scurrying. If there were bins to be secured, detritus to move, she didn't want to be feeling through garbage with nothing but a handheld torch to light her way. That scurrying sound was less likely to be rodents than hapless people trying to find warmth and food, but if she and Meriç had scared them away, they might have left the bin lids loose.

She pulled on a pair of latex gloves, and retrieved her jacket from its peg. She would come back for her bag.

The bolt slid smoothly and the door swung wide.

The kitchen lights threw out a high-powered beam, but failed to illuminate the alley the way she'd hoped. A triangular patch was thrown into sharp relief against huge and impenetrable shadows either side.

At least one bin had been moved. The door bumped into it, wouldn't open flat to the wall.

The shadow to the left was too tall. Not a bin. Had someone stacked one on another? Why? What the ...?

A shape detached itself from the solidness of the shadow. She had barely time to register that this was no thin, shivering down-and-out but a well-wrapped muscular body coming at her out of the darkness.

Instinct and training pushed her into action before conscious thought could catch up. The intent was to hustle her back inside. There wasn't just the one figure. There were more. Couldn't count them.

Go for the unexpected ... make a bid for freedom.

Best chance of escape is before the net has closed.

She'd made this late night exit into a habit ... broken the most basic of rules ... never fall into a routine.

It's just a restaurant, a voice tried to scream in her head, *just a restaurant ...*

She ducked under the outstretched arm, punching hard with her right fist, feeling it plunge deep into soft flesh, using her forward momentum to get out into the night, her left elbow lunging sharply backwards, hitting something, agony screaming through her arm … an 'Uhh!' of surprise and pain from next to her ear.

The only break in her routine had been to swing wide the door with the lights still on. The sudden brightness had blinded them, taken them unawares. It was the only card she held. The route to the main street bulged with ill-defined shapes that could be bins or attackers lying in wait. One side of the alley held the blank wall of the restaurant, the other a tall barred metal gate.

Thank all the gods for a dark dress code, but her jacket was light beige.

She had fractions of seconds before their eyes recovered from the burst of light. No time to scramble round the corner to the safety of a lit street.

The clattering commotion and shouts made it impossible to work out how many of them were down there. Annie clung tight to her insecure perch, face pressed to the rough wall of bricks. From one corner of her eye, she could see the bright arch of the restaurant's back entrance. From uncomfortably close behind came the clanging of the security fence the other side of the alley where she'd thrown her jacket.

A tremor through her limbs mapped the tension of keeping her body braced to hold her feet rigid against inadequate footholds. For balance she had to trust an ancient fall-pipe. She was no more than a metre and a half from the ground, tucked into a corner barely above their heads. From the higher angle the shape of the alley's single streetlight stood silhouetted above the roofline, its glass smashed. They'd planned this; lain in wait, and she'd have been in the trap but for the unexpected blaze of light with which she'd burst out upon them.

Now she had to pray they would fall for that jacket, caught on the sharp spikes of the fence opposite.

'Leave it,' a low voice spoke into the darkness. 'She'll be long gone. Come on.'

The corner of her eye showed her two balaclavaed figures in the light from the open doorway. No detail, no useful characteristics to remember for later. They disappeared inside but she daren't move; couldn't be sure there wasn't a third left behind as lookout.

One of them held her jacket. Her keys were in the pocket; keys to the restaurant, keys to her cramped bed-sit. It was worth the loss to have them believe she'd scrambled over the sharp metal points and got away.

Her fingers grew numb against inadequate handholds, tiny fissures in the bricks. She daren't put any weight on to the elderly pipe or it would clatter down bringing her with it, but if her hand slipped as it threatened to do, there was nothing else in reach to grab. If she fell, her focus must be on a safe landing and a sprint to the street.

Low voices, footsteps. She peered down and sideways to the open doorway. The light vanished. In the cloying darkness a block of white brilliance played behind her eyelids. More voices. A scraping sound. Something had caught under the door as it was pushed shut.

They would use a torch. One upward slant of the beam and they would see her.

The jangling of keys; the snap of the lock's tumblers clicking home.

There was the torch beam, a feeble strand against the imprint of the kitchen's strip lights. An indistinct huddle, a semi-conversation in grunts and mumbles that she could make nothing of. Something was tossed behind the food bins – could it be her jacket or was that wishful thinking? They sauntered off, their footsteps receding, going away from the direction of the road, into the depths of the alley.

Annie had no idea what was up there. Was it a maze of tiny walkways behind the buildings or was it a dead end and would they come back? Were they gone far enough to miss the sound of her jumping to the ground?

She had no choice. Her limbs could not grip the wall any longer. There were no secure holds to let herself down gently. She'd leapt and scrambled this high on a rush of adrenalin. Now she had to risk a jump from high enough to turn an ankle or snap a bone. She did her best to brace against the corner of the wall whose shadows had hidden her but it was an uncontrolled tumble, scraping her leg on a protruding brick and landing her on her back.

She jumped to her feet, listening for running footsteps, indignant shouts. Nothing.

Keeping all senses alert towards the direction in which they'd disappeared, she leant over the food bins, wrinkling her nose at the sweet aroma of decay that floated around them.

She pulled out her jacket. It was what the indistinct shadow-show had looked like, but she hadn't dared to hope she'd been right. It hung heavy on one side. She felt in the pocket. They'd replaced the keys.

She stared into the blackness. Indistinct rustling and distant traffic, nothing else. Careful to make no sound, she slipped the key into the lock and let herself inside.

Once the door was shut and bolted, she allowed herself a moment to lean against the wall and close her eyes. She daren't turn on any lights but used the pencil torch on her keyring to look around.

Tidy burglars and a neat burglary, the only sign some scuff marks on the floor where mud from outside had been tracked in. There was no cash left overnight but there was expensive and reasonably mobile equipment that could have been taken. She sat in the darkness of Meriç's office and thought it through.

A random robbery? If it was a random robbery, she should ring the police and report it. Some gang that had clocked her regular late night exit and planned to jump her the moment she opened the door, not expecting tonight's blinding searchlight to have been behind her. And what had the details of the plan been? Tie her up while they ransacked the place?

There hadn't been much ransacking done. Had they cut it short because she'd got away from them? No, that didn't fit. They hadn't seemed too bothered nor in any particular hurry. Panicked robbers didn't take the time to turn out the lights and lock up behind them.

What if she had got clean away and called Meriç? Should she call him now? He could be here in ten minutes. What would she show him? No sign of a break-in. No missing keys. Annie herself looking like she had had a fall in the alleyway, but otherwise intact.

They'd come in for a reason and she would find it, but not tonight. She daren't advertise her presence by lighting up the windows and she couldn't conduct a proper search with a pencil torch. She had all of tomorrow when the place was closed. For now, she would break with protocol, crack the bolts on the front door and leave that way. Meriç would be incandescent if he found out the front entrance had been left unbolted, but there was no way she would leave again tonight via that dark alley.

Chapter 6

Annie stood in the space between the staff lockers and the heavy door to the cold-store, hands on hips, looking at the ceiling. She'd been at it since before dawn, felt as tired as though she'd already done a full shift, but a smile of satisfaction curved her lips. Good job. No one would know a thing. She couldn't detect any sign of the tiny lens and she'd put it there herself.

The network of cameras wasn't as extensive as she'd have liked, one for the kitchen, one for the dining room, and one in back corridor. She'd had to go with what she could source quickly, locally and discreetly. It had cost more than she'd wanted to pay, more than she could have risked on her own stretched credit so she'd used the business card, the one Pieternel had made her swear was for dire emergencies only.

Meriç would love this set-up. He would want it left intact and agree to pay before Pieternel realised the money had gone.

She flicked her hands down the front of her tabard dislodging some of the dust that had settled there. Absently, she picked up a broom and pulled together the small scatterings of grime that had floated down as she'd been in the loft wrestling with the equipment. The dining room would be easier. She could do that from a step ladder, taking advantage of the intricate coving and dim lighting. Only she couldn't do it now, not with the big windows only semi obscured by their fancy blinds. That would have to wait for later.

Officially, she wasn't here. The restaurant was closed all day and no one was here this morning. She'd studied a map of the city and arrived via the alleyway from the other direction, the direction in which the gang from last night had vanished. It was a maze of back yards, high walls, fences, a lonely pedestrian network especially before dawn. It gave no clue about the people who had jumped her.

A specialist team was due in the afternoon to steam clean the kitchen. As manager she was to arrive in time to let them in. Once they were here, she could legitimately pull down the heavy blinds at the front as though the deep clean was to stretch right through to the front of house. Then she would work covertly while the cleaners were busy in the kitchen area.

Everything in the back of house must be set up before then. She'd fixed the most difficult camera first, crawling through the loft space above the awkward cave of a corridor that held the walk-in, cold-store and office. Just the one in the kitchen to install before the cleaning company arrived. The camera there must give a comprehensive outlook whilst being out of danger of a steamed lens. She manoeuvred the broom awkwardly, pushing the heap of dirt into a dustpan and tipping it into the kitchen bin. No need to bother about the grime she would generate in the kitchen itself. It would vanish under the onslaught from the cleaning crew.

She had a full couple of hours before they were due to arrive. It was less time than she'd originally planned but her schedule had slipped because her first task after ensuring both external doors were locked and bolted, had been a fingertip search to work out what that duo last night had been here for. Nothing missing. Nothing disturbed. Other than the scuff marks on the floor they might have been figments of her imagination. She told herself they'd panicked because she'd got away … expected her to raise the alarm. It didn't wash. They'd been relaxed, casual almost. She glanced at the time. Two hours was ample.

Leaning on the expediting station, gaze on the ceiling to make sure of the optimum positioning for the hidden robotic eye, she was startled by a sudden noise from the back exit.

Someone had pushed a key in the lock and turned it. Now they were shoving the door, trying to open it against the internal bolts.

The gang from last night. They hadn't found what they'd been looking for … had returned for it now. They'd got keys from somewhere … come back … knowing it would be empty.

She clenched her fists and tried to slow the thumping of her heart. They hadn't taken her keys. They hadn't taken the spares from the office. And the impatient rattling was too blatant.

Could it be Meriç or one of the other key-holders on an innocent mission? The noise stopped and footsteps retreated towards the road.

A banging from behind made her spin round. Someone knocking at the front door. Someone who wasn't bothered about being seen in the middle of a busy street. That surely made it a legitimate key-holder.

She slid open the bolts on the back door and retreated. If it was Meriç he would be annoyed that she hadn't come to let him in. He hated using the back entrance. But Meriç wasn't due here till late afternoon.

Voices from the alley … more footsteps.

Treading silently she skipped past the lockers, the walk-in, the cold-store and dived into the tiny office, shutting herself in and putting her eye to the crack where the makeshift door and frame had never fully met.

Annie was aware of a brief muffled exchange mixed with the sound of the back door swinging open. She caught indignation in the tone but couldn't pick out any words. The tiny crack through which she squinted gave her nothing. She stood up straight. Better to rely on sound than to risk cramp by bending awkwardly.

More than one set of footsteps crossed the kitchen. Her mouth dried. Then she felt relief as she heard them go on through to the dining room away from her hidey hole.

An indistinct clatter reached her as though chairs were being moved, or the cupboards in the hostess-stand searched. They wouldn't find anything out of the ordinary in there. She'd given it a thorough vetting in her early morning quest to discover what last night's events had been about.

The footsteps returned. She listened for them to make their way across the kitchen to the exit, but they stopped in no-man's land between front and back of house. Then they moved her way.

A click and a metallic screech. A familiar sound. A staff locker being opened. She made herself push away the paranoia trying to tell her it was her locker being ransacked. Nothing of note in there anyway. It was a staff member coming back for something they'd forgotten. Last night had been busy, everyone had been tired and on edge having Meriç there the full shift.

Two people. Annie could hear shuffling sounds and indistinct grunts. One of them had to be a key-holder which made it the chef or Yağız.

There had been no words spoken since they'd come close enough for her to hear. Someone was raking through a locker. The other was pacing. It might be her imagination but the pacing sounded random, impatient.

As the restaurant manager she had legitimate reason to be in while the place was closed. She could simply show herself and demand to know what they were doing. She held still. If they weren't staff members then she was at a two-to-one disadvantage. And if they were, she didn't want them to know she'd been in. For all that there were no tell-tale wires trailing, she didn't want anyone putting two and two together later.

She'd thought she had plenty of time to complete the installation, but these intruders were eating into it. She needed them gone.

If necessary she'd have to walk out and confront them, but they'd been here a while now making no attempt to keep quiet. It would look odd, would arouse their suspicions for sure.

At last one of the sporadic mumbles she'd been hearing prompted an audible response.

'I know I left it. I missed it almost at once.'

It was the waitress, Carol, and her voice came from worryingly close.

Carol wasn't a key-holder, so she had to be with the chef or Yağız. If she had to show herself, Annie wasn't sure which would be worse. The chef was the staff member who resented her the most, but Yağız was adept at undermining her behind her back. And however she played it now, her appearance would look dubious. They would tell the others.

It was too soon to give up. She'd been in tighter corners than this. As she held herself still and silent almost within touching distance of them, she worked through her story. She would pretend she'd been asleep in the office.

Whatever Carol was looking for, surely she'd found it by now. The lockers were small. No matter how much clutter she had in hers, she'd had time to go through it twice over.

At last, Annie heard the tinny slam of the locker door and the snap of the key securing it. She allowed herself to relax just a fraction.

She wanted the sound of Carol's locker closing to be followed by retreating footsteps. It wasn't. She tensed again and risked softening her knees to see through the gap between door and frame.

Carol was in her line of sight, three-quarter face, her expression puzzled. It wasn't the look of someone who had found what they were searching for. Annie willed her to turn away, to leave. Time was getting on.

When Carol spun round, it wasn't to retreat. Annie felt a hand grip her insides. She and Carol seemed to be eye to eye.

It's dark in here. She can't see me.

Her mind tried to calm her. Even if Carol's target was the office, and it looked as though it might be, she couldn't have seen anything. Not yet.

Carol took half a step, moving away from the bank of lockers, taking herself out of the thin line of sight that was all the crack in the office door allowed.

Annie froze as the footsteps came nearer. She daren't ease herself upright for fear of the creaking floor, but her spyhole showed her nothing. On edge, every hair on her skin prickling as the tension rippled, she prepared herself.

She must leap out on them, not let them catch her. Attack, the best form of defence. She had to radiate indignation, to roar a demand to know what the hell they were doing here. And she had to be ready to yawn and rub her eyes at a key moment to plant the seed that she'd been asleep and they'd woken her.

'I know I left it.' Carol's voice.

At last her companion responded with more than a monosyllabic grunt. It was the chef. 'If it's not in your locker, it's not here. What are you going back there for?'

Yes please, Annie begged him silently. Stop her. Take her away. Carol had chosen to call up the chef rather than Meriç or Yağız to retrieve whatever she'd forgotten. It made sense. Meriç had a keen sense of the restaurant hierarchy. He wouldn't have come out at all, and there was no love lost between Yağız and the wait staff.

She caught glimpses of a tartan gabardine. Carol was dressed up, on her way somewhere special and wanted whatever she'd left behind last night.

'That back door wants seeing to if it's going to stick,' Carol said.

The timbre of the voice told Annie that Carol had turned away to face the chef. She willed her to walk away, to forget whatever it was and go to her special do.

'It was you. You didn't turn the key fully.'

'It still stuck. The lock might be damaged. You don't want to find yourself locked out.'

It hadn't occurred to either of them – why would it? – that the bolt might have been drawn when Carol first tried. The chef must have given her the keys and left her to negotiate the alleyway. He'd intended waiting for her outside. Management protocols were clear. No non-key-holder should be in the building alone. It wasn't something Annie would be able to reprimand him for but she noted it. People got careless when they got comfortable.

A scraping sound and a grunt of effort. Carol was pulling open the door to the walk-in.

'It won't be in there.' Annie heard impatience in the chef's tone.

'If it's not in my locker, I must have taken it out and put it down. Annie or someone'll have picked it up and shoved it away somewhere.

Her heart sank. Carol was right. If she'd left something out, whoever found it would have put it away. It was a matter of seconds or maybe fractions of seconds before Carol realised or the chef pointed out the obvious. Lost property would have been put in the office.

She daren't take her eye from the crack in the door to scan the high shelves, but she reran her early morning search. Her mind's eye would not give her anything that could possibly have come from Carol's locker. The only thing left out had been that freeze-dried apple that she'd told Meriç was tomatoes, and that had been legitimately stashed under the counter. Once she'd extricated herself from this situation she would get that box out again or at least move it to the walk-in. It might not do it any good to be in the cold-store.

She was glad for the reminder but it didn't help her now. Carol wasn't looking for a giant box of freeze-dried apple, she was looking for something that had been small enough to fit in her locker. And if she was stealing ingredients she would surely go for the more lucrative quality spices.

Carol's voice, indistinct from inside the walk-in, regained clarity as she emerged. 'It's not in there.'

''Course it's bloody not!' from the chef. 'Come on. That's enough. You've left it somewhere else.'

'I'll just look in here. It has to be somewhere.' Carol's voice held a level of pleading. Annie couldn't see what she was pointing at but it must be the office. There was nowhere else. 'Did you see those strands under table three?' Carol went on in a more conversational tone. 'Were they saffron?'

Saffron? Annie felt her brow crease. She'd searched the place but she hadn't been looking for random spillages on the restaurant floor. Surely the gang last night hadn't been here for saffron and if so why cart it to the front? It might be one of the most expensive items on the inventory but surely not worth a full-blown smash and grab.

The swish of the door to the walk-in reached her ears as Carol pushed it shut. Footsteps retreated. Not Carol's, the chef's. He was off to check out her claim to have seen saffron strewn under the tables. Annie realised Carol had simply been diverting him to give her time to complete her search.

She came into view through the narrow crack. Annie braced herself. She had to time her move for maximum shock value ... leap out and shout into Carol's face.

It was too late to be pulling the stunt but with the chef out of the way, it might still work. As long as she was fast enough and furious enough Carol would jump and scream before she realised it was Annie. The chef would come running. All would be chaos and Annie would have to maintain the momentum of confusion and anger right past the awkward question of why she hadn't heard them sooner. Then it would be a case of hustling them out while she still had time to set up the camera above the kitchen.

It was Annie herself who jumped at the click of another door, almost expecting to feel the handle she held pulled from her grasp.

But it wasn't the office. It was the cold-store. With more method than logic, Carol was working her way from door to door. Locker first, then walk-in, then cold-store. As if anyone would put lost property in there.

Footsteps. The chef was back. Carol had re-emerged. Annie heard the grunt of effort as she pushed the heavy door into place.

'Was it saffron?' Carol asked.

'It was sunlight through the blinds. Have you found it?'

'No.'

There was a tinge of humour in the chef's voice as he said, 'Addled brain. That's why I'm a top chef and you're just a servant,' but there was a hint of superiority as well.

'Yeah, OK, sorry. You're right. Thinking about it, I stopped off at my sister's on the way home. I suppose I could have left it there.'

Annie held her breath. Surely the tiny office wasn't going to escape scrutiny. It was the obvious place to stash lost property, and yet in the normal run of things it was out of bounds to Carol or any of the wait staff.

She listened to the chef's grunts of impatience as Carol puzzled over whether or not this whatever-it-was had been lost at her sister's. A glimmer of hope sparked. He must have thought of the office but all he wanted was an end to this interruption to his day off. But what about Carol? Even with an invisible wall dividing the place according to Meriç's hierarchies, could she really have forgotten the office? She'd expected to be in here alone. It was the apparently sticking back door that had brought the chef in with her. Had his presence prompted her to end her search?

They were leaving. She tracked their footsteps across the kitchen to the back door, heard it open, close again and the key turn in the lock. She allowed herself a moment to slump in relief, then straightened up to get back to work.

Carol hadn't found what she was looking for. Would it turn up at her sister's? Or had it just become the one thing that had gone missing after last night's break-in?

Chapter 7

'And you can watch these cameras live, can you, from wherever you want?' Meriç's gaze bounced from the screen that showed the back of her head to the ceiling of the corridor outside the office. Annie stood in the doorway, in the camera's line of sight, and watched him stare as he tried to pinpoint the lens.

'That's right.' Annie spoke casually. 'Of course I haven't bothered setting up all the sophistications. No point, I'll be keeping an eye on things from close by.'

Her casual tone hid satisfaction. Meriç was on the hook.

As she watched him, she felt her phone buzz receipt of a text. It would be Pieternel in response to the explanatory email with an urgent tag that she'd left last night. Pieternel would have to wait. She mustn't break the mood by pulling out her phone, not after all the hard work of the past couple of hours.

The kitchen ceiling had almost been her undoing with its maze of ducts for wiring and outlet pipes, but she'd made it – just. The knock at the front door had come as she was placing the final camouflage. She'd had to scramble down to let them in. The fine dust from the holes she'd drilled had rained down and settled widely, but she'd left no sign on the plaster above. The cleaning crew had tried to hide their surprise at the grimy figure that opened the door for them. Annie had ignored the saucer-eyes and acted as though she answered the door like this every day of the week. They'd clocked the strategic mops and buckets that she'd placed about the dining room to give the impression she was doing her own deep clean in the front of house. As she'd shown them through, she'd spotted a mess of footprints on the cooking surface of the flat fryer. Let them think Meriç's standards had fallen. Let them think anything as long as they didn't recognise the clue to what was hidden above.

Once they were in and the operation underway, she found herself with the perfect cover to complete the job in the front of house. The final camera was placed in half the time it had taken her to do the back.

When Meriç arrived, the kitchen was a hazy den of activity, the chemical aroma seeping through the face mask that she'd been given. She'd handed one to Meriç as he'd entered but he'd waved it aside. His restaurant … his air to breathe if he chose.

He'd been prickly, ready to find fault where he could.

Annie smiled as she watched him now with the new surveillance toy. His glee at the possibilities opening up before him had quashed any vestige of bad mood. He was just where she wanted him.

'So I could get a live feed across what distance?' he asked, his glance again flicking up to search the blank ceiling.

'The other side of the city easily,' Annie said. She could truthfully have said the other side of the country – the technology was simple – but Meriç would have assumed her to be exaggerating. The other side of the city amply covered his needs.

'I can see it might be useful in some circumstances.' The studied lack of interest in his tone belied the rapt stare he fixed on the screen.

'I set one up a couple of years ago,' Annie said. 'Not dissimilar to here really. Someone who didn't have time to be in two places at once, wanted to keep an eye on new staff, see how they bedded in, if they were trustworthy, all that.'

'New staff are not my problem,' Meriç pointed out. 'You're the only one on the books who counts as new.'

'What about the young kids you get in to help with prep for big events?'

Meriç's army of casual workers, some of them schoolchildren

who came for cash-in-hand pocket money at weekends or early morning before school, had already been under her spotlight and she'd discounted them. They didn't have the access.

He dismissed her concerns with a wave of his hand. 'They're always supervised. Not here long enough to be running this sort of scam.'

Annie was inclined to agree. Not running it, for sure, but possibly foot soldiers for someone else. And as for supervision, she recalled the chef letting Carol have his keys.

'You'll dismantle it when the job's done, I suppose ...' He let the words fade.

'I could price it up and leave it for you, if you want,' she said, as though the idea had only just come to her. 'I've had to install it all as part of this job so you'd only have the equipment itself to pay for. It's all new.'

'I would have thought I'd already paid enough to have a handful of cameras thrown in. You haven't even found the culprits yet.'

'That's what this is for. We'll have them in a week.'

Again he looked up, running his gaze across the ceiling, as if his next move depended on whether or not he could spot that lens. 'And you would set up the new restaurant as well on the same terms? And my home?'

Annie considered. There was a useful bargaining chip in here if she played it right. And there was another obstacle looming. Even if she found out what was going on, got the culprits bang to rights on the cameras, Meriç would demand his pound of flesh. He would insist the job wasn't done until she'd stayed the full six weeks. He'd have her calculating the options, how and when to proceed, the bad press of a prosecution versus a few quiet dismissals, what to do. She wasn't contracted to stay on and do the paperwork, but by the terms of Pieternel's contract he could insist she did just that.

She glanced full on at the camera's lens, saw Meriç stare at her image on the screen as it stared directly back at him. His head whipped round to try to follow her line of sight.

You won't see it, she thought. I'm good at what I do. And it had given her a foothold, a tiny bit of collateral that might be her early route out of the job. If he let her finish and go, she would set up his surveillance for the bare cost of the equipment. Only with Meriç, the negotiation could not be stated so baldly.

'OK, a week or so to complete what I came here to do,' she said. 'Then once that's wrapped up, I guess I'd be able to kit out the other site and your apartment on the same basis before I left.'

'You told me you'd have the problem bottomed out in two days, didn't you?'

'Strictly speaking I said a week. It was you who gave me two days. Who knows? We might get lucky. Like I said, it's sporadic.'

'So let's say you're done in a week. You spend another … what? … a day maybe on the rest of it? Seems to me the equipment ought to be in the package, given what I've paid.'

He had a reasonable point, if not a contractually enforceable one. She fell back on, 'I'll have to check that with Pieternel but …' She ran the words into a shrug.

'I could easily get in someone local to do this, you know.'

It was a delicate balance. They were a whisker from agreement. She was tempted to say she'd do her bit, and trust to luck that she'd talk the money out of him, but things were tight. If she'd only managed to talk to Pieternel, her hands wouldn't be tied. She had to be sure of the money from one or the other of them, and if Pieternel thought she'd promised Meriç an extra freebie, she might get sticky over company funds.

'Use someone local and word will get about,' she said.

'Is that a bad thing? If the staff know they're being watched they'll be on their toes.'

'In my experience you'll just train them to be smart about what they're hiding.'

Meriç slipped off his jacket, fitting it around the single coat-hanger that swung from the hook on the door. The place was hot with all the activity and equipment running. Almost as hot as at the height of service. His mobile sang out, vibrating the pocket, making the jacket swing gently from its hanger.

He pulled it out, glanced at the screen and red-buttoned the call. 'They must be almost done,' he said.

A clatter from the kitchen cut across his words, spinning them both round. They peered down the corridor to see someone lean over to retrieve a fallen stepladder.

'Let's take a look.' Annie turned to the screen and clicked to the kitchen view.

They watched white-coated figures pulling together their paraphernalia, packing it away under the watchful eye of their boss who leant forward with a gleaming white cloth to dab at already clean surfaces as though x-ray vision had shown some particle invisible to the human eye. It was like watching Meriç at the expediting station with his fussy and unnecessary dabs at the rims of the plates as they went out.

She'd got him. She was sure she'd got him. The degree to which she'd hidden the lenses had been the decider. Her task now was to back off and let him come round in his own time.

'It's looks nice and clean, doesn't it?'

'Don't let the façade fool you, Annie. We don't have our five-star rating without serious hard work, you know. It's the details that count.'

With that, he stalked towards the heart of the operation, to conduct his own meticulous test of the quality of the work. Annie smiled. She'd known he would react that way to her over-bright comment. It got him out of the conversation, left him where he liked to be – in control.

Despite the searchlight brightness from the kitchen strips that leaked through to the dark cave of the office, a subtle background tone was missing. The afternoon light had faded as they'd talked.

As Meriç headed for the kitchen, Annie reran their exchange. Not much to it on the surface, but crackling with intricacies between the lines. She had glimpsed the reasons for Pieternel to tie in this man so tightly, to have insisted on prepayment. He'd have wriggled out of anything less than a straitjacket. And yet Pieternel had left him too much control in determining whether and when the job was done.

She must have his absolute assurance of money for the equipment before she agreed to set it up. In fact it would have to be money upfront again because she couldn't afford to buy new kit for the other premises.

It was an added reminder of times gone by. Completing the job became a formality, her bad credit the real hurdle. This time the memory bolstered rather than depressed her. Things weren't half as bad now as they'd been back then.

Meriç expected her to sit staring at a set of tiny images on a computer screen for at least two days and probably a week. But she barely needed a minute of the right footage. Once she had a handle on what was going on, she'd have it unravelled in moments. But if Meriç thought her tied up watching live footage, all to the good. She had other plans ready to hatch if needed.

A direct line to Pieternel was priority, to get her straight on what this job was and wasn't about. OK, Annie knew her problems were small beer compared to what Pieternel was fighting, but it wouldn't help from any angle if she fell over the lip into a financial black hole.

Meriç's form disappeared round the corner but his voice was strident as he quizzed the boss of the cleaning crew, demanding to see what they'd done. Would footprints on the fryer get a mention? She hoped not. It would put Meriç into a bad mood as well as give him a clue as to where the kitchen camera was placed. He was too pig-headed to ask outright. She intended drip-feeding him the necessary clues as reward for his cooperation with the money and until she had his financial contribution tied in, he wouldn't get to know.

She turned back to the office to sneak a look at her phone, to check the text that had arrived just after Meriç. A new message showed against Pieternel's name.

Yes I understand but you MUST finish the job for Meriç. All 6 weeks. Explain later.

Annie seethed with frustration. Pieternel didn't understand at all. She thought she understood and wasn't going to let in any other thoughts, not even enough to find five minutes on the phone for her business partner. One of Annie's barely hatched plans cracked through its shell. Meriç had guaranteed her two days where she needn't be at the restaurant. It would only take one to travel to London and get Pieternel face to face.

She took a step further into the office, itching to ring Pieternel right now, knowing it would do no good.

And there on the desk lay Meriç's phone vibrating another incoming call.

It took a moment to realise what she was seeing. A name flashing on the handset. *Mrs Peters.*

She dived for the phone, stabbing at it to accept the call and jammed it to her ear.

The monotone buzz of a missed call was all she heard. She stared at it and glanced quickly behind her. Meriç's voice was audible but not nearby.

Grabbing her own phone, thanking every deity she could summon that Meriç disliked smartphones and praying that he left his Bluetooth connection permanently on, she hooked their phones together, bypassed the security code and unlocked it.

As she scanned his phone's log, she felt the weight of her bottom jaw.

Calls from Pieternel to Meriç … calls from Meriç back to Pieternel. She looked at the dates … at the times. Every call had run into several minutes, other than the one Meriç had received and red-buttoned not ten minutes ago and the one she had failed to connect just now.

Chapter 8

Flabbergasted, Annie couldn't prise her stare from Meriç's phone.

The walls of the tiny office crowded her, their haphazard configuration oppressive. OK, Meriç was a client paying a lot of money, but the calls weren't all one-way and this didn't add up.

Her fingers itched to spell out a furious text. *This is Annie. What the* … No, that would simply alert Pieternel, give her time to hone some story that excused the fact she'd been in touch with Meriç whilst ignoring Annie.

Meriç always kept hold of his phone. He slipped it from one pocket to another as he changed jackets or removed outer layers in the sticky heat of a busy service. Today was a one-off; a break in routine. He hadn't realised yet. She watched him on the surveillance screen as he and the boss of the cleaning crew settled up.

This was a now-or-never opportunity but already the screen showed him heading back to the office.

Like seeking footholds on an ice-cliff Annie's mind darted about. There was always something. Use his weaknesses, his overwhelming pride in his operation, his arrogance. Anything to keep him out of the office.

Could she persuade Meriç to supervise the crew as they left? It was a menial role. He would expect her to do it. But if she could plant the right seed … those booths he'd had installed just before she came to work for him … brand spanking new … his pride and joy. Meriç loved new. The intricate edgings around the bar. He stroked them like favourite pets.

She stepped forward to meet him, to block the way to the office.

'Meriç, could you go with them into the dining room, get them to move about a bit? I need to focus the camera in there. It's a golden opportunity to test it out with a group of people.' She was spouting garbage but he wasn't to know that. 'Oh and you might show that guy the booths. He mentioned them when he first came in.'

'Really? What did he say?'

'He was talking to one of the others. I'm not sure. He said about them being new, hadn't seen them before. He kind of whistled under his breath.'

'Did he now?' Meriç gave a short laugh. 'Well, he could hardly miss them, could he? Not that he'd ever admit to me that he's impressed.'

'Oh, I'm sure he was.' Annie stoked Meriç's ego. 'He sounded really amazed.'

Meriç half turned and called to the disappearing crew, 'Don't run out on me. I've something to show you. Give me a minute.'

With that, he swung back towards the office and made to push past Annie.

'Ooh, quick!' She opened her eyes wide, put shock into her tone. 'They nearly had the corner off the bar when that came in.' At random she pointed at two figures efficiently packing hoses on an awkwardly shaped piece of equipment.

With a gasp, he spun on his heel and rushed to supervise.

'I'll watch on the cameras,' she murmured to his retreating back, then dived for the office, pulling out his phone, and punching in Pieternel's number. It was answered on the first ring.

'Everything work out OK?' Pieternel's voice snapped in her ear.

Holding back a furious retort, Annie turned her mouth away from the microphone and grunted in response.

'Did you do what I told you?' Pieternel's tone grew in impatience.

Annie couldn't hold back. 'Pieternel, it's me,' she growled through gritted teeth, wanting to shout, knowing she was on borrowed time. 'What the fuck's going on?'

'Annie! What are you doing on Meriç's phone? I tol–'

The tiny room spun around her, the walls pressing in, the miniature figures of Meriç and the man he wanted to impress moved silently on the screen, unreal, like an old movie. Anger and confusion pushed out clear thought. Pieternel had been going to say, I told him … what?

Her senior partner's voice was back on track now, velvety smooth, expressing regret at having had to keep Annie at arm's length. Annie thought the tone held more irritation than remorse.

'Annie, see it from my side. You know how impulsive you can be. We could lose everything. You know you can trust me.'

'Pah! Don't talk to me about trust! What's going on?'

'It's complicated.'

Annie jerked upright as the figure of Meriç made a move. She had to leave herself enough time not only to cut the call but to erase it from the log. Meriç and his companion walked towards the booths by the front windows. Annie let out the breath she'd hadn't realised she'd been holding.

Complicated? It was always complicated. Should she demand a potted version now or get Pieternel's absolute assurance of a call later? But Pieternel's absolute assurances of contact were what she'd had time and again over the last few days.

'I need to know,' she said. 'And I need to know now. Alternative; I'm on the first train back.'

The darkening shadows pulled in the walls. This was no safe haven, just the slow closing of a trap. Remnants of the sharp chemical aroma hung in the air. Annie shivered at the tang. Was it her imagination or was it water meeting bare wiring … beginning to scorch? What damage had she done clambering over the equipment? Had she opened a route for corrosive chemicals to seep in and initiate a fire? She felt the tremble across every inch of her body. She didn't need imagination. She knew what it felt like to be trapped in a dead end … the smell of fire creeping closer … the case that had precipitated this whole cascading crisis had almost burnt her alive.

'Right now, Pieternel! What's going on?'

Meriç sat close to the table where Ahmed had been with his in-laws. It had been Ahmed's boss who had dragged her out of the fire that day. He'd liked her less than Meriç did, but training had made him seek her out and save her. Meriç wouldn't give her a second thought.

Pieternel was talking, but the sense fragmented as her attention split between the screen and her obsessive sniffing at the air to identify the first whiff of smoke.

She had to listen, to take it in, to filter the real story from the bullshit. Let the imaginary fire do its worst. Pulling in a breath, she turned her back on the doorway, standing side on to the screen. She was experienced enough to be alert to untoward movement catching the corner of her eye.

Pieternel was saying something about the need to be careful over how she moved forward. 'I have to keep the business ticking over on bread-and-butter jobs because … well … are you going to pump in a shedload of money for us to take a year off? No, and no one … else is either. Ticking over but comatose. And the only way to do that is to keep you and anyone personally connected with you at a distance.'

What was that pause, why had Pieternel tripped on her words? But there was sense behind what she said. Who would do business with a firm that was under security services scrutiny? And Annie had been the one to inadvertently put herself in the firing line, but …

'It's not just me,' she pointed out. 'They came after you, too.'

The tiny noise from the handset might have been Pieternel failing to hold back a gasp. Pieternel was terrified. She knew better than Annie how close they'd come to simply being wiped off the map as expendable nuisances.

'I'm keeping my head down as well. And I'm trying to run

the business while I'm supposedly out of the loop. And trying to rebuild. I don't need your paranoia, Annie. I can support you doing this work for Meriç but not if you drop out of it. And when I say support you, that's relative. There's no money for you to go off on one of your extracurricular jaunts.'

Ah, so she'd clocked the use of the company card. 'But I'm going to get more money out of him,' Annie said. 'It'll cover what I've spent and anything more I need to spend.'

'It'll have to.' There was acid in Pieternel's tone now. 'I've stopped the card. I told you that was for emergencies. How is bog-standard surveillance equipment an emergency? You didn't even get a great price on it. Why didn't you ask me to send something from here?'

'I had to–' Annie stopped as a movement from the screen grabbed her eye. The boss of the cleaning crew had shifted in his seat. They seemed engrossed in their conversation. 'I had to move fast, get what I could. I'll need more stuff so yes, you can get it sent on.' Annie dived on the opportunity and outlined what she would need.

'All that?' Suspicion in Pieternel's voice now. 'How big is his place? Single restaurant, single kitchen, he told me.'

Annie gave a mirthless laugh. 'Since when did you rely on client descriptions? You know what it's like. On the face of it, yes, kitchen and dining room. In reality, it's L-shapes, nooks and crannies, store rooms, cold-stores, outside storage, rest rooms. Staff areas, lockers, an upstairs …'

'An upstairs? He definitely told me one floor.'

Annie looked down at the grime on her tabard, the streaks of dust on her sleeves, the feel of grit in her hair; it had been an awkward crawl through the loft space. 'It's not really used,' she said.

Again the screen caught her attention. Though both men still sat in the booth, they looked ready to rise now and call it a day.

'Listen, Pieternel, get me that stuff sorted out. I'll come down and collect it. We can have a proper talk. I don't have to be in the restaurant tomorrow.'

'No, I'll send it. I won't be here tomorrow.'

'The day after then.'

'I'm in Zurich, Annie. I'm staying all week.'

'Why–?' She pulled herself up. Borrowed time. What was important right now? Assuming she didn't get to talk to Pieternel again for another week or two, what did she absolutely need to tie down right now? 'I need that equipment.'

'I'll see that it's on its way first thing. If you'll be at home tomorrow I'll courier it.'

No shortage of money all of a sudden, Annie thought sourly. Money! 'You'll have to put something in my personal account if I don't have the card.'

'Why? What do you need money for? You had money up front.'

'That covered my rent for a fortnight and living expenses. If I end up staying longer I'll be on a park bench.'

'A fortnight?' Pieternel sounded affronted. 'I thought you'd have paid the full six weeks in advance.'

'Why would I? This was never a six-week job. And I need to eat.'

'Come on.' Pieternel laughed. 'You're working in a restaurant. You shouldn't have to worry about food. I'll pay the extra four weeks on your rent. That should be enough.'

Annie bristled as she drew in breath for a furious riposte. A movement from the screen. She barked into the phone, 'When I ring you tomorrow or the day after, you answer. OK?'

With that she cut Pieternel off, scrabbled through the call log to delete all trace.

As she seethed, she played the tiny keyboard, one eye on Meriç who was on the move now. It was clear Meriç hadn't used half the features available to him on this phone. All those scribbled reminders on his desk, but no electronic notes.

Never let an opportunity go ...

Not that there was an opportunity here, just some unwelcome revelations about her business partner. A demon took hold of her, an urge for some kind of revenge on Pieternel. Pieternel hadn't found five minutes for her, but she'd been in daily contact with Meriç. She looked at the unused Notes function. It was foolish to meddle. It would signpost her illicit access to his phone, but then if he never used the thing he would never know. She was on borrowed time now. Meriç had disappeared from the dining-room camera.

Her fingers flew across the tiny keyboard spelling out four simple words. *Message from Mrs Peters*. It wasn't quite a lie. There had been a missed call. She knew it was childish but she wouldn't have anyone meddling behind her back.

There! That would cause consternation for Meriç when he found it. He would take it at face value and suspect Pieternel of hacking his phone. Try trusting her then, Annie thought viciously as she closed the app and threw the handset into the pocket of the Meriç's jacket where it swung on the back of the door.

Footsteps approached.

She acknowledged Meriç as he rushed back in, diving at once for his jacket. Finally he'd missed his phone. Annie was aware of the suspicious glance he threw her as he flicked through it. She'd left a glaring anomaly, but he would find nothing untoward on the log and would have been far more suspicious had he found the phone on the desk where he'd left it, where she couldn't have failed to see it. If he remembered later, he would assume a subconscious act on his own part had slipped it back where it belonged.

Now and then it needed the veneer of a lie to convince someone that a mirage was reality. It was one of the lessons she'd learnt over the years. Another more practical lesson was how to travel far, fast and cheaply. She would have her rent paid, would she? Like she was some junior operative not to be trusted, tied in one place without the money to buy a train ticket to London, let alone to chase Pieternel across mainland Europe.

Pieternel was in for a shock if she thought she'd tied Annie down. She wouldn't wait until tomorrow, she would be back on the phone the second she shut the door of her rented room behind her tonight and if she didn't get answers, she would be in London in the morning and Zurich by nightfall.

'It's all fine,' she told Meriç. 'Working beautifully. I'll just delete the surveillance capability from the office PC and everything's ready.'

'Delete it?'

'Someone else'll be looking after the place while I'm not here. I've no idea how IT savvy they are, but we don't want anyone finding anything. They won't spot the cameras and we mustn't let them stumble on this end of the kit either. You wouldn't normally be in tomorrow, would you? Best to keep out of the way. With both of us gone, someone might take advantage, catch up on anything that they haven't managed to do while I've been here.'

As she spoke she reflected that, according to the figures, her presence hadn't been any kind of barrier to the continued running of the scam whatever it was, but that was a puzzle to solve another day. Her priority was to get back to the relative privacy of her room and make a call of her own.

Chapter 9

Pieternel answered on the fourth ring.

'I've only a few minutes,' she said in greeting. 'I ducked out of something when I saw it was you.'

Don't expect gratitude for that, Annie thought tartly. 'The full story,' she said. 'What's happened? What's gone wrong?'

'Nothing, don't worry,' Pieternel said. 'We dropped off the radar quickly and that's how it'll stay if we keep ourselves under the parapet a while longer.'

Annie listened as her colleague filled in some gaps. Nothing had changed. Essentially they were off the hook but still exposed to reputational damage. It was PR now rather than life or death.

'We're still vulnerable,' Pieternel told her. 'If the wrong people sniff us out, they'll be on us like vultures. We'll be lucky to have the skeleton of a business left.'

The phraseology gave Annie pause. There had been a time when they had been the ones pouncing to pick over the bones of a fallen rival.

'So what's all the subterfuge with Meriç? Why is it so vital I stay buried up here for so long?'

'No subterfuge. He was forever contacting me. I couldn't ignore him. He's paid a lot of money.'

Annie thought back to the call log. The earliest calls had been from Meriç. Maybe she had made too much of it.

'You were answering his calls when you were refusing mine,' she pointed out.

Pieternel let out a tut of impatience. 'I was busy! You weren't going to cause ructions if I ignored you. He was.'

'The occasional text wouldn't have broken the bank.'

'I sent you texts! Annie, there's nothing going on that you don't know about. We need Meriç's money and he was always going to extract his pound of flesh. He'll try and get the money back too once the job's done. I'm relying on you to keep a lid on him.'

The words made sense, and yet there was something nagging at the edges, something wasn't right.

'You can handle him,' Pieternel went on. 'And if you have to stay the full six weeks, what's the bother?'

'Money partly. How am I supposed to live?'

'Oh, come on, Annie. Look where you're working. You're about to uncover some two-bit staff scam. Skim something off the top. No one'll notice.'

Annie felt her lips tighten. This was the side of Pieternel she'd never liked, never trusted, the side that would sell out anyone at the drop of a hat. 'OK, forget Meriç just for the moment,' she said. 'Anyone half competent could do this job. And I could be back in London helping you to rebuild. I want to know what you're keeping from me.'

'Nothing. I just didn't get round to returning your calls. I've had a lot on.'

The response was too hurried. 'Tell me,' she said.

There was a hesitation before Pieternel spoke. 'The best thing you can do, Annie, is keep the money coming in. I've got the rest of it covered.'

The rest of what?

Jumpiness leaked across the airwaves. There had to be something else going on, because what reason could there be for keeping clear water between everyone and their main HQ? Or was it just the ghosts from Pieternel's past? Pieternel had been security services trained. It had given her the skills that had carved out this specialist niche for her and Annie, but the legacy of a horrific hostage incident had left her with a deep vein of paranoia. To have her own operation targeted by special forces had shaken her more than Annie had at first realised. Now she wondered if she still hadn't appreciated the strength of the psychological knock that Pieternel had taken. But she couldn't lose the feeling of something solid behind this. An awful thought struck her; was it all happening again?

'There haven't been any more break-ins, have there?' she blurted out. 'Are you being followed? There's no one behind me. I haven't let my guard down.'

'Nothing like that, Annie. I told you, we're off the hit list.'

That sounded sincere, and yet ... She couldn't let this go. 'Then what is it?'

The hesitation this time was a long one. Annie knew before the words came that she'd broken through the shell at last.

'Do you remember a couple called Dyson and fforbes?'

Without knowing what she'd expected Pieternel to say, Annie knew it hadn't been that. Pieternel was harking back to the first time they'd nearly gone under, when she'd been desperate to secure investment, but then they'd got lucky at the expense of a rival firm. Dyson and fforbes were incidental names bubbling up from that time, two names out of dozens. Her mind showed her a fuzzy impression of an oldish couple.

'From years ago?' she queried, as a hazy memory surfaced. 'Vaguely ... two small f's, wasn't it? Why?'

Pieternel laughed. 'That's right.'

'Weren't they potential investors?'

'That's how they painted themselves but it came to nothing. The thing is, Annie ... I think they might have been behind the break ins.'

'What!' The surprise was so great, Annie almost dropped the handset. 'You mean the recent break-ins ... the ones where ...?' Her head spun. The raids on their offices had been sophisticated affairs that had come close to breaching Pieternel's own security systems. Dyson and fforbes? She'd had them down as an elderly pair of duffers with money to burn. 'But they could barely climb the stairs. Who are they?'

'Oh, they won't have done it themselves but it had their stamp on it. They know people. They work for money. They're completely amoral.'

Annie swallowed an instinctive, *takes one to know one*, and said, 'So they're attached to some big outfit, are they? Which one?'

'Oh no. They're strictly freelance these days.'

These days! thought Annie wildly, feeling herself drowning in potential complexities. She hadn't felt like this since being a complete rookie pitched into a thorny case before she'd had the know-how or experience to cope.

'I'm thinking if they were behind it,' Pieternel went on, 'then they did it for money, bought in the muscle, it'll just have been a job to them. I'll bet they were paid well. But they must have known it might end badly for us and if they've got wind that we're struggling, I'm half expecting them to try to buy their way in at bargain basement rates.'

'Well…' Annie considered. This was Pieternel's territory, not hers, but she remembered a time when Pieternel was ready to welcome Dyson, fforbes and anyone else with a thick pocketbook. And now it looked like finance wasn't the only asset that this particular duo brought with them. 'You said yourself that a shedload of money was one way round the problem. If they're genuine, why not talk?'

'I don't like them. I don't know enough about them.'

Annie didn't know what to say. Pieternel had ways to get at any background on anyone. If this pair of duffers had truly put up a wall against her, then … she couldn't even think about the implications of that.

'They've approached you, have they? What have they said?'

'No, I didn't say that. I just think they're sniffing round again.'

Ah. No actual approach … Pieternel's paranoia working overtime … Was ninety-nine percent of this inside Pieternel's head? Annie reflected that she knew more about Pieternel than almost anyone living but she'd barely scratched the surface.

There was one reassurance. The focus of the problem wasn't her or the job in Hull. It was one of Pieternel's private battles, and maybe one that she should let her fight out alone.

It left her problems unsolved but she wasn't without ideas.

'You said you didn't have to be in the restaurant for a couple of days.' As though reading her mind, Pieternel turned the conversation back to Annie. 'What's that about? Why would Meriç be giving you time off?'

'Not as such. Officially I'm taking the time for personal reasons, but we're both going to steer clear. Those cameras I bought; they're in place so we're giving the staff some rope to see if they show us what they're up to. At least I hope he has the sense to steer clear. He's such a control freak.' *Almost as bad as you,* she added to herself.

'So if the set-up's done, why do you need more stuff?' There was suspicion behind Pieternel's words.

'I've barely got anything covered.' Annie strove for a casual tone as she kicked herself for the slip-up. 'I know for a fact that things are going on in the areas I haven't been able to target. It's subtle. And Meriç is going to want proof. Look, are you sure you aren't being followed or anything like that?'

'I told you, no. Why?'

'I don't understand why you're keeping a distance. If we're off the official radar shouldn't one of us be flying the flag? I don't like the idea of the office running without either of us. I can come back. I'll soon sort something this end.'

'No, Annie …'

Annie smiled to herself as Pieternel scolded her. She had diverted the talk away from why she needed more surveillance equipment to cover a restaurant that was already covered. Her worries weren't entirely made up. She would be happier if she could get back to the heart of things. Her original plan to wind up the job early had mutated into a plan to obtain the ready cash she needed, and as Pieternel's voice washed over her, it changed again – maybe she could put a contingency in place that would cover both angles.

Chapter 10

The winter sun had barely shown its face as Annie strode through the back streets of the old town the next morning, savouring the fresh air after so many days incarcerated in the restaurant. Hull's museum quarter had had a facelift since she was last here, yet the familiar landmarks still stood, guiding her route.

Pieternel's courier had turned up with the dawn, a well-packed box of robust surveillance equipment strapped to the back of his bike. Annie had checked, repacked it and stowed it in the bottom of the wardrobe before setting out.

Meriç would assume her tucked away in a dark hole somewhere, her gaze glued to a tiny reconnaissance screen, but forget that. Everything was being recorded. She would skim through it this evening and ferret out any abnormal behaviour.

Staying to do the job for Meriç had become unavoidable, but she hadn't given up on finding a route to an early release. And he would pay her extra to keep the equipment she'd set up and have similar installed at his home and the new premises. But she had no way to make him to pay out until the main job was over. She hadn't been exaggerating in last night's call. She needed money, ready cash.

The aroma of fresh coffee seeped temptingly from every shop she passed, but she daren't buy take-away anything until she had an income source restored. It was all very well for Pieternel to tell her to pilfer from the business she was here to protect. It wouldn't be difficult but she'd never sunk so low and didn't intend to now.

Moonlighting, on the other hand, was a different matter. As long as she carried out her duties efficiently and well, she had no qualms about finding some short-term cash-in-hand freelance work that she could fit around her hours at the restaurant.

It would be good to savour this as an aimless stroll, an exercise in stretching her legs and breathing some much needed fresh air, but her feet were taking her a route that was familiar from years ago. Not that she knew whether the Thompsons still camped out in that ramshackle bit of office space in a building that should never have arrived in the twenty-first century un-condemned.

As she rounded the corner, she felt a smile break across her face, and shook her head in amazement. There up ahead was the old office building, its façade newly painted. A sign hung below the upstairs window sill, *Thompsons Agency.* The Thompsons had always wanted their own sign but never got round to it. The lettering was professionally done. She shook her head. Money spent and no clue as to what sort of agency it represented. Looking closely she could see the ravages of rot beneath the gloss coat of the window frame that held it. The downstairs windows however – not the Thompsons' – were new uPVC, giving the building an upmarket air.

The owners had done it up, though as far as the upstairs went the transformation seemed skin deep. And the Thompson sisters, with opportunism that surprised Annie, had climbed on the coattails of the refurbishment and hung their sign. She wondered if the inside would have seen equal change.

The downstairs space had been decluttered, painted and left stark and efficient, but the tide of change stopped at the stairs. The new paintwork came to an abrupt halt at the top of the bannisters, showing a crisp clean face to anyone who stayed on the ground floor.

They've done it up to sell, was Annie's first thought. The sisters' realm in the pokey upstairs rooms would be advertised as useful storage space. She wondered if they'd realised, if they had a rental agreement that would offer them any kind of protection. Unlikely.

Oddly it was the downstairs office (hadn't it been a busy accountant's firm when she was last here?) that looked drab and inactive. Attention snapped her way, people looking briefly hopeful as she pushed through the door, then drooping back to listless pursuit of whatever they were doing as she headed for the stairs. It was the first floor that was the source of bustle and activity, the chatter of several conversations growing clearer as she reached the landing.

Annie could see both sisters through the crack in the door. They sat at overcrowded desks, telephone handsets clamped to their heads as they rattled out their one-sided conversations interspersed with sharp comments to each other.

'It was seventy-nine-ninety-nine and we paid it, I remember it from …'

'We could certainly look into that, if you could just let me know … Pat! Where's the diary?'

'I'll look out the receipt if you give me a moment … Open your eyes, Babs, it's right in front of you … You damned well will wait …'

Pat heaved her bulk out of the chair, her eyes narrowed in concentration, her head swivelling towards the door as Annie walked in. 'Take a seat,' she rapped out, pointing Annie to a ramshackle plastic chair. 'With you in a minute. Now, where's that …?' She spun round open-mouthed. 'Good Lord, it's you. Babs, look who the tide's brought in.'

Barbara shot her a fierce glare that morphed briefly to surprise before she returned to her call.

Up here, hidden from public view, decay was apparent in the cardboard tacked across a broken window pane, the back yard it overlooked even more full of garbage than Annie remembered.

'Got the bugger!' Pat wielded a sheet of paper as she snatched up the phone again. 'Now, listen, I have it here in black and white …'

'I'll put that in the diary.' Barbara spoke in velvety tones that vanished as she turned away from her call. 'Coffee?' she fired at Annie.

'Uh … thanks, yes, love one.'

'You know where everything is.' Barbara tipped her head towards the door. 'Black for me. Usual for Pat.'

Inwardly Annie heaved a sigh but she wasn't about to pass up the chance of a hot drink. There would be biscuits too stashed in the small kitchen. She rummaged through the cupboards, a smile of satisfaction curving her lips as she spotted the biscuit tin, scratched and battered but the same one that had done service all those years ago. It was a disappointment to find half packets of value range custard creams and ginger nuts inside rather than the fancy chocolate she'd expected. Maybe this tin had become too battered to be 'best' but she couldn't see another, or maybe value range biscuits were the Thompsons' idea of a diet, much like that sign was their idea of useful advertising.

As the kettle rattled to the boil, her spirits rose. She heard Barbara pick up another call as the second phone rang again. This was as busy as she'd ever seen the place. The money must be rolling in and the sisters hated the legwork that went with it. She could take some of it off them – something she could weave around her restaurant hours – and she would insist on having her fee in advance and in cash. Meriç had hinted he was prepared to stretch her time off to a full week. She could do a lot in a week.

When she returned with a laden tray, their calls were finished. They sat facing each other, eyes locked with an intensity that made Annie pause. A coin balanced on Barbara's crooked thumb. As she watched, Barbara flicked it high in the air. Annie joined them in tracking its spinning progress. It reached its zenith, then spun back towards Barbara's waiting palm. She caught it, closed her hand over it and slapped it on to the back of her other hand.

Barbara smiled. 'Tails,' she said. 'I win.'

'For now,' Pat grumbled, leaning in to check the coin.

Annie found herself doing the same. 'Who's won what?' she asked Pat.

'Nothing.' Pat gave a dismissive gesture. 'It's just a little something we devised to sort out any differences of opinion.'

Barbara pushed her chair away from the desk and lolled back, hands behind her head. 'So, what brings you to this neck of the woods?'

'Just passing, thought I'd drop in and see how you're doing.'

Annie laughed at the quizzical looks that were turned on her. No one was ever *just passing* the Thompsons' office. It was on the way to nowhere in several senses. 'It's a surveillance,' she amended, having worked out her story. 'The guy I'm following is spending a few days here, but he doesn't need watching closely so I thought I'd look up some old friends. You look busy.'

'We're doing OK. Did you see our sign?'

'Yup. Shouldn't it say what sort of agency you are?'

'Oh, everyone knows the Thompsons.'

'And it's missing an apostrophe.'

'Sod that. People can go to night classes if they want grammar.'

'So, what are you working on? Anyone else here or is it just the two of you?'

They gossiped idly as they sipped their coffee and crunched biscuits, swapping information about mutual acquaintances. Annie learned that the sisters worked on their own. Their last employee had given them a dynamic six months of frenetic work and networking before boredom had taken her to pastures new. They referred to bringing in freelances when they needed help. That was encouraging because it sounded as though they needed help right now.

'I enjoyed my time round here,' she said, laying the foundation. 'I could do with something that would get me out and about a bit. This job's like tracking a sloth. If I'm on the guy's tail I'm mainly sitting around and half the time I don't need to be with him at all.'

She reached for the biscuit tin as the sisters exchanged a look. They'd got the message. She was at a loose end with time to spare. Now, offer me some work, she urged them silently.

'And how are you and wossname ... Pieternel ... doing? Got yourselves in deep water, I heard.'

'Yeah, well, goes with the territory. It was sticky for a while but we're fine now. Busy as hell.'

'And yet you've got time to twiddle your thumbs round here?'

Annie shrugged. 'Not really, no, but the client insisted it was one of us on the job personally and she was prepared to pay, so what can you do?'

Another unspoken exchange flitted between the sisters.

'We were like that a few weeks ago, weren't we, Babs? Up to our eyes.'

Barbara nodded. 'Things have eased off a bit just lately.'

Not too much, Annie hoped. 'Still, it must be hard to keep up with everything, with just the two of you I mean.'

'We manage. We keep things ticking over. You're right though, there are times when we could do with a bit of help.'

Annie tipped her head in a tell-me-more gesture, reflecting that Barbara was as relaxed and friendly as Pat. Of course that would change if she put herself back into the hired help bracket. Barbara would get autocratic and distant. She could cope with that. She'd had plenty of practice over the years.

'Vince used to send us stuff,' Pat said, apparently at random.

Annie's mind worked swiftly. Pat and Barbara's father had set up the agency and when he died, his business partner Vince Sleeman had cherry picked what he wanted and left the sisters with the dregs, keeping them in business with the crumbs from his table but never allowing them enough leeway to become wholly independent. Though that wasn't quite true. If the sisters hadn't been so lazy they might have broken free during the time Annie had worked for them.

But Vince Sleeman too was gone, leaving the agency at the mercy of his widow, Leah, and her henchmen. Annie had sometimes wondered what changes that would mean for the Thompsons, and assumed it wouldn't go well for them. In fact, knowing the way she'd last left things between Pat and Leah, she wouldn't have been surprised to learn that Leah had hired assassins to wipe both Thompson sisters off the map. The last thing she would have guessed was their present prosperity.

But why had Pat mentioned Vince just now? 'And do you still get … stuff …' She felt her way carefully, 'from his outfit … from Leah?'

They both nodded. 'Yes,' Barbara said. 'More than we used to. We rarely have time to take on any other work these days.'

Pat barked out a laugh. 'Rarely?'

'OK, never.'

'Some work comes direct to us,' Pat went on, 'but we never seem to have the time for it. We get some interesting cases though, don't we, Babs?'

'Yes, look at that one that came in the other day. Good money. One evening's work. We've not turned it down yet, but we'll probably have to.'

Annie licked her lips. Good money, one evening's work. 'Maybe I can help?'

'Maybe … How long are you around for?'

'At least a week,' Annie replied, keeping her options open. 'This one evening that's needed. Is it any evening or a specific one?'

'Next weekend, big engagement party out in the sticks. This guy needs someone to watch his daughter's fiancé.'

Weekend evenings were busy. Meriç would want her at the restaurant. But she could talk her way out of that.

'Don't know what he thinks he'll get up to at his own engagement party,' Barbara put in.

Pat ignored her. 'They're using outside caterers. He'd organise it that we send someone in as hired help.'

Alarmed, Annie ran a swift mental inventory of Meriç's bookings for outside catering. 'Where in the sticks?'

When Pat named a village out Wetherby way, Annie relaxed. Meriç had a pretty much closed circle for outside events and never went that far. And it felt good to see the enthusiasm that lay behind both sisters' studied indifference. Their new found fortune had all come from Leah who could pull out the rug any time she liked. They wanted to build up the independent business they should have striven for years ago. Better late than never.

'How do I get there?' she said, getting down to practicalities. 'I don't have a car with me.'

'You can take a taxi,' Barbara said. 'It's sixty-odd miles, allow an hour to an hour and a half for traffic and stuff. And you'll need the right uniform so you fit in. You can hire one from …'

'Whoa, whoa …' Annie stopped her. 'Let's just be clear about this. Whatever I need, you're going to have to provide.'

A swift glance speared between them.

'He's offering good money,' Pat said.

'Yeah, you said. What difference does that make? I'm assuming I get a reasonable cut.'

'Yeah, yeah, sure you do. You know us, kid, we wouldn't rook you. It's just …'

'Just what?'

'We were thinking you could kit yourself out, do the job, and we'll pay you when he pays us.'

Annie's smile held no warmth. Typical of them to want to delay payment. There was a time she'd have given in just for a quiet life. They always paid up in the end. Only this time, though they didn't know it, delay wasn't an option.

'This is the deal,' she said. 'You pay upfront, expenses and everything.'

'How about we pay you the day after the job?' Barbara said.

Annie's irritation grew. Barbara always had to win the battle one way or another. She shrugged. 'OK, the fee the day after, but all expenses upfront, taxi, uniform, whatever.'

'Best if we pay everything the day after,' Pat said. 'Keep it simple.'

'What's the fee?' Annie wanted the answer to that question tied down before she gave in and put her cards on the table.

As soon as Barbara named a price, Annie doubled it. Had Pat spoken first, she'd only have upped it by half. Then both sisters jumped in together with new figures, Pat's higher than Barbara's which earned her a glare. For a moment she thought the sisters would start a private bidding war with each other, but they settled for a mutual glower and turned back to Annie.

'OK, agreed,' she said, naming the highest figure so far mentioned, 'but I'm afraid it's upfront expenses or no job. I don't have the money to cover it.'

Pat gave her a piercing look. 'I thought you'd straightened yourself out financially. You're doing well, aren't you?'

Annie nodded. 'Temporary glitch.' She crossed her fingers. 'But there it is. You're going to have to shell out or lose the job.'

'Damn it,' said Barbara, aiming a scowl her way.

Annie looked from one to the other of them, suddenly realising there could be another interpretation to all the sidelong glances. Leah in control of the work flow doubtless meant Leah in charge of cash flow … value range biscuits, not chocolate … they'd all been playing the same game.

'Sorry, kid,' Pat said. 'We're going to have to pass. And we thought you'd been sent from heaven for this one. We've not got the bus fare between us, let alone money for cab rides. We're flat broke.'

Chapter 11

....

Although she'd come away empty-handed, Annie felt buoyed up by seeing the Thompson sisters. They'd had the light of battle in their eyes, and not just for quarrelling with each other; an issue they'd taken steps to address since she was here last. She'd asked about that spinning coin whose path she'd tracked with as much interest as the sisters, though not knowing what it was about.

'We don't waste time disagreeing these days,' Pat had told her. 'We decide by time-out coin-toss. Babs tosses the coin; I call it, and we go with whichever way it lands.'

'Not that we let something like that rule the way we go on,' Barbara had chipped in.

'So you don't always go with it.'

'Not if it's wrong. That'd be daft.'

They certainly needed order in their lives though Annie was sceptical about this new scheme. It was late in the day to turn round the firm that had bumped along the bottom for so many years, but good they wanted to try. Their only way out was to build the independent side of the business, and in typical profligate fashion they had nothing put aside to fund their fight back.

She retraced her route from the Thompsons' to her rented room, using the walk to mull over various options. Were Pat and Barbara bluffing? Could they really be so broke they had to turn down a lucrative contract because they couldn't shell out for a cab? Were they thinking the same about her, holding out for her to say she'd do it with no cash upfront?

Shell out …? Something in the phrase took her mind back to Pieternel, to a time when the firm had operated on smoke, mirrors and thin air, the time from which the shades of Dyson and fforbes had re-emerged to spook the woman she'd worked with for so long and yet barely knew. Was it paranoia or genuine cause for concern? If the latter, then from what angle? She was no closer to answers as she arrived at the dilapidated terrace and let herself in.

Closing the door of her room behind her, she shut out Pieternel's ghosts and the Thompsons. Meriç was paying for her time and deserved enough of it to get his job done.

She fired up her laptop and connected to the cameras covering the restaurant.

The live feed showed her a dining room full of lunch time trade, Carol and Yağız moving efficiently amongst the customers with laden trays, not a value range biscuit in sight. The built-in microphones in the dining room were as good as useless when the place was full; the cameras were too high. What she saw was a mime show. Switching to the kitchen, the sudden burst of sound startled her, but it settled into the clatter of equipment and hiss of steam. She caught a couple of irritated shouts from the chef.

'Who moved those vanilla pods …? What do you call this …?'

But the kitchen was too noisy to pick up anything useful.

Her third camera by the staff lockers, outside the doors to the walk-in, cold-store and office, showed her the empty corridor with a hint of movement at the far end where people moved between front and back of house. The microphone here was well placed to pick up conversation but wasn't somewhere people lingered once service was in full flood.

She flicked to the other cameras and followed the ebb and flow of the operation but when she found herself concentrating more on the food than the people serving it, she stopped.

Nothing would happen at peak times. Everyone was too busy. It was the odds and ends of the day, very early, very late, the lulls between one service winding down and the next starting. Those were the times to watch. The theory didn't convince her. Busy times could be the perfect camouflage, but she hadn't factored in how distracting it would be to watch people eating the sorts of meals that would be beyond her means for several weeks.

Of course as manager she could go down there now, walk in and order food. Full time staff were allowed to take their breaks in the dining room if they stuck by Meriç's strict guidelines; quiet times only, and no breach of the customer/staff divide. If a single real customer was present, any staff member eating in the dining room must be waited on. No diving behind the bar for self-service drinks or carrying trays through and then sitting down to eat. The result was that staff rarely ate there. It was uncomfortable to be waited on by colleagues, and it was unusual for the restaurant to be completely empty once the doors were open. The thought of good food was tempting but she couldn't justify breaching the agreement she'd reached with Meriç that they would both steer clear for two days.

She swapped from the live feed to the early morning to watch the staff arrive. It was a bustle of activity as they poured in through the back door. She fast-forwarded the recordings, concentrating on the flickering images, slowing to real time when anyone ventured out of their normal zone.

The far end of the kitchen was busy with the comings and goings of the casual staff who clocked in to slave over the big sinks and chopping boards. Her camera angle wasn't great. She'd discounted them as viable suspects, but ideally she would get a camera in that alleyway. It was just a shame there hadn't been one out there the night before last.

As people first arrived, she caught their chat in the corridor by the staff lockers; a few morning greetings, some idle gossip as they pulled off their winter coats and tried to stuff them into their tiny areas of lockable personal space. Meriç frowned upon any but his senior team – himself, Annie, Yağız and the chef – using the cramped row of coat hooks outside the office, but at this season of bulky coats and thermal hats, he couldn't impose an outright ban without installing bigger lockers.

Once the bustle of arrival ebbed, there was little reason for anyone to linger in that short corridor and useful sound disappeared. People flitted by as they visited the cold-store or the walk-in, but they were alone so there was nothing to hear.

Annie slowed the recording as Yağız headed for the office. She watched him step by step; the high camera angle accentuating the jet black of his hair. He was acting manager in her absence and it was a legitimate place for him to be. He didn't stay long.

Ten minutes further through the recording a boy of about sixteen, one of the casuals, followed Carol into the corridor. Annie stopped the footage and replayed it. The boy's opening gambit was spoken too low for Annie to catch but it ended on, '... put up with him?'

She saw Carol shrug. 'Annie's taking a couple of days off, that's the story.'

'Has she been sacked?'

'Probably. Yağız has been on at Meriç to get rid of her from the off.'

Annie thinned her lips. He had, had he? She wasn't surprised. Yağız had taken against her before they'd met. He looked upon the manager's job as his own. And it would be, if she showed Meriç he was trustworthy.

As if on cue, Yağız appeared at the entrance to the kitchen. Both Carol and the boy returned to their duties.

Annie let the pictures roll by in real time for a while. There was nothing criminal in one of the casuals catching a break from chopping vegetables, but it was the first time she'd seen one of them as far inside the place. Their work was over by the big sinks. They had no staff lockers, no permanent presence, and came and went by the back door. Clearly the boy had seen Carol going into that corridor and slipped across for a quick word.

But what had Carol gone there for? She'd stopped when the boy approached her and had gone back the way she'd come when the exchange was over. Maybe she'd simply forgotten what she was doing or maybe Yağız's presence had changed her mind. If the latter, that suggested a surreptitious side to her actions.

Yağız had returned to the dining room. Maybe Carol would take her chance.

Sure enough, as Annie watched, Carol reappeared. With a brief glance over her shoulder, she pulled open the door to the cold-store and slipped inside.

In less than a minute she was out again. There was no hidden lens inside and nothing about Carol's reappearance gave Annie any clue as to what she'd gone in there for. Her tasks at this time of day were in the front of house, final preparations before the doors opened. Annie reran the stretch several times but learnt nothing new.

She stayed with the footage from this camera and let it race ahead again, seeing nothing but the blur of figures darting back and forth between kitchen and dining room at the far end of its reach. No one came closer until Yağız's form shot through to the office and out again trailing a wire that Annie recognised as the spare power lead for the POS system. So that was playing up again. She must get on to Meriç. It was a customer-facing system and if it broke down when …

She pulled herself up. The role of manager had burrowed deeper into her psyche than she'd realised. That stuff wasn't important. She was here to uncover a scam.

The next visitor to the corridor was the chef who headed for the cold-store which was a legitimate part of his domain, although unusual for him to go himself and not send a minion. She slowed the recording to real time and reran it.

Almost at once, she clicked pause and rolled it back to catch every second of his brief visit. He strode in slow motion past the lockers and the walk-in, then turned his head, that same over-the-shoulder glance she'd seen from Carol, before entering the cold-store.

No camera inside to let her see what was going on. He was gone for a full minute and then came out at the same moment that Yağız appeared at the far end and glanced his way. The chef's face creased to a satisfied smile and his hand, now holding an apple, rose to his mouth as he took a large bite.

He'd been in there for an apple? It made no sense. Eating on the job was instant dismissal. Meriç guarded his five-star rating fiercely. Annie played that moment again. Something about it made her certain that he'd deliberately taken a bite from the fruit when he saw Yağız watching him. Why would he court disaster like that? He wouldn't have done it in front of Meriç, but maybe this was his way of cementing his place in the pecking order.

He chomped extravagantly on the apple, leaving it between his teeth as he turned his back on the acting manager, pulling out a key and opening his locker. His bulk and the camera angle hid the locker front from Annie's view – and Yağız's – so she couldn't see what he'd taken out or put in, but instinct warned her of some sleight of hand.

It took several more runs through to spot it and it was his entrance to and exit from the cold-store that gave him away. When he strode in there, his chef's whites had been crisp and smooth beneath his huge apron. When he emerged there was a definite bulge in one of his side pockets. Furthermore, once he'd done at his locker the pocket lay flat.

Running it again and again, real time and frame by frame, gave Annie nothing more. That unconvincing apple had been a diversion to draw attention from whatever he'd stashed in his pocket. The by-play between the two men spoke of long-standing tension which interested her. Of course they'd never shown her that side of their relationship. She was the outsider against whom they were all united. But Carol had hinted at hostility.

What would he be taking from the cold-store and why now? He was a key-holder. Why not wait until after hours and go in to get what he wanted? She remembered his attitude when Carol had called him in the day after Boxing Day. He wouldn't bother with after-hours shenanigans. Whatever he was doing he was used to fitting it into the restaurant's quiet times. The whole move had been well-practised.

She would love a look in that locker right now. The master key was in the office safe, not that Annie would need it to tickle open a flimsy lock like that. The problem would be finding a quiet enough moment. And while she was there she could stretch the boundaries by awarding herself a meal break.

No, she couldn't. The chef had had ample time to reorganise his locker since this morning. All she'd seen were scraps of slightly odd behaviour; nothing she could begin to match to the inventory discrepancies. It wasn't reason enough to go down there.

She paused to wonder about the two who had jumped her the night before last. Could they have opened lockers and closed them again? Was that what she'd missed?

And what was it that convinced her she'd missed something obvious? She froze the recording and sat back rubbing her eyes.

Focus.

Carol talking to that casual worker then returning to the cold-store … the chef calling for vanilla pods … Carol distracting him that day, not with vanilla but with the spectre of spilt saffron. Both ingredients were pricey, she knew that from the inventory and wondered suddenly how much someone might make from them. She switched away from the camera images and looked up vanilla pods in various guises, amazed to find that she would have to pay over four figures for a kilogram at supermarket prices. That made them viable as an item for pilfering, although vanilla pods on their own weren't going to provide all the answers she needed.

Her covert surveillance, yesterday from behind the office door and now more comfortably from the hidden cameras, had given her scraps and snippets. Nothing that could be called evidence.

Stray images played in her head. All the ducking and diving to keep Meriç on the right path while she'd been desperate to contact Pieternel. All the tedious hassle of throwing out a suggestion then dropping out of sight to avoid his knee-jerk refusal, allowing him time to mull it over, to work out that it was his idea all along, waiting for him to return and suggest it to her. She'd had to do that the night of the raid; pushed that massive box from under the side in the kitchen to the cold-store. She'd pretended it was tomatoes, that someone had forgotten to put it away.

And the raid. What had that been about? It had had no purpose that she could find … except maybe Carol's lost whatever-it-was … was that what they'd taken? She wanted to ask Carol about it. Could she pretend the chef had told her?

The chef … he'd taken something from the cold-store this morning. She'd seen it in his pocket. He'd taken an apple too as insurance against anyone spotting him.

The chef … crunching on a fresh apple.

That box she'd slid across the floor.

She felt a frown crease her brow. Her jacket lay on the carpet beside the laptop. She pulled it towards her and slipped it on.

Had she got this right? Or was it hunger driving her and the knowledge that a good meal was there for the taking? Appearing at the restaurant would put everyone on their guard.

She could go later tonight, after it was closed. But Yağız would have bolted the front door and she would have to go in by the alley. That broken streetlight had been reported but it wouldn't have been repaired yet.

With sudden decision she snapped shut the laptop's lid and stood up. Something to eat would be a bonus but that wasn't what she was after. It was that huge box she'd used as an excuse to leave Meriç to his musings.

There's a box of tomatoes been left out. I need to put them away.

Of course it hadn't been tomatoes. It had been freeze-dried apple. She'd taken it as good luck to have found something to give weight to her story, had thought no more about it.

She'd used freeze-dried apple with Meriç the way she'd seen the chef use a fresh version of the same fruit to distract Yağız.

And there it was.

Her subconscious had been hammering at her for days that she'd missed something. She'd attributed it to Pieternel's behaviour, to Meriç, to anything but that bland cardboard box.

All those casual workers slaving over the sinks and chopping boards day after day. For form's sake she leant over and opened the laptop again, pulling up the inventory records from the restaurant, but she knew what would be there, or rather what wouldn't.

Meriç might skimp on staff comforts but only the best would do for his customers. She would lay good money that no scrap of freeze-dried fruit of any kind had been used in Meriç's restaurant since the day he'd opened.

Chapter 12

Time had barely crept into the afternoon but an overcast sky laid a heavy blanket that felt like the approach of evening. The air was hard and cold. Annie walked close to the buildings to take advantage of what little shelter they offered. On an official day off she should be able to wear her robust but battered jacket that was proof against Alpine storms, but it would look bad for the manager to call in looking scruffy.

Why do I care?

She almost said the words aloud. It was a matter of guarding her cover, she supposed. A genuine manager would take pains over these things. Of course today she was in the ambiguous position of being the manager who was assumed to have been sacked. A sudden thought. Would they refuse to serve her, thinking she was out to rook Meriç? She drew in a breath as if readying for battle. Let them try.

That box?

There must be more than dried fruit inside but it could have been removed by now, box and all. But what and why and how?

The chef was up to something and he seemed to have pulled the wool over Yağız's eyes, which didn't bode well for Yağız's ambitions to move into a management role, but it looked to Annie like straightforward pilfering. The chef was in a position to falsify things along the way, to disguise the origin of any big discrepancies at the point they were generated.

And what about Carol? It was hard to believe she and the chef were a team. For one thing if that jaunt yesterday held any relevance, then Carol hadn't confided in the chef. She'd had to involve him because he had a key, but if Annie hadn't bolted the back door, Carol would have been in there on her own.

As she strolled through the town, out of step with the general mass of shoppers who raced from store to store outpacing the cold, Annie tried to wind back Carol's story of the mysterious something that she had left at the restaurant on Boxing Day. If it had been that important – and clearly it had or why all that bother to try to retrieve it – what had happened that made her leave it behind in the first place?

The answer might be simple. Meriç had happened. He hadn't been going to be in and then he'd turned up. Maybe Carol hadn't dared to go and rummage through that box with the owner on the premises. She ran the theory through. The box extracted from wherever it had been … ready for … well, whatever it was for … Meriç turns up … the box is pushed aside under the counter by the expediting station. Obvious spot now she thought about it. No one would question a box neatly tucked under there. And Carol had come back for it the following day, but by then Annie had moved it into the cold-store.

She narrowed her eyes as she neared the restaurant. The pieces were beginning to fit.

Carol had persuaded the chef to let her in the next day, hoping it would be a quick in and out whilst he waited in the street, but he'd had to come in too. She'd pretended to search her locker – pointless for a box that size – then diverted him with the story of spilt saffron, as she ducked into the walk-in and the cold-store.

She must have spotted it in the cold-store. The question was had she done anything with it – removed something from it or hidden something in it? Annie wasn't sure she'd had the time. She hadn't lingered, not wanting the chef to follow her in. This morning had been her first chance.

Or so she must have thought.

Annie smiled to herself as she turned the corner and pulled her jacket tighter around her to meet the head on wind that swept down the main street. She could see the restaurant up ahead, its windows steamed, scraps of paper eddying about on the pavement outside. Her inner smile set into a glare of annoyance. Yağız should have had someone on to that. The big façade was the face to the world. It had to stay clean and … She pulled herself up. It was as though Meriç had scripted her thoughts. She didn't care about the restaurant as a restaurant, she reminded herself. Her job was to uncover the scam.

And perhaps she was about to, because although Carol had had time to get at that box again, she wouldn't have found it when she ducked inside the cold-store this morning. Yesterday, concerned that freeze-dried apple ought not to have been stashed at that temperature, Annie had moved it to the walk-in after the chef and Carol had left.

She paused to scrutinize the big windows, to check that the sign gleamed, all its internal lights working and then reached for the A-board to straighten it, stopping herself as a mental image of Meriç popped up. He always moved the thing a millimetre, took another look, and moved it back again. She pushed open the door.

'Good afternoon, ma–' The young girl at the hostess-stand tripped on her words as she recognised Annie, her hand frozen in the act of reaching for a menu, stymied over the uncertainty of Annie's role. Staff members didn't use the front door during service. Annie gave her a nod of encouragement.

'I'll sit over in Carol's section, OK?'

She plucked the menu from the girl's hand and made her own way across. Word would spread. The manager had come in to check up on things.

'Hi, Annie. We weren't expecting you today.' Carol was prompt at her elbow.

'I won't be in town for a couple of days,' she said. 'Family business, but I've had things to sort out before I leave. Thought I'd call in before I go. I'll get something to eat and check out the office. I felt a bit guilty dropping everything at such short notice.' She was pleased with that speech. It established that she was here in her managerial capacity and thus entitled to eat, although it was stretching the boundaries to take a rest break on a fleeting visit and to sit out in the dining room before lunch service was properly over.

'We can cope, don't you worry. Uh … I hope this family crisis isn't anything serious.'

'Oh I'm sure it'll all be sorted out. Right, I'll just have a coffee and …' She ran her finger down the menu, bypassing some mouth-watering delights and settling on a cheaper but substantial main. Pushing boundaries was one thing, breaking them with over-extravagance wouldn't be wise. Word of her visit would get to Meriç.

As Carol turned to leave, Annie called her back. 'You're busier than I expected. I'll get my own coffee.'

Carol gave her a tight smile. Another rule broken. Meriç would get to hear about this too, but, having advertised her presence in the dining room, Annie wanted to infiltrate the back of house while legitimate customers still occupied enough tables to keep the kitchen busy.

She was aware of an undertone of muttering, a hostile vibe as she slipped through and past the kitchen.

'Meriç said you wouldn't be in.' Yağız made no attempt to hide the hostility in his tone.

'Not staying,' she said, pushing past him and heading towards the office.

He spun on his heel and stalked off. She recognised the gesture, turning his back on her, as one of contempt. But he would return to hassle her while she encroached on what should have been his exclusive territory today. She was on her own but not for long.

She caught herself giving that same over-the-shoulder glance she'd seen from Carol and the chef before she pulled open the door to the walk-in and slipped inside.

The box was in the corner where she'd left it but she could see at once it had been opened. The tape flapped free in the breeze from the door. Someone had ripped it back enough to open the flaps. They'd made an attempt to smooth it down again but tape never held its stick once removed.

She heaved it out from the wall and opened the top, unravelling the heavy duty polythene inner liner. It had been cut open and folded down again. Inside lay a mass of what looked like polystyrene packing, but more regular in shape, tiny square bricks. She picked one out and bit into it, tasting the tang of apple. Then she plunged in her hand and rummaged through the mass. This would do nothing for Meriç's five-star hygiene rating and she hoped she was right in her assumption that it would never find its way on to a customer's plate.

The box was empty of everything but freeze-dried apple as far as she could tell without upending it. Carol must have found it this morning. She would study the footage later to see if she could pin point time and detail. Certainly it looked as though something had been taken out. Replacing the flaps and tapes she pushed the box into its corner, stood back to check it looked no different from when she'd first come in, and eased herself out into the corridor.

The bustle of service hung in the air. It was way too early for any member of staff to seat themselves in the dining room, manager or not. Under the general buzz she could hear Yağız's voice … couldn't make out the words, but the tone was light, friendly. He was dealing with a customer. That gave her a few more seconds alone.

… which was all she needed.

She pulled out her phone, flicking it to video one-handed with practised ease. In the other hand she held a picklock … *one second*

... the door to the chef's locker sprung open forced wide by the bulging load within. The tiny space was packed and chaotic. Nothing obvious ... *two seconds* ... a bundled jumper, packets that crunched under her hand as she reached inside, struggling not to let anything fall to the floor, fighting to assimilate the feel of the contents, to impress the shapes and colours on her mind ... *three seconds ... four ...*

She whipped her hand clear and snapped shut the door.

Footsteps from behind.

She strode the few steps to the office and went inside, closing her eyes, imprinting that brief moment on her memory, replaying the colours, the shapes, the feel, to analyse later against whatever blurred images her camera had picked up.

The glory-hole nature of the chef's locker annoyed her. Fresh food was stored nearby. They had a five-star rating to protect. Again she pulled herself up. Something about the ambience of the place had seeped into her. Maybe it was Meriç's pride in his operation contrasted against the haphazard outfit that the Thompsons ran, but she found herself fighting an urge to pen a notice to all staff reminding them that lockers should be kept clean and tidy at all times.

She reached for the PC and scrolled through the system. The morning figures were good, nothing to complain about. Yağız ran a tight ship, though what the bigger picture would show she wouldn't find out until later. She straightened a few papers on the desk and returned to the restaurant, mouth watering at the prospect of a good meal.

'I've put your coffee on your table,' Carol said as Annie emerged from the entrance to the kitchen. A stony voice accompanied the words. Annie gave her a curt, 'Thanks,' and returned to sit by the big window, cupping her hands around the welcome heat of the mug and savouring the aroma of good coffee.

Someone, presumably Carol, had retrieved whatever had been

there to retrieve, but surely the plan would have been to dump the box itself. One stray cardboard carton could stay undetected for a while – under the expediting station, say – but it would be caught in the regular inventory if it stayed too long, and then questions would be asked about who had brought in freeze-dried fruit and why. From the expediting station it wouldn't have taken much to shove it across to join the other garbage on its way out. Especially, she thought suddenly, if one of the casuals was in on it. Getting it out of the walk-in would not be so easy. She would leave as soon as she'd eaten, have a word with Carol or Yağız before she left, make clear that she was off on a long journey. They knew she had family in Scotland. Let them assume what they wanted.

She was biting into her second loaded forkful, savouring the melt-in-the-mouth perfection of the herb-infused lamb when her phone rang. Though tempted to leave it and enjoy her meal, she slipped it out of her pocket and checked the screen, aware of scrutiny from a couple at the table next to hers.

It was the Thompsons' office number which surprised her. She'd half expected it to be Pieternel. She had a private bet with herself that she'd been right; they weren't as broke as they'd claimed, just hadn't wanted to pay in advance.

'Patricia Thompson here from the Thompsons' Agency,' Pat's voice told her.

Patricia? The Agency's full handle? This was Pat's company voice. She was out to impress someone. Annie saw it all. Barbara would be with a client from whom they had expectations. Pat would be audibly occupied on the phone bolstering the make-believe of a busy, well-run outfit. Good strategy. Annie approved.

She shifted the phone to her other ear and raised the fork to her lips. 'What can I do for you?' she said, her voice muffled through a large mouthful.

The adjacent couple shot her a disdainful glance for her table manners. She turned away from them, thankful Yağız was through in the back and that Meriç wasn't here to see her making his customers uncomfortable.

'My partner, Barbara Caldwell, spoke to you earlier about a job we want you to take on.'

'Uh huh,' Annie mumbled through another mouthful.

She wondered if it was a new client dangling the promise of good money upfront, or the original client being persuaded to pay in advance. Whichever it was, Pat's call to Annie was to highlight the vibrancy of their operation, and maybe help to seal the deal.

'... our terms ...' Pat's voice was going on. 'Half the fee upfront.' She named an amount that caused Annie's eyebrows to rise and the fork to pause in mid-air before spearing another succulent morsel. 'And all expenses of course. Can you call in later and we'll do the paperwork?'

Annie strained to hear the muffled exchange that was playing out behind Pat's voice. Barbara's tone was unmistakeable though she couldn't make out any words. A second softer voice wove into the gaps. On this flimsy evidence, and knowing nothing about any of their clients apart from Leah Sleeman, Annie decided this call was designed to impress someone new. She'd nursed a hope it might be genuine until Pat had named that fee, signalling to her audience that the agency was in good shape and paid its operatives well, but they didn't pay that well, never had.

'You're not on speaker-phone, are you?' she murmured.

'No, no, not at all,' Pat's voice boomed.

'That fee was a bit over the top,' Annie said, 'but I'll take it. And don't overdo the successful businesswomen act. Your office is a wreck.'

Pat laughed falsely. 'Not at all, not at all,' she said again. 'Ooh, just give me a second. Mrs Caldwell has something for me.'

Again Annie jammed the handset close to her ear to catch the background exchange.

... of course ... lovely to ... shell ...

Scraps that made no sense. Was that shell out or shell up? That phrase had been playing at the back of her mind since she'd last spoken to Pieternel. The scrape of chairs. Whoever was there was getting ready to go. The tone more than any audible words told her that goodbyes were being said. She caught a woman's voice that was neither Pat's nor Barbara's and adjusted her mental picture, putting the woman in a nondescript coat, giving her a rounded face framed by hair that might have been a wig, not young but hard to put an age to. A man and a woman? Or had that been the same voice as the soft-spoken one she'd heard earlier? She'd taken it for a man but wasn't sure.

'Hey, kid. Sorry about that. Give us a mo. Babs is just showing someone out.' Pat was back in her ear, buoyant and relaxed.

Barbara was Babs again and Annie was kid. Whoever had been there was out of earshot.

'Were you on the level about the job?' Annie asked.

'Sure. We've had a stroke of luck. Someone wants a job doing at short notice, desk-based. They're prepared to pay over the odds and upfront. Me and Babs can sort it while you're out doing the other one.'

Annie heard the excitement in Pat's tone. She was even more desperate to be out from under Leah Sleeman's yoke than Annie had realised. 'Sounds good,' she said. 'And I like the new fee.'

'Ah … well … I was just saying that for effect. Didn't want them to think we were on our uppers,' Pat back-pedalled hastily.

'Where did they come from?' Annie changed tack. They could fight out the money later. Pat had said *they* were prepared to pay. She conjured up the woman in the nondescript coat, and set a man next to her … a soft toned voice, throaty, mellow, unhurried. A wrinkled black face, she decided, hair greying at the edges, suit plain but perfectly cut. She put another forkful into her mouth and wondered why she was envisaging him in such detail.

'Off the street,' said Pat. 'It'll be the new sign.'

A wave of wellbeing enveloped Annie as her body showed its gratitude for an infusion of good food. 'Cash payers?' she asked.

Pat said, 'Yup.'

That made the new clients needy. She would go straight back there when she'd eaten, not just for the money but to try to get more out of Pat, to make sure they hadn't taken on something they couldn't deliver. The woman in the coat, the man with the soft voice. She imagined them strolling away from Pat and Barbara's lair; Pieternel's ghosts leaving the scene.

Why had she thought that?

She was suddenly grateful that Pat hadn't mentioned her name at the start of this showy call. A shiver ran down her spine as her boss's paranoia reached out from across the miles that separated them.

'I'll be twenty minutes,' she said. 'And … uh … who are these new clients?'

'That's for me to know, kid, and you to find out.' Pat was relaxed as she shifted the ground, eased them into an employer / employee alliance.

It made no difference. Whatever there was to find out, she'd get to know once she had Pat face to face. Paranoia did no one any favours. She'd fought countless times not to be dragged under into Pieternel's world of conspiracies at every corner. She should just say goodbye and end the call. Those soft tones …

'Don't tell me,' she said, equalling Pat's relaxed tone and putting a laugh in her voice. 'Two small fs.'

'Oh, right, you know him?' Pat sounded mildly surprised as Annie's heart did a back flip. It couldn't be! 'Quite a character, isn't he?' Pat went on. 'Where do you know him from?'

'I'll … I'll tell you when I see you. Bye.'

She clicked off the call, and stared down at the remnants of her meal. This wasn't paranoia. This was real, but it made no sense. The would-be investors, the ex-security-services pair that Pieternel didn't trust … but then Pieternel trusted no one. The pair whose history Pieternel hadn't been able to find … and Pieternel could unearth anything about anyone. Was this new trouble or a new incarnation of the old? She'd only used the two small fs question because she hadn't wanted to ask outright and it was all she could think of. She had never known which of them was which.

So fforbes – two small fs – was the wizened guy with the greying hair, and Dyson was the craggy blonde with the maybe-wig. Pieternel had been right about them sniffing around, but wrong about where. And they hadn't come all this way to drop work in the Thompsons' lap. It was her they were after. The question was why.

Chapter 13

....

Annie climbed the stairs and let herself into her room. She'd taken a more or less straight route from the Thompsons' office. No one had followed her. She hadn't tried to be incognito since arriving in Hull but she'd been careful. She'd said to Pieternel that she'd been watching her back and she had. Yet Dyson and fforbes must be here because of her, and they must know she'd been to the Thompsons because why else would they have slid their feet under that table? Their intervention was going to give her the money she needed, but what other strings would be attached?

She'd accepted a wad of notes from Pat, her upfront retainer for next Saturday's job. Being solvent again had led to her only detour on her way home, a trip to the mini-market for life's necessities; good coffee and a snack for later, a box of fancy mince pies discounted now that Christmas was over.

She wanted to be sure that this job wouldn't tie her to that shadowy twosome. She'd asked some searching questions. The job had come along before Dyson and fforbes had set foot in the Thompsons' office, well before Annie herself had approached them. It was Dyson and fforbes' money that would make it possible for the sisters to finance the job, but she would be working for the Thompsons' Agency and no one else.

The money was almost a secondary consideration. It was those ghosts from hers and Pieternel's past that she wanted to know more about.

She'd learnt nothing from Pat. As far as Pat was concerned Dyson and fforbes had walked in off the street attracted by the new sign, undeterred by its ambiguity.

Annie had pushed the sisters into doing a basic background check.

'Pat said you knew them,' Barbara had objected. 'Can't you tell us about them?'

'Is there a problem, kid?'

They had both looked worried. They didn't want to see a new cash supply dry up.

'Nothing really,' Annie had said. 'I ran into him one time. Years ago. It's a distinctive voice; I recognised it when we were on the phone. I don't know anything about her at all.'

Pat had swallowed the lie whole and turned to her PC. 'I suppose she's right.' She gave her sister a glance. 'We ought to give them the once over.'

Annie tensed wondering what Pat would find, but it only took moments.

'Average punters. Pretty much nonentities, not from round here.'

'Where are they from originally?' Annie urged Pat to dig deeper.

Pat had pecked at her keyboard. 'Doesn't say. Some database glitch. They're not important enough for anyone to have ironed it out. I told you, kid, nonentities. They're our bread and butter this sort of client.'

She'd shrugged. It had been a long shot expecting Pat to find something Pieternel hadn't.

A part of her had wanted to be on the phone to Pieternel as soon as Dyson and fforbes' names had cropped up, but a voice in her head urged caution. It would mean confessing to having approached the Thompsons, though that was the least of it. Dyson and fforbes signalled dangerous territory.

If Pieternel made the wrong move, their whole operation could go under. And Annie found she no longer had the absolute trust in Pieternel's commercial acumen that she'd once had. Her boss was too ruthless, cut the wrong corners. Everything Annie owned was tied up in their business. She'd sworn that never again would she get herself so far into the financial mire that she hovered at the edge of destitution, yet here she was at the brink with no idea whether the appearance of these two spelt salvation or disaster.

She caught herself raking her fingers through her hair as she paced the tiny room. Who was it who used to do that at moments of stress? Oh yes, Ayaan Ahmed's boss, a detective superintendent someone-or-other. She smiled at the memory and smoothed down her hair. Ahmed's unexpected appearance in her life had become an incidental annoyance. It was hard to believe she'd let it get to her the way it had.

At least she could treat herself to decent coffee while she mulled over her options. She turned towards the tiny partitioned space that served as a kitchen, but as she did so, the doorbell sounded.

There was an intercom but no camera. She imagined a lined black face, greying hair at its temples, a woman of indeterminate age maybe wearing a wig.

'Hello. Who is it?'

'Meriç. I've come to see how you're getting on.'

A frisson of guilt ran through her. She hadn't given him a thought. 'Sure,' she said, buzzing him in. 'Come on up.'

She dived for her laptop, flipping up its lid and clicking it on, urging it to hurry so she could have the surveillance screens live by the time he reached the top floor, thanking every deity she could summon that he hadn't been half an hour earlier and found the place empty. Typical of Meriç to come and check up on her. She should have thought of it and been better prepared.

His nose wrinkled slightly as she let him in. This dingy room contrasted badly with his waterfront apartment. *Location is everything,* she'd told him when giving him her address. *I need privacy and good access to where I need to be.* She'd extracted a solemn promise that he would tell no one where she was living. Her insistence on secrecy had seemed to impress him.

His gaze homed in on the laptop, its small screen split into one large and two small segments as it played out live scenes from his restaurant. He bent down to peer at it. 'Found anything?'

'Bits,' she said. 'Not enough. Not yet.'

'And you have a full record of all these "bits"?'

'Of course.'

'What's going on now?' He stared at the screen.

She moved next to him and watched for a moment. 'They're preparing for evening service.'

'Well I know that. I meant what's going on that shouldn't be.'

'At the moment, nothing.' She pointed at the largest of the split screens. 'It all looks hunky-dory to me.'

Meriç nodded. 'OK, show me what you have. Show me these "bits" that you've found.'

'No.'

'What?' Meriç turned an outraged glare on her at this bald refusal. 'I'm paying your wages. Show me what you've found.'

'You're paying me to uncover the scam. If I show you the half-story I've found so far, you'll go steaming in and give away the whole set up. They'll pack it in and you'll never get the evidence. You'll end up in a tribunal for sacking the wrong people probably.'

'Don't be ridiculous. I'm not going to confront anyone.' Meriç's tone was assertive but he avoided her eye. 'Anyway, I need you back on the floor tomorrow.'

'We agreed a week.' They hadn't quite agreed a week. He'd said yes to two days, but Annie needed longer not only to get Meriç's job done but to do the job for the Thompsons.

'I said possibly a week. And I've come to tell you that your two days are not possible. I have family issues to be addressed. I have to go to Istanbul tomorrow. I'll be gone for a few days.'

'But it'll put the staff on their guard if I say I won't be in then I turn up. I've told them I had a family crisis. They think I'm on my way to Scotland.'

'They'd think it very odd if I were to go away and not call in my assistant manager. And anyway, it's managerial cover I need more than your investigative skills while I'm away. We can pick up the other business when I get back.'

'But surely Yağız can cope for a few days. He's very competent.' Annie kicked herself for all the times she'd implied otherwise.

'No,' he said. 'In these circumstances of course I would cancel your leave. They would think it far more odd if I didn't.'

Annie held her smile through the implication that his family problems trumped hers, and given that hers were make believe and his seemed to be real, she supposed they did, but suspected he'd have taken the same line in any case.

A thought struck her. 'I hope it's nothing serious,' she said. 'Your family problems I mean.'

'Nothing I can't handle.' He waved aside her question.

She couldn't tell if he withheld the detail because he didn't confide family matters to an employee or if there was no detail to confide. Maybe his sudden need to be away was as fictitious as hers. Had he thought through the strategy they'd agreed and decided to pull the same trick on her? She wouldn't put it past him.

'Listen, Meriç, I've an idea. I'll go in tomorrow but I'll be really grumpy about it and I'll find a reason to leave early. I'll make sure they're on their own at the times when I think things are going on. That way we'll have a fighting chance of getting something useful on record.'

'Do you suspect Yağız?'

'No, I don't think he's involved.' Annie spoke with some reluctance but it was the truth. She'd have liked to have unmasked Yağız as the villain but there was no evidence that he'd done more than fail to notice what others were doing – and that was an accusation that could equally be levelled at both her and Meriç. 'The thing is, Meriç, if I go in at your direct order and then duck out, someone's going to contact you and tell you.'

'I should hope so.'

'So the last thing you must do is give them the impression you're going to rush back. We have to give them enough rope or we won't catch them.'

'That's easy for you to say. I'm losing money.'

'You've been losing money for a long time. Believe me this is the way to put an end to it, and to get to know who on your staff you can trust and who you can't.'

He paused to glance around the room again, gazing at the skylight in the sloping ceiling. 'But you have seen something on those cameras of yours?'

'Yes, bits and pieces. Nothing conclusive and nothing that constitutes hard evidence. It's only been one day. When you arrived just now, I was about to … uh … stop watching and put the kettle on. I'll make us both a drink.'

She didn't wait for his reply but turned her back on him and went across to click on the kettle. A decent coffee would relax him and give her time to figure out just how she was going to make everything work.

The best part of an hour later, as Meriç got up to go, he had rearranged her ideas into a plan of his own. She was to go in the next day but as long as things were running smoothly, she could find an excuse to leave.

'Not for the whole day, Annie, just a couple of hours. And if anyone contacts me I will simulate annoyance but I'll make clear I can't come back myself.'

Meriç's 'couple of hours' idea was worse than useless. She was standing at the lip of a gaping chasm, and he was telling her it would be fine to jump half way across.

'They don't like me,' she reminded him. 'They see me as having blocked the promotion of one of their own. If I duck out for a couple of hours, someone'll be on to you to say that I've abandoned the place altogether. Don't let them bounce you into doing anything rash. You can always ring me to check.'

His eyes narrowed a little. He probably disliked the implication that anyone could bounce him into anything. That was fine, a useful image for him to have in his head when Yağız made contact to drip poison in his ear.

If all she was going to take was a couple of hours, she'd be better off staying to manage the place and picking up her undercover role once Meriç was back. From his point of view it was a viable option, but he didn't have Pieternel's ghosts breathing down his neck. Annie didn't want to spend a second longer than she had to wrapping up this job, and she intended having it so tightly bundled that even Meriç wouldn't be able to claim she hadn't finished it.

Forget his couple of hours, she would take the promised couple of days and more, but she needed to be sure he was genuinely out of the way and committed to his trip before she bent his plan back into something workable.

It wasn't part of her role to act as his PA efficiently second-guessing his every need, but it played to his sense of self-importance and was a tactic she'd already used to smooth her path through the minefield of the restaurant's prickly hierarchy.

'Shall I book you a taxi to the airport?' she asked him. 'I assume it's the early shuttle to Amsterdam.'

He softened at her offer, but was there a hesitation? Maybe she'd just surprised him.

'Uh … yes … that would be useful.'

'OK. Four-thirty AM from your apartment and do you have your ticket numbers? I'll check you on to your connecting flight.'

'Thank you, Annie, that won't be necessary. Just the taxi.'

His ticket details would have given her the confirmation she needed. If it was subterfuge on his part, he could simply turn the taxi away tomorrow morning, or even take the trip to the airport and catch another cab back again. But at least he would now think he had the bases covered as far as she was concerned. It wouldn't occur to him that she could cherry-pick a driver who would take a bribe both to tell her where he'd dropped his fare and if it was the airport, to hang around and confirm that he'd actually boarded the plane.

Chapter 14

Early the next morning Annie pushed her way through the alley behind the restaurant. It was piled with garbage, the bins stuffed to overflowing. She felt the urge to kick out at the stack of boxes to relieve her annoyance. She hated working for clients who constantly meddled. This job could have been done and dusted if Meriç didn't keep poking his nose in, withholding information from her.

She rammed the key in the lock. It wasn't only Meriç. Privately she had to admit that her mind hadn't been focused, still wasn't. After he'd left last night she should have been all over the first day's footage like a rash. Instead she'd slammed shut the laptop and gone out for a beer.

What was wrong with this door! She jiggled the key awkwardly with frozen fingers.

Had anyone sorted out an extra garbage collection she wondered suddenly. The Christmas break would have interrupted the regular routine. Probably that was her job, but no one had bothered to tell her.

She yanked out the key to inspect it, knowing it was the right one. And more as an outlet for her growing anger wrenched the handle.

At once her irritation evaporated. No wonder the key wouldn't turn … the door flew open, already unlocked.

What the hell …?

'What are you doing here?'

She jumped at Yağız's voice. He was standing by the big sinks.

Smothering her surprise, she grabbed for a veneer of crossness to garnish her words. 'Meriç cancelled my leave,' she snapped. 'He's got family problems or something.'

Yağız stared at her. 'I know. He came to see me. I told him I could manage.'

Annie gave him a wintry smile. 'Believe me, I told him the same. I could do without this. I really don't need to be here.'

She gave the door a forceful shove, banging it closed behind her as she turned away. Her annoyance abated a little because it had been a useful initial exchange, paving the way for her later exit.

Was he here this early as a conscientious acting manager or was there another reason? The cameras would show her when she got round to watching them.

She marched through the big kitchen casting her glance left and right, checking that everything was in order. Yağız would be watching her. This was a sequence she'd established from day one, scrutinising the place every morning, pouncing on potential violations of procedure but pretending not to notice everything. It bedded in a sense of predictability, gave the staff the feeling that they knew where they were with her. Standard technique for a surveillance that had to be conducted in plain sight. Her assumption before she started the job was that any scams that were playing out would be toned down while they sized her up, worked out what they could get away with. Though from what she'd seen in Meriç's books, her presence hadn't interrupted anything.

She had had confirmation that Meriç had boarded his plane this morning, but she wouldn't risk anyone ringing him during his wait in Amsterdam. He was capable of binning his plans and catching the next shuttle back. She glanced at the big clock. His connecting flight was due to take off at eleven-thirty which, given the time difference, meant she only had to wait until ten-thirty before he was incommunicado and heading fifteen hundred miles away.

Kitchen circuit finished, she moved through to the dining room.

If she'd been alone, she'd have gone to the walk-in first, but with Yağız's eyes on her she mustn't deviate from her usual routine.

He seemed to have lost interest. She could hear him banging about in the kitchen, a brief volley of angry words in a language she didn't understand. Someone else had arrived. She paused at the terse low-voiced exchange, moving quietly to the side of the bar to watch oblique-angled through the mirror. It was the chef. Interesting to see their mutual hostility played out but Yağız must have indicated that she was present. Yağız was withdrawing, one arm orchestrating whatever parting shot he fired. The reflection wasn't good enough to make out facial expressions but Annie could imagine Yağız trying to be authoritative and the chef looking down his nose; her own presence undermining one side and bolstering the other. She'd found this accidental window on the kitchen the first day she'd been here. Meriç would be appalled to know his customers had a view of the workings of the place though Annie doubted any of them had noticed. It was a doubly bounced reflection off a stainless steel back wall and the side panel of the bar mirror that would have shown nothing at all if both surfaces weren't polished to perfection daily. If there was anything significant to glean from the mini-row she would get it later from the cameras.

Back in the short corridor by the lockers she slipped out of her jacket and swapped it for the smart top that marked her as the manager. She clicked open the door to the walk-in.

The box was gone. Other containers had been stacked to disguise the gap.

If she'd done her job properly and skimmed across all yesterday's footage she would know exactly who had been in here and who had shifted the box. Carol presumably, but confirmation would have to wait.

For now she returned to the corridor, had a quick look inside the cold-store – nothing untoward – then made for the office to search for refuse disposal procedures to get that alley cleared. Yağız would know but she didn't want to have to ask. It would be here somewhere. Meriç's documentation was meticulous.

If she went outside right now, she would find the remains of that cardboard box. But what would be the point? If its label survived, she could challenge Yağız about the presence of freeze-dried apple but if he was unaware of the scam, he'd assume it was someone else's trash stacked by the restaurant's bins, and if he was in on the scam, he'd say the same.

She caught the draught of the far doors being swung wide as the rest of the early shift began to arrive.

No one seemed unduly disturbed by her presence and appeared to swallow her sulks and grumpy demeanour as par for the course. It was barely an act. Without Meriç's interference, this could have been the prime moment to leave the scammers the space to incriminate themselves.

When she left, she must be clear she wouldn't be back for three days, but she also had to hope that when this was passed on to Meriç he would believe it to be partly exaggeration from Yağız and partly a double bluff on her part. In the normal course of things, she chatted casually to Carol when she wanted information disseminating on the restaurant grapevine, but for this one she must talk directly to Yağız.

Timing would be key, and it must sound convincing.

She slipped out into the alley and walked away from the door before pulling out her phone and calling the London office.

'Hi Annie, Pieternel's not here.'

That had come rather too readily as though it had been rehearsed.

'I'm not after Pieternel,' she snapped. 'I want you to ring me on the restaurant's landline at exactly ten past ten. Don't say who you are. If anyone pushes, it's personal and it's urgent, OK?'

The timing was perfect. Annie had wandered across to the big windows overlooking the street, ostensibly checking the tables as she went, acknowledging the customers settling themselves for morning coffee.

'Shall I get you a high chair?' she asked a woman manoeuvring a bulky baby buggy between the seats.

'No, he'll be fine on my knee.'

Annie gave the woman a smile as she imagined the crescent of detritus that would build on the floor around them.

'Annie!'

It wasn't quite a shout. It was Yağız's voice raised just enough to carry over the heads of the customers from behind the bar.

He was holding his hand to the side of his head, thumb and little finger stretched to mimic a phone. She hurried over, keeping her front-of-house smile intact but speaking softly from between clenched teeth. 'You know better than to shout across the dining room like that. What is it?'

She was aware of Carol at the coffee machine drawing in a breath as she simultaneously ignored and listened in to what might become an interesting row.

'Phone,' Yağız said, ignoring her reprimand. 'Office.'

'I'll take it here.'

'It's personal … some woman … I told her staff are not allowed personal calls but apparently it's urgent.'

Although Carol had her back to them, she was clearly taking everything in, delaying switching on the coffee grinder that would have drowned the exchange.

Annie pursed her lips, every inch the wrong-footed manager, and without another word, stalked through to the office, shutting the door behind her. That couldn't have gone better. Her only worry was that one of them might pick up the extension in the bar. The lack of background noise suggested otherwise but she didn't risk it and spoke briskly into the handset.

'Listen, I'm not supposed to take calls on this phone. I'll ring you straight back,' and with that she cut the call.

Mumbling to herself in case anyone had their ear to the door, and cradling her mobile ready to jam it to her ear should anyone come in, she rehearsed what she would say to Yağız when she called him into the office in a few minutes. Her own family crisis … he could cope perfectly well … she would cover the extra wage for his acting manager position … Meriç need never know … she would be back in time for the late shift on Sunday.

Of course he would tell Meriç. It was a golden opportunity to be paid extra twice over, but he wouldn't want either of them coming back early so she could rely on him to fudge things just enough.

She watched her phone count off four minutes before she stood up to call him through.

As she re-emerged she saw the chef hurrying towards her, his gloved hand clutching an outsize spatula. This far out of his lair he was either on a nefarious mission, perhaps forgetting Annie was on the spot, or he'd brought bad news. She saw from the satisfaction on his face that it was the latter.

'Neighbours banging on the back,' he told her, 'complaining about trash in the tenfoot. Why hasn't it been cleared?'

Annie let out a tut of exasperation. She'd been on her way to see to that earlier and been diverted. 'I'm on it,' she told him. 'I'm getting it sorted. Tell them it'll be gone by the end of the day.'

'Oh, end of the day's no good. They won't–'

'Tell them it'll be gone!' she cut across him, peering over his shoulder to see Yağız. She raised her voice. 'Yağız!' She tipped her head towards the office. 'I need a word.'

She stormed back the way she'd come. It was all hassle and frustration. This should have been sorted automatically. If she was genuinely running this place, some things would be done very differently, and she wouldn't put up with Meriç's micromanaging either.

'Just let me sort this,' she said to Yağız as she snatched up the phone, leaving him standing awkwardly in the office doorway. She hadn't intended approaching him heavy-handedly but maybe it was the best way to cut through the crap and get things done.

By the time she turned to give him her rehearsed spiel, he was stony-faced, leaning on the wall arms folded.

He heard her out, then stretched one of his hands in front of him, giving his fingernails a thorough inspection as he mulled over what she'd said. After a moment he turned his stretched hand, tapped on the open palm and said, 'Cash upfront.'

Annie hadn't expected this level of directness but was happy to oblige if this was the price of his cooperation. She wondered if he would contact Meriç at all. Yes, of course he would. It was too good an opportunity to miss. A slight qualm rippled through her at the way her advance from Pat Thompson was being eaten into.

'You're not going to ask for a receipt?' he said as he pocketed the cash.

'I don't think I need to.' He could make of that what he liked. They were in the doorway, visible from the corridor; the hidden lens had recorded the transaction. 'Now I'm going to get off. You're in charge.'

'Well, not quite.' He gave her a triumphant look. 'I was coming through to tell you that a customer has asked to speak to the manager. I think it's about organising an event.'

'You can see to that, can't you?'

'I could but it would seem odd. They asked for you.'

'By name?' A few of the regulars had got to know her. She supposed she had better go out and deal with it.

'Not exactly.' The smile that played at the corners of Yağız's mouth was pure amusement. 'The precise words were "the scruffy blonde one".'

Annie tried to stamp down on a flare of anger but could see from the twinkle in Yağız's eye that he'd seen the insult hit its mark.

Why should I care so much?

She looked away and took refuge in an exasperated sigh. She had been called that and worse a thousand times over the years. The rigours of the job made scruffy blonde a pretty accurate description a lot of the time. But it rankled. For all that she'd lost focus on this job to start with, she'd taken pains over her undercover role. She'd not only played the part of manager, she'd looked it, never appearing on the floor with a hair out of place.

'OK, who is it? I'll see to them and then I'm off.'

'They're having coffee at table twelve.'

She pulled in some deep breaths as she stood up tall and walked through, unhurried, every inch the professional, her friendly smile in place. No one would see a chink in her armour.

Four women sat around table twelve, steaming cups in front of them. The one facing Annie, reached across to nudge her companion, to nod her head in Annie's direction. Instead of turning round, the woman lifted her cup and took a leisurely sip. Her three companions watched as Annie came to stand at her side.

'How can I help you?' she asked, smile in place.

The woman set down her cup and twisted her head to look up at Annie. There was no answering smile, just cold disdain as she took her time to run a contemptuous gaze from Annie's head to her feet and back again.

Annie held on to her manager's demeanour but her heart thumped hard as she recognised the woman. It was Ayaan Ahmed's wife.

Chapter 15

....

Thoughts flew through Annie's head. This woman must know who she was … who she really was. She was going to blow her cover, right here, right now.

'I do hope we weren't interrupting anything important,' said Cari Ahmed, 'like one of your many rest breaks.'

'Cari …' one of the women murmured, but was silenced with a look.

So Cari Ahmed knew that she'd had a meal in the restaurant yesterday without working a full shift. Where had she got that from?

'I'm so sorry,' she said, her smile open, friendly. 'I was on the phone when Yağız came to get me. He should have interrupted.'

'Yes, he should. I suppose it was a personal call.'

That was a shot in the dark, Annie was sure. Cari's grapevine couldn't have told her of the call just minutes ago. Outwardly she didn't react, just held her smile as though conversation with Cari was the most interesting thing that had happened to her all day. In a sense that wasn't far from the mark. 'I understand you're thinking of booking an event with us.'

Again the disdainful look raked her from head to toe.

One of the others chimed in to fill the pause. 'Yes, Cari's father suggested …' The words died away as Cari turned a hard stare her way.

'You've met my father, haven't you?' Cari shot at Annie.

'Yes, several times. I've only been here a couple of weeks, but I know that your father is one of our most valued customers. Meriç often speaks of him.' The memory of Meriç's actual words, telling her she couldn't duck away from his regulars no matter how many police officers they had for sons-in-law, added a sparkle to her smile.

She knew she was showing nothing but friendliness and willingness to please. Cari who had arrived with the upper hand was beginning to look condescending and spiteful.

'And you've met my husband too, I believe.'

Suppressed intakes of breath from around the table ... gazes turned away.

This was the nub of it. Annie remembered the look Cari had speared into her as she'd backed off from that unwelcome reunion with policeman Ahmed just five days ago. Had Cari challenged him about some supposed relationship, but if so he surely would have put her straight. Annie's mind flitted across possible responses. She mustn't assume Cari knew everything, but mustn't assume she didn't. She allowed her eyes to lose focus for a second as though seeking a memory.

'DC Ahmed,' she said. 'Yes, I met him briefly last year when I was working in York.'

Cari gave a cold laugh. 'When you were in a more lowly position, I understand. Oh and he's Sergeant Ahmed. How on earth did you land a post like this one?'

That was an interesting turn of phrase – a more lowly position. Ayaan Ahmed had to suspect she was working undercover. Had he warned his wife against exposing her, or had he been less than honest about their previous encounter? With an inward shudder she recalled a shabby excuse for a coffee bar that an old guy had once taken her to in York – insipid instant coffee, sticky sweet pastry. That old guy had been a friend of Ahmed's. Maybe she'd been painted as a waitress in a greasy spoon. Easier than trying to explain the complexities of their genuine meetings, she supposed, and would have put him in a better light.

'It's been hard work along the way,' she said easily. 'But it's always been an ambition of mine to manage a restaurant of this quality.'

'Cari.' The voice was low but assertive. Annie saw a hand placed gently on Cari's arm.

Everyone felt uncomfortable and embarrassed; everyone bar her and Cari. She wasn't even worried anymore because if Sergeant Ahmed had been truthful with his wife, he'd clearly extracted a promise not to blow her cover. And if he'd lied, then Cari had no damaging knowledge to share.

She realised with surprise that she was enjoying herself. Scruffy blonde, was she? Just look at her now. The perfect restaurant manager soothing an awkward customer. Except not soothing. Cari was seething underneath the surface and Annie couldn't be more pleased.

Looking back on the exchange as she unlocked the door to her bedsit, Annie let in a little of the concern she'd originally felt. It wasn't good to have someone like Ahmed hovering at the periphery knowing that she wasn't who she said she was, nor was it a good move to have antagonised his wife the way she had, satisfying though it had been at the time. Interestingly it had elevated the post of restaurant manager in her own head. Meriç's restaurant was a good one, her position required ability and experience. It was remarkable that her skills as an investigator had stood her in such good stead. It hadn't occurred to her that her years in the job might have trained her up for any other role.

Nonetheless she'd messed up in making an unnecessary enemy of Cari Ahmed.

She could ride it out. Cari was an annoyance not a danger. Another four weeks and the time prepaid by Meriç would be up. It wouldn't take her that long to suss out the scam, so all she need do would be manage the restaurant. She'd started to enjoy the job as a job. The extra experience might prove useful.

Or she could call a halt to it right away. No matter how loudly Pieternel had protested that she had to stay the full six weeks, Annie knew she only had to mention the sudden appearance of Dyson and fforbes, and Pieternel would have her out of this contract and out of Hull in minutes. One phone call was all it would take. She glanced at her mobile but made no move to pick it up. It was an option but not one she was inclined to take just yet.

And for now and for the next few hours she had to put all that out of her mind. What she needed was plenty of coffee and a clear head. She had hours of surveillance footage to get through.

Every few seconds Annie eased back her head, twisted her neck side to side and rolled her shoulders. The movements became automatic as the camera footage ran, one window on fast-forward, full concentration, the other two on real time, reliant on her subconscious to flag up any anomalies. Every ten minutes or so she swapped screens so the scene in the biggest, fast-moving window changed from kitchen to dining room to corridor.

She watched without surprise as Carol and one of the casuals, after making much of clearing up packaging from a recent delivery, slipped into the walk-in and emerged carrying the freeze-dried apple box between them. They'd bashed it about a bit, and the top flaps were open with the scrunched remains of other boxes sticking out. To an unsuspecting observer it was a box stuffed with the ripped remains of other boxes and they were just shifting the garbage. The young guy helping Carol was the same one who had approached her on that early footage; one of the incidents she'd had in mind when she'd told Meriç she'd seen bits and pieces but nothing conclusive.

Having played all the cameras up to the last worker leaving the place in darkness on Friday night, and had a last glance at the live action of Saturday afternoon, Annie returned the footage to that stretch where Carol and her sidekick had moved the box. She watched it through in detail again, then stopped the recording and sat back. They were working together. Did that give her a route to flush Carol into the open? When she returned to the restaurant on Sunday, she would dismiss him for his part in blocking the alleyway. Casual workers were easily sacked. It would be interesting to see how Carol reacted.

Chapter 16

Two days later as Saturday afternoon rolled into early evening, Annie felt she'd seen and absorbed all that was there to be found on the surveillance cameras. She'd spent a day and a half, partly watching live, partly rerunning footage from the previous shifts. Nothing new on Carol but she was pretty sure the chef was pilfering supplies. Not enough to account for the black hole in Meriç's books but it looked like he was targeting low volume, high priced produce. A spot check of the staff lockers when his was stuffed with contraband would be the way to catch him red-handed but that was something for Meriç who might decide to write off the losses to date and try a different strategy to put a stop to future stealing. The chef was one of his most valuable commodities and he was certainly no slacker. He'd been clanging about in the big kitchen, sweat rolling from him, the whole of Saturday. He was due a day off tomorrow and always left the kitchen well prepped for his second in command. Watching him, Annie couldn't help being impressed at his industry but also impatient that he wouldn't let go of the reins. He'd never get anywhere if he didn't learn to delegate, and not just the shitty jobs.

She reached forward to close down the laptop. Time to call it a day. She had a job of her own to do for the Thompsons this evening.

The chef didn't usually take Sundays off, but tomorrow was a special day for most of the world. She looked round at the dusty bedsit, its walls papered with cheap woodchip and badly painted. It wasn't that she didn't know what day it was, but the chef altering his routine set things in sharp focus. New Year's Eve and she would spend the evening working. A whole new year due to begin tomorrow. And she was alone.

There was no reason it should get her down. She'd been on her own almost every New Year of her thirty-four years, at least that was how it felt. And would she want to be with her family this evening, her father smothering yawns, faking conversation, pretending he would have stayed up to hear the midnight chimes whether or not she'd been there? Her aunt, invited to stay because that's what you did at New Year, forgetting the date and pottering off to bed at her usual time.

New Year's Eve was always busy in her profession. People let their hair down, let their guard drop. This big do tonight would be no different. She looked with distaste at the dirndl that lay across the bed, bulky, ill-fitting and ludicrous with its full skirt, low cut top, huge apron and large woollen wig tortured into fat plaits. A target to identify, to follow, to check up on. She just wished she didn't have to do it in such an absurd costume.

Looking in the mirror when she'd struggled into it, adding bright make-up as per instructions, and a large pair of glasses, she saw only one consolation. Even Pieternel would pass her by unrecognised, and presumably she would blend into a mass of similarly dressed women once the event was underway.

The taxi driver was monosyllabic, maybe he hadn't wanted to work New Year's Eve. Hard luck, thought Annie, I'm not overjoyed either. The sixty minute ride out of town and across open country went by in silence. As they arrived at an imposing gateway and sweeping drive, Annie thought of Leah Sleeman, the woman whose yoke Pat and Barbara were keen to escape. Leah lived in a remote place like this, long driveway, house hidden behind the trees. But the similarities were superficial. None of Leah's alleged millions showed in the run-down shabby front her house showed to the world with its unkempt hedges and mismatched timbers. Here, a row of lights swept them around the curve of the driveway, discreet illumination emphasising the pristine stonework and mullioned windows. The edges of a manicured lawn peeped out from under the cold hard frost. This place reeked of money.

The taxi bumped off the smooth tarmac turning away from the front entrance, following a track round the side.

'Tradesmen's entrance,' murmured Annie.

The driver gave her a glance but said nothing.

At the back of the big house it was all noise and bustle, cars parked at angles, huge catering pots being lifted from the back of a van, people darting to and fro between the brightly lit opening and the parked vehicles, arms full.

Her experience as Meriç's manager allowed her to run a professional eye over proceedings. She felt they were leaving the set up a little late. The first guests would be here in an hour.

'Pull up over there.'

She directed the driver to take his cab to the edge of the busy hub so she could get out unobserved and slip inside. She had no intention of helping to heft equipment.

If she hadn't been dressed so garishly she might have risked a foray to the front of the house to identify her target, the fiancé whose movements she was to watch. All she'd been given was a grainy photograph of the guy in casual gear, but this was going to be a far from casual do. 'Someone'll have a word when you get there,' Pat had told her. 'They'll show you who the mark is.' Annie had probed further but Pat knew no more than that.

The cold that hit her as she got out from the cocoon of the vehicle made her scurry for the doorway. There would be no outdoor surveillance tonight without the risk of hypothermia.

'Name?'

A sharp voice close to her ear made her jump. She turned and found herself face to face with a short blonde rosy-cheeked man holding a clipboard.

'I don't recognise you from last time. Are you new?'

She gave him the pseudonym Pat had told her to use, and he ran his finger down the list.

'Oh yes, here you are. Put this on.' He handed her a name badge. *Hi I'm Heidi. Happy to help!*

'Is that right?'

He rolled his eyes. 'You're all Heidi tonight, sorry. Orders.'

Annie shrugged and pinned on the badge. The blonde man was signing in someone else, so Annie stepped back into the shadow and watched the comings and goings. Pat had said someone would make contact, help her with getting to the right place at the right time.

'They'll find you,' Pat had said. 'It'll be one of the ones who set up the gig for us.'

That was all very well, but Annie wondered if this contact, whoever it was, would be expecting a crowd of women dressed identically and all labelled Heidi.

Suited wait staff began to congregate, pulling on white gloves. Annie wasn't sure whether she should stay where she was and wait for her contact or to try to explore on her own.

'Ruddy boiler wasn't on,' a voice snapped. 'Look sharp.'

A stream of curses met this pronouncement as a muscular man in a kitchen overall clanged past, a large mobile bain marie swinging from each hand, the edges catching door frames and anyone who wasn't quick to get out of the way. Annie thought of Meriç's complaints about his outside catering operation, how the equipment always came back with dents and scratches if he wasn't on hand to oversee it. When the set up was as late as this, she could see why. And no wonder it was the corners that suffered most, the way the things were swung carelessly through – haste trumping care. But the restaurant manager inside her understood the curses. They'd expected boiling water on tap to fill those bain maries and keep the food hot. Now they'd have to start cold or lukewarm. Not great on the food safety front, but still, not her problem.

The blonde man with the clipboard was still ticking off names as people arrived. She'd seen more Heidis but they wouldn't be needed until the party was in full swing. She kept blondie in her peripheral vision wanting prior notice if anyone went to search his list which would be the only way to find out if she'd arrived.

The huge gastronome pans were coming in now, some clutched awkwardly between two people, some held by one, all faces contorted as they staggered through as fast as they could to get rid of their loads.

She sniffed appreciatively recognising spicy chickpea and walnut sauce, resisting an urge to follow it to the kitchen, to taste and criticise the seasoning. That's what Meriç would do if it was his event.

It smelt good but the bain maries wouldn't be ready. That food would cool before the water reached temperature and heated it again. No doubt that would be in time for the meal later, but the temperature fluctuations would determine the risk. If the staff were offered leftovers at the end of the night, she would have to refuse, couldn't risk food-poisoning or she'd never get this job wrapped up. More pots clanged past, wafting their tempting aromas in their wake. Lamb pilau ... chili ginger ... Good food but potentially ruined by bad organisation. She might have just two weeks' experience as a restaurant manager but she knew she could have run this show much more efficiently.

She stepped back into the shadow experiencing a sudden chill of apprehension. This was too familiar. It was as though the Thompsons' world and Meriç's were colliding with her exposed in the middle. Meriç did no events this far out, but what about their army of casual workers? She hadn't given them a thought. One of Meriç's regulars might be here, dressed just the same way she was.

'Heidis,' shouted a voice. 'Listen up.'

From all sides a sea of brightly coloured dirndls emerged and clustered around the woman who had shouted.

'Now pay attention everyone. No out-and-out soliciting for tips but whatever you make you can keep ...'

Annie gave her half an ear. The task wasn't a difficult one. The dirndl girls were to start their shift as window dressing, moving about through the crowd, 'Keep moving ... smile ...' They would become wait staff once the hor d'oeuvres came out. She moved with the rest of them towards the rear entrance to a large reception room. Dressed as she was, her only way to be discreet was to stick with the crowd.

She had to forget incidental reminders of her job with Meriç. This was work for the Thompsons and she must concentrate on it. Only now she was here, the difficulties mounted.

Even if she could find her target, how on earth was she to follow him? And if all she got to see of him was in the public areas then she was unlikely to witness anything incriminating.

They'd have been better off smuggling her in as a guest or a driver in which role she might at least be able to sidle away from the action unnoticed.

She painted the required happy smile on her face before following orders to mingle with the crowd, but not speak unless spoken to. Look and listen. It was all she could do.

'Sod this for a lark,' murmured one of her fellow Heidis, pausing beside her and glancing back to the door where they'd come in, the dingy portal between front and back of house.

Annie met her eye and asked the question with a raised eyebrow.

'We're not needed before the starters. I'm off to scrounge a drink. You should do the same. You're gonna need it to last the night out.'

'Good plan,' Annie muttered, under cover of a wide smile, wondering if this was her contact. 'Will they mind us leaving so soon?'

'I'm hoping they won't notice.'

Annie held back and watched her fellow Heidi sashay through the crowd, her smile bright, her path towards the exit subtly indirect. She wanted to see if anyone clocked her leaving.

Blondie appeared in the doorway, clipboard in hand, his expression professionally relaxed but his gaze sharp as it darted across the big space. Annie began to weave her way through the crowd, keeping him and the doorway at the edge of vision. She saw the other Heidi make as though to slip through, saw blondie's arm move to block her path.

She peered over the heads of a laughing group. Body language was muted but Heidi was arguing; blondie wasn't budging. Then Heidi backed off, turning to peer into the crowd, no trace of the required pleasant smile. Annie hoped this wasn't the intended contact because if so, the woman's behaviour wasn't professional enough; she needed to blend in before she drew attention. If it was Annie she was now peering through the crowd for, she wouldn't see her. She'd moved and become all but invisible in a mob that became more riotous with every passing second. She saw a waiter jostled, using lightning reflexes to keep his packed tray of drinks upright, before a pack descended, grabbing for the glasses.

It was clear now why they hadn't sent in drinks with the casuals; lithe movements borne of long practice were keeping the packed trays intact, preventing accidents that would smash glassware and spray shards of broken glass far and wide. This crowd looked half cut already and most of them had only just arrived. The evening was not going to get any easier.

As though to underscore her thoughts, a heavy hand slapped down on to her bare back, slipping across to push the short sleeve off her shoulder.

'You look good enough to eat, darlin'. And speaking of eat, when ya gonna feed us? I'm starving.'

A blast of stale breath reeking of something sickly and alcoholic engulfed her as a red-eyed face leant uncomfortably close to hers. She twisted herself into him so they were almost embracing and grabbed his other wrist, wrenching it sharply, keeping the movement hidden between his body and hers.

His colour drained as she smiled into his eyes then pushed her head closer to whisper in his ear. 'You have half of one second to take your filthy paws off me or I break every bone in your wrist.'

An extra twitch of her hand as she spoke and he needed no second telling, staggering back with a muttered, 'Bitch!'

In her line of sight was another Heidi, a young girl, her face scared though trying to hold its smile, being hustled by two men in suits, faces red, eyes glazed.

That instruction about tips returned to her. Had she and her fellow Heidis been provided for more than a bit of colour and some help with the food? The atmosphere in this part of the house was beginning to generate a sinister undertone, an air of recklessness. All the guests were men in suits. There were woman at this gathering too, but they weren't in evidence here. There was more than one type of party going on under this roof.

The prospect of witnessing bad behaviour, perhaps criminal behaviour, in the thick of proceedings had become both possible and probable. But how would that help? This was a cohesive pack, dangerous as they grew more intoxicated, who would surely cover for each other, and she couldn't even get at her phone to take pictures. The dirndl girls were few enough and garish enough that she could feel eyes on her everywhere she walked, hands too reaching out to grab at the stout fabric of her bulky skirt. No way would she stop to pull up the material to access the phone and its camera stashed in her only pocket.

Keep moving they'd been told, and it was the only way to avoid being pawed or pulled into unwelcome embraces. Her protection was that their reactions were blunted by drink and hers were sharp, but that would count for nothing if the mood turned ugly. As yet, it was all drunken bonhomie but it could go sour at any moment.

Finding a target that she had no chance of watching covertly was futile. And in this environment as the volume increased and the ambience grew wilder, she had become the quarry not the hunter. She had no desire to stick around and find out just how nasty this private party would become. One thing her years in the job had taught her was to recognise the necessity of retreat. It was time to leave.

She set her sights on the door guarded by blondie, and shimmied her way through the sweating bodies and raucous laughter. That little squirt with his clipboard had better not try to stop her.

Instead of putting out his hand to bar her way, he twisted round and followed her. 'Had enough?' She heard amusement in his tone.

'I'm leaving,' she said, her gaze darting about to explore the possibilities. If she could find a way to get out of this garb, find something normal to change into, maybe she could explore the rest of the house.

'Oh God,' he said, his humour turning to worry. 'She hasn't seen you, has she?'

'Who?' She looked at him in surprise. There had been no women in that room other than the dirndl girls. Was he talking about the Heidi who had accosted her about trying to slip away for a drink?

'Good, I didn't think she could have found you yet. But listen, I was about to pull you out and you need to look sharp. Here, take these ...' He shoved an envelope into her hand. 'And make yourself scarce. There's someone here out to make trouble for you.'

The envelope was sealed but fat, maybe money. So blondie had been the contact all along. He could have told her sooner. 'What's–?'

He shushed her and pulled her out of the way as more wait staff filed past.

'A woman called Cari Ahmed. Do you know her? She's heard you're here and she's planning to take photos and confront you, make enough of a row that people'll remember you. She thinks you're back in the kitchens moonlighting from your real job.'

Shit, thought Annie, I am moonlighting, but that's not the only cover she'll blow.

'Isn't she with her husband?' Because surely Ahmed would stop her.

'No, she's with a gang of women, one of them's tight with someone in the family.'

Annie's gaze darted back to the doorway through which loud commotion and flashing lights spilled.

Blondie laughed. 'Oh, people like Cari Ahmed and her friends won't be going anywhere near that bear pit. They're round the other side with the proper people.'

Annie remembered the feeling of insecurity as she stood in the shadows when she first arrived, watching the vats of ready-cooked food being raced through. She'd thought the Thompsons' world and Meriç's so far apart she'd had no qualms about being in contact with both, but how could she have been so naïve? The casuals who worked at the restaurant very likely worked these sorts of do's as well. And as for bumping into someone like Cari Ahmed, it had never occurred to her.

If she'd inadvertently forged a link from the Thompsons to Meriç, it was just a matter of time before word of her previous occupation got back to the staff. Some of them wouldn't care but others, Yağız, Carol, the chef … would realise at once that she'd been brought in to spy on them. The resulting row would be a disaster on all fronts.

She looked at the envelope blondie had thrust into her hand.

'What's this?'

'Go on,' he urged. 'Get yourself out of here before there's trouble. There's minicabs dropping people at the front.'

Shivering in the inadequate costume she hurried outside and made her way round the house, keeping to the shadows, watching out for a car to flag down, hoping it wouldn't take forever to talk one of them into taking her as an unbooked job.

Not until she was in a cab and speeding away from the place did she rip open the envelope. Inside was a clutch of photographs. She recognised her target, the fiancé she had been hired to watch but hadn't even glimpsed. If these had been taken tonight, it had been much earlier on, not quite dusk. His glazed eyes bespoke a long and dedicated drinking session, perhaps with more than alcohol thrown in to pep up the party. He was dressed to the nines but the suit looked as alien on him as their tailored garb had on the drunken louts she'd left inside. And in most of the shots, his clothes were dishevelled and hanging half off him, matching those of the dirndl girl who was wrapped around him.

Chapter 17

....

It had been stupid to go ahead with this job once it had become clear it was a catering event. She'd forgotten how much smaller the world was around here than in the crowded anonymity of the capital where she was used to working. She'd allowed her need for ready cash to override a proper risk assessment. And of course it had been like stepping back into the early years of her career, working for a firm that had no real interest in doing things right.

'They certainly go all out when they party back there.' It was the driver, his tone neutral, fishing. He probably brought guests here regularly.

'D'you know the family?' she asked.

'I've brought people here a time or two.' He kept his stare on the road ahead. 'I've heard they throw quite a party.'

'I think there's more than one party going on.' Annie gave him some of the information he was keen to know.

'Is that right? I know they have some real big affairs. Some of the guests turn up with their own security.'

'Yeah? I didn't see anything like that. They're officially celebrating an engagement I believe.'

'Oh, they won't have invited the big guns tonight. They don't approve of the guy the daughter's got herself mixed up with. There'll be no red carpet rolled out. Spoilt brat, she is. Her brother's the same. You do no good with kids if you give in to them all their lives.'

It didn't surprise her to learn he was up to date on the gossip and she gave herself another mental kick. A city of quarter of a million or so people might sound a lot but it was scant cover compared to the millions she was used to working amongst.

'You got kids?' he asked.

'No.' Annie shook her head with an inner shudder at the thought.

For the first time he turned to give her a glance. 'Plenty of time for that I suppose.' She didn't respond, was used to the assumption that her long-term plans included a family. 'They're a worry, I'll admit,' he went on. 'Now my daughter …'

Annie smothered a sigh and resigned herself to his life story as backdrop to the ride to town. Her only regret over her own no-children stance was the ending of the long-term relationship that she'd thought would always be there in the background of her life. She and Mike had lived together briefly before his job took him across continents. Even then, they stayed in touch, got together when they were geographically close enough. But Mike had wanted to settle down, start a family. They'd talked about it. She'd said she'd be insane to emulate the chaos of the family experience she'd grown up with. He'd said it didn't have to be like that. But in the end it didn't matter that he had all the rational arguments. The fragmented memories that were all she had of her own mother struck irrational terror into her at the thought of trying to take on a parental role herself.

The driver was outlining his daughter's travel plans now, somehow linking them to her hair colour. Annie heard paternal indulgence in his tone at the rainbow array of tints she used. 'Now when she goes off to university …'

Annie nodded, allowing herself a smile of satisfaction. He could take it as for his offspring and her multi-coloured hair, but the real reason was that by fair means or foul, the job was done. She had a pack of compromising photographs. Whatever the implications behind the way she'd acquired them, that was all in the Thompsons' world not hers. Her guess was that someone in the family had taken the pictures at a different event but needed to show their origin to be unconnected to them. Maybe they'd hoped she would gather her own set and giving her these was plan B. It didn't matter. She could now exchange the photos for the rest of her fee and then decide what to do about Meriç's restaurant.

Except that she hadn't lost her unease over tonight. Her smile died. She'd left a bear pit of a stag do behind her, a gang of drunken oafs getting rowdier by the minute with brightly dressed women tipped in amongst them as bait. Probably she had been the only one there not clear about their intended role, but that didn't make it right to abandon them. Imprinted on her mind was the young girl whose face she'd glimpsed as she'd manhandled the drunk who'd pawed her. It had been a look of pure terror behind the grimace of the mandatory bright and friendly smile. And fear would fuel that pack.

'Don't ever let your daughter work at one of their do's,' she said, breaking into his monologue.

'Hell, no. I've heard what goes on. Drugs and all sorts.'

She hadn't seen overt signs of any drug other than alcohol but those tired puffy faces bespoke long-term use of stuff the other side of the legal line. She thought again about the young girl, who'd probably been persuaded to go for the easy money. A drugs raid just about now would be perfect. Whether or not there was anything to find, it would break up the party; the seedy side of it anyway. She toyed with retrieving her phone from its awkward pocket, but didn't. She had nothing that would mobilise officialdom and no contacts round here anymore. A face to face report might do it, but she daren't blow her cover.

Although if she could mobilise someone informally …

She turned a speculative eye on the driver beside her, still going on about his blue-eyed girl. Ayaan Ahmed was staying with his in-laws. She had their contact details.

'There were some girls there about your daughter's age,' she said. 'I'm really worried about them.'

'What do you mean?'

She painted some more of the picture, the fear, the trap, the overwhelming numbers, and pretended she knew these girls as she speckled the story with detail that matched the daughter he'd been eulogising for the past ten minutes; hair colour, ambitions to travel, plans for university.

'You need to ring the police,' he burst out, his tone strident indignation. 'Have you a phone? You can use mine.'

She coached him gently over the issues around rich, influential families, scarce police resources and lack of concrete evidence. 'They'd log it but they wouldn't do anything in time. But I was thinking if …'

'If what?'

'I can't let it be known I was there,' she told him, spinning half a story that he seemed to swallow. 'But there was someone there who …'

She fed him the tale of a policeman's wife called Cari; pretended she was in danger of becoming a victim.

'You needn't speak to him, needn't say who you are. One of his in-laws'll probably answer. Just outline the worst of it, say that the name Cari Ahmed was mentioned by one of the drunks. You could say you got the story from a cab driver.'

Later that night, as she sat in the dingy flat composing an email to Pieternel, she wondered if he'd made the call, and whether Ayaan Ahmed had hot-footed it out there. If so, had he gone alone, with family, or had he called on colleagues? She'd met him briefly a couple of times, thought him uptight and prissy. If he'd gone out there, he would have charged in without subtlety, waving his warrant card. The family would probably have been glad of an excuse to break things up, blamed it all on the fiancé if they had their wits about them. Whatever had happened, she could only hope the young girl had got out unscathed.

And if she had, it was more than she could say for herself. Someone might track down the cab driver. They might get as far as blondie and his clipboard. The pseudonym ought to be a dead end but it wouldn't take too much digging to make the link with the Thompsons and then she was centre stage for further enquiries. The edifice was on the point of collapse. Just her luck when she'd started to enjoy the job.

It was her own fault. She'd put everything in jeopardy when she'd approached the Thompsons.

Not entirely her fault. Pieternel could take a share of the blame for abandoning her without any money.

She turned back to the email. There was no need to confess to the moonlighting just yet, but she had to admit to meeting the Thompsons. Several versions had been typed and deleted as she searched for the right words to explain how and why she'd encountered them.

Pat called into the restaurant with a client.

No, that wouldn't do. Pieternel was quite capable of contacting the Thompsons to check.

Annie toyed with a phone call to Pat to ask her to lie if Pieternel got in touch, but she didn't want to admit a rift to Pat any more than she wanted to admit the moonlighting to Pieternel.

I ran into Pat Thompson. One of those things. We were face to face before I could do anything about it.

That was better, and she added that she'd gone back to the office with Pat to say hello to Barbara. Now if Pieternel had the story from either of the sisters, her appearance in their office was explained.

I didn't try the catering cover story on them. They'd never have swallowed it ...

That at least was the exact truth and so was the line she'd spun them about a surveillance; the line that allowed her to be working on their patch without poaching their clients.

It was important that Pieternel didn't suspect her of lying. She'd made too much of her desire to get out of this job early. Pieternel would be on guard and might take mention of Dyson and fforbes as another clumsy attempt, but it wasn't. It was something else that should have had the alarm bells clanging far more loudly.

Turns out it's lucky I got to talk to them. You won't believe …

delete – delete – delete

You won't guess … who turned up on their doorstep.

As she typed the names Annie found herself glancing round as though someone might have sneaked in to watch over her shoulder.

I don't know what their agenda is but it can't be coincidence that they're here. I need to get out.

Watching herself type the words *I need to get out,* increased her discomfort. She looked up towards the light fitting as though to check for hidden cameras. She could leave the email at that. It should be enough. Pieternel would find a way to square things with Meriç. But Annie had already worked it through and wanted to spell it out, to show that she wasn't jumping ship on the back of irrational paranoia. The job was done. What Meriç did about his chef was for him to decide. And as for Carol and one of the casuals, that would be solved tomorrow when Annie fired the guy. Whatever they were doing, she was certain it needed both of them.

I'll set Meriç up with remote surveillance in lieu of the rest of my time. He'll agree.

It wouldn't be quite that easy, she knew, but she'd thought through the angles. Some extra bells and whistles would persuade him. He wouldn't lose the chance to have them installed as part of the price he'd already paid, and she would refuse to do it if he wouldn't sign off the job.

I'll need to show him a couple of gizmos that he won't find elsewhere. Can you send me …?

As she listed the equipment she needed, she imagined Pieternel rolling her eyes, but if Pieternel got sticky over it, it didn't matter.

She could use her fee from Pat Thompson now she wouldn't be staying more than a couple of days.

She looked around the small room again. It wasn't great but up to now it had felt comfortably obscure and insignificant.

The hairs at the back of her neck prickled. Instinct was telling her that she was losing the security of anonymity, that someone was after her.

The email needed a proofread. It was important it came across just right. Pieternel mustn't get the wrong end of the stick. She stared at the screen, then looked round again. Something wasn't right.

She clicked send without reading it through. Her jaw tightened during the fraction of a second delay before the mail pinged on its way. Her hand was on the button to turn the machine off – right off. Phone too. The equipment was shielded but that was no longer enough. She stuffed the laptop into her rucksack, grabbed her good suit from its hanger and rolled it up to go in the top. She had enough money – just – to spend her last couple of nights, maybe three, in a cheap hotel. She'd been careless, allowed things to cloud her judgement. No way would she get cornered in a place like this.

She crept from the room, easing the key silently to lock the door behind her, checking the corridor and stairs. No signs of life. Pausing only to honour a fundamental tenet of fieldwork, and stick a thread, thin as a hair, from door to frame near the top, she made her way downstairs and to the back of the house. It was officially a fire exit and never used. It led on to an alley narrower than the one at the back of the restaurant and would take her behind the terrace of houses and down to the main road.

There might be no one at all in the street outside, no one watching, no one waiting, but at the edge of her mind stood a fuzzy impression of an oldish couple. Dyson, she now knew, was the woman, and fforbes, two small f's, the man.

And if there was one thing she'd learnt over the years it was never to ignore her instinct when it screamed at her this loudly.

Chapter 18

The air was still as Annie walked towards the restaurant the next morning. In her rush to leave her bedsit she'd forgotten her warm jumper and shivered in the chill mist that hung in the darkness. That streetlight in the alleyway would still be out. She would have to negotiate that stretch in the pre-dawn gloom. Her footsteps on the pavement echoed as though she was the only person up and about. Usually there would be a steady stream of early shift workers crisscrossing the roads, on their way to work. Not today. No real point in her turning up at this hour. She could have stayed away till mid-morning, let Yağız open up; Meriç wasn't here to notice.

Yesterday's unease lapped at her feet. Partly she felt foolish, but she couldn't make up her mind that she'd been wrong. She would take an hour's break later, go to the bedsit to check it out under cover of daylight, retrieve her jumper and whatever else she needed. It was a busy area. Even on New Year's Day there would be people about, once they'd recovered from last night's hangovers and got out of bed.

At the entrance to the alleyway, she flashed her torch. It was deserted … cold. The breeze that always flurried between the high fences was muted; early morning damp gleamed like giant slug trails along the ground and walls. But there were also interlinking shadows. Surprise lightened her mood as a glow from round the corner competed with her torch beam. The streetlamp had been repaired. Expectations coloured by overheard complaints about council inefficiency had led her to assume no chance over the holiday period.

She readied the keys. Once she was out of sight of the scant protection of a deserted main road, she wanted to be inside in seconds with the door locked behind her. Pulling in a breath, she lengthened her stride, and headed into the alley.

Nothing but the cold morning and curtained windows watched her as she inserted the key, turned it, moved inside and locked up behind her all in one fluid movement.

The big kitchen sat as it always did, surfaces gleaming, not a pan out of place. She glanced briefly upward; would see her own face looking back at her when she ran through the footage later … if she bothered with that. After all, the job was done. And there was another consideration now. How was she to access the cameras now she had no safe haven in which to fire up her laptop? Both it and her phone had been off since last night. She wasn't going to risk being tracked by someone with Pieternel's level of knowhow. She would turn on both devices here at the restaurant once the place was busy; anyone who wanted could know she was here during the day, but otherwise it would be radio silence. She stuffed her rucksack and laptop into her locker and went to the office where she sat at the PC. The blank face of her phone looked up from the desk. There would be an email from Pieternel waiting but she wouldn't turn it on yet.

The diary said they would be busy, booked to the rafters all day and evening. There must have been a last minute surge. She didn't remember all these. Then she saw the note. Bookings passed on from a restaurant about half a mile away. There wasn't enough information to understand whether they'd overbooked or hit a technical problem but they were off-loading reservations all around the area.

A rattle from the back door had her on her feet, marching to the corner of the kitchen to watch. A key sounded in the lock. The door swung open and Yağız pushed through, smothering a curse and then giving a start of surprise to see her at the far side of the big space.

'Why did you lock it again?' he snapped.

Annie wasn't sure if his annoyance was at the extra seconds he'd had to spend in the cold outside or because he'd wanted to catch her out by arriving first. Certainly he was early for his normal shift, clearly covering the bases had she not turned up.

'If you must know, I don't think it's safe to have it unlocked when there's just one person here. Anyone could walk in.'

For a moment he looked taken aback, then he gave a shrug almost as though to concede the point.

She'd surprised herself by being honest with him, but there was a genuine issue here.

'A few nights ago, there was a gang out in the tenfoot late on. I'm pretty sure they were after jumping whoever came out last. We need to have staff using the front when it's very early or very late.'

Now he looked startled and diverted his course to come closer. 'You never said anything. Did you tell Meriç?'

'There was nothing to tell,' she lied. 'I didn't get a look at anyone. No one got in to take anything.'

Except that maybe they did. That whatever-it-was that Carol had hidden in the freeze-dried apple, maybe that went missing that night.

Yağız looked genuinely worried. 'We'll talk to Meriç as soon as he gets back,' he said. 'OK?'

Annie nodded, agreeing to their first ever act of mutual cooperation. It was a morning for surprises.

Now that she wasn't alone, she returned to the tiny office, pulling the door shut behind her and pressed the button to bring her phone to life.

As soon as it connected it beeped a new email, but she felt a shaft of disappointment to see it was from Pat Thompson. No salutation, no signature, just a one-liner.

How did you get on?

She replied with equal brevity.

Got the goods, will call in this evening.

Reference to the evening was a red herring for Pat, just on the off chance anyone wanted to know when she would be there. An hour's break, Annie thought, just after the lunchtime rush. She could call round to the bedsit, grab her jumper and whatnot. Then on to the Thompsons' on her way back, drop off the photos, pick up the rest of her fee.

As her words vanished into the ether, a new set of emails downloaded and she saw with relief that Pieternel's name was there, and dated from last night; the connections had just been taking their time. Pieternel's note was as sparse as Pat's.

Don't like sound of that. Head down. Sit tight. Later.

Annie felt her shoulders sag, hadn't realised quite how tense she'd been. Pieternel was taking it seriously, looking into it. She'd half expected either total disbelief or an order to leave on the spot. Pieternel was going to make enquiries, find out what was going on.

Don't like sound of that … Strong words for Pieternel. It meant her instincts last night hadn't been over the top. The advice wasn't detailed – *head down, sit tight* – but Pieternel trusted that she knew how to keep herself safe. She hoped the *Later* wouldn't be too much later and that when they spoke Pieternel would be OK with the couple of days that she'd decided she needed to wrap up the job.

There was a knock at the door. Yağız's head appeared. It was progress that he'd knocked.

'We're going to have to call some of the kids in,' he said. 'Don't know who we'll get at this notice. We'll have to pay more. Might try …' He rattled off a list of names that Annie recognised as some of the casuals who came in to help with the food prep.

'But why?' She thought back to the industry she'd witnessed yesterday before she'd left the cameras to get dressed up for the Thompsons' job. 'It's all pre-bookings today, isn't it, and Chef's left everything prepped, surely?'

Yağız's lip curled and for once Annie didn't think it was for her. She'd been looking forward to a day without the chef throwing his weight about, but it seemed he could make his presence felt whether or not he was on the premises.

'Kitchen fire up the road,' Yağız said. 'We've taken some of their bookings.'

'Oh yes, I saw that in the book. So didn't they come in early enough for prep to be done?'

Again that curled lip. 'You'd think. But apparently not.'

'OK, we'll ring round.' She reached to retrieve the contacts sheets for the casuals. Dividing them carefully so that the list she handed him contained Carol's friend, she said, 'You do this lot, I'll do these. Offer them double time. Let's see how many we can get in.'

Twenty minutes later, Annie got up pleased with her own progress, to see how Yağız had got on. While she'd been making calls, she had been weighing the pros and cons of confiding in him her plan to sack the lad who was working with Carol. Would he agree with her … try to argue … would he try to forewarn anyone? If he spoke to Carol, for instance, that would indicate he knew what was going on. That would be useful to know.

'How did you do?' she called out, seeing him emerge from the bar area.

The back of house was bustling now, the sous chef in charge, his face a relief map of worry lines. Once the front doors opened, it would be full throttle until late this evening. She was kidding herself thinking about lulls after the lunchtime rush, but that wouldn't stop her going out for an hour.

'Not enough,' he called back, 'but if you've snared as many as I have we'll be OK.'

They looked at each other's lists, shared a grin of relief and Annie almost raised her hand to high-five him. It was clear they'd both envisaged a day of hard-labour at the big sinks.

He was a different person without the chef on the premises.

There was someone else missing now she thought about it. 'Isn't Carol in today?'

'No. Back Monday.'

'I don't remember her having today off.'

'She asked me while you were gone.'

'You could have said no. We're busy today.'

'No point. She'd have pulled a sickie. She works well when she's here.'

'OK.' Annie shrugged. Again Yağız had surprised her. She didn't have him down as one to indulge the staff however well they worked. And once she'd spoken to Meriç, Carol might be out of a job anyway. Since she wasn't properly his manager it wasn't her place to dismiss his permanent staff, but despite what she was going to tell both Pieternel and Meriç, she wasn't entirely sure of her ground with Carol.

The casual workers were another matter. She pointed to a name on Yağız's list. 'Ah, he's coming in, is he? Well, I won't rock the boat until the work's done but I'm going to let him go. Will you send him to me when he's done?'

His eyebrows rose. 'Good luck with that.'

'You say that like I'm going to need it.'

He gave her his curled lip smile and turned away. 'We have a busy day. I need to get on.'

He was right. They had a busy day ahead. The chef had left a stack of problems in the kitchen and they were without their most experienced waitress. There was no time to concentrate on her undercover role or to worry just how she was going to carve herself a break later in the day. She had a restaurant to run.

The urgency to focus didn't quell a surge of unease. Everything lay finely balanced. Sack the casual worker, prepare for Meriç's return, set up the surveillance equipment in his new premises and his home (she hoped Pieternel hadn't ignored the part of her message asking for the extra gizmos) and then she must go, fade away from here, disappear, drop completely off the radar until the world was safe again.

She thought about the bedsit … tried to imagine sleeping there, but couldn't … the hotel would be safe enough for a couple of nights, three at a stretch before she was out of money again.

One more task before she got to business. She retrieved her phone and tapped out an email to Pieternel. Paranoia perhaps but better overkill than be killed.

New equipment. Send direct to restaurant.

And that would also tell Pieternel loud and clear that her address was no longer safe, something she'd barely known herself when she'd pressed that send button last night. Pieternel would see to it that the package arrived by a courier who would deliver it into her hands and no one else's. If anyone else saw the equipment the job would be compromised. And that was another thing she was keeping from Pieternel, the job was already compromised. Her antics last night at that wild party were bound to leak, not that she regretted confiding in the cab driver; she hoped he'd made the call and that Ahmed had acted on it. Pieternel would be furious if she ever found out.

Chapter 19

Annie held tight to a tray of dirty crockery as she balanced her way behind the bar, squeezing to the wall to allow a terrified-looking server to get past with a laden tray of her own, fresh food steaming from its pristine plates. Annie's glance took in and approved the gleaming white porcelain rims. She'd had to have a sharp word earlier. The sous chef, crumbling under the weight of work, had been dumping food on to the plates with haste and no artistry. She'd heard herself echoing Meriç's testy complaints as she'd rapped out a sharp reprimand.

With no chef and with Yağız unexpectedly cooperative, she felt properly in charge for the first time. People scurried to do her bidding. She had to rein in an urge to throw her weight about just for the hell of it, but the place was too busy for that sort of indulgence. Whilst flitting between front and back of house, she was chatting to customers, clearing tables, keeping an eye on the food as it went out and diving in to fill any gaps that opened. It had become a matter of pride that today would run as well as if Meriç were here, as well as if they had a full complement of staff.

And now, according to the clock, the lunchtime rush was over but pre-bookings had filled every place almost every minute of the day – more than filled. New arrivals were being parked at the bar for drinks whilst waiters diplomatically chivvied the occupants of their intended tables to leave, but the bar was already holding two parties at the other end of their stay who had been persuaded to move for their coffee so their tables could be cleared. The art of booting people out while holding up the pretence that they were welcome to linger as long as they liked was one of the first things that had caught Annie's imagination. It required a delicate touch and a range of skills and, under Meriç's leadership, everyone across the hierarchy seemed able to do it.

'Yağız,' she called, pulling him aside. 'That coffee bar along the way, the independent one, you're friends with the owner, yes? Any chance we might ship out that birthday party for their coffee and cake? Special surprise kind of thing, birthday treat in relaxed surroundings or something like that. We can whip the cake round there, pay for a round of drinks. They're bound to buy more stuff once they're there.'

His initial response was to curl his lip, but she took that as habit rather than comment. 'It'd free up three tables,' he said after a moment's thought. 'And they won't be doing much business up the road. It's not a day for walk-ins.'

That sounded like agreement, which she reinforced with, 'I know Meriç'd say better lose a chunk of profit on one party, than piss off another six. You know them. Will you have a word and see if we can get it sorted?'

Within minutes the birthday party was out of the door, all hands descending on their table, clearing, dismantling, and reassembling the larger structure into three smaller ones. The crowd at the bar ebbed, a glimmer of leeway shone through the unrelenting schedule, people took the time to draw breath, to sustain themselves for the next surge.

'Yağız.' Again Annie pulled him aside. 'I'm really sorry–' She heard the words pop out … hadn't meant to apologise. 'I'm going to have to nip out. I've been trying to wait for a lull, but … well, this is as good as it'll get and it's something I have to sort before it gets any later.'

He looked her in the eye as he digested this. 'Personal stuff, is it? That you were supposed to go to Scotland for?'

She nodded. 'Look, I wouldn't leave now if I didn't have to.'

He shrugged. 'I'd have coped if you weren't here.' His tone wasn't unfriendly.

'I'll be as quick as I can.'

◉ ◉ ◉

Quarter of an hour later she was almost at her flat. She hadn't tried to get a cab, they too would be mostly on pre-bookings today, nor a bus; public transport was on holiday timetables, and instead had reverted to what had been her favoured means of transport around Hull all those years ago. It was a compact city. She simply ran through the streets, taking advantage of half-remembered short cuts most of which were still viable.

At the end of her road, she stopped. A largely residential street it was neither busy nor deserted. She had the option of re-entering the way she'd left, from the alley at the back, but it would be lonely and deserted and if anyone had been watching last night they must know she'd slipped out that way.

She marched down the road, homing in on the front door, scrutinizing everyone and everything as she went, alert for any untoward movement.

Inside, she scanned the shadows of the shared hallway and stairs, listened for the sounds of other tenants. A low bass beat thrummed from somewhere, the fabric of the building creaked as people moved about.

Taking the stairs in twos, she paused at her door only long enough to check the thread she'd stuck across the gap. It was intact.

Once in the room she grabbed for her few possessions, stuffing them into bags. The laptop was safely out of the way in her rucksack in her staff locker. She'd planned to leave anything she didn't need but there wasn't much and it suddenly didn't seem like a great idea to leave any trace of herself behind.

She could go straight back to the restaurant from here. They needed every pair of hands today. But she'd planned to go to the Thompsons, to surprise them by being early. She desperately wanted the money in her pocket, and knew from past experience that it was easier to get cash out of the Thompsons' the quicker she did it.

What would have happened if she hadn't been at the restaurant today? Despite the fact their surfeit of customers was largely from taking on another restaurant's bookings, no one else had thought to reverse the process. If she hadn't got Yağız to get that birthday party out early, the crowd would have become impossible. At least one group would have started to complain, maybe walked out. As it was, not one of the customers had an inkling how close the dam had been to bursting.

The same situation might be arising now. She had to get back to manage the place. Yağız was OK as a manager, but he lacked her flair for coping. Pat expected her this evening; this evening it would have to be, maybe even tomorrow morning.

Everything was now crammed into two carrier bags except for her warm jumper still hanging in the wardrobe. She would wear that. She cast her gaze around the room seeing finger marks across the blank TV screen as it reflected the dull glow of the winter sun. Those fingerprints would have come from previous tenants as well as her own hands as she'd leant across to flip plug switches on or off.

She didn't like the idea of leaving her fingerprints, but it would be absurd to wipe the TV screen before she left. She'd touched every bit of furniture in the place. Who did she think would be here looking for forensic traces? This was Pieternel paranoia. Nonetheless, she slipped on a pair of gloves and whipped out a tired-looking mop head from the cleaning kit under the sink and began to run it over the surfaces from the kitchen cubicle to the miniature shower room, the armchair, table, wardrobe and television. She wafted it at the wall around the plug sockets behind the big screen, but the dust wasn't so thick there.

Memory took her back to the sordid little flat she'd camped in for several years when she'd first lived in the city, scraping a living as the Thompsons' dogsbody. This place was smaller, little more than a bedsit, but it had been clean when she'd moved in.

More than clean. It had been bright. The surfaces had gleamed at her.

She sat at the table where she usually sat. The armchair was uncomfortable. The light from the window caught the TV screen from this angle. Despite her efforts with the mop head, it was still a mess of finger marks. She reached out her gloved hand to the remote and turned it on.

Horse racing from Cheltenham blasted out at her, making her jump, sound bouncing from the walls. The picture lessened the prominence of the marks on the screen but didn't hide them. They were still intrusive. She hadn't had much use for the TV while she'd been here, preferring to use her laptop. Had she even turned it on prior to this?

There was a time when dust and finger marks would have meant nothing to her. The need for cleanliness at the restaurant had sharpened her senses but she still didn't see any real point in housework at home.

And there was a time when she had always watched TV at full volume so that the soundtrack followed her wherever she went. No need for that in this small space, but though her finger hovered over the volume control, she left it as it was and let the commentary pound her ears.

Her mind ticked back over the past two weeks as her eyes stared unfocussed at the screen. She'd never turned on this TV before. This was the first time.

The flat had been properly cleaned before she moved in. She would have clocked those fingerprints before now if they'd been there to see.

She had to swallow as her mouth dried. The thread across the doorway. They'd put it back. They'd known about it and put it back. But they hadn't bothered with dust and finger marks. Annie the useless housekeeper wouldn't bother with those. And they'd done something that had reset the television and they'd left it on high volume just as she used to.

What had she done since she came in? Her mind raced to reconstruct everything. She'd rushed about ramming her belongings in bags, then she'd flown through the place with an old mop head. And for the past few moments she'd been sitting watching a TV set that she was pretty sure was watching her.

Chapter 20

Annie sat still, her expression relaxed, eyelids at half-mast as though dozing. Years of practice had taught her how to turn a relaxed, uninterested demeanour to the world, to hide shock, anger or pain. Right now it was shock that coursed through her.

The watcher watched. How long? Who? How?

Dust motes zigzagged in front of her eyes in the beam of light that emphasised the smudges and swirls on the television screen. She wanted to turn on her phone to see the follow-up email that would have arrived by now.

Pieternel would have dug to the depths of this thing, worked out what it was about; she might already be wondering why Annie hadn't got back to her, maybe fearing the worst.

What was the worst?

This was the worst; not knowing, the feeling of being played at the end of a line that she had barely glimpsed.

She had to get out, but what if they, whoever they were, were watching … waiting for her to do just that?

And once she was out, where then? Back to the restaurant? Ludicrous though it was, she knew the moment she returned to the steam-laden clatter of Meriç's world, she would be sucked into the heart of the gastronomic maelstrom, into her role as restaurant manager.

Gastronomic maelstrom? The phrase caught something at the edge of her mind. She pushed it aside.

Pat. She'd arranged to meet Pat this evening, albeit she'd planned to corner her hours earlier. Whoever was watching her knew about

Pat. It occurred to her that Pat too would have cottoned on about that so-called evening appointment. She knew Annie well enough to expect her far earlier than the time she'd set.

She let her gaze focus again on the muddle of fingerprints on the screen as the thunder of galloping horses played out behind the smudges. Someone with no fear of having their prints lifted. Either that or they were stupid, and she knew they weren't stupid. They thought she wouldn't notice. Of course, if she wasn't sitting at this table, watching from this angle, there would be nothing to see. Maybe they hadn't sat here. After all, why would they?

She was no domestic goddess, but she didn't live in complete squalor these days.

Their research was out of date.

She needed that cash from Pat Thompson. Pat Thompson might be lazy, but she had a sharp edge when she chose to use it. Annie wondered if it might still be sharp enough to be of use to her now.

Even here with that filthy screen in front of her, Meriç kept intruding into her thoughts. Knowing it was irrational, she wanted Pieternel to agree to her staying for just a few more days, to wrap up the job properly, to leave the loose ends tied. And if she got out of the flat today, this would be the last time she was visible outside the restaurant. As soon as she left the premises each night she would evaporate into the ether. That would impede checking the surveillance footage, but she had an idea to get round that.

Since rushing in here, she'd stuffed things in bags, flapped at the dust with inappropriate cleaning equipment and slumped in a chair ostensibly to watch a race meeting. And for all that her intention had been to clear her flat and leave, she could just as easily have been tidying for a guest; the old slovenly Annie to a T.

She jumped to her feet and went to rake through the drawers in the kitchen area, returning with a handful of cutlery that she clattered roughly into three place settings at the small table. Clicking the remote, she put up the channel list which muted the television's intrusive noise. A pretended look at the time, a brief moment of play-acting a search for something – anything – a huff of exasperation, another glance at the time, a grab for her jacket.

Then she walked out.

In the brief moment it took to attach the thread between door and frame, her breathing elevated, she felt her heart thud hard and fast. Instinct shouted at her to run, but she wanted them to think she was coming back. Couldn't be sure if anyone was watching live or if, like her with the restaurant cameras, someone would watch later on fast forward, slowing for the interesting bits.

She took a winding route that allowed her to stop, double back, and check for followers. No sign of anyone, which neither surprised nor reassured her. The watchers, she knew, were confident they could simply drop in and find her when they wanted, but they didn't seem to be in a hurry. She was counting on that to give her the time she needed.

It took a while to find a pub that still had a public phone.

'Thompsons,' said Pat's voice.

'Hey, Pat. Annie here. Just to let you know I'm going to call in this evening.'

'Yeah, you sent me a– Uh … this evening?'

Pat tripped slightly on her words, her tone questioning.

Annie allowed herself a grin and balled her fist at a minor triumph. Pat had remembered. 'Yup,' she said, reinforcing the pointless reminder of an appointment they both knew about already. 'I'm calling in this evening. You got any decent coffee or do I have to bring my own?'

'Cheeky cow! When did we ever run out of coffee?'

Call over, she was off again, jogging through the cold streets, watching ahead, behind … ducking away from surveillance cameras. No one took any notice. Her destination was a remembered café, a greasy spoon, far down the pecking order from Meriç's select establishment, but one whose doors were open similar long hours for a mishmash of punters. Annie felt relief to see the steamed up windows and light from an inadequate bulb as she approached. For those in the know anything was on sale here, or had been years ago. Pushing open the door she met the hopeful gaze of a tired-looking man cradling an empty mug, the only customer, a plate in front of him scraped clean, knife and fork crossed on its empty surface. Under a ragged raincoat, he wore a sturdy tweed jacket straining at its mismatched buttons, its edges frayed. Coat and wearer had seen better times though not in each other's company.

Annie moved to the counter, pulling out a handful of change. 'Get him a refill,' she murmured, jerking her head in the direction of the man.

The woman behind the counter shot her a quick look. Annie read mild censure for her meanness that it was just a cup of tea and not something more substantial. She let her gaze drop, hated the feeling of being forced into small economies that should have been left behind years ago. She moved to one side where she could keep the door in sight. She'd paid for her right to occupy a bit of their space.

She had counted off five minutes and begun to get edgy, when the unmistakeable bulk of Pat Thompson lumbered into view, obscured by the steamed windows. Annie drew further back out of sight of the door.

Pat came in. No sign of anyone with her, body language relaxed but bordering irritable as she looked around.

Annie moved into view, her hand raised briefly in greeting.

Pat gave her an unsmiling nod. 'Wasn't sure where you'd be,' she said. 'I put my head round the door of the Whalebone on my way.'

'I said "coffee". Whalebone would have been beer.'

'It's been a long time. So what's the problem? Why the cloak and dagger?'

By the time she turned on to the main road and saw the frontage of Meriç's restaurant, Annie felt on surer ground. No one had been sniffing around about the job she'd done for the Thompsons, and Pat had coughed up the money. Dyson and fforbes hadn't been back, though Annie was sure they would be. Whatever they were after, they were in no hurry, probably thought she was tied in for a full six weeks.

Annie's mind set off on a different track as her gaze scoured the plate glass expanse of Meriç's restaurant. Were the windows clean, did the sign glow bright, no bulbs out?

Little things, Meriç had told her, *each one trivial, put together they make the difference between top notch and just mediocre. I don't do mediocre.*

She'd been far longer than intended on this excursion, and felt a surge of apprehension. It focused on what she would find inside, whether they were coping, as though she'd crossed a physical boundary that left Pat, the shadowy duo and the invasion of her bedsit far behind. She paused to wonder how she'd come to feel so at home in this role. It wasn't a particularly easy one. Maybe it was because she was good at it. These temporary roles were so often play-acting and bluff.

What was that phrase she'd thought up? A gastronomic maelstrom. That was what she was frightened of finding inside. As she pushed open the door, she smiled. Things looked calm and ordered. Gastronomic maelstrom better fitted the do she'd attended last night, though she'd seen next to nothing of the actual catering. Those huge gastronome pots had been lugged through the crush of helpers and Heidis, zesty aromas trailing behind them as they had been whipped through to the kitchens.

Spicy chickpea and walnut sauce … lamb pilau … chili ginger …?

Who was she kidding? With just two week's experience of restaurant management how could she possibly have identified the dishes so confidently?

She caught a quick word with the woman Yağız had put on the hostess-stand. The place was full but not over-full. Yağız appeared as she slipped behind the bar. She caught his eye. He responded with the ghost of a nod.

'Everything been OK?'

A curt nod. 'Did you get your stuff sorted?'

'Yes ... thanks ...' His enquiry was unexpected. 'Uh ... I'll be in the back. Call me if things get hectic.'

Another curt nod.

She went to her locker, grabbed the laptop from her rucksack and took it through to the office, where she clicked it on, did the same with her phone and left both devices to come to life while she headed to the kitchen.

The sous chef gave her a harried glance as she pushed past to the big cupboards, but it was one of the casuals, not Carol's friend, whose body language radiated worry and guilt as she raked through the outside catering stores. She watched reflections snaking about in the gleaming stainless steel of the cupboard doors. Just one of them with his attention riveted to her activities, and he wasn't trying to communicate with any of the others. Interesting.

All that chaos this morning because the kitchen hadn't been prepared. All that preparatory work that she'd witnessed yesterday.

The gastronome pots were all present and correct but not cleaned to Meriç's exacting standards. She applied her fingernail and scraped a scrap of dried food from a corner. Holding it to her nose, she caught a whiff of chili ginger.

Another piece slotted into the jigsaw.

She'd identified the chef's partner-in-crime, or one of them at least. Just for confirmation, she hauled the bain maries to one side to inspect the corners, seeing the new dents and scratches.

When had they been taken away? They must have been spirited out during service to have made it to the big house in time.

The surveillance cameras would complete the picture, but she wouldn't risk watching them from here. She didn't need her whole laptop, just the software and the relevant files and she could watch from the hotel's business centre, the central library … from anyone's PC anywhere.

It would need a high-capacity pen drive, the sort not routinely available in non-specialist shops, but she had one of those right here.

It was just a week ago she'd prepared reports and data for Meriç to show conclusively – so she'd thought – that there was nothing untoward going on. Thank heavens she'd not shown him. He'd have thought her a complete div. She'd been focused entirely on getting out of the job before she ran into someone she knew. That was why she'd dropped the ball so badly, though the official line would remain that it was Meriç's fault for withholding the detail in the books. Those now useless reports had been sitting on a pen drive at the back of her locker for the past seven days. It would be no penance to delete them and overwrite the whole thing with surveillance footage for later perusal.

She glanced through to the dining room as she returned to the office. Things had settled to a smooth rhythm, the turmoil of the morning forgotten. The atmosphere in the kitchen was more relaxed too as the day wound down.

Back in the office, Annie checked through the laptop, preparing files for transfer to the pen drive, resisting an urge to set the footage running and to watch right now. She'd seen the food arrive at the do last night. It had been late. The chef and his acolytes must have ferried it out of the back door to a waiting van right under everyone's noses. Maybe he'd gone straight from here and been up half the night serving Meriç's food to the ravening hordes out there. All that frenetic activity and so little ready for today. She supposed they'd returned the equipment in the not-so-small hours, probably not long before her own arrival this morning. Certainly the cleaning job had been sketchy. If she'd stayed any later, she would probably have found herself face to face with the chef, though he might not have recognised her in that gaudy costume and pigtailed wig. If he'd been there all night, no wonder he needed today off.

There was a knock at the door. She reached across to pull it open. One of the casuals, Carol's friend, stood there.

'Yağız said you wanted to see me.'

'Yes.' She turned to face him. 'The tenfoot was left in a dreadful state the other day. We have neighbours to think of.'

He let out the whisper of a sigh; didn't quite roll his eyes. 'Well, it wasn't me.' His air was deliberately unconcerned.

'I'm not saying it was all your fault. There have been one or two other things.' She stressed the *other* and held his gaze. He didn't let his eyes drop but she sensed wariness. 'This is everything we owe you.' She handed him an envelope. 'You needn't come back.'

His look was briefly surprised as he took the envelope. 'You're sacking me?'

She nodded. 'I'm afraid I have to let you go.'

He shrugged, half turned away then paused. 'Meriç'll be is back in a few days, yeah? I'll see you later in the week.'

Annie listened to his footsteps recede. Was that bravado? She remembered Yağız's comment. *Good luck with that.*

Chapter 21

Well, it was done now, and when Meriç returned, she would leave. It would be up to him what happened next. She turned to the laptop, wanted to make sure she had all the files she needed. The machine itself could stay here in her locker. No chance then that she'd forget and fire it up automatically. It wasn't the most secure berth, but safe enough, and no one would get through her security if they got their hands on it.

She had everything lined up and was ready to go and retrieve the pen drive when her phoned pinged new emails. As she watched, a stream of them downloaded. There must be something dodgy about the signal from this little cubby hole; she'd had this before. Nothing at all and then a flood. But she'd seen Pieternel in the list. That was a relief.

'Have you sacked him?'

Yağız stood in the doorway watching her curiously. She slipped her phone out of sight.

'Yup, paid and gone.'

'No trouble?'

'Not really ...' She told him about the *See you later in the week* comment.

He nodded. 'He'll beg Meriç for a second chance, or anyway someone will.'

'Then I'll talk to Meriç first, and anyway surely he'd check with me.'

'Anyone else, yeah. He gave that one a job as a favour to Corder.'

Annie narrowed her eyes. Yağız could have told her earlier.

Maximilian Corder was the one with a big enough financial stake to sink the place should he choose to pull the plug. She shrugged. It wouldn't be her problem.

As Yağız left, Annie reached for her phone but then changed her mind. The email could wait. Priority was to get the files transferred so she was ready to leave on a second's notice. She wasn't going to be last one here tonight, leaving on her own into the darkness of the alleyway.

She'd been hidden away in the office for too long and didn't want to lose the new authority she'd gained today. Locking the screen from prying eyes and slipping her phone into her pocket she went out to see what was going on. The dining room was less crowded now, a feel of things winding down. She glanced through the diary. Nothing to worry about.

In the kitchen the sous chef had settled into a routine, calling the orders crisply, inspecting plates before they left. A warm glow of satisfaction grew inside her. Today could have been a disaster even without her extracurricular visit to the bedsit and meeting with Pat Thompson. It could have been a multiple disaster, but she'd kept all the plates spinning. It was going to end well.

The sous chef glanced up as though aware of scrutiny. It wasn't her he looked at. Annie followed his line of sight to catch Yağız standing by the door to the bar watching her. Everyone watching everyone else. She fought back an urge to turn her gaze to the camera above them all, taking in the wider view, and headed for her locker.

As she clicked it open Yağız walked closer, curious maybe about the so-called personal business that had taken her attention. Before today he'd done nothing to try to build up the type of relationship where he could easily ask for detail.

'It's gone well,' she said, forestalling any questions he had been going to ask. 'Good job all round given the circs. What happens when the chef takes holidays?'

'He doesn't take holidays.'

'What would happen if he did? Or if he left?'

Yağız gave her a speculative look before saying, 'He steps up OK for a day,' nodding his head in the sous chef's direction. 'But longer than that, Meriç'd get in someone new. He doesn't promote to senior posts.'

Yağız had of course expected the manager's job that Annie had been parachuted into. There was an edge to his final words, but none of the hostility she'd had from him before today. It felt good that even Yağız was coming round to acknowledging her as good in the job.

'Lost something?' Yağız was watching curiously as she fished about at the back of her locker.

'No, it's nothing. It's just … my bag … fell out …' Annie let the sentence fade into a mumbled pattern of words, a half story that had the air of making sense. 'What time's the last booking?' she asked to avert further interrogation. She wasn't going to pull out that pen drive in front of him.

He gave her a time, adding, 'We know them. They're special occasions only. They'll be punctual and they won't linger.'

'Good,' she said. 'I want you to see we don't take any more walk-ins. It's been a busy one. Once they're in, get the closed sign up and we'll call it a day once they're gone.'

His lip began its customary curl. She could pluck the thoughts right out of his head.

'Meriç wouldn't approve.' She voiced it before he could. 'But Meriç isn't here and I'm not planning to tell him. We've been short-staffed all day, chef left us in the lurch and I think we deserve a bit of a break.'

He gave her a grin. 'My lips are sealed. I'll go and get guards on the door.'

She returned his smile, amazed still at how different he was without his prickly exterior. She wondered if the armour would be back in place when the chef was in the kitchen again. It would be another interesting dynamic to watch. She knew the two men disliked each other, and seemed to have united only in hostility towards her, the incomer. But now she had dropped the glimmer of a hint to Yağız with her comments about the chef leaving. Three days wouldn't be enough to watch it all unfold. She smiled to herself at the irony of maybe wanting to stay on now that circumstances had made it impossible. Pieternel's email was waiting. She might not even have a day left in post.

The lockers were small but deep. There was nothing in hers but her rucksack. Irritated, she pulled it out, careful to check that it didn't bring anything with it, then she shone a torch into the depths. Nothing.

Had it caught on the fabric of the rucksack? The last thing she wanted was to drop the thing on the floor out here for someone else to find. Had she accidentally pulled it out at some earlier point? But she rarely used the locker at all. She hung her coat by the office. It was only because she'd brought her laptop that ...

She stopped, took in a breath, and looked again. It was nowhere on or in the rucksack. The back corners of the locker bounced the torch beam off empty surfaces. She reached in to run her hands all over it in case the pen drive wasn't the colour she remembered and had somehow vanished against the military grey of the locker walls.

She had put it in there on Christmas Day, tossed it to the back ready to be pulled out like a conjurer's rabbit from a hat to astound Meriç. Had she taken it out on Boxing Day? No, but she'd thought about it, remembered seeing it in there, a reminder she hadn't wanted of how badly she'd got things wrong. That wasn't all that had happened. It was that evening she'd been jumped in the alleyway, the evening she'd clung in the darkness as two people barged inside, then off again discarding her coat as they went.

They hadn't stayed inside long, seemed to have taken nothing, left no trace.

She walked mentally through the process; that balaclavaed duo going into the cold-store, ripping open the box of freeze-dried apple … no, not ripping, because it had looked no different the following day when she'd moved it from there to the walk-in. OK, opened it very carefully, then rummaged inside to get at the whatever-it-was. Freeze-dried food in small particles clung on, flew about. It would have been a messy business. They'd been a cool crew, no edge of panic. So they'd opened the box, extracted what they'd been after, cleared up all the mess and resealed the box?

No way. They hadn't been inside long enough.

But they'd had ample time to crack open a locker. The most basic of picklocks would have done the job. And since that night, she had no recollection of seeing that pen drive.

Chapter 22

Maximilian Corder rolled his eyes as he heard his aunt's querulous tones in amongst the raised voices from the corridor outside. What did the old bag want now? Family loyalties were all very well but she knew better than to barge in on him here.

'Let her through,' he shouted, not bothering to hide the impatience in his voice.

She pushed open the door with a triumphant glance over her shoulder. 'Max, Max, let me look at you. Why are you such a stranger these days? How long is it?'

'What d'you want?' he snapped, holding back the more appropriate, *Never long enough!*

'You know I don't bother you at work. Never once have I bothered you at work. You know I wouldn't be here if it wasn't urgent family business.'

His fingers begin an incessant tapping on the table in front of him as he heard the speech she always barged in on. In the right gathering he would make a good story of it, mock her for his own amusement, but just now he felt nothing but mounting irritation. Normally he would have been ahead of her; someone would have warned him which bit of family trivia had lit her fuse. Whatever she wanted, if he didn't immediately give in she would plant herself like a limpet.

Corder watched as she looked round and took a step towards the room's only armchair. At once he was on his feet and at her elbow. 'No, don't sit down. I'm on my way out. What is it?'

'Ah, now Max,' she wheedled. 'Don't rush me. I'm an old woman. I've troubles enough without …'

It took a conscious effort to take her arm gently and ease her away from settling in. Anyone else of this size and stature would be sprawling the other side of the door with a shouted comment to some minion to kick them right out. He heaved a sigh. Anyone else wouldn't have made it through the door in the first place.

He took a stab at the most likely cause of her visit.

'That grandson of yours,' he growled, and saw from the shaft of disappointment in her eye that he'd cut to the chase. 'What's the worthless piece of shite done now?'

'Now Max.' She gave him a pained look. 'That job you got him. He's been doing real well. Barely missed a shift.'

He blew out an exasperated breath. 'Got himself sacked again, has he? I told you I can't keep running about after him. I said no more after last time.'

'Oh, but Max, it wasn't his fault this time. Someone left trash outside and the neighbours complained. That's not his fault. It's not his job to clear the tenfoot.'

Corder felt his eyebrows rise. For once she had a point.

'Meriç wouldn't sack him for that. There must have been more to it.'

'Meriç is away. It was that new manager of his, a woman called Annie Raymond. She's not been in the job five minutes. Meriç'll be back soon. You'll speak to him, won't you?'

Corder raised his glance to heaven. It was a bold move for a new manager. Meriç must have primed her who she could and couldn't push about on her own initiative. He'd thought her harmless but maybe this Annie Raymond merited a closer look. 'It's the last time,' he barked at his aunt. 'From now on, he stands on his own two feet.'

Watching the surveillance footage was suddenly top priority. Annie no longer cared what had happened yesterday – sod the chef and Meriç's losses. She wanted to skim through every second since she'd set up the cameras, which was a day late to catch the raid, but might shed light on what else was going on.

The problem was where and how. If she was right that someone was tracking her through her phone and laptop then her only option was to watch here in the restaurant. The office wasn't private enough to take the time while they were open and if she stayed on she would advertise that she was here alone behind a couple of flimsy bolts in an area that was largely deserted outside working hours.

She needed the files and software. All she lacked was a high-capacity storage device. Where, at this hour on New Year's Day in a city where she had barely any contacts, was she to find one?

The Thompsons maybe, but no, they'd been targeted too. She wouldn't trust any electronics from them. Small games shops … PC repair shops …? There were plenty of those within reach. They'd be closed but surely someone somewhere would have escaped the family holiday on the excuse of stocktaking, checking, catching up. It was worth a try.

With a fleeting apology to Yağız she raced out into the cold January air.

It took the best part of an hour. She found her mark but he was frustratingly stubborn about cooperating. Before he caved in and sold her a tablet – at a price – she had begun to think about sleight of hand and helping herself, not only to the technology but to the half-eaten sandwich on the bench beside him.

There were a lot of files to transfer, huge files. It might take hours. She sprinted back to the restaurant, burst in with barely a word for Yağız or anyone else and pushed through to the office where she set up her laptop and the new tablet. This was not how a professional manager should act. Nor should it annoy her so much.

Managing the restaurant was cover, not her real job. Yet somehow it no longer felt that way.

'Anything I can help with?'

She jumped. Yağız was in the doorway looking at her curiously, his glance flicking to the technology that had so absorbed her she hadn't heard his footsteps.

If it had been Carol she could have said, get me something eat, I'm starving, but couldn't bring herself to try it on Yağız. 'Uh ... thanks, but no. I just want to get everything done that I need to do. It's all in hand.'

'Closed sign's up now,' he told her. 'An hour tops and we're done.'

She gave him a tight smile, feeling his curiosity burning like a laser. Maybe he saw her personal problems escalating to the point she had to leave, then he could step into her job. Don't worry, she wanted to say, the job's yours in a few days.

As he went away she thought about the raid and the locker. Clearly they hadn't been looking for her inept report to Meriç. She wondered what they'd made of it and what they had really been looking for? They might have been at Carol's locker too, but Carol's secrets had still been encased in freeze-dried apple at that stage.

The files were flying from laptop to tablet like lightning which was a relief but no more than she should expect given the amount she'd had to pay for the new device.

She peered into the corridor. No sign of Yağız. Venturing as far as the kitchen she saw the sous chef on his own, applying a brisk polish to the flat plate.

'Good job today,' she said, and received the ghost of a smile in return.

At the doorway to the dining room she saw Yağız chatting with the last couple of punters as he walked them to the exit. The remaining staff were poised to leap upon the final areas to be swept clean.

If that file transfer wasn't complete soon, she would have to stay behind on her own, bolt the front door, make her way into the deserted alleyway. She blew out a breath. They still had the last bits of tidying to do.

She looked around. The till drawer was open and empty, all paraphernalia behind the bar stacked in place and gleaming, not a stray bread roll or piece of fruit within grabbing distance. They were minutes from closure and everything was ready for a quick getaway.

She headed back to the office.

The transfer was almost there, just seconds to go. She grabbed her phone. Both it and the laptop had to be turned off, right off, before she set a foot outside the door. They had to be as dead as if their batteries had been removed. Everything must be packed in the rucksack. No leaving things behind to be tampered with here as she had at the bedsit.

The email!

She hadn't opened Pieternel's email.

Her finger hesitated over the phone, but the process of turning the thing off, completely off, could take several minutes if it chose to be awkward and already the frantic bustle of clearing behind the last customers of the day had ebbed. She could read the email this evening now she had a tablet that couldn't have been tampered with.

The transfer was done. She dived at the laptop to initiate its shut-down sequence, and hopped impatiently as the devices turned themselves off. Don't choose now to update, she implored them. From out in the corridor, lockers creaked open and banged shut.

More voices than usual shouted, 'Bye Annie, see you tomorrow.' They were pleased with her for giving them an early evening.

'Thanks. Good job today,' she shouted back, staring at the technology, willing it to stop its incessant software routines and just die.

Finally, she could stuff everything into the waiting rucksack, grab her jacket and rush out into what was now a deserted restaurant.

The kitchen surfaces shone darkly in the ambient light from the front of house. She was either going to have to go out into that alleyway or leave the front door unbolted.

Her mouth dried. The front door was the only sensible option but she knew she couldn't bring herself to do it. No manager worth her salt would leave her restaurant vulnerable overnight. The cold image of the alleyway with its dark corners, its putrid air of decay, brought sudden clarity.

What in hell do I think I've been doing?

This job had got under her skin in a way no other job ever had before. What Meriç was really paying her to do had become secondary to her role as manager of his restaurant. The vague plan she'd had to be first in tomorrow morning, so as to cover up that unbolted front door, crumbled to ash.

She wasn't coming back. This had been her last day here. She didn't have to have read Pieternel's email to know how dangerous this place had become. It was nothing to do with Meriç but his outfit had become the focus.

She'd thought she could hide out in plain sight for another three days, to get the job done properly. A shiver ran through her as she took a last look around the kitchen. It no longer mattered whether or not the place was ready for tomorrow but she checked anyway.

Someone had left on the light behind the bar. It was a considerate gesture to illuminate her path to bolt the front door before she left.

As she went through, she ran her eye over the bar top, the shelves, reaching high to check for dust.

Then she stepped through into the dining room.

'Ohh!' She leapt back with a gasp.

A silhouetted figure lounged in a chair by the door. It started up at her exclamation.

'Sorry,' said Yağız's voice. 'I must have dozed off. Didn't mean to startle you.'

She felt the rapid flutter of her heart as the shock subsided.

'Go on,' he said, gesturing towards the door. 'I'll bolt it behind you and go out down the tenfoot.'

'Thanks.' She was touched by his thoughtfulness. She'd really turned a corner with Yağız.

She waited outside at the entrance to the alleyway. Within a minute footsteps sounded and Yağız strode towards her.

'All done,' he said. 'Do you want me to walk with you? Not many people about.'

'No, no, I'll be fine. I'll see you tomorrow.'

The words just slipped out. She hadn't meant to lie. There was an awkward pause. Annie knew she wasn't coming back, knew that the story that would eventually filter back to Yağız and the rest of the staff would be something that didn't put her in a good light, something to explain why she disappeared and never showed her face again. She wanted to say something stupid like, it's been good working with you, but that would give the game away and anyway it was only true of today.

She took a circuitous route to the hotel, turning, retracing her steps, watching, aware of everyone and everything around her. If she wasn't being tracked by satellite, then there was no one following.

The last train to London was long gone even before she'd left the restaurant so there didn't seem any point in rushing to get at Pieternel's email. It had arrived hours ago and might say, *Get out now!* But she'd survived the day, she'd made one-hundred percent certain there was no one on her tail and intended to get a good night's sleep before heading out of Hull in the morning.

It was two hours later that she finally switched on the new tablet. She lounged in the hotel's otherwise deserted bar, resisting an urge to doze after having finished every scrap of the bar snack she'd recklessly put on her bill. She'd been lavish in her compliments to the single barman on duty, and appreciative in her thanks for serving her so late. Her short time as a restaurant manager had taught her to value the effort that lay behind a plate of decent food efficiently served. Her effulgence had earned her a full bread basket all to herself, just as she'd hoped. Not a crumb of that was left now.

She watched the tablet spring to life, then thought back to the restaurant as she glanced out of the window at the dancing lights of the city. Did Yağız know about the chef's scam? The idea of that amount of food being prepared and smuggled out on a regular basis without anyone noticing was preposterous. But why would Yağız keep quiet? Clearly he didn't like the guy. Maybe the chef and his helpers had honed their act, making food and equipment vanish, like master magicians.

She looked at the tablet. All that surveillance footage. It didn't matter now though she knew she would go through it if only as an academic exercise, to satisfy her curiosity and give her some concrete evidence to send on to Meriç. She wondered if they would have to pay him back his fee.

She made the connection to her emails and let them scroll on to the screen.

Seeing the rippling patterns of moonlight catching the currents in the estuary far below, Annie knew with absolute certainty that someone out there was looking for her, wondering where she'd disappeared to. She'd cut it fine. Way too fine.

Icy fingers played down her back. Not so long ago she'd thought seriously of going back to that restaurant in the morning, of announcing her presence to the world.

Here in the peace and quiet of someone else's catering operation, empty of customers, she wondered how she could have contemplated something so dangerously stupid. It was all the other stuff that had put her off balance; Pieternel's secrecy, the business on the brink again, having to scrape around for bits of money.

She was on it now. There would be no walking into traps tomorrow morning. Whoever was on her coattails knew she didn't have a car. They would watch the station. She would have to walk, but after a good night's sleep, that would be no penance. A roundabout route out of the city, make her way down to the A63. There were a couple of small service stations. She could target one of the trucks that would have come off the early ferry. Most of them would be heading south.

A phone buzzed from behind the bar. A door creaked open. The barman reappeared. She looked up, gave him a smile that he returned as he picked up the extension and murmured, 'Bar.'

Despite the determination that she would sleep well tonight, a part of her was not going to feel secure until she knew that the city was far behind her.

She clicked on to Pieternel's email and read the short message.

I've looked into it. It's coincidence. Nothing to worry about. You have to stay the full 6 weeks. Stop fighting it.

Annie stared. Coincidence? Stay on? How could she stay after this? Automatically her hand was at her pocket feeling for her phone. But no, that was in her room, turned off and tucked in the rucksack.

She stared towards the barman, who was still talking into the handset. Did that phone have an outside line and could she persuade him to let her use it? She had to speak to Pieternel. Even Pieternel would see that she couldn't stay on after this.

As she waited for him to finish his call, poised ready to signal him over, her mind stalled on a rehearsal of what she would say.

I can't stay on after this.

After what?

My laptop and phone are being tracked.

A sliver of doubt crept in. She had nothing concrete to back that up.

The barman looked her way. She caught his eye and raised her hand. He gave her a nod and a smile as he spoke into the phone.

Someone had been in the bedsit. Those finger marks … the TV adjusted to default to full volume.

Had you ever turned it on before that, Annie? Pieternel would say.

The thread across the door had been unbroken. Had she built this whole edifice out of some smudged finger marks that she'd not happened to notice earlier?

Had you ever sat in that chair at that time of day before? She heard Pieternel's voice in her head.

Footsteps echoed. The barman was at her side.

Before she could speak, he said, 'Your visitors have arrived.'

She gaped at him. 'My … who?'

'They went up to your room, couldn't find you. You shouldn't give anyone your key. That was reception trying to track you down.'

Chapter 23

For a second, Annie could only gape at him. Visitors? In her room? She couldn't have visitors, she didn't know anyone. The Thompsons didn't know where she was. Had Yağız followed her? Not possible. No one knew where she was.

Yet the mental image of these visitors was clear, or clear insofar as she could remember them at all; a dark-skinned man, a blonde woman, both middle-aged. They'd gone to the room where her laptop and phone sat tucked in the rucksack. Were both devices still beaming signals to whoever was listening?

'I didn't give anyone my key.' She heard the catch in her own voice, watched her hand pull out the key card in evidence.

The gloom of the bar with only its night lights and reflections from the big picture windows felt suspended in time, a mirage of a safe cocoon about to shatter.

It was plain from the barman's expression that he'd read her reaction. The shock must be plain on her face. She jumped to her feet.

'Don't worry.' He laid his hand on her arm and gave her a conspiratorial wink. 'I didn't like the sound of them. I haven't said you're here.'

She stared at him, sudden hope that she wasn't yet cornered.

'But they'll come looking,' she blurted out. 'Where else could I be?'

'I said you'd asked about food, and I'd told you our kitchen was closed, but you might find something open down the end of Anlaby Road.'

'Did they … do you know where they went?'

'Looks like they're going to wait in your room. You sure you weren't given a second key?' He glanced at the key card she still clutched in her hand.

'No, just this one. If they've got in my room …' – and she didn't doubt that they had – '… it's not my doing.'

It was the wrong thing to say. She caught a subtle change in his expression. He'd protected her instinctively because she'd been effusive about the food and might leave a good tip.

'Listen, are they trouble? Because we've no night porter. There's no one else coming on till six. We're on our own. Do I need to call the police?'

She could see that wasn't a course he wanted to take. They must be breaching all kinds of regulations with barely even a skeleton staff.

'No, they're not trouble,' she said firmly and saw his shoulders relax. 'At least only to me. I need to get out. When they realise they've missed me, they'll be gone.'

'Well, where will you go at this hour? And will you come back?'

She could see the misgivings stack up as he thought through what he'd done. Was she going to slip away and leave an unpaid account behind her?

'They'll be gone in an hour, two hours tops. And I'll be back tomorrow evening. I'll have sorted it out by then, don't worry. I just need a head start.'

More lies. She wasn't coming back. She was leaving right now, leaving behind her room, her clothes, her rucksack with her laptop and phone. She hoped he wasn't going to push the question of where she was going because she didn't know the answer. The embryo plan to hitch a lift out of the city was impossible when she was this tired, and the weather so cold. Hell, she didn't even have her warm top, so lately retrieved from the bedsit. It was slung carelessly on a chair next to the rucksack and probably being inspected right now by her two unwelcome guests. She had the clothes she was wearing, her small shoulder bag and the new tablet. Everything else was lost.

'Thanks for your help,' she told him. 'I'm very grateful.'

'What room are you in?' He reached out to turn the key card holder to the light as he read the number. 'You can see the entrance from the windows that side. They're probably watching for you coming back.'

That stopped her. Her mind raced over the options. There were two exits, but both on the same side of the building, and she'd have to go by reception. This guy's colleague would stop her, want to quiz her about her visitors, might ring up to her room. Was there a fire door she could use without setting off an alarm … could she manufacture some kind of disguise …?

'There's a staff exit.'

She looked at him. Had he been paid to reel her in? Was she about to walk out of one trap into another? No, that was just paranoia. He was an ordinary guy worried about crossing a line and losing his job. The way he looked at her now it was clear that all he wanted was to see the back of her.

Whoever was up in her room, she thought they probably numbered amongst the few who could crack open devices that Pieternel had secured, but she wasn't going to lament the laptop and phone. These things happened. Her biggest regret as she looked down on to the cold streets was the warm top, but at least she had her jacket.

In response to the barman's follow-me gesture, she slipped behind the bar and into staff-only territory. He led her down an interminable staircase, its treads bare concrete, some landings in darkness, the safety bulbs burnt out. More violations. In her mind she tried to visualise the terrain around the base of the hotel, to work out which way to go, how to avoid being spotted from above. They might have broken into other rooms to keep a watch on all sides. But no, there were only two of them. They didn't have superhuman powers. *Hold that thought,* she told herself, knowing that they'd been a step ahead of her, one step more than should be possible. She'd missed something. And why this pussy-footing about? It was an aspect that worried her more than any other. They could have found and confronted her at the restaurant any time they'd wanted.

'You know where you're going, do you?' the barman said as he punched a code into a key pad and wrenched the bar to open what was labelled a fire door.

She nodded, 'Yes,' and shivered as the night air rushed in.

It wasn't a lie this time. As she stepped into the gloom, pulling her jacket tight, feeling the cold air clutch at her skin as though there was no material to stop it, the answer came to her. It was obvious where she had to go. No decision to face, just a simple Hobson's choice.

Chapter 24

The cubby hole of an office with its windowless walls was a pitch black cave. Annie swung the pencil torch into the corners. Everything was as she'd left it barely a couple of hours ago. The alleyway had not been as threatening to traverse as she'd anticipated. It was once she was inside the restaurant that the hairs on her neck stood up. She daren't put on the lights, but in the kitchen and dining room, the ghostly glow of the streetlamps let her check every inch of the place before she allowed herself to relax.

She had yet to draw the bolt across the kitchen door. That must be done before she found a place to sleep, but she had to wake in good time to pull it back before Yağız or the chef arrived. Either or both of them might be extra early to try to beat her to it, but they mustn't know she'd slept here.

And maybe, just maybe, the phone call she would make to Pieternel, as soon as she had completed her sweep of the premises, would mean she was gone before anyone else set foot in the place.

On autopilot she stowed her handbag in her locker but paused as she reached to put the tablet in with it. There might be more data to capture from the office system so, leaving her keys swinging from the locker door, she returned to the office, stashing the tablet out of the way in the stationery rack as she pushed things aside to make room.

The office computer jingled to life and Annie sat in front of it and set its alarm for five forty-five. Surely no one would get here before that, and if they did she would roll with it. She had to get some sleep. It was tempting to rest her head on the desk right now just for a few seconds but she knew if she did, the next thing she would hear would be that alarm.

She heaved herself to her feet and made for the walk-in to grab a can of something fizzy and a snack before she made the call. Unlocking and yanking open the door she flashed her pencil torch around. At once her eye was drawn to a familiar shape tucked beneath a low shelf. She pulled the door shut and clicked on the light, then crouched to read the tiny lettering, knowing what it would say.

Freeze-dried apple.

But when? How? There'd been no delivery. Had it been there yesterday? Wouldn't she have noticed? She thought of the frenetic rushing about that she'd done, in and out of the place, leaving Yağız to run things. Glancing over her shoulder her gaze met the blank face of the stout door. Though she knew she was alone, she couldn't cope with the thought of someone walking up and locking it from the outside. She stood, brushed herself down, clicked off the light plunging the room into darkness, and stepped into the corridor. That box was intact. Yet another call on her time before she could sleep, but it was an opportunity that could not be allowed to go by. As soon as she'd spoken to Pieternel and bolted the back exit she would rip that box open.

Slumping into the office chair, she pulled forward the phone and lifted the receiver. A scrap of paper that had been caught in the handset fluttered to the floor. The dialling tone buzzed as she drew in a breath. Pieternel's number was in the phone she'd abandoned back at the hotel. But it was also in her head because it was the number that she always had to know. She paused and let her shoulders drop. She was tired and Pieternel changed her phone more frequently than security considerations demanded, but her fingers would remember the sequence. All she had to do was relax and not try to force it. Her gaze focussed on the desk top then slid down to the floor.

With all the rushing about, she might have missed a box in the walk-in, but a piece of paper folded and tucked into the phone …?

No way.

Yağız must have left it deliberately for her to find. He'd offered to walk her home. Had he wanted to say something once they were away from the restaurant? Had he let himself back in and left this note? She laid the receiver on the desk. In a moment its faint buzz would turn to a screechy alarm and that would be the trigger for her subconscious to give her Pieternel's number.

She retrieved the folded scrap and spread it out. The writing was small. She had to squint to read it.

I need to talk. It's got to look like you're telling me off. It's got to be public but somewhere noisy so I can tell you something.

Her tired brain took a moment to catch up. Not Yağız, but a familiar hand.

It had to be someone from the restaurant … didn't it? It couldn't be either of … *them* … Dyson? Fforbes? No, she'd never seen their writing. She'd barely ever seen them.

The handset began to wail its separation from the base unit. Annie clicked it back in place. Pieternel's number popped into her head and so did that handwriting.

She would look in the reservations book to be certain, but it was Carol.

Carol would have heard about her accomplice being sacked. Was she going to confess all to Annie? Had the sacking triggered the note?

Very likely yes, but when? Carol had been off yesterday and she had no key.

Anyone in the restaurant would know Carol's writing. Annie ripped the note into four, shredding one of the pieces to unreadable confetti and letting it flutter into the wastepaper basket as she mulled it over. Another piece was largely blank paper with only the words *somewhere* and *something* legible and whole. She tore it in two, scrunched the pieces and tossed them after the confetti. The rest she slipped into her pocket for disposal later. Would she still be here tomorrow when Carol arrived? Would she have time to find out what she had to say? It all depended on how this call panned out.

She picked up the receiver and reached forward to punch in the number.

As her fingers touched the phone's keypad, she froze.

Voices … nearby … from inside the building.

'Lovely weather for the time of year.' The comment came out of nowhere, incongruous, conversational.

A shiver ran across her skin. She hadn't bolted that back exit.

With great care she eased the phone on to its rest and rose to her feet, holding her breath against squeaky floorboards.

Footsteps now … coming closer …

Holding the office door tight, she pressed herself close to peer through the gap where the frame didn't fit. Voices again … several of them … men arguing. Then a woman's tones broke across them.

Carol.

As she recognised the voice, Carol herself came into view, her face turned away, body language tense, petulant. Annie struggled to make out the words.

Was one of the other voices familiar too? Carol had to be with a key-holder, but which one? It wasn't the chef's voice, or Yağız's. No one else but her had a key … Oh yes they did! It struck her suddenly. Of course there was another key-holder.

⊙ ⊙ ⊙

The church bells outside her aunt's house clanged discordantly. They're chipped, thought Annie, they shouldn't sound like that. They would stop soon. No one went on and on ringing bells that sounded like that.

Not bells … an insistent bleeping …

She shot upright with a start, rubbing at her upper arm where it had cramped. The screen in front of her showed a flashing bell shape. Behind it the incessant beeps went on.

The computer. The alarm she'd set.

Five forty-five!

Could it really be morning so soon?

It hardly seemed a moment since she'd rested her head on the desk. Hadn't meant to sleep like this. She stretched and yawned. Apart from the cramp in her upper arm and an odd feeling of watching the world through gauze, she felt refreshed. Must have slept deeply.

There was a gentle knock at the door.

Annie jumped to her feet. Someone had arrived earlier than expected. Did it look like she'd slept in here?

The door eased open and Yağız's head appeared. 'Ah, you're awake. I thought I heard an alarm. You should have said, you know.'

'What?' Annie stared at him. What was he talking about?

'You should have said you had nowhere to go. I'd have found you a bed. What happened?'

'No … I …' She stalled on a story about having got in early and fallen asleep. The quality of the light … the bustle of movement … She spun back to the PC, knocked the mouse. It said ten a.m.

Ten a.m! But she'd set the alarm for five forty-five.

'Sorry,' she mumbled. 'I'm fine. I'm … I'll talk to you later. Are we ready to open?'

'All OK.' He gave her a grin. 'I covered for you.' He pointed to a sign on the door. *Conference call – do not disturb.* 'No one else knows.'

'Thanks,' she said as he turned to go. It felt like an admission of defeat. He expected the full story from her later. What could she say? She'd think of something … evicted from her flat … whatever. Her priority now was–

She stopped. A voice inside her head tried to prompt her. The gauze shimmered; nothing was quite in focus.

'Yağız,' she called. He turned back. 'Where's Carol? I want a word with her.'

His lip twitched to its habitual curl. 'She didn't show again. She's taking the piss now. You were right. I shouldn't have let her have the day off.'

'OK, never mind, we'll sort it later.' She wanted to say, no, she left me a note, but couldn't put together the jigsaw of when and where.

As soon as he had disappeared into the kitchen, she retreated to the office. Had Carol left her a note? But when … how …? What had it said? Had she fallen asleep while reading it?

She struggled to remember at what point she'd laid her head on the desk. Clearly she'd not bolted the door and gritted her teeth at the potential consequences of that. She'd been tired, overtired, but … she couldn't believe she'd mistaken the time of the alarm.

Ah, that look of kindly concern on Yağız's face. Had he arrived early, found her sleeping so deeply his arrival hadn't stirred her, seen the alarm was set and reset it? Perhaps he'd seen how tired she looked but perhaps he was stacking up evidence to put in front of Meriç to secure himself the manager's job.

Yes, there had been a note. She remembered it falling out of the phone. Or had that been a half-dream / half-hallucination as sleep had overtaken her, because when could Carol have left it? She hadn't been in.

Words on paper in Carol's handwriting. Her memory told her they'd made sense, but all she could see now was an impression of a written note, no coherent words. That made it sound like a dream. If not then where was the evidence? Reaching into her pocket she pulled out her keys, some money and a crumpled tissue. She picked up the wastepaper basket and raked through the bits of paperwork and empty drinks cans. One torn scrap.

... ut somewhere n ... u something

Carol's handwriting. It hadn't been a dream ... *somewhere* ... *something* ... What had the rest of it said? Where was it? Could Yağız have gone through her pockets? Not a chance. She never slept that deeply.

She saw herself last night, sitting here, fighting sleep, reaching for the phone to call Pieternel. The note had dropped out from under the receiver.

The call to Pieternel? Had she made it or had she fallen asleep whilst mulling over the note?

She leapt up again with a crow of triumph, then flinched as the sudden move brought an unexpected wave of nausea. Had she helped herself from the optics behind the bar – a nightcap to help her sleep – and overdone it? The memory would return, but there was one thing that had come back to her. Something she'd been going to do last night and hadn't. She hadn't dreamt that note, and neither had she dreamt that brand new box of freeze-dried apple.

With a quick recce to see where Yağız was, she dived for the walk-in, reaching in to click on the light, ready to pull the door shut behind her. Sleep might have had the better of her last night but she was rested and refreshed now and determined to find out what was in there.

Her hand outstretched towards the door handle, ready to close herself in, Annie stopped and stared. Where her memory showed her a large cardboard box, there were just neatly stacked packets of lentils.

Chapter 25

Had she dreamt that box, too? Had earlier memories superimposed themselves on the fog that clouded her mind? Everything was clean and tidy as it should be, still shining the gleam of a recently washed floor, some swirls from a lazily-brandished cloth reaching partway up the wall and no further. That could be an excuse to give Carol a dressing down. The thought gave her pause. Why was she looking for excuses to tell Carol off? Her unauthorised absence was reason enough. And anyway, the cleaning in here couldn't have been Carol. Maybe Yağız was the one who'd skimped on the job.

Annie stepped into the corridor glancing towards the dining room. The buzz of voices swelled. It would be a busy one, hot drinks and snacks all morning, catering to the shoppers at the January sales. Then punters laden with bulging bags would come in for sustenance after a morning's hard graft. Meriç had been through it all with her; the subtle shifts in furniture to accommodate clients with their loads.

We out-coffee bar the coffee bars, he'd told her. *Fine tuning is all it takes.*

She should go and check that it had all been seen to, though from the noise it was already too late to be moving tables and chairs about. And anyway, she couldn't settle with the events of last night niggling at the edge of her mind.

The phone rang as she pushed open the office door. It was a call that forced her head back into the restaurant's books as she discussed the details of a forthcoming order. She was barely done with it when the phone buzzed again. No room now to think about last night or Pieternel; this would be a continual treadmill at least until lunchtime. She was speaking into the handset and juggling invoices when Yağız leant round the door.

'Customer wants to speak to the manager,' he said as she recited a reference number into the phone.

She replied with a brief shake of her head and upturned palm to signal she was as good as tied to the desk.

'I'll deal.' He ran an appraising look over her before he withdrew. Checking whether she was *compos mentis* enough to do the job, Annie judged.

She just had to get on with things. They were down by one experienced staff member. She pictured herself reaching for the phone to ring Pieternel … the note had fallen out …

Her hand scribbled dates and times, some corner of her attention listened to the person at the end of the line, her own voice recited a reference number as her finger traced its components across the top of an order.

When this call ended she must grab the line and phone Pieternel because the other thing her memory was telling her was that she and Pieternel had already spoken about all this, and Pieternel had had something to say, something firm and concrete, something that would cut away the cotton wool that fuzzed her mind.

'Yes, got that. Tuesday week, first thing,' she said into the phone. 'Bye.'

As she replaced the handset and immediately picked it up again to prevent the next call from coming through, she replayed that image from last night. Her hand reaching out for this same handset … but why?

Why this phone? Where the hell was her mobile?

'Annie, are you there? Can you …?'

One of the servers called to her. She jumped up rubbing at her arm, still sore from where she'd slept on it, and went into the corridor, pushing her hands through her hair, painfully aware that she looked crumpled and dishevelled.

As soon as he saw her, he hurried closer gabbling out a worried query. He gave no sign he'd clocked her appearance, just looked relieved as she dampened down what had only ever been a crisis in his head and told him what to do. He scooted towards the dining room. She followed. Easing the path … being the oil that kept the operation running smoothly. She was doing what a manager should do. But the roles had diverged. The manager post had seemed a perfect fit for this operation, giving her access and authority, but without Meriç on the spot taking the load off her, it had become a fulltime job.

She'd spoken to Pieternel yesterday and been told something concrete. Somehow she'd got herself so over-tired that the evening was a blur. She should phone now and find out; get herself on track. The bustle of the restaurant called to her; her feet turned towards the expediting station, hand ready to reach out with a cloth, to polish the rims of the already immaculate plates. With an effort she stopped herself and marched back to the office.

As she pushed inside, her nose wrinkled at the slightly stale air. No ventilation. The worst place to choose to sleep. She should have curled up on one of the banquettes at the corner of the dining room, invisible from the windows.

Except no, she shouldn't, because it was bad enough that Yağız had found her in the office.

You should have said … I'd have found you a bed …

The memory of his words was slightly unnerving.

Pieternel answered almost at once, with a curt 'Yes?'

'It's me. I need to talk.'

'My email was clear, wasn't it? And why are you on the restaurant phone?'

The events of the evening rushed back at her … email … of course it had been email. She'd read it last night after she'd eaten, then been going to ring, to use the phone in the bar. The message. Her two visitors.

'They … they came after me.'

'What are you talking about, Annie?'

Annie fought to keep her voice calm, not to gabble as the events in the hotel bar rushed back at her. She summarised the unexpected interruption to her badly needed evening's rest.

'You didn't check who it was?' Pieternel asked. 'But it could have been anyone. Opportunist lowlifes caught in the act, pretending they knew you. So you've lost another phone.'

'And a laptop, but I've a new one. And of course it wasn't random. Why would random thieves take the trouble to ask at reception? It was them, Dyson and fforbes, they're targeting me.'

'No, Annie, they're not. If anything they're targeting the Thompsons. God knows why but it's nothing to do with us unless you've been hounding the Thompsons and getting in someone's way.'

'No of course not!' The answer was instinctive, but Annie felt herself colour up. Pieternel had no idea of the extent of her contact with the Thompsons, but surely she couldn't have been treading on *those* toes taking on that job. It had come close to blowing her cover at Meriç's restaurant but it was nothing to do with Dyson and fforbes. 'I don't want to go back to that hotel,' she heard herself say.

'Then don't. You've a perfectly good flat with the rent paid. Go there.'

Annie thought of the pokey bedsit and balked at calling it perfectly good. She wasn't going back there whatever Pieternel said. She shouldn't even be at the restaurant. It was too public. Anyone could find her here. Why had she stayed?

'No,' she told Pieternel. 'There's something else. They …' – a sliver of memory crept in … *Carol* … *voices* … 'They broke in here. I think they broke in here.'

'The restaurant? That makes no sense at all.'

'No,' Annie amended, 'not broke in … were let in. I think they were here after hours with one of the wait staff, the one who's involved in the scam.'

'Does she have a key?' Pieternel rapped out.

'Uh … no. Key-holders are me, the chef, Yağız …' *Someone else … another sliver of memory tantalised her … someone else had a key.* 'Well, Meriç of course but …'

'Well, it won't have been Meriç, will it? He's in Istanbul.'

'Is he …?' Annie murmured. 'I had someone watch him on to the plane, but …'

An indrawn breath answered her. She recognised the annoyance behind it. 'Yes, Annie, he's in Istanbul. How do I know? Because yet again I've let your paranoia distract me. I've had someone check. Could he have left his key behind with someone?'

'I doubt it, not Meriç, too much of a control freak.' Annie let out the words through gritted teeth, smarting at the accusation of paranoia from Pieternel of all people.

'And it can't have been Dyson or fforbes,' Pieternel went on. 'They don't do that stuff, not personally. Tell me exactly what happened.'

Annie tried to remember. The scene came back in fragments.

Carol. She'd definitely seen Carol. More voices, at least one of which she'd recognised. She fought for the memory as she tried to articulate what she'd seen, or thought she'd seen. 'I'm just not sure what happened,' she ended.

Pieternel's tone changed. Her voice held a thread of concern. 'Annie, stop obsessing over Dyson and her sidekick. They're nothing. They're turning you away from where you should be looking.'

'And where's that?'

'How should I know? You're the one who's on the spot. It's tied in with Meriç's restaurant and whatever the scam is or was. You've clearly trodden on some toes and someone's been at some kind of cover up, is my best guess. You're telling me you're not sure what happened. You of all people should know exactly what's happened. You were drugged.'

Chapter 26

Drugged?

It was obvious as soon as Pieternel said it. And Pieternel was right. She of all people, with her past, should have seen it a mile off.

'Shit,' she murmured into the phone, her mind trying to grab for the full picture. When? How? She'd eaten at the hotel but the gap in her memory was too abrupt for it to have been anything that early in the evening. Almost of its own volition her hand crept to the low level ache in her upper arm. With a quick look round to make sure no one was watching she pulled her shirt off her shoulder and stared at the uneven bruise, pressed her fingers into it and felt the sharp stab of focused pain at its centre. A check of her sleeve confirmed it. The rip in the material was barely visible.

Something fast-acting jabbed into her without much care. Had she seen it coming? Had she fought back? She flexed her wrist, wondering if the stiffness was imagined or a result of someone grabbing her roughly until the hypodermic did its job.

'And you're really sure it couldn't have been ... those two?' Even as she asked the question, she began to see the absurdity of it.

'I've made enquiries, Annie. Spent time I didn't have. They're sniffing round the Thompsons for some reason, but I doubt they even know who you are let alone that you're in Hull. You're harking back to that time when ... well ... you're making too much of it. They were a threat back then, but that was different.'

That time when... She shuddered in response to the shudder she'd heard in Pieternel's voice. But she was right, it *had* been different then. Dyson and fforbes had been a threat, but a financial one, Pieternel's territory. The jolt of realisation cleared her mind. She wasn't at fault here. It was Meriç. As business owner he knew the score. He'd brought Annie in to uncover a scam, not to manage his restaurant in his absence. He shouldn't have left, at least not without bringing in someone else to support her. But somehow she'd juggled both roles.

She chuckled at a sudden thought.

'What's so funny?' Pieternel snapped.

'Nothing,' Annie said. 'It's OK. I'm seeing the wood for the trees again.'

'Well, thank goodness for that …'

They talked desultorily before ending the call.

Almost at once the phone rang again and Annie reached for it, pulling up the inventory on the screen. Mondays were always like this, a stream of calls, confirmations and fine tuning to keep the place running at peak performance for the week ahead.

Her laughter hadn't signified real amusement, more dissipation of the tension that had been building with the nebulous threat she'd been facing. Pieternel's doggedness in sticking to her line had finally got through and made the threat tangible. It wasn't some surreal, almost paranormal, force coming after her out of her murky past. It was the people behind the scam in this restaurant. She was at the brink of uncovering something big. And people running big scams didn't like that.

She let her mind run through the stages as she spoke into the phone, verifying orders, confirming numbers. It had been her undercover role that had diverted her in the first place; the distasteful idea of someone she knew believing the cover story, thinking she'd really swapped professions. A stupid conceit that had blunted her edge. Her attention had been on hiding from Ahmed and his in-laws, instead of where it needed to be.

There'd been the unforgivably loose contract with Meriç too. She pulled a face. Pieternel could take her share of the blame there. It had left her worrying about money. No wonder her mind hadn't been on the job. It was that that had pushed her towards the Thompsons and almost under the feet of Dyson and fforbes. Paranoia and not thinking straight had done the rest.

What reason would some outdated duo from Pieternel's past have in terrorising her, in ambushing the restaurant? None whatsoever. But some outfit running a scam behind the restaurant's façade, something that involved Carol and the boy she'd sacked … that was another matter. They'd tried to stop her before she got started. And they'd tried again once she'd got close.

She ended her current call, words coming automatically, fingers playing across the keyboard to record the transactions. She was good at this stuff, being meticulous when it mattered, seeing the detail as well as the big picture, oiling the wheels, managing the ripples of everyday life in a high-stress environment. Trying to do both jobs at once had been her downfall.

The chef's illicit pursuits, if as extensive as Annie suspected, were what was creaming money off Meriç's bottom line. The thing with Carol was something else altogether, something that had not only been worth drugging her for last night, but that was the type of operation where the drug and the means to administer it had been to hand. She took a private bet with herself that Carol's extracurricular activities would not have caused a ripple in Meriç's books but would be of a scale a quantum above anything the chef was doing.

As an efficient manager, her next move should be to call in a private detective. That had been the thought that had made her chuckle as she'd talked to Pieternel. She'd seen herself negotiating with Pat Thompson; imagined her ex-boss lumbering through the door to make a start on the job.

She looked up as she heard footsteps in the corridor outside.

Strictly speaking it had gone beyond that. The attacks and the break-ins made it a police matter. But Meriç wouldn't want that. In this industry behind-the-scenes shenanigans stayed under wraps. It took little to dent the public's confidence.

Yağız was at the door of the office. 'Just to warn you,' he said. 'They're hanging about, the ones who wanted a word. I've said you're dealing with suppliers all morning but they might stick it out.'

'Any idea what they want?'

'Complaint probably. Just don't want you to walk out there when it's packed. They might get loud. Could have done with Carol. She'd have had them damped down in seconds.'

'Is there anyone on the current wait staff you'd promote if Carol left?'

'Have you heard from her?' There was surprise in his voice.

'No, but she won't be back. If there's no one worth promoting then I'll get an advert out.'

Yağız looked taken aback, his mouth half open but stalled on whatever question he'd been going to ask.

'I've seen this pattern before,' Annie lied. 'She's moved on.'

As he returned to his duties and she sighed at the phone shrilling its next call. She'd surprised herself as well as Yağız, but yes, she was sure. Carol had cut and run. Something to do with what had happened last night and the fact that Annie was getting too close.

She dealt with the call, then switched the phone to voicemail. A cup of coffee, she decided, then she would stretch her legs and maybe deal with this complaint before returning to the business of the day. Mondays were bad enough even when she started out well-rested, but it wasn't the general business of the place that perplexed her. Whilst her head swam with inventory and orders, she must carve out some plan for how to deal with the nasty turn that this job had taken.

She took her time in the tiny staff toilet, washing her face, fluffing up her hair, smoothing down her clothes, trying to erase any vestige of evidence that she'd slept rough.

Strolling past the kitchen was reassuring. The chef gave her a narrow-eyed look but not his customary hard stare, even when she stopped to inspect the plates of food ready to go out. He was worried. He'd probably heard that she'd been rummaging through the outside catering equipment.

She moved behind the bar, keeping half an eye on the nearest staff members. They glanced her way but with no hint of a double-take so she took that as confirmation she passed muster and could head out into the dining room.

It was full and buzzed with the noise of dozens of conversations. The tables looked messy, pushed out of line; huge shopping bags lolled against chair legs or up against the sides of the booths. The windows had steamed with the bustle. The door was swinging shut unattended, the hostess-stand pushed back to accommodate another table. No hostess at this time of day during the January sales. Today they were a coffee bar, the busiest in town probably. The thought gave her a satisfying glow as she let her gaze range further, out to the street beyond, clarity lost in the cloudy glass.

Her heart lurched.

A couple were disappearing off down the street. Their moves seemed to match the rhythm of the closing door. She darted forward, snaking her way through the throng, pushing through the entrance, feeling a rush of freezing air envelop her as she craned her neck in the direction they'd disappeared. Nothing. Just a few people flitting from one shop to the next, hurrying, heads down against the cold.

When she turned back, Yağız was making his way through the crush, a tray held high in his right hand, vapour oozing from brimming cups. She felt her face harden as she realised he was heading for her and not a nearby table. *Serve the customers first*, she wanted to snap. He knew better than this.

'Did they catch you then?' He sounded puzzled. 'I didn't realise you'd come out. Was it a complaint?'

'I came out for a break. No one caught me. I was just … uh … getting a breath of fresh air.'

'Oh right, well they've gone. One minute sitting like they were going to block that table all day, next thing they're off like they've been stung.'

'Uh … middle-aged couple were they?' Annie strove to keep her tone casual. 'Her white, him black?'

Yağız nodded.

'Yeah, I saw them leave.' Annie could hear her voice losing focus as her mind tried to fit together the pieces. It had been them, Dyson and fforbes. She was sure of it. But why?

She stared into Yağız's eyes. They looked troubled. Why was he still here?

'Get your customers served,' she murmured through gritted teeth, a nod to the tray.

'No, it's just …' He stepped closer and lowered his voice. 'It looks like trouble. And I'm pretty sure that pair left when they saw it come in.'

'What do you mean?'

He tipped his head and indicated with his eyes. Annie followed his line and saw Ayaan Ahmed, his back to them, standing by the bar with a man she didn't recognise. It was clear in their body language that sloughed off the chill of outdoors that they'd just arrived. She must have passed them in the press of the crowd.

As she'd made a beeline for the door that might have been swinging open from their arrival, they had eased their way around the curve of the tables, taking the customary route to the bar.

She felt a shimmer of anxiety about Dyson and fforbes, but shouldered it aside. She'd done with paranoia. The job had taken a nasty turn that she should have seen coming. She was on top of it now. And as to middle-aged enemies from Pieternel's past appearing at random, there would be a clear explanation ready to present itself the second she had a moment to think it through.

In the time it took her to turn, her mind had plugged together the strands. Yağız had said 'trouble'. Ayaan Ahmed wasn't with his wife or his in-laws. He was with a man whose clothes and bearing screamed on-duty detective. They had collared one of the servers whose face registered uncertainty and worry as she went to look over her shoulder and then out into the crowd, clearly half-remembering that she'd seen Annie just a moment ago.

'Mr Ahmed?' Annie was behind them, seeing relief on the server's face at her appearance.

'Ah, Miss Raymond. This is my colleague–'

'Do come through.' She gave him a glare and all but pushed them round behind the bar, stalking past to lead the way to the short corridor outside the office.

It was hardly private but crowding the three of them into the stale atmosphere of the office cubbyhole would be a last resort. She turned so she was facing the kitchen, ready to scowl away any staff member who ventured into hearing range, and looked Ahmed's companion up and down. He was a burly man, overweight, shirt straining across his chest beneath a thick coat.

Ahmed opened his mouth to speak and she turned her attention to him.

'I don't want names and ranks broadcast in the middle of my dining-room,' she snapped. 'One whiff of trouble in this business and things can turn on a sixpence.'

'*Your* dining room?' he murmured.

She held her expression in neutral. The phraseology had been unintended but fitted her cover story perfectly. Pieternel would have applauded. She had embedded the picture of herself as the investigator who had cut and run from her profession and rekindled her supposed childhood ambition in the catering industry. Annoyance fought with satisfaction at being unexpectedly proficient in both roles.

Ahmed's companion held up his warrant card and introduced

himself as a detective constable from Hull. Annie missed the name as she watched over his shoulder for eavesdroppers.

'Please keep your voice down,' she said. 'What's this about?'

'We'd like to speak to the owner as well. Is he here?'

Annie shook her head at Ahmed's question as another ambiguity popped up. Ahmed was on leave. He worked in York. He had no role in any official enquiry that landed on her doorstep here. 'He's abroad on family business,' she told him.

'When did he go?' The question came from Ahmed's companion, just quickly enough to inject a level of suspicion.

'He flew out from Humberside on the 29th on the early flight.'

She saw a brief glance exchanged between them. *Assume nothing. Believe no one. Check everything.* The mantra ran through her head. So it was serious enough that they would verify Meriç's movements.

'What's it about?' she asked again.

'Is there anywhere private we can go?'

Reluctantly, she moved to the office and pulled open the door. The space was barely big enough for one. It would strain at accommodating Ahmed's colleague.

'We're private enough at this end of the corridor,' she said. 'No one's going to come this way during service.'

'You have a woman called Carol Dale on your books.'

'Yes, she's our most experienced server. She's … uh … not in today either.'

'Were you expecting her?'

'Yes. She took the day off yesterday but …'

Out of nowhere she read their underlying reluctance to talk and found herself staring from one to the other. She began to blurt out a question without quite knowing where it was going, but Ahmed spoke over her.

'Do you have a next of kin recorded in her personnel file?'

'Uh … no.' She'd noted it when going through the staff records, but then few of them were anything like complete. 'Just an address, email and such.'

'Do you know if she had family?'

'*Had*?' She stared at Ahmed's colleague. Ahmed too shot him a look that censured his careless wording. 'What's happened?'

'I'm sorry to have to tell you that Carol Dale has died.'

Her gut had told her what they would say but it still came as a shock. As she listened, she replayed her words to Yağız. *She won't be back ... I've seen this pattern before.* What on earth would he make of her foresight? And who would he tell?

She tried to concentrate on what the two detectives were telling her as her mind tried and failed to fit Ahmed into the picture. They wanted data, files, her views on Carol, anything and everything. Her feet moved her towards the desk to access the staff records.

Found dead in her house by a neighbour. Annie registered the information, wondered who the neighbour was, why he or she had gone to Carol's house in the first place, where had she been ... in bed ... collapsed on the floor ... maybe she'd been spotted through a window?

'How did she die?'

She didn't expect an answer but Ahmed's colleague said, 'We're treating Carol Dale's death as murder, Miss Raymond. Now if you would get us a copy of her personnel record ...'

'Yes, of course ...'

She watched her hand reach out towards the keyboard, just the way she recalled watching it reach out for the phone, seeing that scrap of paper flutter to the floor. It was her last coherent memory from last night before she'd woken to an alarm she hadn't set.

Chapter 27

After they'd gone, Annie sat still for a while before going to find Yağız. She needed an ally. She'd prevented their discussion reaching anyone's ears but hadn't been able to hide that she'd given access to Carol's locker to Ahmed and his colleague. She'd seen the sidelong glances as the servers ferried food back and forth from the kitchen.

At the edge of the kitchen area, she paused, watching the chef orchestrating his team. He was good; a key factor in Meriç's success. And he'd been with Meriç for a long time, since before this restaurant. Annie imagined the small liberties, the bits and pieces spirited away over the years. He'd probably come to see these perks as his right. Maybe he'd always nursed ambitions to run his own show, but preferred the security of a salaried post. Then at some point he'd found a niche, discovered a market that ran parallel to Meriç's clientele but never merged. However it had happened, the scam had crossed the line and now sailed way too close to the wind. Not that he could have predicted her unscheduled appearance as an unconvincing dirndl just two evenings ago, but that event had been practically on his employer's doorstep.

She thought back to the sort of party it had been, and her memory of his labours in the kitchen the previous day; his unaccustomed anxiety. Maybe he'd stepped into territory where he no longer called the shots. Well, that was his look out, but it was clear it was his shenanigans that were gradually crashing the restaurant.

Yet somehow it no longer mattered, because whatever the

chef was doing was small beer compared to whatever she had accidentally come close to uncovering.

This was no ordinary restaurant. It was in the top echelons and held its position through the skill of its staff, the perspicacity of its owner and its use of the very best of ingredients shipped from far and wide. As she automatically counted herself in with the skilled staff, it occurred to her that Pieternel had built more than a clever cover story, she'd plucked things from Annie's past that authentically seemed to point towards a desire to make it big in catering management. Maybe it genuinely was what she wanted to do. Had her early ambitions been derailed in the aftermath of her mother's death, attached themselves to a desire to learn the skills of investigation?

Servers bustling past took her attention. She had terrible news to break to them about someone who had been their friend as well as their colleague. It couldn't be done at the height of a busy service.

And where had her career got her to date? Its starting point had seemed so promising when she'd first signed up with the Thompsons all those years ago, but had led into a dead end. Then an even more promising start with Pieternel with the prospect of excitement as well as riches. The excitement had almost killed her, the riches such as they were seemed to have evaporated and she was still under someone else's thumb, unable to focus on one area, to build her expertise the way she'd always wanted to. Catering was an industry they'd rarely touched, yet now she'd seen it from the inside, from the vantage point of a management position, the possibilities opened up. It was a world awash with opportunities for scammers and fertile ground for the skills she'd honed over the years.

Picking up failing restaurants and turning them around was an industry in itself. Not that this one was failing yet but without her insights it was going to.

She couldn't talk to the staff immediately. Nor could she wait to the end of the shift. As soon as Yağız was unoccupied she would discuss it with him.

Despite the task ahead she felt more secure in this role than she had from day one. The urge to run had disappeared. She knew what she was up against, or rather what she wasn't up against. There was no duo with other-worldly powers stalking her. The explanation for Dyson and fforbes was simple. It had always been simple. They were targeting the Thompsons, like Pieternel said, for reasons of their own. The Thompsons weren't clever at keeping things under wraps – they'd let slip Annie's extracurricular activities – and Dyson and fforbes had come to take a look. She'd have done the same in their shoes. What she was up against wasn't a ghost from the past but standard villains more scared of her than she was of them because she was the one closing in on their scam.

Even the shape of the operation was starting to come together in her head. All those specialist ingredients, the regular consignments, the restaurant's position near a big port. The scope was enormous. She supposed it was drugs. It was usually drugs. High-risk, high-reward and layers of foot soldiers like Carol to take the flak before anyone got near the real perpetrators.

The fact that Carol had been silenced suggested things might already be too hot; maybe the operation had been closed down.

Yağız marched through, his brow drawn into a frown, expression harassed. She signalled to him.

He raised his hand, spread his fingers. 'Give me five minutes.'

She nodded and turned towards the office.

It felt wrong to find optimism buoying her up at a time like this, but it was. Purely by chance she'd landed in a business with real opportunities. Meriç was expanding. He would soon need people to manage his new restaurant. And he wouldn't stop there. He was going places. He had a good brand and he was going to spread it. And after what Annie was going to do for him he would jump at the chance to have her properly on board. It would come as a shock to Pieternel but hell, Pieternel should have seen it coming and treated Annie more like the equal partner she had never really been. Pieternel would manage. She always did.

She stopped at the door to the office and turned to watch Yağız straighten out whatever problem it was that was bugging him with one of the servers. Should she stay on and continue to manage this site or should she leave it to Yağız and go with Meriç to the new one. She was confident she could steer Meriç either way. On balance fresh pastures inspired her more, but maybe she would stay on here a while to make sure everyone's act was thoroughly cleaned up.

As Yağız at last spun round to obey her summons she set her mind on more immediate concerns. What had happened to Carol meant a bumpy road ahead for the restaurant. They were not the sort of place to gain any advantage from the ghoul trade.

That woman who was murdered … this is where she worked … was she poisoned …?

She had turned a cooperative face to Ahmed and his colleague but had withheld vital evidence, and needed to get back to them before the delay pointed suspicion her way. The after-effects of the drug would be her excuse but the reality was that she wanted to remember more, to tell them exactly what they needed to know. She had the key to it all in her head and it was coming back in disjointed flashes of memory. Another few hours and she would know all she needed to. Whoever had drugged her had no clue about her past, no idea of the resistance her body had built up. They probably thought she would sleep for longer and remember nothing.

Hadn't Meriç sacked a previous manager for drinking on the job?

Sound asleep … drunk … couldn't wake him for hours. But when I did I sacked him on the spot.

Carol would have been here back then. She was one of Meriç's longest serving staff members.

So a previous manager had got close, but without Annie's training and skills had been effectively silenced. That wouldn't happen again.

The memories would return and give her everything she needed.

Meantime Meriç might be back any moment. Once he knew what had been going on and that she had uncovered the scope of it whilst keeping the restaurant lucratively afloat, he would probably see the possibilities without her having to spell them out, though she would drop a hint at what she could do for him. In a couple of years they might have spread this franchise far and wide. Her reputation would grow as a manager / trouble-shooter. And once she'd made a solid name for herself – two years would do it – then she could strike out as a freelance, maybe even take her skills abroad.

How often had she talked about trying her luck the other side of the pond? As an investigator it was a whole different ball game, different rules, different regulatory system. She would have to fight her way up from the bottom and might never surface. But with a track record in managing the hothouses that were high-quality restaurants, and a solid reputation as a trouble-shooter … It was the opportunity she'd never realised she'd been waiting for.

'They were both coppers, weren't they?' The words came from behind her.

She sensed hostility as she turned to face Yağız.

Chapter 28

The resentment in his tone opened a gulf of antagonism between them. In a heartbeat she had become the enemy again, the alien interloper; he the representative of an aggrieved body of staff.

Even if she couldn't be as frank with Yağız as she could with Meriç, they'd built up some kind of rapport these last couple of days, and Meriç was out of reach. With the effects of the drug still with her, dulling her senses, she felt vulnerable and alone, desperate for someone to talk to.

'Carol's dead,' she told him. Hadn't meant to blurt it out like that. 'It was her locker they wanted to look in. I had to let them. I …'

She stopped. Yağız stared, his face draining of blood as she watched him. He grabbed at the office chair, slumped into it, and put his head in his hands.

When he looked up at her again, all trace of hostility was gone. All she saw was shock.

'I'm sorry.' She tried to apologise for the way she'd broken the news, struggled not to show her relief that he was back on side, that they could talk.

He reached out to grab her arm. Her instinct was to pull away but he seemed oblivious of his own actions. 'Carol? How …? When …?' His voice was a whisper.

She pulled the door to and perched at the edge of the desk as she told him what she knew. It wasn't much, just the skeletal version she'd had from Ayaan Ahmed.

'They're coming back to take statements,' she ended. 'I had to agree to that. We'll close early, hold a staff meeting, tell them about Carol so they're forewarned.'

Yağız sat shaking his head slowly as if unable to comprehend what she was telling him. 'Did they say … how …?'

'I don't think it was a violent attack or anything like that.' She saw a sliver of relief in his expression. 'They didn't give me any detail of course, but just from something they said, I think it was drugs.'

'An overdose? Carol?'

'They say it's murder.'

Ahmed and his colleague had given nothing away. She was building a picture out of what she knew about last night – all the things she'd yet to tell Ahmed; the things she daren't confide to Yağız, not yet. He knew she'd slept at the restaurant but he didn't know Carol had been here. The police didn't know that anyone had been here overnight. She'd been drugged in the expectation she would sleep for so long the memories would never come back. That option hadn't been available to silence Carol.

As they talked, Yağız recovered something of his composure and embarrassedly slid away his hand from where it had rested on her arm. Between them, they agreed what time they would close and what story they would tell. The staff would be alerted to a last-minute meeting, everyone to attend even the casuals who would be called back in.

'They'll assume we're cutting staff or wages,' Yağız told her. 'Have you ever had to do anything like this before?'

Annie wasn't sure if he meant had she ever broken the news of an unexpected death or had she dealt with redundancies. 'I'll tell them,' she said. 'But I want you next to me. I don't want to be one person facing everyone else. They resent me as it is, I don't need anyone blaming this on me too.'

Meriç pushed through the doors, swapping his phone to his other ear as he stepped out into the fresh air, needing the space to stride out his exasperation and annoyance.

Good money had changed hands on the promise of a competent manager for his restaurant. He'd thought she was doing a pretty good job, better than he would publicly give her credit for. If he'd had doubts he'd never have left her to her own devices; he'd never left another manager in sole charge so soon after their appointment. The Peters woman had told him Annie had all the relevant experience from an earlier career but that she wouldn't want to talk to about it – should have enquired more closely into that.

Of course, it was a full time job being a good manager. So when did she fit in the investigation side of things? Nights, he supposed. Maybe that was why she was always so spiky. Lack of sleep. She must have loads of support and backup from the Peters woman; probably had an office full of minions at her beck and call analysing findings from afar, all that sort of stuff.

The archetypal private investigator was a loner who drank too much. He hadn't seen that in Annie; wouldn't have entertained her for a second in a position of trust if he had. Though it should have occurred to him that these stereotypes often had a basis in fact. And poor Carol. She'd been a good worker.

'Why is it you telling me this, Yağız?' he asked into the phone. 'Why hasn't Annie been in touch?'

'She's struggling, Meriç, out of her depth. I'm doing what I can to support her, but …'

Of course Yağız was distressed about Carol and not as careful as usual in what he was saying.

His views were understandable. Next in line for a management post, he hadn't liked it when Annie had been brought in over him, but to his credit he'd worked well under her, never showed any resentment, just looked after the restaurant's best interests.

Carol had been a loyal employee. It was unusual to keep a

waitress on her wage for any length of time. Having someone experienced on the floor made a difference. He felt a moment's regret for Carol that would doubtless blossom into genuine sorrow once he was back on the spot with the reality of her fate in front of him. For now it was his business interests that were at the forefront. Instinctively his gaze flicked upward, catching the flat blue of the sky above cotton wool clouds. If Carol could see him, she would understand. She knew the importance of running a tight ship.

Meriç knew his staff, which was how he sensed it, even over a less than perfect phone line. Yağız was holding something back. He pushed for answers and eventually Yağız cracked.

'It's not my place to criticise,' he said, his voice worried. 'If it wasn't for Carol … well … I'd have waited till you were back.'

Meriç smiled to himself. He didn't want his staff gossiping behind his back, so he'd come down heavily on one or two nonentities over the years. Bad mouth your line manager and you're out on your ear; that was the message. Word spread. It worked a treat. Made everyone careful what they said to whom; and made them especially careful of anything that might be interpreted as criticism of him. The fact was, though, that he did want them to dish the dirt. He wanted something on everyone who worked for him. Not the trivia, not the gossip and silly squabbles but the real stuff. He knew how to read the signs, how to sense when someone had something to say.

'I understand,' he told Yağız. 'I appreciate your loyalty to your immediate boss. It's a trait I admire, but there are times …?' He let the words fade into the ghost of a question and Yağız became putty in his hands.

His eyes narrowed as Yağız's recital unfolded with its obfuscation and sudden stops. Yağız was at pains not to criticise Annie or say more than he should.

'She's always insisted on making her own coffee, and the other day I … uh … well, I don't know for sure …' Yağız's words faded, but Meriç knew just where he'd been going. Annie was helping herself to something stronger than coffee.

'And then this morning …'

Meriç felt his fists clench as he listened. Yağız had found her slumped in an alcoholic stupor, had had to cover for her, do her job all morning as well as his own, until the police arrived and made a scene about Carol.

'I got them off the floor as quickly as I could,' Yağız said, 'but with Annie not on top of things, I know people were talking.'

'I want you first in every morning, Yağız, and last out at night until I'm back. I'll sort you out for the extra hours.'

'Yes, I've already … yes, of course. That's no problem.'

The pause told Meriç that Yağız was already taking on the manager's hours, had probably been doing it all the time he'd been away.

He would have to hope Annie Raymond had done the other side of her job properly because the sooner he was rid of her and had Yağız officially in the role, the better. It was a timely warning and he blew out a small sigh of relief. He had begun to wonder about using Annie once the new place was ready to open – on a very different footing of course. That wouldn't happen now.

His business here was done. He'd hoped for a couple of days to relax with family, but he had to get back.

He shook his head. Yet another drunk for a manager? Talk about bad luck!

Chapter 29

....

It was relatively early still but the winter sun was long gone and no moonlight leaked through the clouds. The street outside wore its mid evening air. Other than Yağız, the staff had gone home. The meeting was over; the detectives had been and gone.

Ahmed's colleague had arrived with a woman Annie hadn't seen before. Ahmed himself hadn't returned. Once Annie had gleaned they were focussing on Carol's long-term friends and colleagues, she had interrupted them to say, 'You'll want to talk to me again when you've done with the staff.'

She'd overlain the words with a touch of arrogance, the air of someone who thought themselves more important than they were.

'We have all we need from you,' the woman had told her putting on a professionally sympathetic smile. 'You can go home if you like.'

Annie had allowed her expression to harden. 'I have to close up when everyone's gone. I'll be here if you need me.'

She had retreated unsmiling and prowled the kitchen and bar area watching the clean up that was going on simultaneously with the interviews conducted in the dining room. Yağız had tucked the detectives discreetly in one of the corner booths. 'It's more private here,' he had said.

What he'd meant was less chance of prying eyes seeing them from the street, but they weren't where Annie would have put them. She hadn't been quick enough. She'd fought the sluggishness enveloping her thought processes. She should have seen that they were closer to the hidden surveillance camera, close enough that its microphone would pick up their words.

The drug, presumably cocktail of drugs, still coursing through her system had tied her tongue. This leaden effect so many hours later surely meant they'd intended her to be out for far longer. Had they expected her to wake at all? She thought of Carol and shivered.

Once again, Yağız had taken charge, settled the two detectives as though seating new customers, drawn Annie away to the back of house. 'Let them get on with their job.'

'The notice is up, isn't it?' Annie had tried to grab a modicum of control but it was a foolish question. They could both see the notice prominent on the door.

Sorry, we are closing early today, business as usual tomorrow.

It was a professionally crafted sign from the back of a cupboard. Meriç believed in being prepared. It struck Annie that he'd made no provision for having to close the restaurant on a day when he wouldn't be open *tomorrow*.

'You've sorted the reservations?' she'd rapped out, knowing that that too should have been her job.

'Yes, yes. All regulars. I've called them all and spoken to them personally, told them about Carol.'

'You didn't tell them …?'

'No, no. Just that she'd died suddenly at home. They all know her. They understood it was a mark of respect.'

The staff interviews had dragged on longer than the time it took to clean the kitchen. Those who had been spoken to were allowed to leave. There had been discontented muttering as the restaurant hierarchies were not respected and some of the casuals released before the chef had been seen.

Annie had been surprised to see the boy she'd sacked. Certainly she hadn't called him in. Yağız must have done it. He'd looked white-faced, shaky, and avoided her eye. If she hadn't felt mentally on the floor, she'd have challenged him, done her own impromptu interview about his extracurricular activities with Carol. But she hadn't felt up to it, had had to retreat to the small office as a headache threatened. If Meriç kept decent beer on the premises she would have been sorely tempted to pour herself a glass, but he didn't. The beer he served was bottled, too light and fizzy.

Then it was over. The two detectives bustled about as the last staff members collected their belongings. If Annie had pushed, she could have forced herself on one or the other of them, but there was no obvious moment where she might have grabbed a word.

Tomorrow – and tomorrow was the absolute latest it could be – she must go to them and spin a yarn about why she hadn't told them about Carol's appearance in the night. That she'd been drugged and not remembered anything properly was her only excuse and she could say semi-truthfully that she'd tried to get a private word with them. The long-lasting effect of the drug gave her some hope that she might be believed.

Now it was just her and Yağız. Annie slipped on her jacket and slung her bag over her shoulder. She missed the bulk of her rucksack on her back, not just to hold the tablet that she had tucked awkwardly under her arm, but for the extra layer of warmth.

The orange glow of the streetlamps lit the dining room as Yağız turned off the lights and came to stand beside her in the shadows behind the bar.

They watched a couple approach the front door and read the sign. The man reached out to rattle the handle.

'Like that'll light the lights and fire up the grills,' Yağız murmured. 'You need a drink?' He tipped his head towards the optics.

Annie half smiled but shook her head. A beer would have been good, but not the alcohol that was available at Meriç's bar.

'OK,' she said, stretching and standing up straight. 'Let's get on our way. Do you want to go through the front? I'll lock up after you.' She wanted to show him she wasn't scared of the dark alleyway.

He misunderstood. 'You can't stay here, Annie.'

She rolled her eyes. 'I've no intention of staying here. I wasn't here all night last night, believe it or not.'

He didn't try to hide his scepticism, and deciding she hadn't the energy to pick a fight over it, she snapped, 'OK, lock up behind me. I'll wait for you,' then stalked to the front door and slipped out into the night.

The street was quiet but it wasn't quite chucking out time for the local pubs. It might get rowdy soon. She had to spend the night somewhere and had a stark choice ahead of her. The restaurant was out. So was the hotel. The barman would have regretted the help he'd given her and they would be sure to demand payment of the bill so far. It was a park bench or return to the bedsit, and as she pulled the jacket around her against the chill night air and tried to shield the tablet from the damp atmosphere, she knew the bedsit was her only option.

All that funny business with the TV must have been Dyson and fforbes checking her out. They were from Pieternel's world, the sort to go for over-elaborate gizmos. It wasn't her they were interested in, it was the Thompsons. They'd even come to speak to her openly until chased away by Ahmed's untimely arrival with news of Carol's death.

She was not going to feel comfortable, but was reasonably sure that Carol's accomplices had not targeted her outside the restaurant. She could make the bedsit safe enough to get a decent night's sleep.

A movement caught her attention and Yağız appeared from the end of the alley. He marched up to her and said firmly, 'I'll walk you home. It's been a bad day.'

As she opened her mouth to tell him no, he turned, crooked his arm towards her and said, 'It's this way, isn't it?'

It wasn't the right way, but it was the direction she always took when she left. He must have been watching her. For a second she stared at the offered arm. The gesture was so unexpected, yet his misplaced gallantry wasn't unwelcome. A cocktail of drugs still swirled inside her, dulling her senses. The cold was beginning to creep to the centre of her bones. It had not just been bad, it had been a terrible day.

'No,' she said, as she let her hand rest across his arm. 'I'm fine getting home, but I could do with a breather. Let's find somewhere that didn't close early.'

For a while they walked in silence, then Yağız said, 'Poor Carol. Why would anyone do that?'

'I guess she got herself involved in something she shouldn't have,' Annie said.

'What do you mean?' His tone was sharp. 'Do you know what it was about?'

'I've no idea.' She glanced at him, uncomfortable suddenly at the anomalous hand lying across his arm as they walked along. Pulling free she made a pretence of searching her pockets, whipping out a tissue to wipe her nose.

'Why did you say drugs?' he asked.

She struggled to remember what she'd said ... what she'd told him. 'I don't know. That's what I thought ... something they said. Maybe there's a crap batch of something out on the streets. She might not be the only one.' The picture in her head was of someone stabbing Carol with a syringe, maybe the same syringe that had punctured her own skin, but she tried to convey a more arm's length affair.

'Did they find anything in her locker?'

'Not that I could see, no.'

He grunted and they relapsed into silence as they followed a route that was familiar to Annie from many years ago, the route to a favourite pub on a back street, to ale brewed on the premises. She hoped it was still there. It was just the lift she needed.

She hid a smile of amusement at the dismay on Yağız's face as she guided him into the dark deserted road that led to what would have been a bustling dockside a century before. She had the impression that he wanted to hang on to her arm now, rather than offer her his.

'Meriç might serve the best food in Hull,' she said, 'but his bar leaves a lot to be desired and after the day we've had, you and I need a drink.'

'I don't drink, Annie.' His outstretched hand stopped her as she went to push open the door.

She held back an irritable expletive. Of course he didn't drink. She knew that. He must have thought she'd meant a coffee bar, not a pub. But the promise of shelter and the smell of hops were too close for her to forego them now. Firmly, she moved his arm out of the way and reached again for the door. 'Sorry, Yağız, after the day we've had, I need a beer.'

'A beer?' He looked relieved. 'I'll have a beer with you. I thought you meant the hard stuff.'

Taken aback, she watched him march up to the bar and order two glasses of the local bitter. He was a mass of contradictions. She knew less about him than she'd realised, but then they'd barely made any real connection before this last couple of days. His choice of beer was OK though she chafed a bit that he'd made the decision without asking her. However, there was one matter where she intended stamping her mark.

'Pints not halves,' she said to the barman across Yağız's shoulder, ignoring the look he turned on her. Heading for a nearby table, she left him to pay.

Annie took a long slow draught of the smooth liquid, relishing the feel of its cool passage down her throat, and knowing that it would envelop her in warmth by the time she was a third of the way down the glass. For a while, neither of them spoke as they relaxed and savoured the robust ale. When she glanced at him, she saw his expression was troubled.

'Did you know Carol well?' she asked.

'I've known her a long time, but I'd not seen much of her outside work lately.'

It surprised Annie that they'd had any kind of contact outside the restaurant. 'She lived a good way away,' she said, remembering the address in Carol's personnel file.

'The other side of the city. Nice house.'

'You … uh … you've been there?'

He nodded as he looked into his drink before raising the glass and draining it.

'Did she live on her own?' Annie asked, remembering the gap where a next of kin should have been recorded.

'Yes.' Yağız's eyes lost focus as he stared into the middle distance. 'I'm just trying to remember anything she said about her family. I don't think they had much. She was married once, but a long time ago. Maybe he was rich, gave her a good settlement.'

Annie watched as he turned over the ideas in his head. 'And maybe he wasn't?' she prompted.

'Yeah, exactly. Waitress wages all these years. A house like that.'

Annie shrugged. 'Could be all sorts of reasons,' she murmured, wanting to remain noncommittal, unsure if he was working these things out for himself or if he was fishing to find out how much she knew.

She finished her beer and put the empty glass on to the table. She wouldn't be tempted into a second pint.

Yağız pushed aside the empty glasses then said, 'We could get a cab.'

'I'm fine from here, thanks. I'll walk.'

'I meant to Carol's house.'

'To Carol's? Why would we …?'

He paused then said, 'I know one of the neighbours, from going to see Carol I mean. It's not too late to call.'

Annie sensed the curiosity that motivated his suggestion. This could be the neighbour who had found Carol's body. A voice in her head recited the reasons she should have nothing to do with his plan: it was outside the remit of her case; she wasn't on top of her game; she didn't trust Yağız; the police might still be there; she had already withheld information from them …

But curiosity was strong in her too and they were in the cab and on their way before something else occurred to her. Yağız hadn't said specifically why he wanted to talk to this person, but that thing about Carol having been found by a neighbour … that was something the police had told her. She had no memory of passing it on to Yağız.

Chapter 30

Annie let herself rest back into the plush floral-patterned softness of the cushions, happy to play spectator and watch how things developed. It was clear from the off that Yağız knew this woman far better than he'd implied.

'Yoci! Am I glad to see you! It's been awful. So good of you to come round. You must be devastated. I'll make coffee.'

And also that this was the neighbour who had found Carol.

'It was terrible. I can't close my eyes without seeing her lying there. I can't bear to talk about it.'

She took Annie's presence for granted. 'Oh yes, Annie. The new manager. Isn't it dreadful?'

Yağız and the woman shared memories and speculation as Annie sat cradling her cup and watching them. This was a new side to Yağız. Stripped of his work persona he became just an average guy coming to terms with the loss of a good friend. How good, Annie wondered? Clearly he knew both this woman and Carol far better than he'd led her to believe, to the extent she began to think he'd been involved more than platonically with one or the other of them – maybe both at one time or another.

She wanted to push for detail, but would have to pick her moment. As she listened to their gossip, she glanced around the room. It was lavish, crowded with furniture and ornaments, but it was less the room dressing that interested her than the room itself. This house was the mirror image of Carol's semi with which it shared a wall. This was the prosperous end of town. These dwellings cost serious money. Had Carol owned hers or was she renting it; maybe her side of the big building was split into flats. As she listened, the to and fro between them strayed into the territory she'd been wondering about.

Yağız had no inhibitions about prying into Carol's affairs, and asked outright how much equity she had in the property.

'Oh, she paid her mortgage off years ago, lucky thing.' The words were followed by a sudden pause. Not so lucky after all.

'Poor Carol,' Annie murmured into the silence as she framed the question she wanted to ask, but before she could open her mouth again, the woman had jumped to her feet and grabbed the coffee pot.

'Refill?' she said to Annie.

Annie smiled and held out her cup. It felt like a diversionary tactic but the coffee was welcome. She would wait until the hot liquid was out of the woman's hands before probing further. *I can't bear to talk about it*, was clear enough, but Annie would not let it stop her trying.

Leaning over to return the coffee pot to its tray, the woman reached to pull a cord that drew the curtains. As the thick fabric swished around the curve of the bay window, Annie caught the glint of stars. It was a clear night.

Again she opened her mouth to speak, but this time it was Yağız who dived in, cutting across her. 'What about her family? Was she in touch with them?'

The woman shrugged. 'There was a cousin ... I don't know really. I suppose the police will find out.'

It felt as though Yağız wanted to turn the conversation, as though he was aware of what she wanted to ask and was having sudden scruples. She shot him a glance. He wanted to know the detail as much as she did. He just didn't want to be tarred by the brush of ghoulish interest.

She approached from a different angle. 'Have the police arranged for you to have counselling if you need it?'

'I don't think so. I'm not sure. Someone gave me a leaflet.'

'You should consider it.' Annie ignored a disbelieving sniff from Yağız. 'It's traumatic to lose someone close, especially when you're the one to find them. Believe me, I know.'

'Well …'

'What made you go round?' Annie persisted. 'Wouldn't she normally have been at work?'

'It was her car. It was parked outside.'

'Carol never came to work by car,' from Yağız.

'No, and she never left it on the street unless she was coming right out again. She always put it in her garage. It was there when I woke up in the morning, and when it was still there hours later, well … I knew something was up. I rang her but I just got the machine. She didn't answer the door so I got my key. We have each other's spare keys,' she added defensively and Annie surmised she'd been grilled on that by the police.

'Where was she?'

'In the kitchen round the back. Lying inside the door.'

Something sparked in the sluggishness of Annie's brain. She wasn't sure what, so asked, 'Did you know at once that she was … I mean did you think she'd just collapsed?'

She was fishing to find out if there had been any previous episodes, anything that might be related to drug overdoses. Remembering the smallness of the bruise on her own arm and the imperceptible rip in her sleeve, it was unlikely this neighbour would have noticed anything like that.

'Oh, I knew at once. It was clear from her injuries. Her head was … half of it … it was as though she'd smashed into the corner of the mantelpiece. I even looked to see if there was any blood up there.'

'And was there?'

'Oh no. There was no blood at all.'

'On the mantelpiece?'

'Anywhere. A bit of a stain on the newspaper under her head but nothing much. If there'd been … I just can't imagine what I'd have done. I know I'd have fainted.'

The colour had drained from the woman's face. Yağız too looked like he was trying to back away from the images conjured in his mind.

'That probably means it was really quick,' he said, his voice unsteady. 'Doesn't it?' He appealed to Annie.

She couldn't tell if he was looking for reassurance for himself or the neighbour, or how she had become the authority on violent death.

'Yes,' she said, giving him the answer he wanted, no idea whether or not it was true.

Desperately she prayed for the fog in her head to lift, to give her the space for clear thought. She'd had the information she'd come here to get, and it had told her something unexpected, something she prayed would not occur to Yağız.

It was hard to pick up any kind of conversation after this. Yağız didn't try so Annie didn't either. Carol's neighbour glanced at the clock, made as though to rise and offered to drive them both back across town.

'It's late. You'll not get a bus at this time.' She gave Yağız a speculative glance that made Annie think she might be weighing up whether or not to ask him to stay. It might be her own presence that was the bar.

As Yağız raised his hand and said, 'No, no. We're fine,' she turned to Annie. 'Whereabouts do you need to get to?'

'Don't worry,' Annie replied, naming the street the restaurant was on. 'I'll ring for a cab.'

But I'll have to use your phone, she added silently, I've lost mine.

Yağız shot her a sharp glance. Was that because she'd ducked out of saying where she was going or that she hadn't included him in the putative cab? Maybe he too had glimpsed an embryo invitation to stay and didn't want it to go anywhere. Perhaps that was why he'd brought Annie with him in the first place.

In the end, Yağız made the call. As they said their goodbyes on the doorstep Annie could sense the woman's relief. She'd been pleased enough to see them, to see Yağız anyway, but was happy to see the back of them.

'You've lost your phone, haven't you,' Yağız said to her as they sped through the dark streets.

She replied with a grunt. She wasn't sure how he'd guessed but it was somehow the least of her worries. She needed a good night's sleep. Could she persuade herself even to catnap at that bedsit? Then there was the police interview she had to have first thing. The longer she left it, the clearer headed she'd be, but the evidence would be gone from her system. She wanted to know … wanted the proof. What if they didn't order blood tests? Should she do it privately? How would she pay? What if it was too late? Would they believe she'd been there simply as a place to sleep? Why should they buy that when she had a bedsit rented in her name? What if they found out about the hotel? No way would she be able to rest with all this in her head, no matter how securely she barred the door.

'I told you yesterday, Annie, I'll find you a bed for the night.'

Yağız seemed to pluck the thoughts from her head. She turned to look at him. His skin pulsed orange and dark as streetlights slid past leaking weird shadows into the back of the cab. She saw concern in his expression.

'No strings,' he said. 'Just somewhere you can get a good night's sleep. Somewhere you can be warm and safe.'

The words reached out as though to coil around her … reassurance or a trap ready to snap shut?

She struggled to formulate the reasons she must be firm and say no. The words kept repeating in her head … *Be warm and safe … warm and safe … be warm … beware …*

Chapter 31

As Annie surfaced from a deep sleep, she savoured the sensation of waking naturally, of feeling properly rested. The bedding that entangled her legs as she stretched was heavy, unfamiliar.

She snapped fully awake. Her memory replayed the night before. She'd been tired … too tired … not in control. Her mind was alert now, all that leaden sluggishness gone.

Waking from a proper sleep was too much of a luxury to spoil with regrets. The other side of the three-quarter bed was empty, the pillow bearing the imprint of the head that had lain there.

The curtains hung in folds, the same garish pattern as in the living room. A gap near the top showed no trace of light but sounds from elsewhere in the flat of water running, pipes clanking, told her it was time to be up.

The previous evening as he'd let them into the flat and flicked on the lights, Yağız had pointed to a bed-settee in the small living room, saying, 'I can sleep there.' He'd made no effort to sound sincere, and had rummaged in a cupboard, bringing out glasses and a bottle of decent single malt. 'Nightcap? It'll help you sleep?'

Annie had taken the glass from him, knowing he would read her acceptance as more than just for the whisky. She remembered laughing at him, asking some pointed questions. As far as she could gather, his philosophy on alcohol had more to do with who would witness him drinking than any principled stance.

His obvious assumption that yes to hard liquor implied her agreement to share his bed had chafed a bit, but only in the way she'd been mildly annoyed at his choosing which beer to order in the pub. Like he'd said when they left the restaurant, it had been a bad day. She supposed he'd seen sex as a useful relaxant to augment the whisky, and she was his only option. She'd felt pretty much the same towards him.

As she looked out of the window on to a city still sleeping, she reflected that they'd both needed the catalyst of strong booze but she suspected he'd needed it more.

She pulled on her clothes, eased open the door and listened. The rattle of a kettle coming to the boil reached her ears. He might be planning to bring her a hot drink and might only have good intentions but she would face him fully dressed and away from the bedroom. She moved silently to where she could peer through to the kitchen. He had his back to her, and looked somehow vulnerable as she watched him unobserved. This wasn't like following his movements on the hidden cameras. At the restaurant he always looked sharp, alert. Here at home he was relaxed, not so polished and formal. He leant on the surface by the fridge, poring over something. Her eyes narrowed as she realised what he was doing. Making no sound, she withdrew a step and reached behind her to push shut the bedroom door with an audible click.

The sound provoked a sudden scurry and thud that she interpreted as him hastily putting something down and returning to the hot drinks.

'Ah, there you are,' he greeted her, a half glance over his shoulder, not meeting her eye. 'Tea or coffee?'

Annie saw her new tablet lying beside the fridge on the room's only unoccupied flat surface. Its cover was down but a tell-tale glow at the edges showed it had been open seconds ago. And anyway, she'd left it in the living room.

She allowed herself an extravagant yawn, pulled out a stool and sat down. The edge of her vision showed the bright glow fading as the screen turned itself off.

'Coffee, thanks. Do you think Meriç'll be back today?'

'How would I know?' He answered a fraction too quickly, his eye meeting hers as he looked round.

She'd said it more as something neutral to say than that Meriç was in her mind, but his reaction surprised her.

Absently she rubbed her arm, nodding her thanks as he placed a steaming mug in front of her. With studied carelessness, he pushed her tablet out of the way. She felt him watching for a reaction. Some instinct had told him there was gold dust on there but she knew he wouldn't have been able to access it. She wondered how long he'd been trying ... how early he'd been up.

It was still dark outside, a good three hours before sunrise. They needed to set out soon for the restaurant. Leastways one of them should.

What were the chances of him allowing her to stay behind in his personal space? It was going to ride on how many secrets he had hidden here. She wondered about that sudden look when she'd mentioned Meriç; it had been close to a guilty start. Had Meriç been in touch? Was he on his way back? If so, Yağız would love nothing more than to be there to greet him whilst Annie was absent.

She rubbed at her arm again. It might already be too late to detect what had been jabbed into her but she had the bruise and the tiny rip in her sleeve as evidence. She had to find Ahmed or one of his colleagues and tell them everything. And it had to be today ... this morning ... it couldn't be left any longer.

'Yağız, will you be OK if I'm late in today?'

A suspicious glance, then a shrug. 'Why? Why would you be late?'

She told him that she had to go back to the police, implying without spelling out the lie, that it was a prearranged appointment.

'Only can I stay here and tidy myself up, get a bath? I'll be back for the lunch rush ... well, I hope so.'

She saw the struggle behind his eyes as the different implications unfolded. He turned away. Weighing up what damage she could do here on her own, she thought, and also what damage he could do to her through her absence at the restaurant.

◉ ◉ ◉

An hour later, Annie sat on the bed settee, wrapped in a dressing gown she'd found hanging on a door, rubbing her hair with a towel. Yağız had set off far too early so she hadn't rushed things, convinced that he planned to come back, to check out what she was really up to. She'd been relaxing in the hot deep water when she'd heard the click of a door. It had been creepy to lie there, not knowing if he could see her through some gap in the flimsy bathroom door, or even if it was Yağız at all. She'd splashed a bit and hummed to herself and there had been no more sounds.

It was pointless leaving too early. Ahmed's colleagues had been on the late shift last night. She would go in a couple of hours. It didn't give her much time to do what she needed but it would have to be enough.

Instinct had told Yağız that her tablet held something important. He hadn't been quite right. Any internet portal would do the job. The real key was what she had in her head; usernames, passwords, IP addresses. That was where she would find the answers.

She thought back to the night she'd clung to the flimsy ledge in the alley, the abortive raid, and her regrets that the cameras hadn't yet been installed. Well, now they were, and whatever had happened two nights ago would be recorded, and if it had happened in that short stretch of corridor it would be recorded in detail.

It was another thing she couldn't keep to herself. The police had to see the footage. She would have to give them the security codes … everything. She wasn't sure what they would do with it, but she doubted they would let evidence sit on the servers for her to peruse at her leisure. If she wanted to see whatever was there to see, it was now or never.

She logged on to the system and paused before opening the archived footage. What time would it have been? Her mind had been so fogged by later events, she'd lost track. She clicked to the live cameras, flicking from corridor to kitchen to dining room, her heart skipping a beat as they all showed empty. Where was Yağız? Was he right here watching her?

But no ... she breathed again. There he was pushing in from the back door. He'd been clearing some boxes. OK, he was there. She was safe.

Back to the archive, to the night before last. She decided to work backwards and homed in on the early morning. Yağız had taken to arriving extra early whilst Meriç had been away, as though keeping an eye on the place. Sure enough, the back door opened and he stepped inside. She fast-forwarded his to and fro from the lockers, turning on the lights, to his visible start of surprise as he opened the office door. The picture didn't show the inside of the small space but from what she could see, he'd been robust in trying to wake her.

She ran the footage backwards, fast, watching the hours unwind until there were people in the frame again. It was dark; indistinct shapes bustled back and forth. She flipped to the kitchen camera. Those same shapes, the pinpoint light of a pencil torch, quickly extinguished. The back door already swinging open.

She hustled the recording back through time and suddenly the kitchen lights were blazing.

Stopping the backwards blur she allowed it to play straight. This was too blatant. Who were they that they could be this confident? There was Carol, looking hard-faced and cross; no sign of the pleasant smile Annie had learnt to expect. She stalked into the heart of the restaurant. Another figure crossed paths with her. Boxes were carted back and forth. They kept their heads down, concentrating on the loads they carried. Two men Annie had never seen before hefted a large box across the kitchen, and out into the darkness of the alley. She froze the image to try to grab more detail but everything was covered. There was just one moment where one of them tipped his head backwards, and gazed upwards at the lens. She drank in the man's face, impressing his sallow features on her memory. He might be the one who'd stabbed a hypodermic into her … or the one who'd killed Carol.

Seconds later the lights were out again, but the door still swung wide.

The figures blended into the darkness … someone came back in … it might have been any of them, Annie couldn't tell.

Flip to the corridor lens. Voices. She replayed a few seconds. The door to the walk-in was half open.

Backwards again. She wanted to see what had happened to her … when had they found her?

The darting figures flitted with staccato reverse movements in and out of the walk-in, backing off the edge of the frame towards the kitchen. She switched briefly to the kitchen view and saw the matching moves … figures scurrying across the space between the door and the edge of the frame that took them in range of the corridor camera. This was the to and fro to cart away whatever Carol had stashed for them in the walk-in, not only that big box, but piles of other stuff too. She played through their last moments in the restaurant. The door to the cleaning cupboard swinging open. More to and fro. The lights stayed off. Nothing was distinct.

She skipped the footage to the other end of their visit to see them arrive. With a larger monitor she could have split the windows and watched two cameras at once, but it was hard enough to get any clarity on the tablet's small screen. She ran the different cameras and swapped between them.

She looked covetously at Yağız's television. What she would give to attach the images to that widescreen … Pointless, she didn't have the means to hook it up.

Two figures scooted backwards across the kitchen, one of them taking a reverse diversion to the side and the lights blazed on. Two more appeared.

Why were they so damned quiet? She wanted to hear them speak. Again she paused the footage and ran one part of it over and over, then moved it forward and replayed a second stretch. They weren't quiet. She could detect voices, but not within range.

It was as though they knew about the surveillance equipment. She brushed the thought aside. The background hum of voices came from inside the walk-in. It was logical that they talked in there, and probably outside in the alley, but not while they carted the stuff through.

Annie made what adjustments she could, but had nothing sophisticated enough on the tablet to pull out coherent words. She toyed with contacting Pieternel, getting her to access the footage, analyse it.

But no, she wasn't running to Pieternel anymore. Pieternel wouldn't stop at analysing the sounds; she would grab copies of the footage, hide it away, get them into unnecessary trouble, endanger the licences they relied on to be able to operate. Wasn't that how all their current troubles had started?

She took in a breath. Maybe on this one occasion she was being unfair to her senior colleague, but it was always secrecy, conspiracy … she was fed up with never quite being fully in the loop.

The police labs could analyse the sounds. As it was a murder enquiry she supposed they would find the resource to do a thorough job.

Time was getting on. She moved to the kitchen camera and spun the footage back in a blur until a lone figure appeared that she recognised as herself.

She stopped the recording, trying to tell herself that a fresh coffee would be good, but knowing it wasn't coffee she wanted, it was to put off the moment of seeing herself attacked. The view of the restaurant kitchen showed her nothing, but the corridor camera was not going to be easy watching.

Taking the timestamp, she flipped to the corridor view and set it the same. Watching in real time she felt her shoulders tense. It seemed ages before she appeared. She had checked out the rest of the place before heading to the office. Her figure too was indistinct in the darkness. She watched herself move off the edge of the frame into the office.

How long now? How long had she been in there before she'd heard voices? Had voices been the first she'd heard of them? The memories reconstructed themselves as she watched the empty corridor. The bolt on the back door. She'd been going to slide it across but not until she was sure the place was empty.

Then there was a figure in the corridor. A lone figure, moving softly. No voices. But surely she'd heard voices. She stared hard at the hazy image. Whoever it was, stopped at the lockers. Was it Carol?

The figure retreated. Empty corridor again.

She'd missed that. There was nothing in her memory that matched what she was seeing.

Movement. The lone figure was back again. She watched its progress, slow, gentle steps as it eased its way along the corridor. Surely not Carol. Whoever it was pressed themselves to the far side away from the doors to the walk-in, the cold-store, the office, continuing their careful way until almost out of range of the lens, lost in the very far end of the corridor where no one went but the few people allowed to hang their coats on proper hooks.

Now there were voices. The words came across clearly, spoken at normal conversational volume.

'Lovely weather for the time of year.'

'Lovely for Polar bears. I can't stick this cold.'

'Days getting longer, or is it shorter? I can never tell.'

'Hard to know, but ...'

One voice was Carol's. And one of the others had a familiar ring. *Key-holder ... one of the key-holders.* It was nothing to do with what she was seeing, it was the memory coming back to her. Something about key-holders.

Her mouth dried as she watched.

They were talking at random, making no sense. She was there in the office, off camera, watching them through the crack in the door. There was no vestige of memory that she'd clocked that other shadowy figure, the one who had glided silently past her to the other end of the corridor.

All the time they'd known she was there.

She expected it now but when it came it made her heart lurch. A shadow detached itself from by the coat racks and stepped fully into view. It swung open the office door. She glimpsed her own face, shock blossoming ... saw the stab of a fist into her upper arm.

Her body slumped off the edge of the frame, all but her legs. The figure stepped over her, and a moment later her crumpled legs were whipped away as she was pulled into the office.

'Get to it!' It was a low growl, none of the fake bonhomie of the earlier exchange.

She replayed the sequence, this time watching Carol as closely as the gloom would allow. Carol threw one careless glance in her direction as she was ambushed, then snapped to attention at the growled order and they began the sequence that Annie had already sampled of a swift to and fro between the walk-in and the back door.

Lovely weather for the time of year ... get to it!

Was there something familiar in the timbre of the voice or had she imagined it?

The sudden ring of a phone made her jump. Yağız's landline. She leant across to look at the handset and recognised the restaurant's number on its screen. Yağız checking up on her. She debated leaving it, pretending she'd already left, but for all she knew he had a neighbour watching out. She picked it up.

'Hi, Annie,' said Yağız's voice. 'You've not left yet then?'

'Uh … no. I was just about to.'

'Well best not go yet. Meriç is back. He's on his way round to see you.'

'Shit!' She jumped to her feet looking down at the oversized dressing gown that was all that covered her. 'When? Why did you tell him I was here? Why didn't you stop him?'

'Sorry,' he said again, sounding genuinely contrite. 'I didn't speak to him. It was a message.'

'OK, see you later,' she snapped, thumping down the phone and rushing to grab her clothes.

In less than five minutes she was back in the living room, fully dressed and a little breathless. She looked round. The tablet lay open on the table, its face showing a hazy still of the restaurant corridor. She flipped shut the cover. She would show him if he needed to see it, but was wary of him trying to persuade her to keep quiet about the cameras.

The doorbell buzzed. She blew out a sigh, relieved not to have been caught in nothing but Yağız's dressing gown. It had been close.

Before reaching to unlock the door, she leant forward and put her eye to the spyhole.

Through the magnifying glass, the distorted features of a man swam into focus. He stood at the head of a trio, his bulk all but blocking out Meriç and whoever the third man was.

Key-holders!

She realised who she'd seen … heard. Not the chef or Yağız. Not Meriç. The other key-holder. The man now standing on Yağız's doorstep.

Chapter 32

Annie stared as though hypnotised. It was too late to run. Nowhere to run to. No other way out.

Fragments flew into place in her head. The raid … the men in the alley. So that was what it had been about.

She watched through the distortions of the spyhole as the man's hand, grotesquely huge, rose again towards the doorbell.

Her thoughts raced. She'd never missed her phone as much. With a few clicks she could have sent an alert to Pieternel.

Email!

How quickly could she get back into the living room, wake up the tablet; it was already attached to Yağız's wifi … The thought was fleeting, dying as it was born. She held a single card, and it was as flimsy as the physical barrier between her and the man on the step.

No choice. She had to let him in and play her card as though it was an ace.

He didn't know she knew. He'd never expected her to wake up from that jab in the arm. His accomplice would be in trouble for failure to administer it properly, but he knew nothing of her abnormally high resistance to drugs. Should have done your homework, she thought, as her hand rattled the lock and his hand withdrew from its intended assault on the doorbell.

As she turned the catch, she realised she had another card. Meriç.

Meriç knew nothing of what had been going on, because if he had he would never have employed her. They wouldn't do anything in front of Meriç. While he was with her, she was safe from physical harm.

Trying to slow the thumping of her heart, she pulled the door wide. 'Hello.' She put an element of surprise into her expression as she gave the man her friendly smile. 'It's … uh … Mr Corder, isn't it?'

'Max, please. And can I call you Annie?' He smiled expansively. 'Forgive the intrusion, Annie, but I have a lot invested in Meriç and his catering venture. I need to know what's been happening.'

'Well … uh …' She found herself retreating as the bulk of Maximilian Corder advanced.

'No beating about the bush, Annie. I know why Meriç employed you.' He gave her a wink. 'And it wasn't to manage his restaurant.'

'Uh … you'd better come in.' He was already inside but she wanted at least a pretence at control.

She led the way to the sitting room. Footsteps followed. She hadn't acknowledged Meriç, hadn't even looked at him.

Her tablet lay on the table. It was comatose now and would have locked itself but the stills from the night she'd been attacked lay waiting behind the passcode.

Aware of Corder's bulk behind her, she thought about the first raid. Those men pushing their way in from the alley, relaxed, blasé. Why would they worry? They'd been Corder's men sent to find out about Meriç's new manager. They'd been in her locker and found that pen drive, the one that held the original flawed surveillance, the files with which she'd planned to convince Meriç that nothing was wrong. One glance at those reports would have told Corder exactly what her role was. Maybe that card was closer to an ace than she'd thought. He'd seen evidence that she'd found nothing.

We weren't after you, she wanted to tell him. It was the chef's scam that was creaming the money off Meriç's bottom line.

Corder's felony had never made a ripple in the books for all that it was the big one, the nasty one, and he must have been running it ever since he got his hooks into Meriç.

Act normally. What would she do now? Any embarrassment or awkwardness could be explained by them finding her in Yağız's flat. She should offer them a drink.

She'd been so transfixed by Corder that she'd still not acknowledged Meriç or the third man, not even looked at them. She should ask him about his trip.

'Can I get you coffee?' she said as she turned to face them.

The third man was over by the door, clicking it shut. Meriç had moved out of her line of sight; her peripheral vision showed him homing in on the tablet.

No, Meriç, not that. Not now.

Her mouth dried as the man by the door looked round. The sallow features she was staring at were the ones she'd impressed on her memory not ten minutes ago. Working her lips around a pleasant enquiry about his trip, she spun towards Meriç, and stared horrified at a hand flicking open the cover of the tablet. Every muscle in her body tensed, suddenly convinced that it hadn't had time to auto-lock, that it was about to flash the picture of the attack for them all to see.

As its bland screensaver flared to life, she fought to hide a wave of relief.

'How was your trip?' She looked up into his face.

'My what?'

He stared back. It wasn't Meriç. It was a stranger.

'Where's Annie?' Meriç barked the question at Yağız as he let himself into the restaurant.

'Um … she's not here yet.'

Meriç looked all around. Everything seemed to be in place, the kitchen was a scurrying hive of preparation. He knew to the second what time it was but stared at the clock to underline his words. 'We're due to open in less than half an hour. When will she be here?'

'When the police are done with her I guess.'

'Why? What do they need to know? Why would they keep her when she's needed here?'

'Well … uh … didn't she say?'

'Say what? When? What are you talking about?'

'The phone message. I thought it was you.'

Meriç stared. Was Yağız about to fall apart? 'Don't stand about doing nothing,' he snapped. 'We're down an experienced server as it is.'

Yağız flinched at his words. Meriç felt a flash of pain constrict his own throat. Carol had been part of the bedrock on which this place had been built. But that didn't mean they should let it crumble just because … she wouldn't want that.

As Yağız hurried away to oversee the preparation for opening, Meriç thought back to his first meeting with Carol. Carol and a sallow-faced man. They'd come together, recommended by Corder in fact. He'd been concerned that Corder would turn into the sort of investor who meddled, especially when he'd had to let the man go as worse than useless. Carol's job too had hung in the balance but it turned out she and the man weren't any kind of item.

Never set eyes on him until Mr Corder had us both meet him here … the day you gave me a job.

He recalled her words, the relief that he wasn't going to have to sack her too, the worry that Corder would blow his top, but thankfully he hadn't, because even back then Carol was showing herself to be the most valuable of assets, a real workhorse with no ambitions to move on.

And now they must do without her. This was no time for his manager to be swanning off. And no time for Yağız to go wobbly on him either.

He heard the ring of the phone. Fingers crossed it was a booking, not a cancellation. Word got round. Carol's end had been violent. Poor Carol.

Chapter 33

Nothing overt had been said or done. On the face of it, Annie could slip on a jacket and simply walk out. That was what Corder wanted her to believe. He hadn't made up his mind. She'd seen this type of stand-off too often not to know exactly what the stakes were and how high they were stacked. Corder didn't know how much she knew. That's what he was here for. It was always less hassle to let someone go innocently on their way, but if he had to silence her, he wouldn't hesitate. For whatever reason, Carol had turned from trusted ally to liability and he'd wasted no time in silencing her.

No one had responded to her offer of a drink and she'd tried to brush off her mistaking the third man for Meriç with a muttered, 'Sorry, thought you were someone else.'

She knew she'd behaved awkwardly, but then they'd surprised her in Yağız's flat at a time when she should have been at the restaurant. She put a touch of defensiveness into her tone and said, 'I've arranged with Yağız that he's in early today.' Let them think that time-keeping was uppermost in her mind. She toyed with using the excuse she'd given Yağız; her putative appointment with Ahmed's colleagues. But Corder's gaze was laser-sharp. She daren't be caught out in a lie. He was the restaurant's major investor. The police might have talked to him. He might know exactly who they'd seen and who else they wanted to see.

He pointed at the tablet. 'That thing working?'

Looking at it blankly, she shrugged. 'I dunno. It must be Yağız's.'

It wasn't the best thing to say because Yağız knew it was hers, but it was all she could think of.

Corder reached into his pocket and pulled out his phone. Toying with it he looked her in the eye, nodded and said, 'Yes, why not?'

She returned the look, not understanding what he was saying. Had he seen through her act or ... what? He glanced all around the room. Annie felt obliged to follow his gaze. Seeing it through his eyes, the outlandish patterns on the curtains were suddenly prominent. She half expected him to ask why she'd picked it. It's not my space, she would say, it's Yağız's.

'Yes,' he repeated. 'We'll have coffee.'

Without any attempt to hide it from her he tipped his head to sallow-features in an unmistakeable gesture to act as chaperone.

They don't know I know. She kept the mantra running in her head. *They can't know how much I know.*

The phone was at his ear. He snapped, 'Corder here,' and barked out a demand to, '... speak to your head waiter, Yağız.'

She remembered Yağız saying sorry. Had he meant more than regret for giving away her whereabouts to Meriç? And where was Meriç anyway?

As she moved across the threshold to the kitchen area, her sallow-faced guard at her heels, the question was answered.

'Meriç?' Corder's tone was both surprised and indignant. 'I said I wanted to speak to Yağız.' A pause. 'Assume be damned! I expect to speak to who I ask to speak to. Now fetch me that head waiter.'

So Meriç was at the restaurant and he wouldn't like that peremptory command. His presence had been a surprise to Corder. That surely meant Meriç knew nothing about any of this. Was there a way to let him know that she was with Corder right now?

Clicking the switch on the kettle, she rummaged for cups.

'Has he put this thing on speaker?' boomed Corder's voice. 'Then–' the sharp sound of a profanity being swallowed, then the words were quietly spoken and measured. 'Then turn it off speaker.'

Corder had asked a question, but his voice was muffled against the steady rattle of water coming to the boil. Sallow-features leant on the worktop picking at his teeth with his finger nails, watching her.

She shovelled coffee into a cafetière, hearing the rumble of speech from the living room but failing to pick up the words. Hot enough, she decided, it didn't do to pour boiling water on to coffee, and as she flicked the switch to cut off the noise, she heard Corder say, 'Oh, it's Annie's is it?'

He'd asked about the tablet. She felt blood prickle her skin and made much of swishing the liquid to keep her back to sallow-features while she composed herself. Then she turned and pushed three empty mugs at him. 'Take these through, I'll bring the coffee.'

Her mind spun through the options. She was holding a full jug of almost boiling liquid. It was a weapon of sorts ... a last resort.

But when they entered the living room, it was to see Corder's expression hovering somewhere between angry and amused. He took the phone from his ear and stared at it, then shook his head and produced a short mirthless laugh.

Speaking into the handset again, he said, 'Be quick. I'm a busy man.' With that he pressed a button and the unmistakeable background sounds of the restaurant reached Annie's ears.

'Annie, your boss has a query for you.'

As though walking through a dream, Annie reached to take the phone from him but he made no move to hand it over, so she held on to the cafetière while she spoke.

'Hello?'

'Ah, Annie. I heard your name mentioned.' Meriç's voice came at her with a familiar overlay of impatience. 'You've locked all my worksheets and whatnot behind a password ...' Did she imagine minor emphasis on *whatnot*? 'I need to get at them. What is it?'

She stared. It made no sense. There were no worksheets. He was the one who'd hidden the paperwork from her. Instinctively she played for time. 'But I ... I gave it to you.'

'You didn't. And if you did, I don't know where it is. Tell me again.'

What was he playing at? There was nothing hidden behind passwords other than– It dawned. The surveillance footage. He was after the surveillance footage but he didn't want Corder to know. If he was to watch it and see the attack … then surely … could she rely on him to do the right thing?

And could she pass on the access codes under Corder's nose? Wouldn't that be giving the game away? And the codes on their own were no good. Meriç might think he knew where to find the footage but he didn't.

She'd wanted him to know that she was with Corder; thought that would give her some protection. Now he knew. Corder himself was holding the phone while they spoke to each other. She felt no safer.

Her mind flew across the alternatives. Meriç was listening. So was Corder. What could she say? She might shout for help but Corder would shut her up in a second. She needed to give Meriç something that sounded like a passcode, something that would alert him to something wrong. As the ideas flashed back and forth, she thought of her phone, the lost phone that would have allowed her to alert Pieternel. The phone … a revenge demon whispering in her ear … a habit learned from Pieternel of grabbing every opportunity … there might be a way.

'I … I don't know. I can't remember. But I know you have it. You … you wrote it down when I told you. You put it in your phone. In the notes section. I saw you do it.'

'Annie, I didn't. I …'

The rest of his response was cut off along with the background clatter from the restaurant as Corder clicked the button, reclaimed the conversation, and demanded that Yağız be put on again.

'What were you saying, Yağız? It's Annie's is it?' As he spoke, he turned his gaze towards her, one eyebrow rising slightly.

She gave him a puzzled glance … *he doesn't know I know* … ready to ask the question, *what's mine?* … the coffee pot still clutched in her hand.

Corder listened for a moment, impatience clouding his eyes. 'On the small table by the settee,' he rapped out. 'Blue cover.'

Once he'd said that, Annie had to look too. Everyone's gaze converged on the tablet that sat between them like a ticking bomb.

Yağız's voice played from the handset, barely audible, recognizable from the pitch more than the words. She thought she heard … *Annie's I suppose* …

She met Corder's eye, gave him an enquiring look.

I don't know what he's talking about … it's not mine, it's Yağız's. It's his flat.

Corder picked up the tablet in one hand and shook the cover open, holding it out towards her. 'Open it, Annie.'

She tried to look mildly surprised as she pressed her thumb on the home button, then hovered her finger over the keypad as though waiting for him to tell her the code.

A glance bounced from Corder to sallow-features. There was a clink of crockery as sallow-features banged down the cups he'd been carrying. Then Annie felt her wrist grasped as each of her fingers was pressed in turn on to the button.

'For heaven's sake!' she snapped. 'It's not mine.' But she allowed him to go through the charade of waiting for it to recognise one of her prints, swapping the steaming cafetière to her other hand as he tested those digits too. And although she knew there was no match to find, she felt blood pounding as her skin rested against the plastic.

'Well it doesn't seem to be Annie's,' Corder said into the phone, his tone measured.

Again the echo that had the timbre of Yağız's voice … *must be … nephew's* … And in her head Pieternel's voice resonated from a time when everyday technology was far more basic. *Never program in your biometrics, Annie. You want people to have reason to cut off your damned fingers?*

She pulled her hand away from sallow-features and gave him a glare. Corder cut the call and skimmed the tablet into a corner where it clattered to the floor in amongst a heap of magazines.

Corder's demeanour had changed. For a moment it was more irritation than menace. Annie moved fast to consolidate whatever ground it was that she'd gained. Reaching forward and tapping the table top, she ordered sallow-features to, 'Bring those cups over here so I can pour.'

Sallow-features obeyed, and she filled the three mugs. It was the tiniest show of authority, but it helped to paint the picture of her as remote from their real agendas.

'Not having one yourself, Annie?'

'Had mine earlier.' She opened her hands in a questioning gesture. 'What's this about?'

Corder sat down in an armchair and accepted his coffee. His gaze skimmed the table top where the tablet had rested, but Annie held her concentration on the hot liquid.

'You're a private detective,' he said. 'Tell me exactly what you've been doing for Meriç.'

Chapter 34

Annie wanted Corder to think she was surprised but not overly alarmed. With no idea whether she had caught the right balance, she let her attention move away from him as she sat down on the only vacant chair, a hard upright one. The three men had taken up all the room on the settee and in the armchair. It put her in the position of an errant schoolchild, here for a telling off. She regretted bringing only three cups. The fact they cradled drinks and her hands were empty exacerbated the picture of them in control.

Sallow-features smothered a yawn and let his eyelids droop. No surprise he should be tired. He'd been doing night shifts with Corder.

Corder raised his coffee to his lips, his gaze steadfast on Annie's face, waiting for a reply. As she met his eye she forced her mind not to linger on what would happen if he found out about the surveillance cameras and saw the footage of his own night time appearance at the restaurant.

It would be pointless to deny his assertion. She would normally take refuge in client confidentiality in circumstances like these, but she'd be mad to take that line with Corder. Except no, she wouldn't. Acting normally was her only way out, the only hope she had of winning this hand.

'Meriç is my client,' she told him, climbing on to a high horse of professional discretion, hoping his first move would be to persuade her with reason not force.

It was impossible to avoid glancing at sallow-features, now close to genuine sleep.

The chair cut into the backs of her legs as her muscles tensed. She needed to relax but couldn't. The light had changed. Time marched on. How long had they been here?

Her sole aim now was to get out from under the cloud of Corder's suspicion. He needed to be sure and wouldn't wait around forever.

She narrowed her eyes at him. 'I'd need his permission to discuss details with you.'

'You admit you're not a restaurant manager, then?'

'I'm that too.' She put a dash of pride into her tone that wasn't a sham. She'd made a bloody good job of managing the restaurant and was pretty close to deciding that she would go with Meriç to his new place and step into the real manager's role there – it would be a relocation that distanced them both from Corder. 'I'll ring Meriç and run it by him.'

As she spoke she leant forwards a little, preparatory to standing up.

The move from Corder was barely discernible. A spark. The room crackled with sudden tension. Without moving a muscle, sallow features snapped from half asleep to fully alert.

She'd said the wrong thing, pushed the wrong button. Corder was about to call her bluff, reveal his hand.

She was already raising her own hand to ward them off … an instinctive defence that she couldn't stop.

They don't know I know. They can't know I know.

'Ah, sod it!' She spoke louder than she'd meant to, barely knowing what she was saying … anything to distract, to divert, to keep up the charade. As though an autocue had failed at just the point she realised she didn't know her next lines, she fought against a tide of dread.

She couldn't have stood up now if she'd wanted to. Her legs had gone to jelly beneath her. Flapping her hand in a dismissive gesture, she sat heavily on to the chair.

'You're the major investor … your money on the line …' she babbled, stabbing her finger towards Corder, scrabbling in her head for what to say, how to cram the lid back on to this whatever-it-was that had just happened whilst maintaining the pretence of a normal conversation. 'Meriç needs to tell you anyway before the whole shebang goes tits up.'

Corder sat up and stared at her. 'Meriç needs to tell me what?'

Sallow-features relaxed, eyelids drooping again. Annie fought not to slump with a sigh of relief.

'The chef,' she said. 'Meriç's chef.'

Fighting every instinct that shrieked at her to recoil from Corder, to avoid his gaze, to shrink from notice – as if that was even possible – she leant forward and looked intently into his eyes, injecting her tone with the self-righteous gratification of one who enjoys delivering bad news. 'He's got the business on its knees.'

'Tell me more.'

As though the autocue had sprung back to life, Annie immersed herself in her role as the words tumbled out, making the worst possible case against the chef for his outside catering shenanigans. She talked about the anomalies in the books … a tip-off she'd had about a big do out in the sticks … how she'd followed him there. As she spoke, stray images clicked together in her mind.

On the floor behind Corder, mostly hidden under a heap of magazines but one corner just in her peripheral vision, lay the tablet he'd slung down there, and behind its locked screen lay a frozen image of her being ambushed by a man with a hypodermic.

That wasn't all it had shown her.

The pictures played out as she talked about scratched equipment … expensive ingredients … damaged reputations … flashy parties with hired dirndl girls …

Carol and her sallow-faced assassin carting boxes to and fro. Not only boxes. That large something-or-other carried by sallow-features and the other man. The third man, the one she'd mistaken for Meriç, the one sitting watching her and Corder now. He must be the one who had ambushed her.

She didn't want to work through the chronology with Corder's hard stare in her face, but her mind wouldn't cease its slide show of fragmented imagery.

Carol's neighbour. *Her head was ... as though she'd smashed into the corner of the mantelpiece ... there was no blood at all.*

Out of nowhere she understood the atmosphere of discomfort from the two men. They didn't want Corder with them. They would do his bidding efficiently and competently, but they wanted him to be hands-off. And who could blame them? Corder was a thug, a maniac. And one who was used to getting his own way.

'He's been at it for years,' she declared, with an extravagant sweep of her hand. 'Bloody good chef, of course, but hell, no business can take that level of pilfering.'

The slide show rolled on. Carol back and forth with sallow-features. On their own. Together. Back and forth. The footage was clear.

'Have you any idea what saffron costs? Meriç doesn't buy from bargain basements!'

The words babbled out. Horrified she watched them stray towards Meriç's suppliers. It was their diversity and far-flung origins that had given Corder his opening to run his own side-line right on top of the restaurant's legitimate business.

He didn't react, in fact she had the impression his eyes were beginning to glaze over. Was he swallowing this flamboyant story of the private detective who had unearthed the wrong crime?

She'd watched him on that footage too. Without watching it again it was hard to be certain which of them had been where.

'I never thought much of his hygiene standards.' Corder finally broke into her frenzied monologue. His voice was calm with the hint of a laugh that was echoed by an answering chuckle from the settee.

Annie smiled, trying to join in a joke she didn't get.

Carol and sidekick to the walk-in. Sidekick out again. Sallow-features to and fro. Corder back in.

That unexpected dance with the cleaning materials. The smears of an inadequate wipe down where she thought she'd seen a box that shouldn't have been there.

What had Carol said or done to enrage Corder?

It hadn't been sallow-features. He was the trusted lieutenant, used to sweeping up after his chief's irrational furies. Carol to and fro … the two men … Corder. The other two had gone out.

Hygiene standards? He was going to get Meriç to have the whole place emptied and steam cleaned, no matter that it had only been done a few days ago.

It had been Corder who had been inside with Carol.

And after Corder had marched back into the walk-in, Annie hadn't seen Carol come out.

He'd killed her right there in the restaurant. Annie had watched his sidekicks carrying the wrapped body out through the kitchen.

Chapter 35

Annie fought back the fear that rose inside her. They were no more or less dangerous than they'd been just because she'd worked out what had happened. Corder was listening to her. She was making headway. With no way to time herself she felt she'd been rattling on for hours with geek-like absorption in her topic, leaning forward towards Corder, ignoring the other two, ticking off the points on her fingers.

'Hygiene, you said it yourself. It was the state of the outside catering equipment that alerted me.'

'Alerted you when?' It was Corder's first intervention for a while. He fixed her with a sharp gaze as he spoke.

Why had he asked? What was he thinking? He wanted to calculate the timeline. Annie's mind skipped across the pieces that Corder had in front of him. He'd seen the report she'd never shown Meriç, the one that said the books balanced, that nothing was wrong. And now she was telling him of a scam that had caused serious damage to the restaurant's bottom line.

'I saw what he was doing,' she said, 'but I couldn't figure why there wasn't any damage. Financial damage, I mean. That was before Meriç showed me the real books.'

'You didn't know he kept two sets of books?' His tone was mocking, bordering on suspicion again. Had she overplayed her hand?

'I didn't expect him to hide the real picture from me,' she shot back, layering her voice with indignation.

He gave a half shrug as though accepting what she said. His air of menace had subsided. At any rate, she was no longer its focus. If anything she'd told the story too well. He was becoming interested in the chef's shenanigans.

It felt like stalemate. She didn't want to keep talking. The more words that came out of her mouth, the greater the chance of saying something foolish. But she couldn't sit in silence and pretend everything was fine. He still wasn't quite sure.

She sensed that safe ground was within reach, but if she didn't do something decisive they might skirt a safe refuge and veer back to the heart of the danger zone. With an inward girding of loins she prepared for what might be a reckless leap over a chasm too wide to cross.

'I planned to catch him in the act,' she said. 'Couple of nights ago. I heard there was an event on. Decided to stake the place out overnight.'

As though she'd put a match to a flare, the tension blossomed. All three of them were wide awake and watching her.

'And what did you find?'

She gave Corder a glance, then looked down as she ran her hand through her hair and rubbed the side of her nose. 'Look, I was tired.' She spoke defensively. 'It had been a long day. I had a drink. I don't know. I fell asleep.'

'Did the chef turn up?'

'I don't think so. Nothing had been moved. And anyway it doesn't matter. I've enough for Meriç to act on. I've got the smoking gun. I don't need to catch him with it in his hand.'

She maintained her slightly embarrassed stance that allowed her to avoid Corder's eye, and was aware that the three of them exchanged glances.

Had she said enough? Or was it too much? Had she explained away all the questions they'd come here to find answers to?

Sallow-features stretched and sat upright. She was aware of

an unspoken exchange. The tension seeped away. She felt elation begin to build inside her.

'What d'you think?'

It was Corder's voice. What was he asking? She looked up. His gaze was on the third man, not on her.

The man leant forward and pushed his mug on to the coffee table. 'Time's getting on,' he snapped as he pulled himself to his feet.

Now they were all standing. Annie got up too, reaching to gather together the used coffee cups. She would busy herself in the kitchen while they left.

'There's plenty of time,' said Corder.

Annie had the impression he said it to wind up the third man who was now jigging impatiently.

'Waste of bloody time, if you ask me,' the man growled, taking the bait.

Corder looked daggers at him. For God's sake, Annie wanted to shriek, don't push him! He had only just swallowed her story and, being Corder, might easily spit it out again.

'Ever been to the warehouse, Annie?'

The tension was back. The air zinged with it. She and Corder were its focus.

'Max!' It was sallow-features, voice low and furious, his outrage reflected in the hard glare on the third man's face.

They'd been convinced by her act. All three of them. She knew they had. But now Corder had crossed a line, and whatever line it was, he intended taking her across with him.

'The warehouse, Annie,' he repeated. 'Have you been there?'

Caught by the intensity of his gaze, she could only stare back as she shook her head.

Meriç watched the wait staff scurry to and fro. Since speaking to Annie he'd felt oddly superfluous in his own restaurant. Confusion battled with anger as he thought about Corder's peremptory demand to speak to Yağız. What was going on? Had they been in touch with each other while he'd been away? Was it a longstanding arrangement? Yağız was … had been … one of the few he'd thought he could trust.

He'd deliberately pitted Annie against Yağız, knowing it was unfair on them both, but what had fairness to do with business? Annie wasn't his real manager and Yağız should have been promoted. He'd wanted to make Yağız all the more hungry for the job when Annie left, had even thought of taking him to the new place. But if he was hand in glove with Corder …? He watched now as Yağız fussed at the expediting station. Safer to leave him here if he might be in Corder's pocket.

As for the new place … the new manager …

He thought of Annie, of the unexpectedly competent job she'd done. He'd been critical but only to keep her on her toes; hadn't expected her to function as a manager at all, but she'd done both jobs. And there had been an element of relief in having someone on hand that he could talk to frankly. He had a suggestion for her, wondered how she would react. It was over and above what he'd paid her to come and do.

Irritation welled up again. How could he put anything to her when she wasn't here?

'Yağız,' he snapped, tipping his head to call him over.

'There's a woman in the corner by the window,' Yağız began, his tone low and urgent. 'Blue coat. She came in just a–'

'Never mind women in blue coats,' Meriç snapped. 'Where's Annie? When's she coming in?'

'Oh … uh … but she's the same one that … Annie? I'm not sure … I … uh … She told me she'd try not to be long.'

'Not to be long where?' Meriç's confusion grew. Why was Yağız looking so shifty? He'd been pleased as punch to report her absence when Meriç had first arrived.

He listened to Yağız's mumbled answer – the police wanted to see her – but his mind skipped on to other things. Yağız probably felt caught out. For starters, Annie had a reasonable excuse to be late, which was not the implication Meriç had had from him earlier and secondly, that call from Corder might be playing on his mind. Leastways, it had better be playing on his mind.

'I don't see why they should have to take her away in working hours,' he grumbled. 'And what woman? What blue coat? What's that about?'

'I think she's … just a minute …' Yağız sidestepped to intercept one of the waiters. 'Did you take the order for the table in the corner, woman in a blue coat? Let me see the ticket.'

Meriç watched as Yağız read the order then swore softly as he held it up for Meriç to see.

A latte and a salad. Meriç creased his brow as he looked the question at his head waiter.

'Fairly soon after we opened,' Yağız said. 'That woman who got food-poisoning. Do you remember? You got Max Corder to smooth it over. It could have closed us down.'

Shock shimmered down Meriç's spine. 'Same woman? You're sure?'

Yağız nodded emphatically.

'Then oversee her order yourself and don't let her out of your sight. Is she on her own?'

'I'm not sure. I just clocked the face.'

Meriç was sure without going to look. There would be two of them. One to be poisoned, one to be witness. He remembered it like it was yesterday. Corder smoothing things over? He supposed it must have looked like that to Yağız who was the only one Meriç had confided in. It had been after he'd sacked the man Corder had recommended, the one who turned out not to have been a friend of

Carol's. Carol had known about it too, now he thought back. How had that happened?

And yes, he'd told Yağız that he'd tapped the big investor for a solution, but he hadn't. Max had been on the phone to him. What had he said? *It's a bad idea to kick out good people* … In the shock of it all, it had taken a while for him to make the connection, then he'd been back on to Corder to suggest he re-employ the man. But Corder's tone had changed. *If he can't do the job, he can't do the job. Who wants passengers?* Meriç, now thoroughly confused and wondering if he'd misread the thing from start to end, had mentioned the complaint, the food-poisoning. Corder had dismissed it. *Storm in a teacup. Ignore it. It'll go away.* And it had.

With a sense of foreboding creeping through his veins, he stepped to the corner of the bar to watch the woman's order make its way across the space, Yağız holding the tray high as he threaded his way through the tables. After serving the woman, Yağız moved to an adjacent table and started to clear crockery. Meriç moved out into the crush to get a clearer view. Yes, the woman had her cup to her lips but she was watching Yağız, maybe waiting for him to go away. Meriç moved closer. The woman was nibbling a lettuce leaf that she held between finger and thumb. Her companion watched, as though hungry but not allowed to eat. They turned to each other, shielding their movements and their conversation from Yağız, but Meriç could see them clearly enough.

As the woman twisted her head in Yağız's direction and raised her hand, Meriç skipped nimbly through the crowded room to field the complaint that her coffee, 'tasted funny,' and that she wasn't sure the lettuce in her salad was fresh. With one hard look at Yağız to keep him quiet, he leant over the two women and slid a banknote on to the table between them.

'No charge, of course,' he murmured, 'and you can redeem this in any other restaurant in town. You won't be wanting anything else here.' He leant closer and widened his smile for the benefit of any customers who might be watching. 'Now get the hell out of my restaurant and don't come back.'

The woman glanced at her companion and briefly raised her eyes to heaven as they both rose. Meriç watched them leave then spoke to Yağız, a whispered aside, 'She slipped something in the coffee. Get rid of it and sterilise the cup.'

They both looked at the plate, now topped with a limp green leaf that had not seen the inside of their kitchen. 'I'll bag that,' Yağız muttered, 'and take it out to one of the street bins.'

Meriç nodded. He didn't think a lab would find anything too noxious but it was as well not to take chances. He was pleased that Yağız had cottoned on so quickly.

As they pushed through to the kitchen, Meriç felt a stab of anxiety at the sight of orders stacking up. He didn't want Yağız taken away from his duties and wondered about sending one of the juniors. But no, that would be asking for trouble.

'Is it Corder?' Yağız shot at him as they reached the relative quiet of the kitchen station.

'Service!' roared the chef, glaring at Yağız.

'I'll deal with Corder,' Meriç said, pleased to see a look of relief on Yağız's face. Whatever overtures had been made, they'd surely come from Corder not Yağız.

'What about Annie?'

'For pity's sake, come on!' shouted the chef, as another of the waiters hurried through dumping a tray laden with dirty crockery and grabbing at the new orders.

Meriç stared at Yağız. 'What about Annie?'

'She's with Corder. Is she all right?'

'You said she was going to the police.'

'Yes, but when you spoke to her earlier ... I don't trust Corder. I think he's had Annie followed.'

'Ah ...' Light began to dawn. That made sense. Corder had got wind of Annie's real identity. He'd been to confront her. Meriç shot a sudden look of alarm at the ceiling, seeing Yağız follow his stare and look puzzled. He should have come clean with Annie. Corder had been adamant about any kind of security cameras. He'd had some facts and figures about employee morale, about better ways to counter pilfering. *Not this sort of business where you're so hands on. Counterproductive. Believe me, I know.* Meriç hadn't been bothered either way, hadn't really considered surveillance until Annie had come along. But what if she'd told Corder?

Was that what his stooge in the blue coat was all about?

No, it wasn't, because the woman's move would have been caught on the dining room camera.

'Don't worry, I'll sort it,' he told Yağız.

Yağız dumped his tray, clamped a clean plate on top of the offending salad, grabbed it and the coffee cup and headed to the back of the kitchen to dispose of the evidence.

'Get these orders cleared,' Meriç barked at the chef who was gaping at Yağız.

The chef turned his outraged stare on Meriç, opening his hands in a gesture of despair. Meriç ignored him and headed for the office. Annie wouldn't have let on about the cameras. If she had, she'd have been open with him, not given him that garbage about passwords being in his phone.

As he pulled out the handset, he gazed for a moment at the Notes icon, finger hovering to click on it. He'd never used it. Why would he? The thought crossed his mind that Annie herself might have put the passwords on there, but to do that she'd have had to have her hands on his phone and it never left his side.

Changing his mind he punched in Corder's number and waited to hear what the latest hoop would be that he had to jump through.

Chapter 36

This had become some kind of power play between Corder and his acolytes. Annie continued to act dumb, bustling round the flat, gathering the cups together, wiping the surfaces, brushing down her jacket.

'Right then.' She tried to inject a brisk tone into her words. 'I need to be on my way. The restaurant'll be busy.'

The two men continued to snap at Corder, short phrases, disconnected words, hiding coherent meaning from Annie but clearly telling him to back off whatever edge he was pushing them towards. She heard the taunts in the tone with which he responded. He enjoyed winding them up, but he was also on the verge of saying more than they wanted her to hear. The term, 'warehouse,' might have crossed that boundary already. It was as though he'd caught the taste of blood with Carol's killing and wanted there to be no choice other than to shut her up too.

No response to her words, so she headed for the kitchen.

This time no one followed her. All their attention was on each other. They'd fallen for her act, but only on balance. One wrong move and the façade would crumble. She considered the distance from where she stood to the front door. Too far. They might be taking no overt notice of her but they weren't amateurs; they were sharply aware of their surroundings. Speed alone would not get her out, and she would show her hand if she tried.

'Annie.' It was Corder's voice calling her. She moved to the doorway to face him. 'You'd like to see the warehouse, wouldn't you?'

'No,' she shot back at him. 'Meriç deals with that side of things. I need to get into work.'

Sallow-features reacted with an ironic smile to her mention of Meriç. They were still buying her story.

'OK,' said Corder, suddenly compliant. 'We'll drop you at the restaurant.'

Sallow-features looked as distrustful of him as Annie felt. She'd played on the urgency of getting there; leaving herself no plausible reason to refuse the offer of a lift. 'Thanks.' She gave him a nod and a brief smile.

He was playing games with his two henchmen, but his mood could turn in an instant. She would go outside with them, then pretend to have forgotten something. There was a good chance that Corder's impatience would do the rest and they would simply go and leave her behind.

Sallow-features went first. Corder, in a mock chivalrous gesture signalled her to go ahead of him so she was flanked by the two of them as they stepped out into the street. The cold air pressed hard against her skin, the day unseasonably bright. Tiny crystals tracked lines down the walls and pavement, a sparkling boundary between hard frost and winter sun.

Parked cars crowded the road, but Corder's wasn't hard to identify. A sleek black diamond amongst lines of standard family saloons.

This was the moment to turn back, to say, 'I promised Yağız that I'd check the ...' but she got no further than a glance over her shoulder. They were on full alert, mistrustful, wary. Corder was winding them up just for the sport of it, but he didn't really want to have to deal with Annie. They had the length of the journey for him to reconsider. He would enjoy her discomfort and theirs but he would drop her at the restaurant and go on his way. This was not the time to plant any doubts in his head.

'What's the matter, Annie?' He reacted to her brief glance,

his voice playful on the surface, rippling with lethal currents underneath.

'Did you check it was locked?' She aimed her question at the third man.

'Of course he did, Annie. Now, in you get.' The back door of the sleek black car slid sideways. She barely had to duck her head to climb in.

'Meriç went to some trouble to get you,' Corder said as he eased in to sit next to her. Sallow-features perched on a pull down seat facing her. The third man acted chauffeur. A darkened glass partition separating the passenger compartment showed the back of his head as an indistinct outline.

'How do you mean?' she said. 'He got in touch and signed us up just like anyone would.'

'He could have had someone local. It would have been cheaper, I'm sure.'

'I think someone recommended us,' she said vaguely, whilst weighing the pros and cons of an honest answer. Sticking to the truth added credibility and she saw no reason to sidestep this one, though she might be doing Meriç no favours. 'It was to keep it hush-hush,' she told Corder. 'I think he wanted it sorted before he had to come to you about it, and someone local ... well, there might have been links back to someone who'd have blabbed.'

'He was going to tell me all about it, was he?'

She shrugged and gave a mirthless laugh. 'Probably not, if he could have got away with it, but the guy's taken him for some serious money. I don't know how he's fixed financially but if he's really in the shit, who else would he go to?'

Again she felt the tension lessen. She'd hit just the right note to reassure both Corder and the sidekick. If she could just sustain this tone, she was almost home and dry.

'What's he paying you, anyway?'

Unease shimmered through her. She didn't want him to know

the inflated price that Pieternel had coerced out of Meriç. There was something dangerous in giving him that knowledge, though she couldn't immediately pinpoint it, and anyway he might already know. If she lied he'd catch her out. If she refused to tell him, he'd get angry. If she said she didn't know, he wouldn't believe her.

She gave him the truth and watched his eyes open wide in surprise. Even sallow-features sat up. She watched as the two men's eyes met, and knew she'd made the wrong decision.

'I don't deal with the money,' she added. 'My boss sees to all that.'

It chafed to call Pieternel her boss, but it might help if they saw her as the valued and expensive employee of someone who might come looking for her.

'Not an amateur outfit, then?' The words came from sallow-features; the first he'd spoken directly to her. She didn't like the way his contribution changed the vibe, didn't want to be drawn into conversation with him.

'No.' She looked out of the window as she spoke. They weren't far from the restaurant.

'What's your boss's name?'

'I'm sure you've done your homework.' She felt no need to mollify Corder's sidekicks and was aware that Corder smiled, amused at her put down.

Sallow-features moved so fast she barely saw it. Her jaw was clamped in his fist, her head twisted to face him. The seatbelt cut painfully into her side, locked by the speed at which he pulled her towards him.

'I want to hear your boss's name from you.' He spoke from so close she saw spit gather at the sides of his lips, fine lines bunch the corners of his eyes.

'Mrs Peters.' Shock forced out the words. No time to wonder whether or not it was the name to give them. It was the name Pieternel went by these days.

Sallow-features' fingers squeezed tight, drawing a gasp from her. Then he pushed her away.

'So that's it, is it?' he said to Corder, who shrugged.

Annie's heart thudded as she rubbed at her jaw, struggling to suppress the shakiness that rippled through her. What were they saying? What did it mean?

At the end of this street was a left turn and then they'd be at the restaurant.

She'd misjudged the dynamic between sallow-features and Corder. Corder hadn't answered the question. They'd just looked hard at each other. The air crackled with silent communications, insight she wasn't allowed to share.

The hand that had come close to snapping her jaw, reached up and back to slide open the partition that separated them from the man at the wheel. Once again, a short monosyllabic exchange.

The detail was hidden from her but the wider picture became clear. As she'd surmised, they had done their homework. Quite why sallow-features needed confirmation from her lips, she wasn't sure, but he'd veered to Corder's point of view. For reasons of their own they were about to make her complicit in their agendas. She couldn't guess what role they saw for her – willing accomplice, hostage or maybe simple patsy – and had no idea if any option left her with a way out.

The partition slid shut. The car slowed, but instead of swinging left, it described an arc and turned through three-hundred-and-sixty degrees.

As Annie stared at the familiar streetscape, a string of lights flared to life above her, the buildings faded to fuzzy outlines and then disappeared as the glass in the windows darkened to an impenetrable shiny black.

Chapter 37

Corder hadn't taken his call. Meriç looked down at the phone wanting to try again, to impress on Corder that this was no game. But getting on the wrong side of his major investor would be worse than not getting in his story first. He wondered what version the stooge in the blue coat would spin. And he wondered where Annie was.

'Meriç, your friend's arrived.'

He looked up sharply. The girl who had brought the news hadn't lingered, probably sensed his mood. He'd said to let him know, not fully expecting his regulars to be back into a routine this soon after the festive break. He wanted to ask were they on their own, just the parents, or had they brought their daughter and new son-in-law too, the supposedly on-leave policeman from York. Yağız said he'd been one of the pair who had broken the news about Carol.

He sauntered towards to door that would show him the dining room. It was the policeman who held the information he wanted, but Meriç didn't want to see him there. He wanted to see the parents-in-law on their own. He might get some information then. Ayaan Ahmed would tell him nothing.

Better than he hoped. His old friend was alone, looking lost without an entourage. He supposed his wife would be busy with family at home. He put on a beaming smile and strode across.

His welcome had to be tempered as he received his friend's condolences. Carol had been a favourite with the customers, yet somehow her grisly end kept being pushed out of his head by more immediate concerns about the business.

'Your son-in-law came round to tell my staff about it. Very thoughtful of him. I was still away.'

That took the conversation nicely into the right territory and Meriç let his mind race ahead over the moves needed to arrive at a bald request for the new son-in-law to be contacted and squeezed dry of any information that might circumvent future trouble for the restaurant.

◉ ◉ ◉

It was impossible to follow the twists and turns of the journey whilst fielding the questions that Corder and his sidekick fired at her, but Annie tried anyway. They were professionals. They wouldn't make it easy. It was already clear from the sharp turns that the driver followed a circuitous route.

Sallow-features wanted chapter and verse on Pieternel and how long they'd known each other. Annie batted back the queries with shrugs and half-truths, no detail … *we go way back … she used to work abroad … I can't remember …*

Corder pulled out his phone. Annie sensed the vibration from the handset and with pretended indifference glanced as though to look out of the window. The mirrored black glass, polished to perfection, gave a clear image of the car's interior. The screen on Corder's phone was tiny, moving with the motion of the vehicle. She had only a fraction of a second to take in the image before Corder red-buttoned the call. A brief glance was enough. It had been Meriç.

Not Corder, Meriç. Ring Pieternel.

The questions continued. It interested her that they knew more about Pieternel than about her. She was used to it being the other way round. They didn't know she'd worked in Hull early in her career, and she weighed up whether or not she could use that.

Corder grunted in exasperation as his phone vibrated another call. The reflection showed her nothing this time. Corder took the call and put the handset to his ear.

Sallow-features spoke but she ignored him. She wouldn't sing to his tune while the organ-grinder wasn't watching. Risky tactic because she hadn't fully fathomed the dynamic between them, but after his painful attack on her, it fitted the role that she continued to play. He shrugged and turned away.

Corder tutted impatiently and then threw back his head and roared with laughter. 'Meriç? Priceless.'

Meriç! Annie teetered at the brink of firing an answer at sallow-features. Any answer ... loud enough to flag her presence to whoever was at the other end of Corder's call. She held back. He'd said, 'Meriç,' as though talking *about* him and not to him.

'Our timid restaurateur has managed to grow a pair,' Corder said as he ended the call.

It was impossible to say whether the comment had been aimed at her, sallow-features or whoever had been on the phone. Annie didn't react. Neither did sallow-features.

The journey continued in silence. The black mirrored windows were disorientating. It was hard to judge speed, but Annie felt the car transition to a smoother, faster road. The A63 maybe.

Somehow they'd moved beyond the point where she needed to play dumb about their activities. They had believed her act but still drawn her into their world. Her welfare was no longer reliant on her playing a part. She had become a pawn. No illusions. Her safety now relied upon her getting away from Corder. But without help, she couldn't see how that would happen.

Annie thought she sensed salt in the air. A warehouse by the docks? The smell of the sea?

Corder moved suddenly, an irritable shifting in his seat. It made both Annie and sallow-features jump.

'I'm going to ring Meriç back,' he said.

Here was a small chance. Some innocuous message so that at least Meriç would know she was still with Corder.

'Can you tell him–?'

He cut her off with a look. She swallowed her planned words. His stare held her for a fraction of a second and then flicked to sallow-features. His head barely moved, but Annie read the message as clearly as if he'd written it in blood. Sallow-features had been told to make sure she kept quiet during the call, and she saw in his smirk that he relished the task.

She could only listen to Corder's side whilst pretending indifference. He said nothing that surprised her, but because she was still playing her role, she felt she should allow her eyebrows to rise when she heard him say, 'Annie? No, we left her back in that waiter's flat.'

Whatever Meriç said in response made Corder's lips tighten.

'I've no idea,' he snapped into the phone. 'I didn't ask.'

As he clicked off the call, he said, 'Now why would Meriç ask me if you'd gone to the police?'

'Statement,' Annie said, fighting to maintain a couldn't-care-less demeanour. 'Routine. One of our waitresses died.'

Corder grunted and relapsed into silence.

The car skidded round a tight left hand bend. Annie threw out her hand to stop herself cannoning into the window. Sallow-features, on the pull-down seat, had braced himself for the manoeuvre before it happened. It made Annie wonder if they were following a familiar route, rather than random twists and turns to prevent her from mapping the journey in her head.

Her hand jarred painfully, catching in the door pocket. With sudden hope that she might feel a blade beneath her fingers, she felt around the inner surface. Gravel scratched her skin. Useless as a weapon but she palmed what she could anyway and slipped it into her jacket. It was scant consolation to imagine that forensics might tie her body to Corder's vehicle through a handful of pebbles.

The car gave them a smooth ride but the road surface had deteriorated; their speed fell.

After a minute or so they slowed almost to a standstill, then jolted over a series of obstacles that felt like severe speed bumps. A short stop, maybe to open a barrier. Now they were climbing a steep hill. Annie stored the images but could make nothing of them.

A sudden halt. Had they arrived? No, because after a few seconds they were moving again but the surface had changed, the vibration quite different. She wondered if they were off road. Yet another series of speed bumps bounced them about. Annie counted the same number of jolts but noted these were less severe and taken at greater speed.

Then Corder was at her again, questions about the chef's scam. 'A lot of hard work for little reward,' he commented.

'Oh, I don't know,' said Annie. 'Very good margins, especially if you're nicking your raw materials.'

They stopped abruptly. Again it was only Annie who was taken unawares and thrown forward against the tension of her seat belt. Now what? This time she had a sense that they'd arrived.

The car jigged back and forth as though manoeuvring through a tight opening. Then they were going backwards. She felt the vehicle tip as it crept down a slope. Then the whine of the engine took on a higher pitch. Still in reverse, the car picked up speed and seemed to describe an arc, as though they were being driven in decreasing circles.

She stared hard at the blackness of the glass beside her, desperate to see something through it that would ground her. The motion brought on nausea.

Disorientated, she didn't realise the car had come to a halt until sallow-features reached across and clicked open the door. He climbed out. Corder signalled her to follow.

Relief at being on solid ground was short-lived. The only illumination was from the car's interior and that cut out when the door was slammed shut. Ambient light crept in from somewhere, but very little. She blinked to try to adjust her eyes.

'Here we are,' said Corder, and Annie could tell from the echo that they were at the heart of a huge indoor space. This must be the warehouse.

◉ ◉ ◉

'Full deep clean?' said Yağız. 'Again?'

'Yes, again,' snapped Meriç. 'Overnight. I'm not losing trade for it. I've organised everything and if Annie doesn't show up, you're to stay and oversee it. Not the front of house, just the walk-in, corridor and kitchen.'

'But we've only just …' Meriç watched light dawn on Yağız's face as he pulled his mind back from a busy service to this latest development. 'Ah, the woman in the blue coat. But even so, surely …?'

'You know the deal,' Meriç said. 'Corder can close us in the blink of an eye and he will if we don't jump.'

'The new place …?' Yağız spoke tentatively, testing the water Meriç thought. He wasn't used to being the confidante but he was de facto manager in Annie's absence.

'You'll be manager here.' Meriç told him what he wanted to hear. Hadn't meant to show his hand so soon but he needed Yağız on side.

Ayaan Ahmed had been unexpectedly accommodating, and told his father-in-law that his colleagues were done with the restaurant staff; official enquiries were heading in a different direction. That left a question unanswered.

'Why was Annie at your flat?'

'Oh … uh … she needed a bed for the night. Some problem with her place.'

Meriç fixed him with a hard stare. 'So where is she now? She's not with the police.'

'Is she still with Corder?'

'He says not.'

Meriç told himself that Annie wasn't his problem, but he saw his own unease reflected in Yağız's eyes. He wanted to get at those surveillance files, but he'd had a go and couldn't access anything useful. She should have left him the password.

You put it in your phone. In the notes section.

He hadn't. He knew he hadn't. But he pulled out his phone anyway.

Chapter 38

Corder and sallow-features moved away from the car, heading towards the ranks of long racks that ran from floor to ceiling. Annie tried to hang back, but daren't let the distance between her and the two men grow too big. Sallow-features might have his attention elsewhere but a part of him was clocking her movements. While they thought her compliant they wouldn't hold on to her, and if they weren't holding on to her, she could grab the chance to get away, supposing such a chance ever came.

The third man either hadn't left the car or had disappeared before Annie had regained her equilibrium. She'd glanced back at the vehicle but could see nothing through the darkened windows, and the only sounds were their own footsteps and the impersonal creaks of the building's fabric.

As they neared the metal shelving a long strip light flickered on above their heads throwing a line of light along a short stretch of one aisle.

Corder spun on his heel and marched back to the car. Sallow-features stayed put so Annie remained where she was, wary, trying to watch them both. The burst of light hadn't shown her much, but there was no sign of cameras in here; little chance of some bored security guard spotting them on a bank of screens, but then Corder would have had all that kind of thing in hand. She saw him lean in to the car's window. Then the engine purred to life, idling for a moment then it roared to a crescendo as it set off in a spray of dust and grit as Corder turned away. Annie stared. Whichever way it went was the way out.

Her shoulders were gripped hard enough to for her to gasp in pain. She was pushed and spun round. Disorientated, she felt hands on her arms and upper body, holding her upright at the same time as forcing her to spin.

She would have recognised the grip even if she hadn't seen his laughing face close to hers as he tipped her off balance and then let go, leaving her to stagger and slip as she fought not to fall. The thin strip light clicked off again.

So soon after that unanchored circling in the blacked-out car, the nausea rose again and she had to breathe hard.

Corder ignored the byplay and began snapping queries at sallow-features. Too much was left unsaid for Annie to unravel any meaning, but she could sense that their talk centred on her. Or was it Pieternel? Or maybe both of them. But why?

She had to get away. The hum of the car's engine was gone. It had died while sallow-features spun her to dizziness. She'd heard no break in rhythm to signal its traverse through a doorway; no creak that might have been an entrance opening or closing; and seen no change in the ambient light.

'You like money, Annie?'

She answered Corder's remark with an indeterminate tip of her head. Again, his observation was just off kilter. She wasn't the one who liked money in the way that his tone implied. That was Pieternel.

In turning his attention to her, he stumbled on a small pile of dust and detritus that looked like the result of a half-hearted attempt to sweep the vast floor.

Sallow-features smirked. Corder lashed out, his booted foot swinging through the heap careless of any bricks or glass that might be concealed there. Annie jumped at the sudden move but was behind the arc of spraying debris. Something sharp caught sallow-features' ankle and he swore. Corder's turn to smirk.

A larger fragment flew through the gloom and clanged off the metal shelving. At once, a strip light flickered on giving them a view down a canyon walled by boxes. Something ricocheted and the neighbouring gangway lit up.

With a flurry of movement two cats shot out from beneath the racks and sped down the edge of the space, pursued by a sharply flung object hurled by sallow-features.

Annie watched the cats' grey forms blend into the darkness as they skidded round a corner to vanish back into their dark world. She supposed they were a form of pest control.

Keeping her head towards the two men she swivelled her eyes to see what she could. The light was confined to the nearby stretch where the stones had hit. The brief view of a high narrow corridor walled with boxes melted into darkness without showing her any hint of an exit or even how long these gangways stretched. Was each one a single long passageway, or were there gaps connecting the lanes? Surely there would be gaps. She imagined taking off and sprinting into the heart of the warehouse, dodging down the gangways, diving through the openings from one corridor to the next. As an idea it was a non-starter. The automatic lighting would map her exact path.

They continued to trudge across the uneven floor, Corder expressionless, sallow-features tight-faced. Annie nursed a hope that the stone Corder had booted into his sidekick's ankle had done some real damage.

As they passed one of the racks, sallow-features swerved to back-heel a metallic stanchion. The automatic strip flickered to life. He was rewarded with a sharp yowl and one of the cats streaking clear to skid round a corner and vanish into the inky blackness beneath the lowest shelf in the neighbouring gangway. Annie's gaze tracked its escape.

As far as she could judge, these lights stayed on no more than a couple of seconds, but she supposed that if someone was working and moving within their sensors they would stay on longer.

She was directly behind Corder, a couple of arm's lengths away, as he snapped at sallow-features to, 'Stop pissing about!'

Her stare never left the backs of their heads as she moved fractionally sideways.

The far wall began to define itself. There were metal stairways, high walkways and haphazard heaps of boxes, maybe awaiting their slot on the ordered metal shelving.

The friction between Corder and sallow-features, apparent since they'd walked into Yağız's flat, bubbled close to the surface. Annie caught fragments of a furiously hissed exchange. This time she made no effort to interpret or decipher individual words. All that mattered was that their attention was on each other and not on her.

Maximilian Corder sauntered a little behind his associate, watching the man's determinedly couldn't-care-less posture. He'd suffered a burst of annoyance when he'd tripped on stuff that should have been swept out of sight, but his kicking out at the heap of garbage had been a deliberate tactic to bracket together minion and trash. The sharp-cornered brick fragment was an unintended but happy outcome that had shut up the mouthy git.

It was hard even to feign annoyance. He'd sussed out a prize catch in Annie Raymond. She could so easily have slipped through his fingers before he'd realised she was attached to the Peters bitch.

The gloom of the place was broken only by the occasional splash of light from the automatic strips reacting to carelessly flung stones or marauding cats. They were insulated in here; immune from the weather, from the city that would be waking all around them, from the vessels out on the river not a stone's throw away. Hidden too. No one had seen them enter and no one would see them leave. It was an environment he loved, where he could do as he pleased.

Annie Raymond was his route to the enigmatic Mrs Peters. He

would give a good deal to have someone like her on his books. He might even forgive her the initial rebuff and her deceit in sending a lackey in to keep an eye on him via Meriç's restaurant.

He wasn't going to kill Annie Raymond, nor even harm her, but he would make both her and her boss believe that he was. He would make them plead and bargain. And eventually, when the message had been well and truly rammed home, then he would let her go. When he offered to do business with someone, that business would happen.

The warehouse was never quiet and never dark. Low level lighting burned twenty-four hours a day. Their progress was accompanied by creaks and groans as the fabric of the place stretched and contracted. Occasional scurries came from the resident cats and their prey. Normally at this time, the place would be bustling with the clang and crash of forklifts, people working up and down the rows, strip lights blazing. The background breathing of the empty building cosseted him as he walked towards the gangway where he would make his move. Annie Raymond's footsteps pattered trustingly behind him. That comment from Meriç had rattled him; her going to the police to provide a statement. It would be garbage, just like the trash all over the floor, he was sure of it, but it didn't hurt to check. He fingered the phone in his pocket, waiting for the vibration of the call that would signal the all-clear.

As though in response to a telepathic command, the buzz zinged through his fingers and he pulled out the handset.

'Yes?' He spoke tersely, aware of his associate turning away, still sullen over that well-deserved clout to the ankle.

A clatter like a mini-avalanche sounded from the walkway. Corder glanced as he listened to his phone.

'They're not looking at the restaurant premises.' The voice was gruff, no wasted words. 'They've fallen for what we left at the house.'

'OK.' Corder half smiled. No surprise there. If anyone got round

264

to considering the restaurant as a crime scene, the evidence would be long gone.

He expected the call to be cut, but there was a pause, a sound that might have been a throat clearing. 'What?' he prompted.

'I threw in a bit about the chef, all that stuff she told us about him running his own show on the quiet.'

Corder tensed. He hadn't said to dig further. On the other hand he hadn't said not to. 'Well?'

'She had surveillance cameras installed. Meriç told the police but they can't find any archive footage as yet. It's not hooked up locally. It's been beaming it somewhere remote.'

Corder felt his blood turn to ice. He choked off an expletive and barked, 'When? Where? How long?'

'Dining room, kitchen, staff corridor. One week ago.'

One week! Shit shit shit...

He held very still, had to think this through. Whatever her cameras had caught, she hadn't seen it or she'd never have behaved so casually around them, but then even if his dumb-assed hired help couldn't stab someone's arm with a needle properly, she had to have ingested enough to have befuddled her brain. She had no idea what had happened.

He wondered if that archive footage had been beamed anywhere at all or if it was just set up to look that way. If anyone had seen it, it would be the Peters woman. Maybe she would see it as a bargaining chip.

Change of plan.

No one had seen the car arrive and no one would see it leave. If Mrs Peters wanted to play hardball, she would find herself playing out of her league. She could have had a scared and roughed up colleague to deliver the message, but now she would have a body; her colleague at the bottom of a high metal staircase inside a locked warehouse; killed in an accident of her own making after she'd broken in.

That scurrying sound again. He cut the call without another word.

There shouldn't be anyone else in here but he needed to be sure. He turned. The gofer could climb up there to check while he watched Annie Raymond. More than watched. This was his last chance to squeeze anything useful out of her.

He put on his friendly voice, the tone that lit fear in people's eyes.

'Now, Annie, while–'

He stopped. Then spun through 360 degrees … saw the gofer do the same … felt his mouth drop open.

Annie Raymond was gone.

Chapter 39

Initially disconcerted, Corder's mood turned to amusement as he watched his companion's panicked rush towards the nearest bank of metal shelving.

'I told you to stop pissing about,' he barked. 'What are you doing, turning all the lights on so we can't see which way she goes? Are you trying to help her?'

'No, Max. Don't be daft. Of course not.' Corder smiled to see alarm veer in a new direction. No one wanted to be thought disloyal. Just look what had happened to Carol.

'Then let's see where the bitch has got to, shall we? You go up top.' He indicated the metal stairway, and when the man hesitated, added, 'That's where she went. Didn't you hear it? I was busy on a call. You should have been paying attention.'

'Nah, she can't have made it up there.'

Corder shrugged. 'OK, then go up there and keep a proper watch. When a light comes on, I'll go in and get her.'

'But what if …?'

'What if nothing. There's no way out till we open the doors. She can't get away.'

He saw the man's agitation subside in the realisation that Annie Raymond was just as trapped whether or not they could see her.

As his companion relaxed, Corder's mood darkened. A shadow had crept over his day and he didn't want to be only one weighed down by it.

'The bitch installed surveillance cameras in the restaurant a week ago,' he said.

The man's face drained of colour. 'Cameras? Working cameras?'

'Of course working cameras.'

'Where? What's she got? Who else has seen it?'

That was better. His companion's rising panic would allow him to keep a lid on his own.

'No one yet. They're getting footage off it now but only because they're capturing it. The Raymond bitch had it set up to send remotely.'

'Who the hell to?'

'Who knows? Maybe no one. Maybe she was just cutting corners.'

The man went to speak but then paused, taking his time to stare all around into the gloom of the warehouse. 'That stuff she told us about the chef running his own show; that was a paper trail from the books and a tip off. It didn't happen in the restaurant.. She didn't get any of that off surveillance cameras.'

Corder felt his lips curve to a smile. Observations like that made him remember why he put up with this mouthy git. He had a brain when he thought to use it. There was still an outside chance that the footage had been beamed to somewhere other than a virtual trash can, but she hadn't been doing it to further the job for Meriç, probably some scam of her own she was trying out on him.

'If it's gone anywhere,' he said, 'then we know one person who'll have access.'

'We do?'

'Mrs Peters.'

'Oh God! The one …?'

'The one who wasn't inclined to play. And if she thinks she has a bargaining chip then we have some useful collateral too.' He raised his voice a little so that the echo carried further through the maze. 'She destroys the footage. We send her colleague back intact. All we need is Annie to make the call.'

He'd spoken louder in case Annie Raymond was still in hearing distance, but knew how this maze of boxes smothered sound. Best case, she gave herself up on the promise of doing the deal with her boss. Then it would be a judgement call as to whether to kill her here or take her away and keep her on ice before dispatching her. Least risk, least hassle was to do it here, but he'd rather be sure she was dead before they left, especially after her coming round so soon the other night.

Decision made he raised his hand and signalled his companion closer so he could lower his voice. 'If we find her, we call Mrs Peters from here, do some kind of deal.'

'Yeah, but what if she–?'

'She won't. She has too much to hide. Anyway, deal or no, if we find the bitch, she's going over the top.' He tipped his head to indicate the high walkway. 'And if we don't find her ...' He shrugged. 'Either way ... find her or not ... we're having the place fumigated as soon as we leave.'

'That'll pee off a lot of people; twenty-four hours without access.'

'Longer than twenty-four,' Corder said with a half-smile, 'after they find someone made an error with the mix. No rats, human or otherwise, will wake up after this one.'

His half-smile was returned as the man headed towards the steps, saying over his shoulder, 'I don't think she's up there. I don't see how she could have made it without us seeing.'

'We were distracted. She was quick.' Too quick, he thought to himself as he pulled out his phone. Maybe she *had* seen that footage. 'Call me and keep the line open. I'll go to the car. If she's down here and she moves, you'll see the lights. Let me know and we'll go in and get her.'

Corder's handset buzzed the incoming call. He opened it and set it to speaker. 'She might be up there,' he said into it. 'Watch your back.'

Annie lay cramped beneath one of the metal racks, her face uncomfortably close to a mess of cobwebs packed with the tiny remains of hundreds of insects. The rule was that when you got away, you went as far and fast as you could. You scrambled to get outside the boundary of your pursuers' viable search area, put in everything you had and more to be a mile distant while they thought you were still in the room with them. And if you couldn't immediately get clear, the rule was to be invisible and immobile right under their noses, fool them into widening their search area beyond your hiding place before they started. Then it was a cat and mouse game of keeping one step ahead, always being in a place they thought they'd covered already, waiting for the search to move away.

This would be cat and mouse but she now knew she was playing it within a sealed perimeter. Corder's feet were clearly visible. Sallow-features was walking away. She'd heard everything they'd said apart from a whispered exchange, and she could hear them both now through the speaker of Corder's phone.

She shouldn't be surprised that Meriç had confessed to the police about the surveillance cameras, but who had told Corder? Surely Meriç or someone would ring Pieternel and she would give them access. Wouldn't she? What had all that been about?

The one who wasn't inclined to play … some sort of deal …

So they thought she was trapped, did they? Given free rein she'd like to bet she would find a way out, but how long did she have? She didn't like it that Corder hadn't been bothered by her disappearance; had expected them both rushing into the stacks to try to chase her, confusing the possibilities as they lit up the aisles. Sallow-features had come close enough in that first rush that she could have reached out and grabbed his ankle.

But Corder had fallen for her ploy and now she could hear sallow-features' feet clanging on the metal steps. He was right. She'd never have made it up there unnoticed. It was the handful of gravel and stones from the inside of the car door that she'd lobbed up over their heads while they had their backs to her, and the second their attention had been caught by the clatter, she'd thrown herself at the nearest rack and slid under it, working herself away from the edge.

The cats had shown her the way. They had scurried at ground level in darkness, only activating the lights when sallow-features chased them higher. Maybe the swirling dust and debris used to trigger the sensors too often, and they'd been realigned. Whatever the reason, it gave her a low and cramped corridor along which she could wriggle unchartered by the automatic illumination.

As Corder began to move, Annie screwed up her face, fighting a compulsion to clear her throat as another layer of dust swirled around her head. Her options were limited. She could stay where she was – they would never think to look for her this close to where they'd been standing – wait for them to leave, then look for her own way out, or for a phone. Surely this place must have some kind of office somewhere, maybe up on that high walkway. She didn't like it that Corder didn't seem to care about giving her that option. She could stand up, call out to him, tell him she would speak to Pieternel, do this deal whatever it was. The dryness in her throat wasn't just the dust. She remembered sallow-features and the other man on the footage, struggling across the dark restaurant kitchen with the awkwardly-shaped package that could only have been Carol's body.

Or she could slither from aisle to aisle, pressing her body to the floor, crawling under the racks, praying she was right about the sensors, trying to be fast enough to keep pace with Corder and quiet enough that he wouldn't hear her. He'd told sallow-features he was heading for the car. That was the way out.

She twisted to watch his legs recede. If she came out from under the shelf to cross an aisle before he'd gone right past, the movement might catch his eye, so she would have to be well behind him. And there would be no leaving the sanctuary of the maze of racks because sallow-features was up on the walkway with a bird's eye view. It was hard to imagine keeping pace with him even for a minute, let alone for long enough for him to traverse this huge space. Already his footsteps echoed in a way that made it hard to pinpoint the right direction.

She pulled herself on her elbows out from the protection of the shelf, across the scratchy concrete of the aisle and into the blackness of the next rack, feeling silk sheets of cobweb tangle in her hair, trying to feel forward with just one arm so she could keep her hand over her nose and mouth.

Beady eyes gleamed from the darkness just in front of her face. She couldn't stop a shocked intake of breath that almost closed her throat. Squeezing her eyes tight shut, clenching every muscle, she was aware of scurrying, felt something brush past her arm.

Corder's voice … indistinct … sallow-features response echoey and unintelligible.

She'd let him get too far. She fought down the urge to cough, kept her breathing shallow, took as much of a look ahead as she could see and then put down her head. This way she was moving blind but not taking the worst of this subterranean world full in the face.

As fast as she dared, she dragged herself across the concrete in the direction she thought Corder had gone.

Chapter 40

Meriç rapped sharply at the front door of the restaurant, ready to escalate his unease to bad temper if he was left standing on the street. A chance encounter with a fellow city trader had made a satisfying start to the day. Officially he was exasperated with the council for the timing of their city centre road works. In fact, the diverted pedestrian traffic had worked in his favour. If it hadn't been for his disloyal snake of a chef he would have been coining it in. Yağız, alerted by phone to his early arrival, was prompt with the bolts and Meriç entered.

He and his chef had already had words. Meriç hadn't meant to do it, but fury at the man's disloyalty had overcome him. He'd cornered him in his own house before dawn with every intention of painting as bad a picture as possible in front of his wife and family. A voice of caution had reined in the worst of his planned tirade – he needed this man's skill for another few days – and in the end made it more effective. Whilst letting on that he was aware of a scam being played out, he had left an element of doubt that he hadn't quite plumbed its depths, that there might still be time to cover things up, to find a scapegoat to take the blame. Without fully articulating the lie, he implied that he suspected the boy Corder had shoved on to him, the one Annie Raymond had sacked; and that the chef's crime had been to be blind to the wrongdoing. The man had tried to ask questions but Meriç had put on the cloak of arrogant owner, not in a mood to listen.

And now he pushed past Yağız, ignoring his greeting, and made straight for the back of house. He stalked deliberately across the length of the big kitchen aware of the spike in tension from the casual workers as they bent their heads over the sinks and chopping boards. He never came this far inside the workspace at this hour. He led from above and at arm's length. Their chain of command went up to the chef. To underscore his point, he pulled open a cupboard and took a look at the pans inside, tipping them, clanging them together as he rummaged.

'You!' He picked one of them at random. 'Tidy up that lot.'

He walked as far as the back door, opening it briefly to take a glance down the alleyway, then as he marched back he barked, 'I don't want to see a scrap of mess in that tenfoot today.'

There was satisfaction in seeing how they all scurried to do his bidding. It was at his whim whether or not they ended the day with the jobs they'd had when they woke. But the atmosphere was tighter than that. They'd seen their boss, the chef, kowtowing too, none of the banter he usually shared with Meriç to mark his territory as top of the heap. On balance Meriç knew he shouldn't have said a word, not yet. If the man thought he'd be sacked, heaven alone knew what damage he might do in the interim.

It took time to recruit a top rank chef. And although he was lucky to have possibilities in the pipeline for the new place, chances were he would have to bridge a gap of a few days with his sous chef in charge. The sole reason he'd not sacked the traitor on the spot but left him with a spark of hope was that he didn't want an inexperienced pair of hands at the helm for the weekend trade. Thursday today. He wouldn't sack him until close of play Sunday.

It had been Mrs Peters who'd told him what Annie had found. She'd had no explanation for that *Message from Mrs Peters* that he'd found in the notes section of his phone, just saying Annie must have done it.

'But how?'

Mrs Peters had brushed it aside as unimportant but Meriç kept rerunning the scene in his head. Him talking to Corder on the restaurant phone, Annie in Yağız's flat. How could she possibly have accessed his phone from there and left that note? And if she could do that, why hadn't she done it again to let him know where the hell she was. The Peters woman hadn't known either.

'I spoke to her on the phone this morning,' he'd said.

That had been Tuesday. Not a peep out of her in the two days since.

Not that he'd had time to chase her. Wednesday had been a nightmare of fielding detectives in and out. They wouldn't agree to use the back door either. One big man, shirt straining at its buttons, had seemed to crowd out the office the whole day. They'd wanted to take his computer away but he'd argued the toss, and in the end they'd had someone in to take a proper look.

'No stored footage,' the woman had said, 'Looks like it was beamed remotely, but I can't follow any coherent trail. More likely it was hooked up to a laptop. Do you have one? Did she have one?'

Her presence had been such a relief from the monosyllabic man-mountain that he'd told her all he knew about Annie Raymond, not that that included anything about a laptop, but he was able to pass on her address. The woman had stayed on, and Meriç found himself responding to her friendly chatter as she worked. Thinking back, he wasn't quite sure how it had happened, but she'd got to know all about the business, the shenanigans that Annie had unearthed, even the new place. She'd made the feed work, so he could now sit in there and watch what was happening.

He could have retreated to the office now and watched everyone covertly, but he stayed by the expediting station, a visible presence.

And when a sharp rat-a-tat sounded from the front door, he was on the spot to march through. Police again, he supposed. No one else knocked on a closed sign with that level of confidence.

He paused and signalled Yağız forward. The door opened on a tall woman dressed in a long well-tailored coat that screamed understated wealth. Something about her luxuriant light brown hair drew his eye. Without any evidence, he decided it was a wig. He met her gaze, realising that he'd learnt a thing or two from Annie Raymond about appraising people. This one was fake from head to toe. He would lay money the frames of the spectacles she wore held plain glass. Even as he scrutinised her, he knew he'd have difficulty recognising her again.

'How do you do, Meriç.' She took a step forward and offered him her gloved hand which he took in a brief handshake.

He was aware of Yağız, by the re-locked door, watching them with saucer-eyes.

'Two coffees, Yağız,' he rapped out, and signalled his visitor to the corner table. He would look a fool if he guessed wrong, but the timbre of her voice was the clincher. They'd spoken only a couple of days ago. As he eased out the chair for her to sit, he returned her greeting, 'How do you do, Mrs Peters?'

She acknowledged him with a half-smile.

'Please say nothing about what we talked about,' he murmured as Yağız moved away. 'I need my chef on point for a couple of days yet.'

'Sure. And you've told the police about the surveillance cameras. Have they found any archive footage?'

She seemed especially alert to his answer, keen to know. 'They were here most of yesterday, but ...' He glanced over his shoulder. Yağız was setting the second coffee cup on a tray. 'I don't think they found anything. I asked them to be discreet. The staff only know that my computer has been inspected. I believe the rumour is that Carol Dale was running some manner of fraud, but as far as I'm aware no one has picked up any hint about hidden cameras and I want it to stay that way.'

'I'm not here to tell tales to your staff, Meriç. I'm here to find out what's happened to Annie. She probably had footage on her laptop.'

'The police looked in her locker,' said Meriç, 'and her flat. They didn't find a laptop as far as I know. Yağız ...' Meriç looked up at his head waiter who had arrived with their coffee. 'Did you ever see Annie with a laptop?'

He shook his head. 'She used the PC in the office.'

They both watched Yağız as he walked away, then Mrs Peters leant in and said, 'Her locker and her flat, you say. Where else would she have put a laptop if she'd had one with her?'

There was something about the way she asked the question that made Meriç think she already knew the answer and was fishing to see whether or not he did. It annoyed him. This wasn't the time for game-playing. 'They didn't find her phone either,' he said.

She held the cup to her lips and sipped coffee through the foam. 'Oh, she had her phone stolen when she was going round town or something.'

'She didn't tell me that.'

'She told me. Now I have a few photos I'd like you to look at. Might be completely irrelevant but do you recognise any of these people?'

She laid out four small printed photographs, pushing them across the table towards him. He could make out three men and one woman. All but one of the faces was indistinct, turned away, obscured by low lighting. He pointed to the one whose features were visible. 'I don't know him.'

She pushed across the one that showed a woman's form. It was little more than a blur. 'That might be your waitress. The one who was killed.'

'Are we opening as usual?' Yağız was at his shoulder, his gaze running over the photographs.

'Of course,' snapped Meriç. Then on impulse he slid the picture of the woman towards Yağız. 'Is that Carol?'

Yağız gave Mrs Peters a curious glance then reached forward. He scrutinized the photo, twisting the print to catch the light. 'Could be,' he said doubtfully. 'Uh … Meriç … could I have a quick word. It's about …' He tipped his head towards the back of house.

'Can't it wait?'

'Not really …' Yağız jigged awkwardly.

Mrs Peters gave them both a gracious smile as she pulled out her phone. 'Go ahead. I'll check my emails. I'm on a deadline. It's not that tight, but don't be too long.'

Meriç followed Yağız to the middle of the dining room. 'Well?'

Yağız leant in close and lowered his voice. 'I wasn't sure what I should say in front of her,' he whispered. 'Is she one of Carol's relatives? Why's she asking about Annie?'

'Never mind who she is. What is it?'

'You asked if Annie had a laptop. She did. Well, it was a tablet. She had it when she came to my flat. I should have said before but with all the rush yesterday it slipped my mind. I mean if anyone had asked, I'd have remembered, but no one did. I don't even know if it's still there. Max Corder asked me about it. That time he rang and he wanted to speak to me, remember?'

Meriç gave a terse nod.

'I told him I thought it was Annie's, but then she'd obviously said it was mine, so I said my nephew had probably left it.'

'Corder bought that, did he?'

'He seemed to, but I can't remember seeing it again so he probably took it anyway.'

'You two! Here!'

Meriç spun to face Mrs Peters who had her hand raised. Automatic subservience to someone in the guise of customer had them both return to the table, but Meriç met her eye with a hard look.

'Enough with the games,' she said and pointed at Yağız. 'You need to get back to your flat and find that tablet if it's still there. How far is it? How long will it take?'

He and Yağız stared at each other. How had she heard them?

Meriç swallowed an irate response. There was an urgency behind her words that seemed to supersede other considerations, at least for now. 'All right,' he said, jerking his thumb towards the door. 'Go on, but be quick.'

'I don't even know if it's there.'

'Max Corder doesn't nick tablets from kids,' Mrs Peters said. 'And if he hadn't bought your story, you'd have known about it. Either Annie took it with her or it's still there. I need to know which.'

Meriç felt the weight of his bottom jaw. Annie's boss, Mrs Peters, knew his major investor, Max Corder. What was he to make of that? So much for employing someone from far away so that Corder wouldn't get wind of it. He began to wonder if he'd been set up from the start.

Yağız hadn't moved. Still that uneasy fidgeting. 'Well, go on,' he urged. 'Don't be all day.'

Yağız looked from one to the other of them. 'There's something else.'

They both watched as he reached forward and pointed to the one photograph that showed a clear shot of its subject's features. 'I've seen him before. Tuesday morning when I left the flat. There was a big limousine thing parked up, out of place in our area … darkened windows … He was leaning on its bonnet, smoking.'

Chapter 41

From putting on an angry front but feeling satisfied with the world, Meriç's mood flipped. The anger was real now, but in danger of being overwhelmed by trepidation. He felt something approaching dread for the woman who sat at the table cradling her coffee. Was she human or some kind of robot? No one could have heard that whispered exchange with Yağız.

'I'm worried about Annie too,' he told her, 'but that doesn't mean you can come in here and order my staff about. I've a business to run.'

She rested her gaze on him for a moment as she lifted the cup to her lips. Her expression told him nothing but he felt foolish anyway. He had already allowed her to order his head waiter off the premises in the run up to opening. 'If Annie took the tablet from that man's flat ...' She paused. 'Are they having some kind of thing, by the way, Annie and that waiter?'

Meriç shrugged. 'I understand she had nowhere else to go.'

Mrs Peters rolled her eyes. 'Annie and her paranoia. Anyway, if she took the tablet with her, then she left without Corder. If it's still there then she went with him. I need to know. How long'll he be?'

Meriç thought quarter of an hour but said, 'Twenty minutes.' He wasn't sure why he'd added the extra time but again it felt like something Annie might have done. Maybe he was trying to buy himself a few minutes. 'I've things to see to in the office,' he said rising.

The quarter hour had ticked away when Mrs Peters called him back to the dining room.

'I'll need to know where your overseas stock comes in, what's the route … I assume Corder's outfit sees to the shipping and so on.'

Meriç sat down opposite her. He didn't want to discuss Max Corder with this woman. She was fishing, using stuff Annie had passed on. 'I don't get involved in that side. It's all delivered. It's not just this place. He has a whole network.'

'Hmm …' For a moment her gaze lost focus.

He watched her hand, still gloved, resting on her phone where it lay on the table. A thought struck him. Once again he felt Annie Raymond's influence shaping the way he looked at things. She'd been a more useful person to have around than he'd realised. He'd been right to think about keeping her on.

Annie's boss was as human as he was. He recalled the way she'd ushered him and Yağız away when Yağız had wanted to talk; her outstretched hand inviting them to go and talk in private.

It seemed an audacious move to try to fool this woman, but she was in his restaurant calling the shots and he didn't like it. Without giving himself time to think, he sat up with a start and half-turned to towards the kitchen. 'Who's that coming in at this time?' He injected worry into his tone and made as though to rise.

As he gained his feet he twisted round letting the movement take him back where he'd started, in the chair facing her. 'Oh well,' he said. 'They'll sort it out.'

He thought her eyes narrowed a little, but he didn't think she'd guessed. Distraction and diversion were what this was all about. She'd invited them to go and talk in the middle of the dining room, and they'd followed her misdirection like sheep, putting themselves under Annie Raymond's hidden camera and microphone.

Her hand covered her phone as she clicked off the screen, but he'd caught a glimpse as he'd spun round. She had a feed to his surveillance cameras right there on her handset.

He was on the point of saying something, but then Yağız

reappeared, slightly breathless, a computer tablet under his arm. 'Here.' He passed it to Meriç. 'It had been chucked in amongst the magazines.'

Mrs Peters pulled it out of his hand and flipped open the lid.

'It's locked,' Yağız said.

She gave no sign she'd heard him, just pressed buttons and played her fingers across the keyboard. They both saw the screen flare to life before she snapped it shut again.

'Shouldn't we look at it?' Meriç asked, aware of Yağız still at his elbow.

'No,' she said. 'It should go straight to the police.'

No one was that uncurious. 'Get through there,' he ordered Yağız. 'Make sure we're ready.' And as Yağız retreated, he hissed at Mrs Peters, 'You've seen it, haven't you? The lost footage from my cameras.'

She neither admitted nor denied it, saying again, 'I need to find out where Annie is. If she's got herself the wrong side of Corder … well … I suppose she wasn't to know.'

'Know what?'

'Where does Corder hang out around here? Where does he stash his … no, you wouldn't know. Who would know? Who can tell us where we need to look?'

'Shouldn't we see about getting that footage to the police?' Two could play the game of ignoring the other's line of discussion.

'They'll get it,' she snapped. 'Now who would know where to look for Corder? I don't mean Corder himself. I can contact him any time. I mean someone who knows his haunts, knows where he does business, knows where he goes to ground. Come on, Meriç, think. We need to shortcut this. I've a feeling time is tight.'

'Carol,' he told her coldly. 'She would have known; she was one of Corder's. Oh, wait a minute … there's always the boy Annie fired. A phone call will get him in.'

'Then get to it! Wait … tell him to arrive by the back way … and make him hurry. We need to know where we're going before he gets here.'

'Before who gets here, the boy? And who's going where?'

'No, Max Corder. You, me and Corder are going for a ride together, but I need to know where to. He sure as hell won't tell us.'

'Max is on his way here?' Meriç's gaze snapped towards the door. He didn't need a row with Corder, not just now with all this going on. Thank heaven he'd had that deep clean done. It had been in his mind not to bother.

'Not yet,' Mrs Peters said, still fiddling with her phone. 'Go and get that boy to come in. Do whatever it takes to make him rush, but I don't want him in here. We'll meet him in the alleyway. Can you set someone to watch out so we don't miss him?'

'We'll see him arrive from here, and he knows to go round the back.'

She turned her full attention to her handset.

They'd be opening soon.

He left her and went behind the bar to make the call. Corder hadn't yet been on to him to have the boy taken back, but he would be. It chafed to reinstate a bad worker but he might as well anticipate the inevitable. The phone was answered at once and he snapped into it, irritability getting the better of him, as his attention focussed on his unwelcome guest at the table by the door.

It didn't register until he'd returned the receiver to its rest that the boy had sounded uncharacteristically grateful. Maybe Uncle Max hadn't intended playing ball this time.

Yağız bustled through, pointing one of the servers to remove the empty cups from in front of Mrs Peters. He met Meriç's eye, a brief unspoken question. Meriç tipped his head towards the door. Yes, open up now.

Bolts drawn back, blinds up, sign flipped. Extra light flooded the place as Yağız adjusted the window screens.

For a few minutes, the emptiness of the place felt inviolable.

It was a familiar feeling. He'd experienced it every single day since he'd opened his first café. Today would be the day when no customers crossed the threshold, zero. In all the years he'd been in business, the nightmare had never materialised and he recognised the irony that today was the one time when he hoped it might.

The first few through the door were nonentities, hurrying to the bar for drinks to go.

'How long'll that boy be?' It was the first thing Mrs Peters had said for a while.

'There's a bus comes by about five past. He'll be on that.'

'Don't miss him.' And she went back to her phone.

He was aware of a group approaching the door and his heart sank. This was not the day for idle gossip with his regulars. And they were earlier than usual. Mrs Peters glanced at him as he stood to greet them. What else could he do?

In the jumble of smiles and how-are-yous, he caught that they too had noted the early hour but, 'Cari and Ayaan insisted.'

'You didn't have to come with us, Dad.' Cari's voice held an undertone of exasperation.

Then unexpectedly, Mrs Peters was in the conversation. 'Sergeant Ahmed, thanks for coming,' she said, offering her still gloved hand in a brief handshake.

'Mrs Peters, I assume.' His voice had a hard edge. 'We've only ever spoken by phone.'

'Well well, you two know each other, do you?' Meriç felt the inanity of his words as they came out. Of course they knew each other. Annie had told him that. He found himself tongue-tied. The only conversational route from here led to Annie and some past case in York, neither of which he wanted to mention in front of Ahmed's in-laws.

Mrs Peters turned to him. 'Is that the bus?'

'Yes.' He saw the double-decker turn in at the end of the street.

'Waiter!' Mrs Peters called out, raising her hand to summon

Yağız. 'Coffees, whatever … all round.' She turned to Ahmed, pushed the tablet at him. 'Annie's surveillance footage is on there. I've unlocked it. And I've some intel on your target, but we're going to have to act fast. Give me a couple of minutes.'

'Hey, give the boy a break.' Ahmed's father-in-law spoke easily. 'He's enjoying a holiday with his new family. He's not here to work.'

'That might the official line,' she snapped back. 'But he's actually here as liaison with a team after a guy called Corder. Meriç and I are about to get the info that could prevent something very nasty. You'll need one of your colleagues on standby, Sergeant Ahmed. Come on, Meriç.'

She grabbed his arm as she strode away, leaving him with no choice but to hurry after her if he didn't want it obvious that he was physically being dragged.

Anger began to burn inside him. He'd seen hurt betrayal on his old friend's face; he'd had no idea of his son-in-law's covert role. Cari's expression on the other hand had betrayed to the whole group that she'd known all along. In that one curt speech Mrs Peters had sown seeds of mistrust that might flourish for years.

Chapter 42

Meriç shivered as the breeze from the estuary cut through the inadequate cloth of his coat. A bleak industrial landscape, several big warehouses ranged around them. All focus was on the one directly ahead, its doors still sealed from recent fumigation.

He glanced uneasily at Max Corder who was muttering into his phone, his body language surreptitious, curved away from the car Ayaan Ahmed had just returned to. 'Stick to Corder like glue,' Mrs Peters had told him. 'He needs to keep up the front while you're around.'

It wasn't clear to him how she'd persuaded Corder to drive out here with her. From the little he'd heard of the call, she'd got him to the restaurant with a mix of threat and promise. Ahmed and his new family had left by then; hadn't stayed for the drinks Mrs Peters had ordered for them, but had swept out in a flurry of low-voiced recriminations leaving Meriç to wonder if he'd ever see any of them again.

Whatever story Mrs Peters had used to coax Corder into her car, it had worn thin long before Ahmed turned up with a colleague on this austere industrial site.

Meriç felt annoyed with himself. If he'd had the least bit of gumption, he'd have left her to drive away with Corder. There had to have been a limit to how forcefully she was prepared to order him into the car, because at that point she'd still been putting on a front for Corder. The fact was, though, that she'd not needed force. He wasn't going to argue with her, not after what had happened in the alleyway behind the restaurant.

The boy had put on a swagger as he'd rounded the turn that hid the road from view and seen both Meriç and Mrs Peters standing by the trash bins.

'Don't let anyone out of that door,' she'd murmured as she stepped forward.

The memory sent a fresh shiver through him and he glanced around.

Corder had spoken to him just once since they'd arrived, had pulled him aside. 'Ah, Meriç, my friend.' Nothing outside the raw words gave a hint of bonhomie. Voice lowered, 'That deep clean. Is it done?'

'Last night.'

The grasp on his arm had slackened in what Meriç read as an expression of relief. A nasty possibility was beginning to push itself forward. Yağız was in charge back at the restaurant. If need be, he could ring ... tell him to get everyone out, to close up. Better for people to see shuttered doors than hear scandal.

He wondered where Mrs Peters had disappeared to. Ahmed had been furious with her and no wonder. Meriç too had felt a rush of anger at the way she'd deliberately wrong-footed everyone; from her terse comments to Yağız, making clear she'd overheard their conversation, to the way she'd spilt the detective Ahmed's secrets for all to hear. And then she'd slammed that boy against the wall of the alley, the flash of something at his neck that Meriç had deliberately looked away from.

Now, as he stood in the chill breeze with only Corder nearby, Meriç saw her actions differently. It was foolish for someone in her position to broadcast her secrets. She could have been subtle. Mrs Peters was in a hurry ... more than that, she was in a panic. Whatever she was after, she thought she was too late.

A man and a woman wearing holster-pocket trousers and branded tabards strode towards Ahmed's car. Meriç sidestepped to be within hearing distance.

He had already gathered that the big warehouse up ahead had been undergoing fumigation and there was some query over when it could be opened up; something about a mistake in the mix.

'It should have the full extra twenty-four hours,' he heard someone say.

'We need to see what's in there,' Ahmed said. 'We must be to time by now and you've got protective gear, haven't you?'

'Bloody foolish venture, if you ask me.' Meriç jumped. Corder had moved close enough to mutter the words without the group by the car hearing them. 'I don't know what they think they'll find.'

He looked into Corder's face but didn't reply. Behind the façade he could see the worry. Corder knew exactly what they thought they would find and was desperate not to be here. Mrs Peters' initial move had seemed random but he was learning she did nothing by chance, and she'd manoeuvred them into an awkward spot for a discreet withdrawal. Presumably that was part of why she'd told him to stick with Corder. The problem was that Corder was on the brink of asking for help and Meriç knew better than to say no to him. He had to find a diversion, daren't let Corder ask the question, because it wasn't rocket science to work out what everyone had avoided putting into words. No one had seen Annie for two days; the exact length of time that warehouse had been sealed.

He stepped closer to Ahmed and the warehouse workers. The closer he was to them, the less chance Corder would risk propositioning him.

Ahmed looked round. 'Mr Corder, would you mind …?' Ahmed's tone was pleasant and slightly deferential as he called Corder over; an officer of the law addressing a pillar of the local community. 'I understood you had space in that warehouse.'

'No, sergeant,' Corder replied striding forward. 'You've been misinformed. On several counts, I imagine.'

The place began to bustle as more people appeared, some in heavy protective clothing, homing in on the warehouse doors.

Meriç saw Ahmed frown at a sheaf of paperwork in his hand as he leant to check the screen of a PowerScan inventory device held by one of his companions. Whatever he'd expected to find in the records wasn't there.

There was a light touch on his arm and Mrs Peters was beside him. 'They're not finding Corder in there,' she said as she drew him away from the group by the car. 'He has no goods stored; hasn't had for years. Was that kid on the level?'

He looked at her coldly. 'Believe me, that *kid* told you everything he knew about Max Corder. And anyway, if you really think that he's … that they're going to find … that … well why would he use a place with his name all over the paperwork?'

'He's done it before. The kid knew about it.' They both spun to stare at the sound of a door swinging open. The seal had been broken. Heavily garbed figures were disappearing inside.

'What do you mean, he's done it before?'

'You heard how many deaths there've been in that place over the past ten years.'

'They said accidents.' As the words left his mouth he knew what sort of look she would give him. It was on the tip of his tongue to tell her about Corder demanding that deep clean. Instead he said, 'He won't stick around, you know. If it's true, they need to arrest him now. Why don't they?'

'I know.' Her own glance mirrored his concern as it flicked towards Corder. 'But there's nothing to link him. They've just pulled the CCTV. His car came in a couple of days ago but way over the other side, nowhere near here.'

Meriç looked at the cameras high on poles by the warehouse entrance. 'Nothing on those?'

'Zilch. Normal traffic in and out, vehicles and people. At the time they can track Corder on the site, he stayed the other end, did some routine business in one of the offices over there, then he left.'

'This fumigation business …?' He let the query trail away.

'Not ordered by him,' she said. 'Some kind of rat infestation that needed to be cleared pronto. The paperwork's messed up, not up to date. That's hardly unusual in this sort of set-up.'

'So it might be nothing to do with him.'

'Of course, it's him,' she snapped. 'I thought he'd acted on the spur of the moment, cut corners. But it looks like I was wrong. Only if it was pre-planned … that means … but why? I thought he'd use her for a bargaining chip. I never thought …'

She was talking more to herself than to him now. He took in a breath, almost spoke but then held back. The activity up by the big warehouse was taking on a more intense air; more people, more commotion.

He heard Corder's voice, measured, conversational. 'I'm happy to help officer, but I have businesses to run. You have my number. You can always call me back if you need me.'

He felt Mrs Peters tense.

'Yes, of course,' Ahmed said smoothly. 'I won't be long. I see they've opened the place now. Give me a minute or two and I'll give you a ride back to town.'

'He doesn't want to stay, does he?' Mrs Peters murmured.

'No,' said Meriç, 'and he's been on his phone. He'll have called someone to come and collect him.'

She turned her gaze in the direction of the main road access, out of sight from here. 'They can stop cars getting down this far. They just need long enough to find a reason to hold him. I was hoping the paperwork would do that.'

'Meanwhile, he can just walk out and no one can stop him.'

'He'll keep up the pretence as long as he can,' she said. 'He doesn't want to burn any bridges.'

Meriç kept one eye on the comings and goings at the warehouse entrance. After a few minutes, Corder wandered away from Ahmed and came closer. Mrs Peters stepped away.

'Damned waste of time,' murmured Corder to Meriç. 'I need to be elsewhere and I'm sure you do, too.'

'I'm stuck until someone gives me a lift,' Meriç said. 'It didn't occur to me to bring my own car.'

'And it's bloody freezing. I didn't dress for this.'

Meriç nodded. He could agree on that point.

Corder gave him a speculative look and started to speak, but then Mrs Peters stepped closer to join the conversation. Corder gave her a glare and turned away.

Meriç thought he could track Corder's line of thought and his intended escape route. It was easy enough to stop vehicles getting down here if they put someone on the main gate, but harder to stop people walking out. Corder's glances towards the nearby buildings gave him away. He would draw Meriç with him so far, on the pretext of finding shelter in the lee of one of the smaller huts. From there it wouldn't be hard to manoeuvre himself out of Ahmed's line of sight, leaving Meriç as the decoy. Then he would simply walk off between the buildings and rendezvous with his associate who was probably up by the main road.

How long did it take to search a warehouse?

Corder meandered away, pulling a handkerchief from his pocket and coughing into it. He had his back to them. Meriç was fairly sure he was talking into his phone again.

'Another ten minutes should do it,' murmured Mrs Peters.

Meriç thought they would be hard-pressed to keep Corder tied down that long.

For a while they stood in silence. Corder's mini-coughing fit took him a little further, nearer to the shelter of that wall. Meriç wasn't sure that Mrs Peters had noticed. Her stare was on the warehouse entrance and had intensified as someone rushed out pulling their face mask aside, revealing the features of a young woman who gesticulated wildly, pointing back to the interior. Two or three others fell into a huddle with her, their glances shooting towards where Ahmed and his colleague stood. Ahmed too was watching intently, taking a step forward, breaking into a jog and he headed for the group.

Meriç, with Mrs Peters at one side and Corder not far away on the other, felt himself trapped between two irrationally violent people. How had it come to this? He wouldn't admit it openly but he would be relieved if Corder disappeared. He didn't want to be in the thick of a suddenly-exploding crisis. They could always go and find the man again, arrest him quietly without making a song and dance.

His attention too was caught by the unfolding drama. He swallowed against a suddenly dry throat. Ahmed was with the group. They were pointing. The woman who'd torn off her face mask was crying.

'This fumigation business,' he said to Mrs Peters. 'Corder ordered something similar at the restaurant. He demanded we steam clean of the back of house.'

'What?' She jumped as though stung. 'When? Have you had it done?'

He nodded. 'Overnight.'

She closed her eyes for a second and let out a sigh.

'It doesn't matter, does it?' he said. 'The police have Annie's computer device.' He paused, but he had to know. Ahmed was coming back towards them. 'What did you see? What was on the footage?'

She gave him a bleak look. 'Not enough. Not if you've had the place deep cleaned. Well?' This last was to Ahmed, who was hurrying towards them.

'Cats,' Ahmed said. 'They're supposed to chase the cats out before they seal the warehouse. It wasn't done this time.'

'Sod cats,' Mrs Peters snapped. 'Did they find … what else did they find?'

'Nothing so far. It'll take time to get in every corner. It's a big place. But so far no sign. I'm going to have to let–' He looked around as he spoke, stopping abruptly. 'Where's Corder?'

'He was over there I think.' It felt to Meriç as though the words popped out with no conscious thought from him. He saw the line of his pointing finger, saw both Mrs Peters and Ahmed turn trustingly to follow his misdirection. Corder's network reached too far and too fast. Much as he wanted to see the man's power base broken, he didn't want to be part of his destruction.

Chapter 43

Maximilian Corder scrambled through the mud between the buildings. His target was the perimeter fence where it was least visible from the centre of the site. Everything was in place; had been for years. But if they found her body before he got away … no, it wouldn't happen. They had nothing. If they arrested him, he'd get bailed, and that was all he needed. The spectre of incarceration loomed; his meticulously planned route within sight but out of reach.

Thank God for her own feeble escape attempt. Otherwise he'd have had her chucked off the walkway and she'd have been right there in plain view when the doors opened. Sweat trickled down his neck. For all the cold of the day, he felt hot, enclosed. Checking the lie of the land, he crossed a pathway and ducked behind another shed. Where was she? What had she done? Once the process started, she'd have found the gas vents and got herself as far away from them as possible. She might be curled up under a rack right in the middle of the place. It could take days to find her.

Maybe they'd stop looking. What evidence did they have that there was anything to find? Mrs Peters' random accusations? She was hardly a reliable witness. Was there time to sow the seed of some feud between himself and her? And another between her and Annie Raymond? Paint her as a time waster?

His problem was that they would find her eventually, even if it was some punter unearthing her rotting remains when he went to collect his gear. And because of Mrs Peters they would shine a spotlight on him.

There should be nothing in the warehouse to tie down to him; the restaurant had been deep cleaned; so had the car. Even so, he couldn't feel secure. That little bitch had set up CCTV inside Meriç's place.

The Peters woman thought she'd cornered him, but she'd chosen badly. He knew every blade of grass on this site. He cut between two small buildings and veered off to the grassy slope that rose up to a line of shrubs and the high security fence. A flash of light on metal betrayed the location of the biker tucked in the scrub beyond the wire.

Corder gave a low whistle as he pulled his phone out of his pocket. The figure eased into view, showing the blank silver sheen of a full face helmet. It scanned the site behind him, then gave a quick nod. Corder angled his arm and threw the phone. It arced high over the wire. The biker sidestepped and reached out, catching it easily in one hand, then lifted his bike free of the bushes and disappeared.

Corder slithered down the slope to the cover of the buildings, stopping just once, easing himself next to one of the power hub connectors. It caught the light when seen from the forecourt. Anyone standing next to it was invisible from down there.

He knew he was right, but felt his breathing elevate as he stood up straight. A calculated risk.

There they were, Meriç looking uncomfortable. Mrs Peters gabbling on at him. The policeman Ahmed heading towards them from the warehouse entrance. He glanced towards the scene of the crime and read distress in the body language of the group by the door. Shit, they must have found her.

And there was Ahmed spinning round, his line of sight too low, but Corder had to grab at every ounce of self-control not to duck down. A sudden move could be fatal.

Meriç pointed the other way. They all turned to look.

The man was far enough out of his depth to be thoroughly

confused, and maybe he genuinely believed that was where Corder had gone. But it was almost as though Meriç was covering for him. The thought disturbed him. Why would Meriç do that unless he knew way more than he should?

No time to puzzle it out. He set off again. One more corner, one more pause to check no one was in sight, and he strode to a padlocked door, clicking in the codes, then punching in the lock sequences – one lock, then the second, then the third. It took time but the only other way in was to open the big garage at the back, and that might draw notice. The morning light vanished as he slipped inside and pulled the door closed behind him. The air held the chill of winter. He fumbled to reset the locks; too risky to use the lights in this space. Once satisfied he was locked in, he felt his way across to the inner door.

The key codes came easily to his fingers. Again he slipped through the gap, closed himself in and reset the lock. The dark was total now, no windows, no outside walls. He clicked the switch, blinked in the flood of light, and moved to the control panel to deactivate the alarms and movement sensors.

With the inner sanctum sealed against the world, it could be any time of day or night. Corder glanced at a wall clock. He'd always hated the insecurity of not knowing where and when he was.

The movement sensors wouldn't summon anyone untoward, but he didn't need people rushing down here thinking the place had been broken into, drawing attention to it.

His hand hovered, momentarily confused. Focus. Concentrate. Had he flipped the switch or hadn't he? Either his fingers had walked through the familiar sequence without conscious thought, or the last person out had forgotten to set it.

He let a spark of anger ignite as a useful antidote to the tension. This wasn't the time for careless mistakes.

Consciously taking in a couple of deep breaths, he allowed himself to relax. He might be holed up within a stone's throw of the drama at the warehouse, practically on hand for when they dragged out Raymond's body, but no one knew. If they tracked his phone they would find it on its way back to his office in town. It was tempting to think he might even brazen this out. What did they have to link him to anything? Annie Raymond's restaurant footage was the curveball, and she would have had time to scribble a note once she knew she wasn't getting out. Mrs Peters' interference meant he hadn't been able to control who had gone in first. That didn't mean he might not get lucky. There were several people who would discreetly dispose of a note on a body, for all sorts of reasons.

Meriç had had the restaurant cleaned. He'd ordered the car to be done too, and that was something he could check.

Access from the central hub led to the workshop, where he didn't flick the switch for the fluorescent tubes, just left the door wide to allow in enough ambient light. Not that this space led directly to the outside but there was a small skylight high in the roof. The sudden blaze of light from an empty building might be noticed. Hard to imagine they'd called in aerial support, but you never knew.

The car sat shrouded in heavy-duty plastic sheeting. He lifted one corner and clicked open a door. The smell of recent chemical cleaning was unmistakeable. He wrinkled his nose and drew back, satisfied. The sort of forensic examination that would get any trace from this vehicle had to be way outside anyone's official budget. And anyway, the moment it could be unobtrusively moved, the car would be on its way to a new home overseas.

He walked right round the vehicle, stumbling in the dim light over something lying by the exit. Kicking it aside with a curse, he saw light gleam on the polished metal of a wrench as it clattered against the wall. A crisp packet rolled lazily across the floor. Corder noted these small slip-ups with distaste. The whole place needed tidying. Someone had been getting too comfortable in here, helping themselves to things that weren't theirs. He could see his driver – and it could only be him – bringing the car into the inner workshop, closing the doors, then sitting back for a leisurely break before getting on with his job.

On impulse he reached out to pick a plastic cup from a shelf. One sniff was all he needed. The bastard had been at his good malt. This place was a bolthole, rarely used for more than car repairs, but always ready. That was a problem with employing people with no vision, no thought for the future. They took advantage, shortcuts.

But now was not the time to distract anyone with reprimands. He had larger fish to fry.

At last, the sound he'd been waiting for. A discreet buzz signalled the phone ringing in the inner-office. He returned to the central hub, flipped the switch that opened the keypad and punched in the code. He didn't hurry, and moved around the desk to sit down before reaching for the receiver.

'Well?'

'They brought dogs in.'

He tensed. 'Dogs?'

Could dogs follow his trail?

'Yeah, to shortcut the search of the warehouse.'

Yes, of course, the warehouse. Not him.

'But won't that … that stuff, whatever it's called, confuse any scent they try to follow?'

'Yeah, that's right. I hadn't thought of that.' The voice broke into a laugh. 'That'll explain why they've called off the search.'

'They've called it off? That quickly?'

'Well now, this is surmise you understand, but we're thinking the copper's decided he's been duped by the Peters woman, or she's got it wrong or whatever, so now they're not expecting to find anything. So they get the dogs in to do a quick sweep. And if the body's somewhere inaccessible, out of sight, and they've not caught the scent anyway because of the other stuff. Game, set and match.'

'For now. She's going to be found eventually, and then they'll be back. Maybe I should have stayed.'

'No, too risky. That copper Ahmed's already rung your phone.'

'When? What did he say?'

'Don't worry, it all went like clockwork. You'd diverted your phone while you were out at a meeting. He says that he is your meeting and you've left. So we say that you'll be on your way to the office for your eleven-thirty. He didn't ask you to ring back.'

'Don't get comfortable. We've dodged a bullet here, and we're not waiting around for anyone to reload.' He thought about the warehouse, about the body that must be in there somewhere. It was human nature to hide. The gas vents were at the perimeter. Once she was out of other options she'd have retreated to the middle of the place, tried to find clean air, climbing higher and higher. Probably the topmost rack in the very middle of the place was where to look.

'Have they gone?'

'Ahmed's gone. Peters and the restaurant owner had a bit of a row, then he set off walking, and she went and got her car and picked him up. They're all off site.'

'Get someone down to the reception, side car park, right now. I'll be there in five minutes.'

Having replaced the phone on its rest, Corder strode to a corner cupboard, selecting a pair of brown overalls and a cap that sprouted its own scraps of hair. He stepped into the overalls and pulled on the cap. After a quick glance in the mirror, he added a pair of glasses, thick frames, empty of lenses. It was hardly robust but it didn't need to be. It was to cater for anyone who glimpsed him or any CCTV that caught him on the way to the car park and freedom.

He shut the door to the inner office, rattled the handle to make sure it had locked itself, then opened the control panel to activate the alarm and movement sensors. The machine began to beep the twenty seconds it allowed for him to get clear before it classified him as an intruder.

Inner door shut. Locked.

Six strides to the outer door.

Easing it open cautiously he checked to make sure no one was nearby, then slipped through into the cold brightness of midday. Reset the locks … click home the padlocks.

Tucking down his head, he made for the car park.

Behind him, within the inner hub, a hand reached out to open the control panel, to flip the switches back and deactivate the alarm.

Annie stretched out the cramp from where she'd crouched in the maintenance cupboard, and looked around. Still trapped in this windowless series of rooms. She'd already investigated every possible escape route, including taking a wrench to the big doors of the echoing workshop where the car was parked. But now she had the key code to that other heavy door, the one she'd thought was a safe, and she knew there was a phone inside.

Chapter 44

'Your mate looks pissed off,' said Yağız, as he set food in front of Annie.

The plate was heaped beyond standard portion size. They all assumed she was starved after her two-day ordeal and had tutted sympathetically over Ahmed and his colleagues keeping her so long after they'd extracted her. She didn't put them right. Proper food was welcome. A diet of crisps, biscuits and fizzy canned drinks had been monotonous but she'd weathered worse.

She followed the line of Yağız's gaze to where Pieternel had walked away to take a call. She gave him a smile, not so much for the food, but for the fact he'd referred to Pieternel as her mate and not her boss. Not that he knew any better but it made a refreshing change.

Pieternel's feathers were ruffled. And serve her right, Annie thought as she stacked her fork. The first thing Pieternel had said to her had been, 'Why didn't you ring *me*?'

'I'd no idea if I'd triggered an alarm going in that inner room,' Annie had responded. 'And you've not been answering your phone.'

'But Pat Thompson of all people!'

Pieternel had let it lie and Annie wondered if she guessed how much of the truth had come out since they'd last sat face to face.

She'd learnt a lot, most of it in that first uncomfortable ten minutes.

'I followed him by keeping close to the floor,' she'd told Ahmed and his colleague, explaining about the automatic lights. 'On the way in, we'd driven up a steep hill, stopped for a while then carried on – it felt like a different surface. I thought we'd gone off-road. Then after a while we stopped again, and the car reversed down a slope. Then there was a lot of fast driving and skidding about, just to disorientate me.'

'His car came on to the site,' Ahmed had told her. 'But over the other end, nowhere near the warehouse.'

'That's where you're wrong. Corder's been pulling this trick for years. I'll bet he's never been seen in or around that warehouse.' She'd thought of the play-acting in Yağız's flat. No wonder they'd all been so jumpy when he started talking about the place. They knew he wasn't after reeling her into their operation; he'd got the taste of blood and saw her as a loose end to be tied – as well as a message to Pieternel.

'That steep slope,' she told Ahmed. 'They drove the car into the back of a truck. I'll bet you have the truck on the cameras. That's why it felt like a different surface. It was the lorry that was moving not the car.'

'And you hid in the lorry to get out?'

She'd had to suppress a shudder as she'd remembered the sequence of events. Half-blinded by dust and cobwebs, things crawling against her skin, she'd despaired of keeping up with Corder, but had scrambled from one rack to the next. 'I thought I'd lost him,' she said. 'Thought he'd got too far ahead of me, but then it all changed.' She'd been within a whisper of slithering out into the open, thinking she was heading for another set of shelving. 'It was a wide open space,' she told Ahmed. 'I suppose a loading bay or something, and there was this tall lorry. I didn't realise straight away. Then someone called out. It was the driver, the third man. He sounded impatient. Corder marched off round the front of the truck. I just took my chance.'

Corder's move had lit up the area. Annie had pulled herself free and raced for the cover of the vehicle.

'The car?' Ahmed had asked.

'I wasn't thinking about the car. I went to the back of the truck, keeping low in case anyone was in the cab … mirrors. The ramp was down and there was the car inside. I didn't have time to think. I was inside and there was nowhere to go. My only choices were in the car or under it.'

Annie re-lived the way her mind had raced. Touch the car door and an alarm might shriek. Slip underneath and be a rat in a trap when they backed off. But underneath had seemed the best bet. She had imagined lying stock still, face down, as the vehicle backed off; timing her move to slide to a corner as the wheels hit the steep ramp and the headlights tipped upward. Maybe the shadow would be deep enough if she could find the right spot.

Then she'd seen that one of the doors was ajar. It wasn't locked, wasn't alarmed.

'It's a big car, but three of them were going to get in. There was nowhere to hide except …'

'The boot?' Ahmed supplied.

She nodded. It was simple enough to say. She'd been trapped in a car boot once before, some years ago. Memories of a horrific ride, being battered from all sides had made her pause, made her think again about risking the floor of the lorry and praying that the shadows would be kind.

'Yes,' she said. 'It was the only option.'

Ahmed shook his head. 'And after all that they took you to a building practically next door. Did you realise how close you were to where you'd started?'

'I knew it hadn't been a long journey, but it's not easy to judge when you're crouched in a car boot.'

She'd held back the detail. The journey had been smooth enough, the truck doing the work, not the car. Their voices had been clear, Corder and sallow-features arguing the toss about how much trouble Corder had made for them by leaving her in the warehouse. He seemed to think none at all; just a case of making sure the right people found her and cleared up any untoward evidence. Then they'd talked about Pieternel, referring to her by the only alias they knew, Mrs Peters. Corder had been courting her network for a long time. And Pieternel had been stringing him along as she always did, checking to see what was in it for her before she tossed him aside. She must have had her eye on several of Corder's assets, and it seemed as though Corder had cottoned on. They'd been playing each other at the same game.

For a while Annie had wondered if Pieternel had sent her to Hull as bait for Corder, but she didn't think it had been quite that deliberate. It was clear Pieternel had wanted her out of the way for a few weeks, and had seen the job in Hull with its link to Corder as a happy coincidence.

'I was curious how he'd react,' Pieternel had admitted. 'But I swear, Annie, I had no idea he'd go after you the way he did.'

On balance Annie believed her, but it didn't alter the fact that Pieternel could have acted sooner and faster. And could have been more open from the start.

The experience at the warehouse would play out in her head, but she would get past it; she'd got past worse than this and come out unscathed. The difference was that this time she had options.

'Eat while it's hot.'

It was Yağız's voice. He was watching her, his expression both concerned and curious. He barely knew half the story. She tapped the seat beside her. 'Sit down.' When he hesitated, she added, 'The place is closed. Meriç isn't going to mind.'

'OK.'

'While I eat, tell me what happened here. How come we have a new chef? I thought the chef might have gone but ...'

The restaurant was closed. Other than Yağız and the new guy, everyone had been sent home. The small group still on the premises couldn't help but be aware of the forensic team's activity in the walk-in.

'Don't worry about that.' Yağız dismissed her concern. 'But why are they in there? You know what happened, don't you?'

'Yes, but I've been told to keep my mouth shut. That's why I don't think it's a good idea to have someone so new–'

'He's not new. I mean not to Meriç. He'll be chef at the second restaurant. Meriç brought him in here to keep an eye on things for a couple of days before he fired our chef. He told me all about it, what you'd found out. Why didn't you tell me? Did you think I was involved?'

Annie shrugged. 'I didn't know what to think.' She hadn't asked Yağız to sit down and talk just as a snub to Pieternel. She wanted someone to bring her up to speed. What had Meriç said to whom? It seemed that he'd kept quiet about her undercover role, but what about her new role? 'About the second restaurant …' she began.

Yağız gave her a smile. 'Meriç told me. It'll be good to have you on board.'

Annie couldn't help feeling absurdly pleased at this endorsement. Her conversation with Meriç had been fleeting. 'The new place,' he'd said. 'I'd like you on the team. I don't mean as an investigator.'

She'd made sure of the basics, that he knew this was an agreement between her and him; that Pieternel was out of the loop.

'Will the police want to see you again?' he'd asked. 'Only I need you at the new place tomorrow. We must get started.'

'I'm sure they will, but my work for you will take precedence. I'll be there tomorrow.'

'Is it true,' she asked Yağız, 'that this place will be closed for a week?'

He nodded. 'Meriç has let it be known we'll be closed for several days out of respect to Carol. Carol would have laughed at that. I don't know how he'll square it with his wife.'

'What do you mean?'

'There's no way Meriç would close the restaurant for one of us unless there was more than employer-employee going on, if you take my meaning. He doesn't like it but for some reason it's the angle he's going with.'

That meant Meriç knew what had happened back there. She'd assumed so but hadn't been sure. She wondered if Ahmed had told him or if Meriç had guessed. Meriç would find any excuse to avoid it becoming common knowledge, yet it was bound to come out eventually. At Corder's trial, if nothing else. But it was clear that Yağız didn't know that Carol had been killed in the walk-in. Annie wouldn't be the one to tell him. It might be a long time before Corder came in front of a court. They had to catch up with him first.

Pieternel had told Annie about the deep clean. 'There's nothing distinct enough on that footage,' she'd said. 'And now there'll be no forensics.'

'Of course there will,' Annie told her. 'I've seen how they deep clean and I know that walk-in.' She remembered the smears on the wall … the description of Carol's injuries from her neighbour. 'The blood will have seeped through. I can tell them exactly where to take up the floor.' And that's what she assumed they were doing right now.

But everything was low key. Other than Pat Thompson and Ahmed's team, the only people who knew where she was, knew she was alive, were the ones with her now.

She'd asked Ahmed about Corder. He'd been noncommittal at first.

'He's given you the slip, hasn't he?' she'd said.

Ahmed had given her a speculative look. 'Not overtly. He's been in meetings or not answering his phone … no one we speak to is quite sure where he is … a very busy diary apparently.'

'I suppose he doesn't want to declare his hand and do a runner until he really has to,' Annie had said.

'He's waiting to hear that your body's been found. The circumstances of that will dictate his next move.' Ahmed had paused at that point, as though inviting Annie to say more.

'What if he gets to know that my body isn't going to be found? Will that make him feel safe enough to risk showing his face?'

She could see she'd guessed his line of thought, and supposed he wanted to be able to say the suggestion had come from her. 'He'll not show his face anywhere near me,' Ahmed said. 'But …?'

'If I was to contact him, hint at blackmail …?'

'He might agree to meet you but it wouldn't be to congratulate you on your escape.'

Annie had given herself a moment to work through the scenario. Money. A lot of money. A pay off to keep quiet. Corder was loaded. A cash injection was what she needed to start her new life. She could almost persuade herself it was a viable option. And if she could persuade herself, she might persuade him. 'He'd probably send a lackey,' she said. 'And either way, it's a big risk.'

'No one's going to ask you to go and meet him.' Ahmed had sounded shocked. 'But we might get you to make that call. We have a few hours, maybe a day if you keep your head down and no one talks. I'd need time to get a team in place.' She'd seen concern in his expression for budgets and resources.

They'd left things there.

Meriç's snappish tones floated through from the kitchen.

'I hope he's not going to piss off the new guy just because he's in a mood,' Annie said to Yağız.

Yağız laughed. 'He's had to let everyone take a week off on full pay. That's what's hurting him.'

Annie laughed too. 'You'll be taking over here when it re-opens. Does that bother you? I mean would you rather have had the new place?'

'No, no. Better the devil you know.'

Yağız jumped to his feet as Meriç appeared from behind the bar, turning to speak to Pieternel who was just putting away her phone. Annie watched but their voices were too low to make out any words.

It was time to tell Pieternel. She didn't want them to part on bad terms, not after all these years, but events had snowballed. Meriç wanted her to start tomorrow. Her old boss and her new boss were engrossed in a tight-faced conversation over by the bar. Annie hoped Meriç wasn't spilling the beans. She'd asked him not to. Now the phone was ringing. Yağız went to answer it. While she had a moment to herself Annie surrendered to the plate in front of her and savoured the last few mouthfuls.

It was as she leant back, full to bursting, every scrap gone from in front of her, that she realised Yağız was coming towards her holding out the handset.

'Police?' she mouthed.

He shook his head. 'Thompson agency or something.'

She took the phone from him. 'Hi, Pat.'

'It's Barbara.'

The tone sounded as tight-lipped as Pieternel looked. So much for Ahmed's hopes of people keeping quiet. Pat had told Barbara … and Barbara would spread the word to all and sundry probably including the Sleeman clan from where it was a stone's throw to Corder's contacts. She wondered if she should let Ahmed know, see if he wanted her to try this sting on Corder right now … but she felt too tired to bother. And tired she might be, but where in hell was going to feel safe enough to rest her head tonight?

'What can I do for you, Barbara?'

A pause. 'I wondered … we wondered if you'd like to call in to the office this evening.'

Annie felt her eyes open wide. Under what circumstances did Barbara think she would have the least inclination to traipse to their cold uncomfortable office tonight? She bit back a sarcastic response. In less than a day she would no longer be based in London working for Pieternel, she would be based in Hull working for Meriç. And if she wanted to develop the type of working arrangement she planned, she would need people like the Thompsons.

'This evening's difficult,' she said. 'Can you tell me what it's about?'

'Yes, we're offering you work.'

So the Thompsons had netted another random job that they didn't want to do and thought they could palm it off on her. Those days were gone. 'I'm afraid that was just a one-off,' she said, lowering her voice and checking that Pieternel and Meriç were out of earshot. 'And anyway ...' she allowed a bit of real feeling to push aside the professional veneer, '... you haven't got any money to pay me.'

'We have now. We've a new investor who's brought work as well as finance. And I didn't mean a one-off. I meant come and work for us full time. You must be fed up of singing to Mrs Peters' tune. You could be your own boss here. You know the territory.'

It was as though Barbara was reading from a script. She sure as hell didn't want to be saying these things. Maybe she and Pat had tossed a coin over it. 'I'm sorry.' She cut the conversation short. 'I'm going to have to go. I'll ring you back.'

Barbara started to say something else as she clicked off the call. Annie looked round for Yağız to give him back the handset, but it was Pieternel who approached and pulled out a chair.

'I've wound up the job here,' she opened.

Not as far as I'm concerned, thought Annie, but said only, 'Glad to hear it. No problems, were there?'

Pieternel shook her head. 'Uh ... Meriç has told me about the new restaurant, Annie.'

In all it was a relief not to have to broach the subject herself, and Pieternel's tone was mild, perhaps a little shocked.

'Yes, sorry, I wasn't expecting it to happen this quickly. But it's been building for a while and after all that's happened here, I ... I'm sorry, but I'm finding it very hard to trust you these days.'

Pieternel looked down and picked at her nails. 'Tell me the detail, Annie. I'm not sure I've got a clear picture from Meriç. What is it that you're going to do?'

'I'm going to manage his restaurant. To start with. It's a whole new world to focus on. You wouldn't believe what goes on under the surface and someone with my skills has a lot to offer. It's specialist but it's going to be big.'

Pieternel looked perplexed. 'But our business back in London ...?'

'We'll sort something. You'll have to buy me out.'

'On paper, Annie, there's no–'

'I know, I know,' Annie interrupted, annoyed. She'd wanted to rehearse this conversation, not ad-lib it. 'On paper there's nothing to buy out, but you know as well I as I do how much I've invested in this business. I don't just mean money. And I don't care if ...' She checked herself as her voice rose. A row was the worst way to negotiate with Pieternel.

'OK.' Pieternel raised both her hands in surrender. 'Cash settlement for a clean break. I'd better get something drawn up pronto if you're starting your new job tomorrow.'

It took a determined effort to keep her expression in neutral as she tried to read Pieternel. A cash settlement? With so little argument? With intimate knowledge of her partner's skills in these matters she had already resigned herself to walking away with nothing. Did Pieternel have a heart, after all? No, of course not. The answer was right in front of her.

'You've been planning this!' Annie snapped out the accusation, ready to ride roughshod over Pieternel's denial, but it didn't come.

Pieternel just shrugged. 'Seems we've both been planning it, Annie. We both know it's time to part company. If I'd known you felt like this, I'd have come clean with you from the start.'

'Why didn't you?'

'Didn't want the fight, to be honest. I thought if I offered you cash we could part on good terms. We've been a team for a long time. I needed you out of the way to sort stuff out, get new people on board. Frankly, to work out where the business is and where I'm going to take it. You're quite right. There's no money really. But I have plans.'

'Plans that don't include me,' Annie huffed, narrowing her eyes.

'You're too high maintenance, Annie. You always have been. You won't chase down a job with just the money in mind. You always want the truth, the real story.' Pieternel drew in a deep breath. This was territory they'd been over too many times in the past. She reached into her inside pocket and drew out a sheet of paper, slapping it on the table in front of Annie, placing a pen beside it. 'I was going to pretend to nip out and get this drawn up but I brought it with me. The settlement's bigger than it ought to be. I didn't want money getting in the way. I thought it'd be the break that we argued about, but you were right. I should have trusted you to be on the same page. Let's just do it.'

Annie looked at the paper she was being asked to sign. She tried to show no emotion, wanting to gauge whether or not Pieternel expected her to haggle. It wasn't much for all that she'd put in over the years. Thank goodness for Meriç. If she'd been cast adrift with no new berth, she would have had to go cap in hand to the Thompsons as well as volunteer to chop vegetables in someone else's restaurant. Pieternel didn't want the hassle and loose ends of a dispute between them. It wouldn't keep her off the streets for long but it was better than nothing.

'OK,' she said. 'When do I get the money?'

'I'll put it in your bank now.' Pieternel reached for her phone.

Annie picked up the pen and scrawled her signature. She felt an air of urgency without quite being able to pin it down. Pieternel had been worried, unsure when she made the trip whether Annie would be alive to sign anything. Maybe it was conscience money and if she didn't grab the chance, it would evaporate.

'Thanks,' Pieternel said. 'I'll email you a copy. You need to get yourself a phone. Drop me a line. Let me know your new number.' With that she raised her hand briefly as she stood up, tucked the paper in her pocket and made for the door, signalling Yağız to follow and lock it behind her.

Annie stared after her. Was that it? That might be the last time she and Pieternel ever saw each other. A brief wave was the extent of their final leave-taking after all these years. She felt numb.

Better than squabbling like the Thompsons, she supposed. And if things didn't work out with Meriç it looked like she had a job there. She pulled a face at the thought of turning the clock right back to working under the thumb of the Thompsons. It wouldn't come to that.

'Oh hell!' She jumped to her feet, staring at the door, trying to see through the slatted blinds.

The Thompsons! Barbara!

Shock rippled through her. Pat and Barbara had known Pieternel for years.

She was aware of Yağız turning her way, worried, asking, 'What's the matter?'

How had she missed it? Barbara ringing her, not Pat … the ludicrous story of an investor … and when had Barbara ever called Pieternel, Mrs Peters?

'I misjudged Barbara Caldwell,' she said as much to herself as to Yağız. 'She was trying to warn me.'

Chapter 45

'Meriç, I need to borrow your mobile. Quick! It's important.'

Meriç looked surprised, and gestured towards the handset that Yağız still held. 'No, that won't do … uh … please, Meriç. I need to go somewhere and I have to have a phone. I've lost mine.'

'And I don't need to lose mine.' His tone was severe but he seemed to react to the urgency in her voice and pulled it from his pocket.

She snatched it from him, fighting an urge to open it herself. Don't burn bridges. There was a bit of time yet. She held it out. 'Unlock it for me. I have to make a couple of calls. I'll get it back to you, as soon as …' She let her voice fade as he clicked in the code.

Her jaw tightened as she listened to the ring tone, begging silently for them to answer, for it not to be too late; all the time watching the front door, listening for commotion from the back exit.

'Thompsons.'

'Barbara, it's Annie,' she rapped out. 'I've had a change of …' letting the words blur … 'I'll get to you soon after seven, before seven-thirty, OK?'

It took a fraction of a second for Barbara to respond. Long enough for Annie to imagine her voice saying, *Oh, it's too late now …*

'Make it seven. We don't want to be here all night.'

She allowed herself a small sigh of relief, though she couldn't be sure. Thoughts chased through her mind. … *rat in a trap* …

'See you soon.' Before anyone could make a move to stop her, she tucked the phone into her pocket, strode to the door and let herself out.

Gaze darting all around, she marched down the street. Putting distance between herself and the restaurant was priority, but so was her call. She thought she caught sight of Pieternel up ahead. It gave her pause as she was about to punch in Ahmed's number.

Ahmed needed to know, but …

… and on the other hand, would Pieternel answer a call from Meriç's phone?

She did, but her tone was wary.

'What is it, Meriç? I can't–'

'Barbara Caldwell rang me,' Annie interrupted, and raced through a summary of the brief conversation.

'Uh …? Caldwell offered you a job? Oh well, if it doesn't work out with Meriç–'

'No, no,' Annie said impatiently. Pieternel's mind was clearly on other things. 'She called you Mrs Peters.'

'So do a lot of people.'

'Not Barbara Caldwell.'

'So what? She prob– Oh my God!' Now she'd caught on. 'That must mean …?'

'Yes,' said Annie. 'It's Ahmed's sting, but it's Corder who's pulling it. He's heard that I got away, and he's using the Thompsons.'

'Christ! Then you need to get out of that restaurant. He could be on his way.'

'Don't worry, that's why I grabbed Meriç's phone. I'm not far behind you.' She looked ahead at the crowd into which she thought Pieternel's form had blended. Nothing to see now.

'You need to get on to Ahmed, Annie.'

Annie hurried on, dodging the early evening shoppers. 'That was my first thought. But listen, if I tell Ahmed, you know what'll happen. How's he to raise a posse at short notice, even for Corder? They'll send a squad car or something. They'll blow it. We don't even know if it'll be Corder at the Thompsons.'

'So they mess it up. What's it to you?'

'If I'm going to work round here again, I don't want it to be with Corder like a bloody spectre at the feast. It was Vince Sleeman before. I'd like to start with a clean slate.'

'So why have you rung me?' Sudden suspicion flared in the voice in Annie's ear. Annie smiled.

'We can do it. Between us. Last job together. Get Corder properly in the net and then call Ahmed in. That way it sends a better message to Corder's hangers-on.'

'That's a ridiculous risk.'

'Are you saying you're not up to it?'

Pieternel laughed. 'And you wonder why I don't want to work with you anymore. I've got lackeys to do the field work these days.'

'Bollocks,' said Annie rudely. 'You've missed doing this stuff. And you're good at it. You'll never be someone who does the job from behind a desk.'

'Not while you're around.' Pieternel gave an exaggerated sigh. 'You'd better get on to Barbara, hadn't you?'

'Already done. I said I'd be there soon after seven.'

It was a back route to the Thompsons' office, one that Annie had used several times in the past; long enough ago that she'd worried the narrow alleys and derelict gardens might be blocked or redeveloped. Every step evoked memories. The time she'd parked her car out of the way to avoid anyone seeing it outside the sisters' place; another time she'd been with a guy who had things in common with Ayaan Ahmed, though none of Ahmed's ambition. They'd fled down this maze of back streets and alleyways with Vince Sleeman's henchmen on their heels. She'd always known that something nasty would fly in to fill the vacuum left by Sleeman's death. The squabble that had ensued over his sphere of influence had thrown up Corder and probably more like him. The thought bolstered her. Corder was no Sleeman.

The phone vibrated a text. Pieternel's number.

How close are you?

TD, Annie texted back. Touching Distance.

Having agreed to help, Pieternel had mapped out a simple plan. They would go in fast, right now, and well before the appointed meeting time. She would be first to suss out the lie of the land and signal to Annie if she should follow her in, lie low, or simply alert Ahmed.

'One of us needs to stay out of reach,' she'd said. 'Corder's too unpredictable. I'll play it by ear, see if I can get in to make sure. No point moving too soon. If Corder's expected, we can wait for him to show. He might come in person if he thinks you'll be there.'

'But Corder knows you,' Annie had objected.

'If Corder's there, he won't know it's me,' Pieternel had said. 'Neither will anyone else.'

Annie thought of Pieternel's words as she approached the end of the alley. It was an amateurish thing to do, to poke her head round the corner to peer down towards the Thompsons' but she couldn't resist. She was confident she'd recognise Corder or his acolytes. They wouldn't bother with any disguise.

The street was busy with people heading to town. This was still the run-down area it had always been but it was catching the wave from the burgeoning arts community, might even snare a measure of regeneration money in a year or so. Would that be good for the Thompsons or would it see them out on their ear?

She was too far distant from the shabby entrance to make out faces, but there was no one with Corder's swagger, no flashy cars parked. And no one who looked remotely like Pieternel but Annie knew better than to let that fool her.

Another vibration from the phone.

Someone up there with them. Downstairs office busy. Going in to check now.

Annie felt the tension. She wanted to text back, *Be careful,* but that would be foolish.

Her gaze raked the width of the road. From where she was standing, she didn't have a clear view of the stretch beyond the Thompsons' door where Pieternel must be. She would spot her though. There was only one way in. A bouncy gaggle of teens meandered untidily spilling on to the road, catching up and subsuming a laughing crowd of middle-aged women, everyone pleased to be released from the day's work, heading for home, for the bus station, for a night out.

The briefest of shadows shimmered at the edge of the throng. The Thompsons' door swung open spilling out a shaft of light. Annie blinked. Was that Pieternel ducking inside … had she painted herself a polychrome teen or a stout older woman?

The door closed. The background rumble of traffic overlay the chatter of the crowd.

Vibration from the phone.

It's not Corder. You're on your own.

Thoughts flashed through Annie's head as she leapt out from her hiding place, sprinting towards that office doorway. Pieternel wasn't going to wait. Corder was momentarily irrelevant. Pieternel said it wasn't Corder, so it wasn't Corder. But why did her ex-boss feel the need to flee without a proper goodbye? It was that same sense of urgency that had had her scrawl her signature so readily. She'd thought she was doing it to secure the money while it was still on offer, but now it felt that it hadn't been her urgency at all.

Her stare remained fixed on the wooden panels as she ate up the distance. One way in and one way out. Even Pieternel couldn't disguise herself as a wraith or walk through walls. Annie was going to corner her in the Thompsons' office and get an explanation.

She burst in a little out of breath. Faces from the downstairs workplace snapped up to see who had crashed in so late in the working day. Her gaze raked every expression, looking for a hint of furtiveness or discomfort. There were no corners by the door. If Pieternel had spotted her coming and hidden down here, she'd pushed past several desks to do it, and Annie would see it in their faces.

There was a moment's silence as everyone stopped to stare, then a man said, 'Woman with the headscarf?'

Annie nodded, thinking of the plump middle-aged bevy in the street outside.

The man tipped his head towards the stairs.

Annie took them in twos, throwing open the main office door at the top, aware of both Thompson sisters staring blankly at her. 'Where is she?'

She didn't wait for a response, ignored Barbara's testy, 'You said seven!' and raced along the landing to the small kitchen and bathroom, all the time keeping one eye on the head of the stairs in case Pieternel had taken refuge in the back room. It looked like that was exactly what she'd done because the rest of the place was empty. Annie returned, more slowly now she was sure of her ground, and marched past both sisters towards the tiny back office.

'Where is she?' she asked again, her hand reaching for the door handle.

'Where's who?' Something in the blankness of Pat's response reminded her of the times she'd wanted to avoid someone when she'd been working here. She'd forgotten that space by the filing cabinet; how she used to press herself back against it as Pat showed someone in, then slither round the edge of the door to slip away.

As she spun round, a voice spoke from the far side of the room, from the space where the filing cabinet used to stand. A man's voice. 'She couldn't be here this evening,' the voice said. 'You'll have to make do with me.'

Chapter 46

....

Time lapse.

Pieternel had taught her to work on an automatic time lapse. Arriving before the due appointment ... staying one step ahead ... keeping everyone looking just the wrong way. Yet still she'd fallen for it, though it showed progress that she'd managed to spot Pieternel at all. That swift-moving shadow, the door swinging open. When Pieternel had texted to say she was going in, she'd already been inside and was ready to leave. That had been her on the way out, blending with the crowd and vanishing. And here in front of Annie was the reason, stepping towards her, his hand outstretched.

Annie took in his features. She wanted to impress them on her memory, to know she'd know him again. This was the first time they'd met face to face.

'Miss Raymond, how do you do? Or do you prefer Ms?'

'How do you do, Mr fforbes?' Annie took the proffered hand. 'I'm usually Annie.'

He gave a half-smile, seemed as relaxed as if they'd met incidentally on a sunny afternoon in a park. 'You're a hard person to track down.'

She noted that he hadn't shared his own first name. 'You came to the restaurant, didn't you?'

'We had hoped for a quiet word in plain sight since you were reluctant to meet anywhere more private.'

She remembered that fleeting glance, the couple who'd left

when Ahmed and a colleague came to break the news about Carol. *Reluctant to meet anywhere more private?* 'It was you at the hotel then?'

'Yes.' He turned and walked to the hooks where a bulky accumulation of Pat and Barbara's coats, jackets and umbrellas crowded the corner. He lifted out a cloth bag with a shoulder strap. 'When we realised you'd gone, we took these for safekeeping.' She reached to take the bag and peered at the jumble of leads. 'The phone'll need charging.'

It was her stuff. For a moment she couldn't put together the pieces to work out if it had all come from the hotel room or if they'd been in the bedsit too. She wouldn't be able to rely on it. They could have done anything, laden it with trackers, booby-traps.

Pieternel had known these people for a long time and didn't trust them. She rummaged through the bag. Her ex-boss didn't trust anyone, and she worked for Meriç now.

She caught a movement and looked up to see fforbes check his watch. Rolex, she noted, old and a bit battered but sure to be genuine. 'I was curious to know if you would show,' he said to Annie before turning to the sisters. 'Mrs Caldwell, Miss Thompson. We'll be in touch.'

'Uh … yes … right.' Barbara struggled to half stand. 'Yes, Mr fforbes. Mind how you go.'

She slumped back into her chair as footsteps receded down the stairs.

'It'll be good to have you back, kid,' said Pat. 'Won't it, Babs?'

'Well, if we're going to be pulled out with work …'

'Whoa! Hold your horses,' Annie interrupted. 'That's not why I'm here. So he's your new investor, is he? Him and his sidekick.'

Pat nodded. 'They'd heard about us, wanted a foothold in the area.'

'Heard about all the great work you do, I suppose?' Annie said, but saw the sarcasm lost in the affirmative nods from both sisters.

'We told him about you, too,' Pat added. Barbara shot her a

narrow-eyed look. 'No, fair's fair, Babs. They were interested in who we'd worked with. We told them about you and all the others and I said you were back in the area.'

Annie wondered if there was any way to stop this deal. Dyson and fforbes wanted a foothold, did they? It might bring temporary prosperity but there would be a price down the line. And they'd checked up on her because of her approach to the Thompsons. Maybe they thought Pieternel had sent her to see what they were up to.

'Look, you called Pieternel, Mrs Peters. What was that about?'

'Oh, they know all about her, can't stand her. You'll be able to tell us what it's about. They wouldn't spill the beans.'

'No, I mean why did you call her Mrs Peters? You know that's not her name. You've never called her that before.'

Barbara looked blank. 'Did I? Well, it's what they called her.'

'Nothing to do with Corder then? Max Corder.'

Pat looked at her. 'That's the name you mentioned when you rang me. I passed it on. Why would it be to do with him? Who is he?'

Annie relaxed. They didn't know Corder. This was nothing to do with him. Corder was no fool. He'd be miles away by now.

'But you're going to come and work for us, aren't you?' Pat asked.

Annie held back an emphatic no. She would be based in the area, might need to call on their services. She needed to decline this offer with tact. 'No,' she began. 'I'm not, but that doesn't mean we won't be working together at some point ...'

Several good things had come of this meeting. She'd got back her phone and laptop – worrying over what that duo had planted in her tech was a concern for later – and she'd found herself clear in her mind about Corder. He was gone. Long gone. His gofers would have their hands full with damage limitation from the discovery of the secure warehouse. Her bedsit was safe. And she badly needed a good night's sleep.

As she left the Thompsons, she wondered if she should phone Ahmed or if he had figured it for himself. Probably he had. He wouldn't be back to try his sting. It was too late. They would have to chase Corder the hard way.

Now it was time to look towards her own future. Tomorrow her relationship with Meriç would undergo a fundamental change. It was important to start out on the right footing, to be at the top of her game. She allowed herself one 'what if' shudder of horror. What if she hadn't been planning the break from Pieternel while Pieternel was planning to cut her adrift? Winding back the clock and becoming the Thompsons' lackey might have been her only option. Except no, it would never have come to that. She would have washed dishes in the back of a restaurant first.

The following morning saw Annie up and about long before sunrise. She'd slept well. The malaise that had blanketed her since her kidnap by Corder was gone. She felt ready for the challenge of the day ahead.

And it would be a challenge. When she'd returned his phone, Meriç had confirmed the where and when of their first meeting at the new premises, adding, 'You've met my cousin, Aydin?'

'Yes, pleasant guy.' She'd nodded, remembering a quiet man who'd been in a few times.

'I should warn you that he doesn't approve of my picking you. Doesn't think I've known you long enough.'

'He can't veto your decision, can he?'

Meriç had laughed. 'No, no. You're on the team, but I wouldn't put it past him to try to trip you up. Just be on your guard.'

She had been extra careful with her outfit, needing to look every inch the professional when she arrived on her new turf.

The place was shuttered, looked abandoned, encased in stout

wooden boards impervious to prying eyes. Not yet time for the 'opening soon' stickers, not until the outside face looked more inviting. She knocked at the makeshift door.

It was Yağız who let her in.

Annie took in the wide expanse. The blanked off shop-front had not done it justice. This would be a much bigger enterprise than Meriç's joint venture with Corder. If this one took off, it wouldn't matter if the original was scuppered by the fallout from Corder's criminality. She wondered if this had occurred to Yağız. He might not resent her now, but if he ended up out of a job it would be a different story. She wasn't sure how much he'd been told and it wasn't her place to enlighten him.

'It'll be a busy day,' he said now. 'Meriç wants us to find another chef.'

'He does indeed.' Meriç emerged from a back room, giving Yağız a hard look, and turning to Annie.

'I thought you'd found a chef.'

'Yes, yes. I mean for the other place. I have that traitor to replace. And I'm relying on you to spot any bad apples, Annie. I have to admit I wouldn't have suspected him in a million years. He played on old friendships.'

Annie smiled but said nothing. Meriç was banking rather more than he should on her ability to spot wrongdoing. I had surveillance cameras and luck, she wanted to say, I can't just look in their eyes and suss them out.

Or maybe she could. Her years with Pieternel had fine-tuned her paranoia.

'You know my cousin.' Meriç drew her forward. 'Aydin, you know Annie.'

This was the man who planned to trip her up, was it? They exchanged a handshake.

'Let us show you round, Annie.'

She followed. It became a guided tour. It was clear that Aydin was familiar with the place but she and Yağız weren't. Dust sheets were lifted so that veneer could be admired, cushions prodded and equipment marvelled at. The deeper they moved inside the building the more advanced the renovations. She found herself asking questions, querying the siting of some of the equipment, suggesting minor amendments.

Meriç beamed throughout, proud of his new domain, and accepting her suggestions as good sense.

'Come through here, Annie. What do you think?'

This was more like it. Annie found herself returning Meriç's beaming smile as she stood in the doorway of a substantial manager's office with a good-sized desk, comfortable chair and large window. What was Yağız thinking? Was his mind drawn, as was hers, to that claustrophobic cubbyhole back across town?

'I think it's superb.' She answered Meriç's question.

'Right, well, time's getting on,' Meriç said. 'We'll see people in here.'

'These are for you, Annie.' Aydin held out a sheaf of papers, his face wearing its bland smile.

Annie took them, catching sight of a chef's CV. The bundle she held was the twin of one that Yağız was taking from an envelope. Meriç had one too. The difference was that they were pulling their copies from envelopes they'd had in their pockets; the papers they held were crumpled and folded. They'd had the stuff for a while. On this flimsiest of evidence she surmised that Aydin had put together the chef's CVs for the interviews, had given Meriç and Yağız their paperwork in advance and made sure she didn't get hers until … she glanced at the itinerary on the topmost sheet … five minutes before the interviews were due to start. This was his plan to wrong-foot her.

He'd picked the wrong person and the wrong tactic. She could skim the cream off this lot several times over in five minutes.

Moving to one side, she began to flick through the sheets. Meriç's shortlist was long. He was picky, would probably waver back and forth over the final decision. Yağız had said it would be a long day.

Half way through the heap, one of the CVs brought her up short. She stopped skimming and read the detail. It had the feel of someone linked to Meriç and Aydin, a family member. Was she here as the outsider to prevent the rubberstamping of a job for a relative? Meriç would want genuine talent in his kitchen, and there was no culinary expertise on this résumé. In fact – she looked closer – this wasn't a chef's application at all …

She thumbed through the rest of the applications. Some were applying for the head chef position and some …

There was enough at her fingertips now to grill the candidates convincingly. Suddenly that didn't matter.

The top sheet … the itinerary … she read it word by word.

Her mind skipped back over her conversations with Meriç as her heart began to pound … every conversation she'd ever had with him had been fragmented, cut in pieces by the demands of a busy restaurant or some other crisis.

Annie, I'd like you on the team … It's important, Annie … a key role … I can't risk some new scam going undetected. I need you … need your expertise …

That urgency she'd felt from Pieternel … wanting that paper safely signed.

Meriç has told me about the new restaurant, Annie … Tell me the detail, Annie … I'm not sure I've got a clear picture from Meriç.

She'd had a clear picture all right, and instead of coming clean, she'd grabbed her chance.

Annie thought about how much had happened … how tired she'd been … all the distractions …

She'd just accepted that everything was panning out the way she wanted. But it wasn't. Of course it wasn't.

She looked at the neatly typed list and the itinerary. All very professionally done.

He wasn't asking her to be his manager. He'd never even registered it as a possibility. He'd been asking her to sit on the interview panel. Her new job for Meriç was for today only. It would be over by sundown.

'Are you ready, Annie? Our first applicant is here.'

She straightened her back and turned to him, arranging her mouth into the semblance of a smile before she made her way to where Aydin had ranged chairs for the four of them to sit.

Chapter 47

The day was over. The last candidate had been shown out. For Annie it had gone by in a blur as though she was an automaton whose sensory awareness had been switched off.

Meriç had provided sandwiches for a brief half hour's lunch during which she had excused herself and walked outside the plush office. She'd clicked Pieternel's number into her phone, not quite sure why or what she would say, but all she'd heard was the continuous tone of a non-existent number.

She'd returned to join the discussions on each of the morning candidates, holding her own when Aydin tried to highlight her unfamiliarity with the CVs he'd so painstakingly collated. That had back-fired because it was Meriç flying by the seat of his pants on that score, going by instinct not by paperwork.

The afternoon was filled with interviews for the manager's post, the job that Annie had thought was hers. By the end of the day she couldn't have told anyone a single thing about any of the candidates for either position, but she knew she'd played her part.

'Well, well …' Meriç rubbed his hands together. 'Good work. Thank you everyone. Thank you, Annie. I hope you'll call in one day and sample the new cuisine.'

'Thank you, I'd be happy to.' She stood up and reached for her jacket. 'Well, if you'll excuse me, I've a call to make.'

'Of course, of course …' Meriç saw her out into the empty space that would soon be a busy restaurant.

Annie listened to the wind whistle across the wooden cladding. 'I'll stay in here if you don't mind. I'll not hear a thing out there.'

She could have walked to the bedsit or to a nearby pub, but knew she must make this call right now or she wouldn't make it at all.

'Thompsons. Pat speaking.'

'Hi, it's Annie.'

'Annie!' Before Annie could draw breath to speak, Pat was in full flow. 'Listen, Annie, will you reconsider? I'm sure we can come to some arrangement. We really need someone and …'

Annie listened and felt lead begin to flow in her veins. She'd vowed she would wash dishes in the back of a restaurant before she would work for the Thompsons again. As she listened to Pat's pleas, she realised there was no way she could make it work with the Thompsons …

… unless …

She narrowed her eyes.

Why were they so desperate? Was their so-called new investor going to pull out if they couldn't get help on board? Why the rush? Dyson and fforbes were the real reason she should be running from this as fast as she could, but it was the thought of the Thompsons that rose up as an insurmountable obstacle.

'They're sleeping partners, that's all,' Pat was saying. 'Rich playboys with money to burn. They'll leave us alone.'

Sleeping partners, thought Annie. Did she really think that? Dyson and fforbes had reeled them all in with the expertise of poachers after prime wild salmon. That party … her absurd dirndl costume … They'd hijacked that job somewhere along the line, as well as planted the evidence and a patsy to hand it over, because the job wasn't important. Its purpose was to give her the evidence to wind up her own job with Meriç; evidence she'd come close to missing. And all so that she could be tempted to join the Thompsons again on the back of their money.

How speculative was their investment? How soon would the

duo return to extract the price and how high would it be? This was a conversation she wanted to have with Pieternel but that wasn't going to happen.

'There might be a way.' She cut across Pat.

'What? Come on, kid, don't keep me in suspense. What've you got in mind?'

'I'll call in. We can talk. But you need to know that I'll only work for you if …' Annie paused. Yağız had appeared at her elbow. 'Just a sec …' She turned to him.

'Long day.' He mimed raising a glass to his lips. 'D'you want to go for a beer?'

'Maybe,' she said. 'Give me a sec.'

She turned away from him, lowering her voice as she spoke into the phone.

The gasp from the handset echoed. Barbara had been listening in. She cut off an outraged, 'No way!' as she closed the call.

'Yes,' she said to Yağız. 'A beer is exactly what I need, only I have to go and see someone first. I'll meet you at the pub.'

◉ ◉ ◉

The door swung open. Annie climbed the staircase and pushed into the office. The sisters sat behind their desks and glowered at her as she came in.

'They're threatening to pull out, aren't they?' Annie opened.

Barbara shrugged. 'We don't need them.'

Pat's gaze flicked towards her sister but she said nothing.

'On the other hand …' Barbara glanced down and inspected her nails. 'A cash injection is always welcome.'

'They'll want a return on their investment,' Annie said.

Both sisters shrugged. She supposed they saw their new backers creaming profit off a successful business as the years rolled by. Sleeping partners, Pat had said. It wouldn't be the investors who were the sleepers, it would be the agency – her, Pat and Barbara. Sleepers for a duo that Pieternel ran away from. She couldn't begin to imagine what price they would ultimately be asked to pay, and no point even trying to have this conversation with the sisters yet awhile.

'Like I said on the phone ...'

Pat and Barbara glanced sideways at each other. The anger still simmered but they'd had time to dampen their initial outrage.

The truth was that she couldn't wash dishes in the back of a restaurant. Private investigation was all she knew, and her association with Pieternel meant that no one she wanted to work for would touch her with a bargepole. To be at the Thompsons' beck and call, even for a few weeks while she scrabbled about for employment elsewhere would stifle her, might lead her down the same road they'd travelled, falling into malaise, indifference and probably alcohol.

She pulled out a chair and sat down. 'Like I said, I'll come back and work here, but only if I'm in charge. I'm the boss, or no deal.'

Her hope was that she was their only shot at this new money, that without a third person on board, Dyson and fforbes would disappear. Barbara would love them to be financially secure, though Pat was the one more likely to concede that Annie would make a good job of running the agency.

The sisters sat in silence, stares locked.

Barbara shook her head. 'No way.'

'I'll go for it,' Pat said.

'You'll change your mind.' There was a sneer in Barbara's voice.

'I won't. I think she can do it. I don't mind a bit of a shake-up. It'll do us good.'

A glimmer of hope. Something sparked within Annie. Suppose they agreed, it might be years before Dyson and fforbes showed their hand; might be never. They must have spread their bets far and wide. And meantime, she could do wonders with this outfit if she had a free hand and some financial backing. There was a fire within her that she hadn't felt for a long time.

But if they held firm, she would have to cave in and be their employee. A ton of sand smothered the embryo flame.

'We're not going to agree,' Pat said with a finality that snapped Annie's gaze to her face, but it wasn't Annie she was looking at. It was Barbara.

Barbara pulled in a deep breath, narrowed her eyes and shifted in her seat so she could reach into her pocket. Annie saw the coin lifted between Barbara's thumb and forefinger, twisted towards Pat, as though they both had to check it was for real.

Pat leant forward in her chair. Annie found herself doing the same. Barbara balanced the coin, sat up straight and flicked it high in the air.

'Heads,' called Pat.

Annie's stare held like glue to the silver disk that shimmered against the light as it spun in an arc, *hope – nightmare – hope – nightmare* – breath held, she waited for its decision on her future path.

The End

Author's note

....

Syrup Trap City is set in the UK in the northern port of Hull. It opens as Hull's City of Culture year dawns. But in order for it to be published in that same City of Culture year I had to write it in advance. In the summer of 2016 I was writing about the winter that was yet to come, studying long-range forecasts and praying that we wouldn't have snow, which would have added an extra dimension to one scene that would have been akin to giving Hercule Poirot's contemporaries mobile phones.

From the start, I nursed an ambition that I kept from my publisher. I intended grabbing the manuscript back out of production at the last minute and adding something iconic that marked Hull's birth as UK City of Culture. Every publisher's nightmare, the author who insists on last-minute changes.

Nonetheless, I intended doing it, but what would it be? I wasn't going to bend the plot. I just wanted that iconic something in there. It would have to be an episode from early in the year, so as to disrupt, as opposed to kill dead, the production of the book.

And the good people of *Hull UK City of Culture 2017* presented me with the perfect event.

Blade, conceived by artist Nayan Kulkarni, was one of the first of a programme of temporary artworks created for the city's public spaces.

The Blade was a 75 metre long, 25 tonne rotor blade; the world's largest, handmade fibreglass component, and one of the first made at the Siemens factory in Hull. On the night of January 7th, it was transported secretly in an incredible feat of logistics and engineering, to be installed in the town centre bisecting Queen Victoria Square, reaching from Savile Street to Carr Lane, rising to a height of over 5.5 metres at its tip, allowing double-decker buses to run beneath.

The only dilemma for me was whose story should intersect with the Blade's epic journey? Someone needed to spot that giant convoy in the small hours and wonder about it for a moment. Annie maybe; she tends to be out and about at night. Or restaurateur, Meriç, who would officially disapprove of the disruption and secretly delight in the extra publicity. It could be head waiter, Yağız, out trying to track Annie. Perhaps Ayaan and Cari Ahmed could come across it whilst out for a romantic stroll late that night. It might even be Max Corder striding the city streets as he checks his many and varied investments.

To decide who would have the job, I checked to see who was where, and who would be best in the role. I expected to have many options. I'll bet those engineers thought they would have options too. But much in the way that the Blade would fit one way, and one way only, in Queen Victoria Square, it turned out that the Blade would fit one way, and one way only, into *Syrup Trap City*.

The story of *Syrup Trap City* began on Christmas Eve and ends … oh no … two days before the Blade left the Siemens factory.

None of the characters could have seen it. As Annie and Pat watch the coin spin from Barbara's hand, the Blade is yet to leave its berth on Alexandra Dock.

The only place the Blade will fit into this book is here in the author's note at the end. Not what I originally had in mind, but at least it's here.

This leaves me, as the author, pondering that epic journey from Alexandra Dock to the town centre and wondering if it might make an unusual opening for book eight.

… but no, wait a minute …

Is *Syrup Trap City* the sixth or seventh book in the Annie Raymond mystery series?

Answers on a postcard, please. It isn't that straightforward a question.

Annie's career was kick-started in Hull by what she initially saw as a lucky break in *Like False Money*. After that *The Jawbone Gang* saw her settling into her new role but with seriously itchy feet. These took her both south to London and north to Scotland as she faced an appalling dilemma at the start of *The Doll Makers*. An odd set of circumstances landed her once again in Hull in *Where There's Smoke*, facing down an enemy she'd not seen since her early career.

Buried Deep took Annie to York from her London base and was a crossover book that for the first time put a police investigation front and centre alongside her own work. This was the book that introduced DC Ayaan Ahmed and Det Supt Martyn Webber. *Tiger Blood*, the next in line, took a step sideways and majored solely on a network of police investigative work, following the tangled career paths and personal lives of Ahmed and Webber. Despite it being advertised as the sixth Annie book, she gets no more than a passing mention.

Syrup Trap City returns both to Hull and to Annie although Ahmed, now a sergeant, has a role. It is Webber who becomes the unnamed passing mention.

Where next? It's a major career change for Annie, and not the first time she's become involved with the shadier side of life. The difference this time is that she walked in with her eyes open.

Watch this space.

The Annie Raymond Mysteries
Book 1: Like False Money
Book 2: The Jawbone Gang
Book 3: The Doll Makers
Book 4: Where There's Smoke
Book 5: Buried Deep
Book 6: Syrup Trap City

The Webber/Ahmed series
Book 1: Buried Deep
Book 2: Tiger Blood
Book 3: Syrup Trap City

If you have enjoyed this story, please consider leaving a review for Penny to let her know what you thought of her work.

You can find out more about Penny on her author page on the Fantastic Books Store. While you're there, why not browse our delightful tales and wonderfully woven prose?

www.fantasticbooksstore.com

www.ingramcontent.com/pod-product-compliance
Lightning Source LLC
Chambersburg PA
CBHW070642180626
46817CB00006B/2216